THE
OLD
ENEMY

Also by Henry Porter

THE
OLD
ENEMY

HENRY PORTER

Atlantic Monthly Press
New York

First published in Great Britain in 2021 by Quercus Editions Ltd
An Hachette UK company

Published simultaneously in Canada
Printed in Canada

First Grove Atlantic hardcover editon: June 2021

Library of Congress Cataloging-in-Publication data is available for this title.

ISBN 978-0-8021-5865-9
eISBN 978-0-8021-5866-6

Atlantic Monthly Press
an imprint of Grove Atlantic
154 West 14th Street
New York, NY 10011

Distributed by Publishers Group West

groveatlantic.com

21 22 23 24   10 9 8 7 6 5 4 3 2 1

For Charlie P. and Charlie K.

PART ONE

CHAPTER 1

Berlin Blue

He had made it into the spring – three months longer than they gave him. And here he was, out on the peninsula in the early-morning light, feeling okay and in some ways happier than he'd ever been, though, of course, it was not Robert Harland's custom to examine his state of mind too closely. He was alive and painting – that was enough. And a kilometre away, on this crooked finger of land that pointed north into the Baltic, his wife, Ulrike, was at their cabin, by now tucked into her spot between the porch and timbered wall, sheltered from the wind. She'd have a book in her hands and a shawl around her and she'd be looking out to sea, sometimes peering at the insects that were blown round the porch and came to rest beside her on the bench.

In a moment he'd sit in the camp chair and maybe smoke one of the three cigarettes in the breast pocket of the old field-coat he wore, ignoring her strictures without much thought. For there was work to be done to the small oil sketch in front of him, which, like the others in the series, had been executed rapidly with some of the basic colours of the seascape mixed the night before. He looked up. The continent of cloud suspended over the ocean was about to deliver shafts of light that would reflect from the sea and spread through the spray-mist above the waves. With a brush clamped between his teeth and more brushes and a palette in his hands, the old spy waited, looking and looking, hardly breathing.

Ulrike would never know what made her open her eyes at that moment. She was plunged in the terrible finality of their time together, these days of being alone when, if Bobby was feeling strong, he would go out early with his paraphernalia loaded on to the light handcart that he was so pleased with, returning only when he was too tired to carry on, or he'd finished the painting. In the evenings, they were together. She'd cook – not much, because his appetite had gone – and he'd sit with a whisky looking at the day's painting and peering intently across the scrub to the sea. Later, they'd lie in bed, mesmerised by the dancing shadows thrown by an oil lamp, the smell of which filled the cabin. Sometimes they'd go back to events three decades before in Leipzig and Berlin and, later, in Tallinn – the cities that marked chapters in their lives – and to the people they'd known and lost, and occasionally murmuring their love for each other. When he slept, she kept watch, wondering what she'd do when he was gone; what it would it be like without him beside her. Before dropping off the night before, he'd muttered, almost angrily, 'I'm sorry, I had no idea this would be so ghastly for you!' And, grazing her forehead with his lips, 'You know that no one is more loved than you? You know that, don't you?'

'Yes,' she said eventually, and, using the German for her usual reply, '*Ja, und ich liebe dich auch*,' – and I love you, too – then she asked, 'Are you happy out here? You don't want to be doing anything else? Go home?' She worried he was pressuring himself, because he was so short-tempered in the mornings.

'The work's got to be done.' He'd been promised an exhibition in late May and he knew that was what kept him going. He needed twenty-four decent canvases to add to the works on paper that were already framed at the gallery in Tallinn. She reckoned he had nineteen, maybe twenty-two at a push. He wasn't so sure.

He slept, but she did not, so now she dozed in her spot, smelling the resin in the wood heating up when the sun came out. The only sound came from a lark suspended in the sky, way off to her right, and the wind nudging the porch door. What made her start she could not say. But she sat up, filled with alarm. She shielded her eyes against the light and looked around. A figure was moving purposefully along the track by the shore; hard to make out because of the dark rocks, but occasionally a silhouette flashed against the breaking waves. She stepped inside and unhooked the binoculars they'd inherited with the cabin and trained them through the kitchen window. This individual, certainly a man, was carrying something, but not fishing gear, not a hiker's backpack, not even the wildfowler's shotgun under his arm; more like a case slung over his shoulder. She lost then found him again and, without thinking, pulled her phone off the charging lead, went outside and dialled her husband's number. The call didn't go through. She moved to a rise a few metres away and phoned again. This time the call was successfull but he didn't answer. She waited a few moments, because there wasn't anywhere with better coverage, and searched the shoreline with the binoculars, but saw nothing. She dialled and this time got through but was cut off. Then she dialled again.

He felt the vibration in his pocket but didn't answer. The clouds had spilled a pool of light and he had caught it because he was waiting and the few brushstrokes applied automatically were so certain. To respond to nature in real time, almost as quickly as film, was what he was still alive for and, when he got it absolutely right, it was thrilling. The second call came and he put the palette and brushes down on the collapsible table – another piece of equipment that gave him huge satisfaction – and fished out his phone, smearing the screen with the paint on his fingers. He could hear her moving and called out her name – maybe she had dialled him by mistake. But she spoke, breathless. He couldn't hear her because of the noise of boots in the dead grass. He waited and implored her to stand still – Goddammit! – and speak to him. He heard the crunch of the hard-core track beneath her boots then she said something. 'What?' he bellowed. 'I can't hear you.'

'Someone's out there with you. I don't like the look of him, Bobby. Where are you?'

'Just beyond the wreck.' He pushed up his blue tam-o'-shanter, looked around and saw nothing, except the light-fall from the clouds, which now had the faintest yellow tinge and made the spray glow. He caught his breath. It was too late to change his painting and, anyway, that was then; this was now. He grappled with the phone to take a photograph, hoping that he wouldn't lose Ulrike. He took several because the scene was developing every second. Then he returned the phone to his ear: she had gone, so he called her back. 'I can't see anyone.' But at that moment he spotted a man moving by the rocks at the water's edge, right in line with an illuminated patch of sea. 'Ah, I've got him!' he exclaimed. The figure hesitated then moved off to the right to take the track to the lighthouse that ran across the peninsula between him and Ulrike. 'He's going the other way,' he said, letting himself down into the camp chair. 'Let's have a brew-up! Come and join me. I want you to see what I've been doing. I think it's rather good . . . well, it's not bad.' He was never sure what he felt about his work. Elation was often followed by a crash in spirits. She hung up and he reckoned he'd got about ten minutes to get the water boiling and smoke a cigarette. He leaned forward and yanked a camping stove from his bag, lit it and placed a small whistling kettle on the flame. There was just one enamel mug for them, but he had tea, milk and a silver-and-glass hip flask that he had inherited from his father, together with the taste for a dash of whisky in his tea. They often shared a mug beneath the Baltic sky, Ulrike making a rather too penetrating appraisal of his latest. She could go easy on him, he reflected, but that wasn't her. He sat back and ran an eye over his work, an unlit cigarette in his hand. Some sketchiness in the foreground, where the paint was thin, worried him, but he decided he liked the effect, and he was glad he hadn't done any more to the light on the sea. She'd stopped him overworking the scene.

The roar of the camp stove obliterated all other sound, so he would not hear her call out, which she always did with a wave when she reached the brow. He looked to his right and lit the cigarette discreetly, inhaled and let the smoke dribble from the corner of his mouth. It was stupid to pretend he didn't smoke. What bloody harm could it do now? But it made her very angry indeed, because she quit her tiny ration of smokes when he received the diagnosis. He took another drag and leaned forward to remove the kettle, which was beginning to tremble on top of the stove. As he did so, something very powerful hit the aluminium frame of his chair and threw him on to the grass to his right. He rolled on to his front. A man was moving towards him, marching robotically, with the scope of a rifle pressed to his eye. A second shot hit the table and Harland thought, *fucking amateur.* But he had nothing to defend himself with, and nowhere to go and, besides, he wasn't up to running, not over this ground, not with his lungs, not with his aching bones. All he hoped was that Ulrike wouldn't witness this. He rolled again to search for his phone. He needed desperately to speak to her, to say he loved her, because this was it: they'd found him and, however incompetent the assassin, he would certainly take what little life remained to him.

The third shot tore across the back of his left calf. He writhed in the grass, as much from anger as pain, and at the same time realised the prescribed morphine was suppressing the effect. He'd started the course, without telling Ulrike, three days before when a deep internal pain made it hard to concentrate. He reached for his sketchbook, the pages of which were fluttering in the breeze, and, half noticing that the burner was on its side and scorching the grass very close to the turpentine container, he scrawled 'Berlin Blue' on the back of the pad, ringed the words, then wrote in block capitals 'LOVE YOU'.

An idea flickered in his mind. He seized the turpentine bottle, un-screwed the top as he rolled on to his left side, which caused the pain from his leg to surge upwards. He didn't yell out. Not now. Not after a life of fear and pain and self-control – he just waited. The man was twenty paces away: black beanie, an unexceptional, fleshy, mid-thirty-year-old face, gloves and dark brown lace-up military boots. He lowered the rifle. Why? To enjoy the moment, or make sure his rotten aim wouldn't fail him again? Harland flung the bottle. It Catherine-wheeled through the air, spraying turps, and hit the man in the groin. He followed that with the burner, which fell short but did its job of lighting the turps on the ground around the man, and instantly his legs and midriff caught fire. Harland groaned an expletive and collapsed on to his back and looked at the sky. The heightened awareness that came from concentrating on nature, which always remained for an hour or so after stopping, was still with him, and the sky at that moment seemed impossibly beautiful. Four shots were loosed off chaotically, one of which entered his heart.

CHAPTER 2

GreenState

Paul Samson was familiar with her routine. Before leaving the sixties block on the fringes of Westminster, where GreenState's campaign headquarters were housed, Zoe Freemantle would go over to the water cooler and fill her flask. She'd return to her desk, then work her phone and slip her laptop into her shoulder bag. After checking her phone a few times, she would get up without saying anything to those around her and head for the stairwell, which she used in preference to the lift. All this gave Samson a head start, and by the time she pushed through the double doors on to the street he was wearing his helmet and had started the bike. He was sure she hadn't been trained in counter-surveillance, yet she was good. She would walk for about half a mile with her big stride and air of imperturbable self-possession until she suddenly stopped and got into the ride she'd hailed twenty minutes before. She never used the same rendezvous and always chose a spot where the driver could slip into what was for London relatively fast-moving traffic. She usually included a dry-cleaning move in the route and twice Samson had lost her because he couldn't follow her on the bike, although without it there was little hope of keeping up with her. On this occasion, she walked along the Embankment and at the last moment jogged up the steps and into the main entrance of the Tate Gallery. Samson turned right and stopped on the street corner so he could watch the front and side entrances of the gallery simultaneously. Ten minutes later, he caught sight of her long suede coat ascending the steps at the far end of the side entrance. He followed her through Pimlico, past Victoria Station, to a small triangular park, which she crossed, and, on the far side, climbed into a silver Prius hybrid.

She retraced her route to Westminster. The car crawled through Parliament Square and headed east along the Embankment, towards the City of London. But just as it reached the intersection near Embankment station, he saw the rear door open and Zoe hop out and plunge into the crowds converging on the Underground station. It was a smart move. There was access to Charing Cross main-line station and two lines ran through the Underground station. He parked the bike and locked his helmet in the seat box, but it was already hopeless. There was no guarantee he would find her, or that she wouldn't walk straight through the main-line station and exit towards Trafalgar Square. There was, as he had discovered when losing her twice before, little point following her on to the Tube. He would have to guess at her eventual destination, which a couple of times had been the Edgar Coach and Engineering Works, a large industrial building on an intersection known as the Junction, north of the City of London. She was probably headed there, so he would go there, too. And if she had given him the slip again, well, that was on her.

It was less than ninety seconds before he mounted his bike. He didn't take particular note of a much more powerful bike that roared up with a pillion passenger and lingered under the rail bridge, but he would remember it later.

He arrived at the Junction twenty-five minutes later, stood the bike in a cobbled passageway called Cooper's Court and entered the Lina Café and Bakery, diagonally across the intersection from the Edgar Building, which he had used on the two previous occasions. He certainly wondered what went on inside, but it wasn't his task to investigate Zoe, or find out the reason she was at GreenState. He was employed to watch for any threat against her, report back and make sure she didn't get hurt. He hardly saw himself as that kind of muscle and, in truth, the job was rather below him, but Macy Harp, head of the private-intelligence firm Hendricks Harp that he often worked for, said it required brains and a keen eye. Besides, he'd negotiated a very good rate with the individual who wanted to keep Zoe Freemantle alive. He stressed over and over that it was a question of life and death, although he couldn't, or wouldn't, say what the threat was.

Samson found her on social media under her cover name, Ingrid Cole. As far as he could see, Zoe Freemantle had no presence whatever. Ingrid, however, was on three big platforms, a dedicated environmentalist, animal lover and climate-change activist who frequently linked to her own website. This consisted mostly of photographs of her work, dating back several years – he admired the care she'd taken in pushing back the history of her legend – and some deadly-dull screeds about big tech, poverty and media ownership. Photographs of her were few, except those in which she was wearing round dark glasses or her face was partially hidden by her long brown hair, which, at work, she wore in a knot, or rather haphazardly clipped. Her wardrobe was unvarying – light brown, calf-length suede coat, or a navy-blue blouson with the GreenState bird logo hot-pressed above her left breast. She favoured well-cut trousers, never jeans, and ankle boots, which pushed her height an inch over six feet, or black trainers, which he came to recognise were a sign that she'd leave the office at some point during the day.

He had no contact with her at GreenState – his was a lowly volunteer's job replying to questions on the campaign website with a set of standard responses that were designed to elicit money – but he was in a position to observe her most of the day, and he was pretty certain that she had not yet noticed him. She was self-contained and never involved herself with office politics. Her colleagues were wary of her because of her sharp tongue and she was no respecter of status or the conventional NGO politesse where everyone's opinion is indulged, however empty or lacking in evidence. He heard her murmur to GreenState's director of campaigns, a man named Desmond who Samson heartily disliked, 'We're doing good work, but that doesn't mean I'm not going to call you out when you're talking crap.'

Her behaviour was tolerated because she was good at what she did. She had fluent French and German and often appeared in the morning having completed, overnight, the work that would take others a couple of days. She wrote video scripts, advertising briefs and focused on GreenState's messaging, for which reason she often took meetings outside the office with agencies providing their services free. No one asked where she was going, or why. Not even the ridiculous busybody Desmond.

Samson resigned himself to a fruitless wait and let his gaze travel the breadth of the five-street intersection. The regulars on the street were beginning to be familiar to him – addicts, with sleeping bags round their necks, scrambling for deals beneath the rail bridge, north of the Edgar Building; an abandoned young man handing out religious leaflets on the traffic island; two glacially moving homeless men; and the team of Roma beggars who looked as though they might all be related. The Junction was a twenty-minute walk from the vast wealth of the City of London, but a different universe. No one made much money here: the buildings were tired, rubbish was piled everywhere, and people struggled. But for all that, it had a palpable life force that Samson admired. It reminded him of the Middle East – his native Lebanon.

The thin drizzle outside turned into rain, but it was lunch hour and the streets weren't any less busy. His phone went. It was one of Macy's assistants, asking him for a meeting, or conference call, at 7 p.m. Samson opted for the meeting. He wanted to be in the room for the call with the States.

'What's going on, Imogen?'

She ignored him. 'Seven p.m. prompt, Paul, so if you have any concern about not being here, I'll send you the dial-in.'

Samson glanced at his watch – it was 1.30 p.m. – and he assured her he'd make it. 'And you can tell Macy that we'll need to review the current job,' he added.

As he hung up, a big, freakish fellow wearing a black leather kilt, panel leggings and a filthy American sports blouson, appeared outside the café and looked through the window, trying to see past his reflection. His face was broad – vaguely Slavic. Samson noted a missing upper-left tooth and a pierced nose. The man turned away and, with a kind of jig, began thrusting a crumpled cup at passers-by, who had absolutely no problem ignoring him.

'The state of that!' said a woman behind the counter. 'He was some-one's sweet little baby once. Imagine!'

Samson wasn't interested. Something had made him straighten in his chair.

No conscious process in him asked: am I watching a surveillance opera-tion here? But the conviction that he was arrived fully formed in his mind. Two men, across the street, one with his hand in an empty knapsack, kept glancing at the Edgar Building then looking away. An Asian couple on his side of the street pretended to talk but were surely communicating with others – both wore microphone earbuds. A fourth and maybe a fifth were separately threading their way through the stalled traffic towards the gates of Mo's Tyre and Body Shop, which lay between the Edgar Building and a rail bridge to the north. The whole thing could be accidental, but the choreography looked right, and the operation seemed to be focused on the Edgar Building. He paid up without removing his eyes from the street then walked to the door. Still inside the café, he craned to see north and south of the Junction, wondered if either of the illegally parked vans was part of the surveillance team and whether the operation had been mounted by the police, MI5, or was a joint endeavour. There were at least eight watchers around the Junction and he even considered the beggar capering a few paces away might be part of the team.

The thought that he didn't want Zoe walking into this situation arrived a few moments before a cab pulled up awkwardly at the mouth of Cooper's Court, by which time he had taken out two phones, copied the number for Zoe that he had acquired at campaign headquarters from his personal phone into the field of a new text message on a burner phone and written, 'Do NOT enter the Edgar. Leave the area now!' As he looked up, the cab came to a halt and he saw someone paying. A flash of the suede coat inside the cab – it was Zoe. He sent the text. She got out and looked around in preparation to cross over to the Edgar Building. Samson decided he would have to break cover and get her away from the building – some change in the barometric pressure around the Junction, which maybe only a former intelligence officer would be aware of, told him that the team was ready to make a move. He stepped out of the café and went three paces, but saw that she had pulled out her phone and was reading as she walked. She stopped suddenly on the pedestrian crossing, looked around and turned to head back to Samson's side of the road. He moved back. At the moment she reached the curb, as yet apparently without recognizing Samson, who was no more than a few metres away, he became aware of a blurred movement in his right field. The beggar was on the move and coming towards them fast. His hood was raised against the rain; both arms were bared and he now wore gloves. In his right hand, held low, there was a blade about six inches long.

Samson's basic knowledge of self-defence came from a course taken as an SIS officer. He'd only made use of it properly once – in Syria, a man came at him with a knife when he was carrying cash to help trace and free the Kurdish-American doctor Aysel Hisami. Samson had seen that attack coming and had had time to step outside the thrust of the knife, seize the man's wrist with his right hand and go to work on his face, clawing at his eyes with his left. It had proved remarkably effective and he'd quickly disarmed and knocked out the young fighter, a member of his escort into ISIS-held territory who had been looking for an opportunity to get Samson alone for the previous twenty-four hours. Now Samson had less warning and he had no idea which way the man planned to go. He instinctively blocked the way to Zoe, on his left, and shouted for her to run, but that meant he was still inside the line of thrust. Someone screamed. Samson moved to his right, grabbing the man's upper arm, forcing it away and, at the same time, delivering a punch to his Adam's apple, then several rapid upward blows to his chin with the heel of his hand. He was much stronger than Samson and he easily wrestled his arm free. Samson moved back. The man came at him again and Samson aimed a kick at his groin and, taking hold of his upper arm for a second time, headbutted him in the face. These two blows did something to stall the attack, but he was aware that his back was against the café's window and he had nowhere to go. People had scattered from the pavement and there was now no sign of Zoe. He ducked to his left, but the man pursued him with a boxer's dance, jabbing the air with the knife. Samson was aware of two new sounds – a woman behind him shouting for the man to drop the knife and the roar of a motorbike that had mounted the pavement and skidded in a 180-degree turn to face away from him. He looked round to see one of the watchers aiming a gun at the beggar, feet splayed and both hands holding the gun. She was a police officer and knew what she was doing. He looked back for the man's reaction. He simply shrugged and began to back away, smiling with the certainty that the officer could not possibly take a shot at him with so many people about. The beggar leapt on to the back of the bike, took the helmet handed to him by the driver and they sped along the pavement, cleaved a path in the lunchtime crowds then darted through a gap in the traffic and went south.

It was the same motorbike Samson had seen waiting in the tunnel by Embankment station, a ten-year-old Suzuki with the maker's blue-and-white livery beneath the grime – as old and unremarkable as his own lowly Honda. He had obviously been followed, because the knifeman had arrived outside the café before Zoe. This interested him, for at no stage on his journey from Embankment station had he seen the bike in his mirrors, which led him to one conclusion – his Honda must have been fitted with a tracking device. This thought was followed by a more arresting one – unless they were using him to lead them to Zoe, which was, at least, a possibility, he was the target. But this made no sense whatsoever. What mattered was that Zoe Freemantle had got away from the vicinity of the Edgar Building unharmed and unidentified by the police. That was what he was paid for.

The woman officer who had drawn her gun was anxious to get back to her operation and hurriedly took down his name and address and said someone would be along to talk to him about the 'incident'. Samson gave her false details and, as soon as she had left, went to his bike, unlocked the helmet box and placed the key in the ignition. Whatever the police presence around the Junction, it wouldn't be long before the bike, together with the tracker, was stolen from Cooper's Court. He checked that no police had gone back to the café then left the area, noticing that the minor matter of a knife attack at the scene had not disrupted the surveillance operation.

He went straight back to Westminster because he needed to check whether the GreenState building was being watched and he also wanted to know Zoe's reaction to finding him at the Junction. She may not have recognised him immediately, but he had shouted her name during the attack, so she was bound to have spotted him and it would be immediately obvious that he'd been shadowing her. That meant this particular job was over, which was a relief to him, yet there were questions he wanted answered. She took care with anti-surveillance routines, but was she aware of regular attempts to follow her? Had she ever seen the man in the black leather kilt before? And what was going on in the Edgar Building that interested the police so much?

There was no sign of any surveillance outside the building, so Samson entered and went back to his desk in the volunteer room, which also served as an overflow for the digital department, and returned to where he'd left off addressing inquiries to the organisation's main site. GreenState's purpose was to advocate a revolutionary new deal, zero-growth economy and a transformation of the way people live and consume. In reality, it was a number of different campaigns all housed in the same building – there were the GreenState Economics Foundation, GreenState Water, GreenState Climate Research, GS-STOP, which campaigned for a total ban on trophy hunting, and GSMedical, which sniped at big pharma. The organisation, Samson realised, was very large, given its humble origins as an NGO limited to activism in the state of California, very rich and also all rather opaque. But in its private mission, GreenState was unwaveringly clear. As a likeable volunteer organiser named Rob had explained during Samson's first week, GreenState only gave a damn about three things: data, getting things for free and looking after its own image. Rob cheerfully admitted that the climate emergency and mass extinction of species probably came fairly low down the list of the organisation's priorities because, well, it was like all campaigns – the success of the organisation rather than the crusade mattered most to the senior people.

GreenState had a thirst for data, for which reason Samson's job this past three weeks had been to answer every incoming email with a customised appeal for money, followed by a request, delivered in the most unctuous and manipulative language, for the correspondent to complete a questionnaire on their lifestyle, beliefs, income, social-media engagement and environmental activism that would allow GreenState 'to better serve the planet and its people'. It was surprising how many of those who turned down the request for an immediate donation were happy to complete the detailed survey. 'If we don't get them to donate now, we get them later,' Rob told him while going through the procedures for replying to emails and Web enquiries. 'Whenever there are floods, wildfires, news stories about the unprecedented release of methane from the tundra, etcetera, we bang out appeals to different groups of respondents based on the data they've given us in the questionnaire. It's pretty goddamn effective.' In the guileless responses, which included mobile numbers, private email addresses and income, and at times ready donations, Samson saw Rob was right. GreenState was a cash cow with a lot of political power that could be deployed internationally, nationally, or at constituency level, although it never actually caused much trouble to the government. 'We work on the inside to reform,' said Rob.

The operation intrigued Samson and when he was waiting for Zoe to make a move he researched the company structure. He used to do this in his brief career as a banker before being recruited by SIS, and he was surprised to find that there were no annual reports because GreenState was now owned by a series of private companies, the original evangelicals having long since been removed. The whole was controlled by an American parent company called GreenSpace Dynamics US Inc., which in turn was run by a tiny board of business figures, about whom there was also very little public information. GreenState made a lot of noise about the good it was doing but was remarkably silent about its own affairs.

Late in the afternoon, Zoe appeared in the office, looking stricken. Samson wasn't close enough to see if she had been crying, but thought she might have been – maybe she had been shocked by the attack in the street and thought that she was the target, but that didn't seem in keeping with the character he'd observed. Instead of removing her coat, she strode down the aisle of the open-plan campaign centre with her bag slung over her shoulder. A few minutes later she came back and went straight to the exit without stopping. He couldn't follow without making it obvious and, besides, she seemed too upset to have the conversation he wanted.

A minute or two later, Desmond appeared. 'A word with you, Mr Ash, if you wouldn't mind.' He signalled to the two youths from Digital, who made themselves scarce, and checked his reflection in the glass partition. He sucked the ends of his reading glasses, toyed with one of the grey curls that framed his face then regretfully left his reflection to its own devices. 'We have had a complaint, Mr Ash. I'm afraid I have no alternative, as Director of Campaigns, but to ask you to leave.'

Samson said nothing.

'Did you hear what I said?'

'Yes, that's fine – I'll leave.'

'You don't want to hear the nature of the complaint?'

Samson shook his head, got up and hooked his jacket over his shoulder.

The Director of Campaigns was not going to be deprived of the pleasure. 'I'll tell you anyway. We've had a complaint from a member of staff – a much-valued and trusted member of staff – that you have been stalking her during your time here and that, further, she believes you volunteered at GreenState in order to carry out your campaign of harassment. It will be obvious to you that we cannot allow this situation to continue. I will inform Security that if you try to gain entry to these offices, or are seen loitering in the vicinity, they should call the police. Is that clear?'

Samson shrugged and smiled.

'Have you nothing to say?'

'Nope,' said Samson, brushing past him.

'There's one other thing. We're aware that you have used your time here to investigate the organisation – Web searches are recorded, as I'm sure you know. We had you marked down as an undesirable and you would, in any case, have been told we no longer required your services at the end of the week. GreenState will defend itself, Mr Ash. Do not trifle with us.'

Desmond's neck was flushed and his Adam's apple was working furiously. Samson smiled from the doorway. 'You look like you need a rest, Desmond. Have a good evening.'

As he left the building, the burner phone in his pocket pinged with a message from Zoe. 'Now please fuck off, whoever you are, and leave this to me.'

He replied, 'Thanks for that. Whatever you're doing in the Edgar, you're being watched. Stay safe.'

CHAPTER 3

Survivors of the Bridge

It was still raining when he arrived in Mayfair. The bookings for his restaurant, Cedar, were not good for that evening and it seemed unlikely that there would be any change, unless there was late trade from the Curzon Cinema nearby. Ivan, who had worked for Samson's parents before him, and without whom he couldn't run what was described as Mayfair's premier Lebanese restaurant, appeared five minutes later and hovered at the door to the office as Samson began to go through the day's invoices. 'What is it, my friend?'

'Mr Nyman is downstairs. He's been waiting half an hour. I have served him coffee.'

'Jesus, that's all I need. Let's make him wait a bit longer.'

'He knows you're here.'

'Tell him I'm busy. I don't want him thinking he can drop in any time.'

'He's booked a table for later. He is to be joined by a lady friend.'

'Nyman with a woman! It can only be his sidekick, Sonia Fell. Make sure they order the '89 Musar. That should deter him from coming again.' The materialisation in his life of Peter Nyman, now of indeterminate status at SIS but always capable of making trouble, was never good news.

After being shot or, rather, winged in a street in Tallinn, Nyman and his colleagues had tried to put the blame on Samson and have him arrested by the Estonian authorities. The last time Samson saw him, he was cowering in the street outside the club when Adam Crane – aka Aleksis Chumak – was lifted two years before.

He looked down at the message notifications accumulated on his phone. 'Give me a quarter of an hour, Ivan. Thanks.'

There were two texts from Macy Harp and one from Macy's assistant, Imogen, all of which told him that Macy's and his conference call with Denis would now take place at nine that evening, and several texts on an encrypted app from Detective Inspector Hayes, Samson's friend in the Met and occasional lover. 'Call me!' they all instructed.

He dialled Hayes's number. She was busy and said she would call back, which she did in under a minute.

'Samson, were you in north London this afternoon?'

'Why?'

'I bloody knew it was you.'

'What're you saying?'

'You wrestling with a lunatic in a skirt and with a bloody great knife.' She paused to wait for a response, which wasn't forthcoming. 'Look at your email – there's one from my private address.'

He opened his laptop, found the email and clicked on the attachment, film taken with a phone camera. Someone outside the café had caught part of the fight and had evidently moved to get a better shot of the incident, although it was jerky footage and Samson was unrecognisable. There was much more screaming than he remembered and his assailant looked bigger. The man's escape was filmed, too. And the number of the Suzuki was clearly visible.

'You watching it?'

'Yes.'

'I knew it was you because of that jacket I gave you.'

'Ah.'

'Well, at least you're wearing it. I thought you didn't like it.' He didn't, but had worn it to GreenState because it was so unlike anything he would choose for himself. 'You're the anonymous hero of social media – the man who saved lunchtime crowds from a knife-wielding crazy. The Met wants to interview you – this is a serious incident, Samson.'

'Have you said it was me?'

'No, because I know you are up to no fucking good. What were you doing?'

'Waiting for someone.'

'Right!'

'Why do they need me? They've got the bike's registration.'

'And they know who he is.'

'Who is he?'

'You're not getting that information so easily, Samson. I want to know what you were doing at the Junction before I tell you any more. There's a lot of interest in that particular location and I guess that's actually why they want to interview you. I'll see you at your place later.'

'I've got something on . . .'

'I mean, later. I'll stay the night so you have time to tell me what the hell you're up to. That okay with you?'

'Yes – I guess.' This was characteristic of their relationship. It wasn't love, by any means, but a friendly arrangement that suited them both and was the best distraction he had from his perpetual yet now diminished ache for Anastasia Christakos, who had returned to America and her marriage to Denis Hisami after the ordeal of her kidnap and violent release. On the bridge at Narva they had been injured by the same bullet and after that they spent two agonised, blissful weeks of recuperation together. Jo Hayes was smart and uncomplicated company. He admired and liked her a lot, but there was no question of love. There never could be with anyone else.

'And Samson,' she said with a note of admonishment.

'Yes?'

'This man isn't your ordinary crazy. He's a really bad'un. Not good. Look after yourself. I'll see you about eleven thirty.'

He buzzed down and told Ivan to send Peter Nyman up.

Nyman had been to his office twice before and each time his appearance augured disruption in Samson's life. It was Nyman who hired him to find a young Syrian refugee named Naji Touma on the migrant trail through the Balkans, and then, three years later, he blundered into Anastasia's kidnap by Russian hoods. There was one thing you could say about Peter Nyman; whatever his failure to understand the thing that was staring him in the face, he never lost an unreal self-belief.

Samson didn't get up when he entered but gestured to the chair Nyman used before, where he let himself down with his customary disregard, causing the whole thing to groan and the cushion to wheeze.

'New suit?'

'As a matter of fact, yes,' Nyman replied. 'I got it in the sales and have only just come to like it.'

'I can well understand it took time,' said Samson with a straight face.

'Well, I think it works quite well,' said Nyman. His eyes went to the floor. 'I don't suppose you have a drink available? I believe we are both going to need it.'

'What do you want?' Samson swung round in his chair and went to a small inlaid drinks cabinet that his father had bought in Istanbul twenty years before. 'Scotch? Gin? Cognac? We can get the mixers sent up from downstairs.'

'Brandy – I'll have it on its own.'

Samson handed him the drink.

'You will need one, too, Samson.'

'Too early for me.'

Nyman filled his mouth and held it there with his cheeks slightly in-flated before swallowing. 'Robert Harland was killed this morning, shot dead by an assassin in Estonia. He was alone with his wife at some sort of country retreat, a cabin apparently, and the gunman killed him when he was outside, painting.' He stopped and took another mouthful. 'Good painter, Bobby.'

Samson took a moment to respond. He was genuinely shocked. 'Any idea why he was killed?'

'There are theories.'

'Does Macy Harp know? They were friends for over forty years.'

'Yes, he must do. As you say, they were in our service together for many years. In some ways, they were a vintage generation – end of the Cold War, beginning of the modern era of espionage. Everyone is very upset . . . very troubled. Bobby was a hero to us all, as you know. As intelligence officers go, Bobby was the gold standard. The best.'

'Gold standard? I don't remember you being very flattering about him in Tallinn,' said Samson.

'Operational tensions – all part of the life we chose.'

'What are the theories?'

Nyman put his glass down and pulled out a handkerchief to dab his nose then clean his glasses vigorously. 'The theory is that this is just one of the hits planned against all the survivors of the bridge.'

'By which you mean?'

'The people who had anything to do with freeing your friend Anastasia and the death of Adam Crane – their top man, Aleksis Chumak, so, that would be Harland, yourself, Denis Hisami, and your young Syrian friend Touma; in fact, anyone who was on or near the bridge at Narva. That may include your friend Anastasia Hisami, I'm afraid.'

Estonia had been a disaster for Nyman – he had been wrong at every turn and paid for it with his position in SIS, though, somehow, he had managed to hang on to an unspecified but reduced role. Against Harland, Nyman was unimaginative and mediocre, which contributed to Samson's suspicion that Nyman felt some kind of perverted vindication in report-ing Harland's death. 'What's your evidence, Peter?'

'Chatter. We knew they were mightily put out by what had happened, especially about the money and the release of all the names of far-right activists.'

'They weren't activists – they were white supremacists and anti-Semites and all were potential terrorists, Peter. Let's not sanitise what they stood for. They were genocidal killers in the making.'

'That's as maybe, but it doesn't stop them being extremely annoyed and, well, they want to teach us a lesson and the first part of that lesson was killing one of the most talented spies of the last half-century. They are sending a message. Robert Harland's death is proof that they can do these things with impunity.' He took up his glass and studied Samson. 'You haven't had any trouble of that sort, have you, Samson?'

He shook his head. 'Running a restaurant doesn't expose you to a lot of risk.'

'But you're someone who likes risk. It's no secret that you've had a bad run at the tables and are, in consequence, forced to take on menial work to pay off your debts. You know how people will gossip about these things.'

Samson smiled. There had been an episode and he had lost big time – exactly £74,500. But that was a year back, when the ache for Anastasia was much stronger and the pain of losing – the counterintuitive thrill of it – made him forget. He couldn't say whether he had lost intentionally, whether his subconscious had pushed him to defeat in the high-rolling backgammon games that had been a disaster for his father, too, but he understood that the prospect of selling the restaurant and losing much else besides had made him snap out of this funk. 'You don't need to worry about me, Peter, although I know you've always had my best interests at heart. Now, if you don't mind, I'm going to call Macy. It will be very hard for him.'

Nyman showed no sign of taking the hint, so Samson rose. 'Oh, I'm forgetting, how rude of me.' He sat down again and leaned forward. 'You never come up here without wanting something. What is it?'

'Harland knew he was in danger and was, in effect, hiding out on that lonely stretch of land where they hunted him down and ended his life. We want to know why. Was he threatened? Did he have intelligence? There is evidence that he was working on something. You were close to him, Samson – in many ways, you were very alike – and it has occurred to our people that you were aware of the danger he faced, and perhaps had some intimation of a threat to yourself, as well as the other survivors of the bridge. We would like to catch these people. We can't let them think that Britain is so weak that they can continue to murder our citizens at will. We have to put them on trial.'

'You don't seem to have had much success with that so far and, anyway, Harland was an Estonian national. He renounced British citizenship. He didn't like this country; thought it was ludicrous and posturing.'

Nyman looked around and sipped his brandy. His eyes came to rest on the photographs of Samson's father and mother as newly-weds and the gap where he'd removed the little framed picture of himself and Anastasia in Venice, the one he had forwarded from the phone he found near a deserted track in Italy where she had been abducted. 'I get it,' said Samson, heading off Nyman's question about the gap or his usual observations about his parents' life in Beirut half a century before. 'You want to use me as bait.'

'I wouldn't go that far, but you're the one they're likely to come after next, and we'd like to monitor you and prevent that attack.'

Samson got up and walked to the door. 'Peter, you can tell *your people* to stay away from me. I'm not bloody playing. Now please leave.'

Nyman got up regretfully, knocked back the brandy and came towards him. 'Nevertheless, we'll keep an eye out for you.' He searched for Samson's hand, but, not finding it, tapped him lightly on the chest. 'No harm in that, is there? I'll be downstairs in the restaurant, should you want to talk further.'

Now that Nyman had gone, he'd have that Scotch. He poured the drink and tipped his chair back. Robert Harland's murder appalled him, not because an attempt had been made on his own life, which added weight to Nyman's theory, but because he liked Harland and in their two meetings since Narva, once during the summer in Estonia and another in Berlin when the German government marked the thirtieth anniversary of the fall of the Wall – poorly, in Harland's view – he had come to see that the old spy's life added up to something heroic and steadfast, which was rare in their business. He hadn't clung to the job beyond the end of his personal mission, or his usefulness. He didn't need SIS, or his country. He'd found another life in another country, as well as a deep love with Ulrike. He'd become an artist, reclaimed his freedom, lived on his own terms. He wasn't someone who told you much about his inner life, but on the Berlin trip Samson noticed how often he used the word 'freedom'. That was what Harland fought for – his and other people's freedom.

He held the glass up to the desk light and pondered the glow in the liquid. Out loud to the room, he said, 'To you, Bobby. I'm so very sorry.'

Then he pulled his laptop towards him and searched for the live stream from the Congressional Committee on Foreign Affairs in Washington DC. It was the second day of hearings on America's relations with the Kurds in northern Syria and, in particular, allegations that the Kurdish-American billionaire and Anastasia's husband, Denis Hisami, was helping to finance military action against US forces and their Turkish allies. Hisami had been caught out by the sudden change in US policy on the Kurds. They were no longer America's ally in the region and Hisami's donations had become the subject of outrage in the White House and hysterical attacks on websites. Hisami maintained that the money had been donated before the administration's abandonment of the Kurds and in any case was being used for humanitarian purposes, such as the rescue and rehabilitation of women enslaved by ISIS. Samson had watched for half an hour the day before and had glimpsed Anastasia sitting with Hisami's aide, Jim Tulliver, behind Hisami as he was cross-examined by an aggressive congressman from the South. She was as beautiful and composed as ever, but the strain of the last few years was showing and he thought she'd lost too much weight and maybe that the humour had left her eyes.

They hadn't seen each other in two years. They'd talked and emailed frequently after her return to the States, but then she seemed to suffer a precipitate collapse, not surprising, given what she had endured at the hands of her tormentor, the man she knew as Kirill but who was in fact a sadistic Russian brute named Nikita Bukov. She called Samson one night, distraught and quite unlike herself, and said it would be better if they didn't speak for a while: she needed to straighten things out in her head; she couldn't sleep or focus on her work. She told him she'd been traumatised by the events in Macedonia when she, Samson and Naji Touma were all nearly killed, but this was far worse. There were moments when she had no orientation with the real world whatsoever, like when she was imprisoned in a container on the ship, then a metal box. That confinement and the terror were always with her. She couldn't rid her mind of them.

This exchange was extraordinarily painful for Samson. They loved each other, but there was absolutely nothing he could do, and she wasn't strong enough to deal with being so frequently in touch yet also separated by five thousand miles. Her husband, now free of the particular round of persecution by the US authorities, had got her the professional help she needed – a new treatment, she implied – and was caring for her with all the love in the world. She said it would be for just a few weeks, but they hadn't spoken since. The only news he had of her was when she returned to Lesbos, the Greek island where they had met and where the Aysel Hisami Foundation, under her supervision, was trying to deal with the scale of mental-health problems of the people who'd been in the camp for over five years. He had toyed with the idea of flying out to see her, but she hadn't told him she would be there – he'd just seen her quoted in a story on the CNN news site.

His eyes went to the gap in the photographs on the wall. He'd removed the picture of them on the evening he'd agonised about going to Lesbos. Eventually he'd told himself that if Anastasia was well enough to return to work yet had not contacted him to say she was in Europe, there was no future for them, and he certainly wasn't going to embarrass them both by dropping in unannounced. He took the photograph down and put it in a drawer and, from that moment, the pain had begun to leave him.

Something had moved in him when he caught sight of her in the proceedings the day before, but now he simply wanted to check she was all right. He found the stream from Congress on C-Span. However, although it was past two o'clock in DC, there was no sign of the session starting. Staffers were milling around the committee room as if they didn't expect the hearing to restart soon. There was no sign of Hisami and Anastasia, and no commentary to say what was going on.

He turned the sound down, took out his phone and composed a text message to Jim Tulliver. 'Robert Harland is dead. Maybe a threat to others involved with the Narva affair. Call me urgently – Samson.'

Then he finished his drink and dialled Harland's greatest friend, Macy Harp. This wasn't going to be easy.

CHAPTER 4

Room 2172

Among members of Congress, the offices in the Cannon Building, on the south side of Independence Avenue, had the reputation of being the worst on Capitol Hill, and those on the fifth floor of that 120-year-old building were known as 'Siberia'. Originally attic storage space, the fifth floor had been converted to offices to accommodate the newer representatives, and this is where Shera Ricard, the freshman member for California's 14th District, ended up after winning her election. The offices were cramped, generally had a poor view and were several minutes' walk from Room 2172 in the Rayburn Building, where the House Foreign Affairs Committee held its hearings. The Cannon was the only office space not served by the Capitol's underground railway, and a seemingly endless programme of renovation meant that the thud of jackhammers and drills was transmitted through much of the structure's fabric.

But for all this, Shera Ricard, one of the youngest members of the new intake, remained upbeat and smiling, and she was more than happy to play host while one of the major donors to her campaign, Denis Hisami, was appearing in front of the committee, of which she was a member. She had helped plan his evidence, which had now lasted four hours, and the responses to questions, but the afternoon session, delayed by half an hour already, was going to be the toughest for Hisami.

There were seven in the young congresswoman's offices – Anastasia, Hisami, Jim Tulliver, a lawyer named Stewart Steen, Ricard and two members of her team. Anastasia said nothing, though occasionally nodded to her husband when he glanced at her to see if she agreed. She was worried for him. After investigations and court appearances lasting two years, he had become gloomy and defensive in his manner, and he wasn't coming over at all well on TV.

'You have a lot to talk about with the foundation's work,' said the congresswoman brightly, 'a proven record of humanitarian care. I guess you need to refer to Anastasia's background and the projects in the Mediterranean and then you call these fucking guys out. They're mostly lawyers and they've done damn all to help their fellow human beings.'

It was at this point that Jim Tulliver, who was sitting next to Anastasia, withdrew the phone from his inside pocket to read a text. Anastasia couldn't help but see Samson's name and the brief message about Robert Harland's death. She touched Tulliver discreetly on the arm and shook her head to tell him not to show her husband then shrugged helplessly to apologise for reading over his shoulder. He nodded and returned the phone to his pocket. The news was indeed bad – she was fond of Harland and Ulrike and he, of course, was partly responsible for saving her life – but why did Tulliver look so devastated? As far as she knew, he'd never met Harland.

The planning went on for a few minutes more before one of her staff appeared to say that the session was due to commence in ten minutes. 'Okay, so we better get our asses over to the Rayburn,' said the congresswoman. 'Remember, there's no elevator from this floor.' She glanced at the lawyer, who was still looking put out at her remarks about his profession. 'Come along, Mr Steen – we all know the world needs lawyers, just fewer Southern trial lawyers and the ones that defend the coal industry.' She dived into her desk. 'You people go ahead and I'll see you in 2172.'

She straightened and gave Hisami a brief hug. 'That's on the taxpayer. You'll be fine, Denis.'

Four of them hurried along the endless corridors towards the northern foot tunnel, the southern one being closed as part of the renovation works. When they reached it, the Capitol Police told them there was a demonstration – climate-emergency protestors had positioned themselves at the far end of the tunnel – so it was going to take a lot longer to reach the Rayburn. Tulliver explained that they were in a hurry and an officer led the way, breaking through the line of demonstrators, who were in the process of gluing themselves fast to the walls, the railings and each other. When they emerged in the hygienic sixties splendour of the Rayburn and started to push through the media scrum, they were already several minutes late.

Anastasia caught hold of Tulliver's arm. 'What's going on, Jim? They weren't here this morning.'

'Maybe they've been tipped off about questions we haven't anticipated. I'll talk to Denis.'

'And what was that about Harland?'

'Later,' he said.

Hisami had gone ahead with Steen, forging through the crowd of reporters with the help of the officer, nodding but refusing to answer questions hurled at him about his past as a military leader in Iraq. She saw him stop as a thickset man in a suit and tie blocked his way and thrust a bundle of papers into his hands, as though he were delivering a subpoena. Hisami glanced at the papers, shook his head with irritation and looked up to try to find the man, who had retreated into the crowd. He passed the bundle to Steen, who clamped it under his briefcase arm and pointed ahead to the committee-room door.

The hearing started sedately enough, with the chair of the committee, an old Democratic congressman from New York named Harry Lucas, making a short opening statement about the delay caused by protestors all over the Capitol. Hisami sat alone at the table with a few papers in front of him. Anastasia and Steen were a little to his right, while Tulliver took the chair immediately behind Hisami. As Lucas consulted a member of his staff, he leaned forward and whispered to Hisami, who listened without turning round.

It was the turn of Ranking Member Warren Speight, the representative for the First Congressional District of Louisiana. He had an easy, pleasant manner, but the day before had twice caught Denis out and made him look evasive.

'Mr Hisami, you told us this morning that you and your wife have spent millions of dollars in the provision of psychological and therapeutic care, is that right? Speight did not look up to see Denis nod. 'And this foundation of yours was set up in the memory of your sister, Dr Aysel Hisami, correct? Would you care to tell us a little more about her, Mr Hisami?'

'Yes, she was a dedicated doctor. She worked with children undergoing treatment for cancer. In 2014 she returned to our homeland in northern Iraq to help treat the huge number of battlefield casualties in the war against Islamic State. She was taken prisoner and died in captivity. We don't know exactly when that was, but her death was eventually confirmed by women who were held with her. My wife and I wanted to keep her memory alive so we set up the Aysel centres to deal with the trauma experienced by refugees – from torture, the loss of loved ones, and the hardship of leaving everything they know behind. My wife is a psychologist and was an aid worker in Greece, and this was an area where we knew we could make a real difference.'

'And you have started working on the border with Mexico. That's much more controversial territory. You have come up against ICE – Immigration and Customs Enforcement – right?'

'It's a pilot programme. We're working through the issues with ICE.'

'Tell me about your sister. You were close?'

'We went through a lot together. We were also once refugees.'

'When you were defending yourself against allegations made by ICE, in effect the Department of Homeland Security, in New York two years ago, the court heard evidence about your past as a commander in the PUK – the Patriotic Union of Kurdistan. That was when you were known by your birth name, Karim Qasim, is that correct? Your sister changed her name, too.'

'Yes.'

'Because she was also a fighter with the PUK, a front-line combatant.'

'Yes, for a short while.'

Anastasia saw the way this was going. Speight was drawing a picture of two fanatical young Kurds who had laundered their reputation in the States but remained committed to the armed struggle for Kurdish independence. The mention of the tiny operation on the Mexican border, which had been her project, was only meant to stoke opposition to her husband. She glanced at Steen, who shook his head and then did something odd. He got up, stretched to the witness desk and grabbed the water carafe that was set in front of the empty chair beside Denis. Harry Lucas looked over his glasses disapprovingly but let it go because Steen looked like he really needed it.

'And there were photographs shown to the court of you at the scene of a war crime,' continued Speight, 'where scores of Iraqi soldiers had been massacred.'

'Yes, I was in the company of the CIA officer named Bob Baker, who's in the photographs and gave evidence in court. That was at a time when the United States and the PUK worked closely together. We were allies. Regrettably, on that occasion, we were too late to save those men from being murdered.'

'It is fair to say that you are a fighting man. You were a successful commander – you're someone who knows how to handle himself in a war setting.'

'That *was* true, yes. But not today . . .'

'Yet you believe there are times when only aggression – that is to say, military action – will get the job done.'

'I suppose so, yes.'

'Like the time when you avenged your sister by killing the men whom you believed imprisoned her. That was in Macedonia, sometime in 2015, right?'

'There were reports, but they were inaccurate in almost every respect.'

That at least was true, thought Anastasia. The one site that eventually reported the events in the remote farm in northern Macedonia had got almost everything wrong, except Denis's presence.

A point of order came from the congressman sitting next to Ricard to the effect that this was not relevant to the matter in hand – namely the allegation that Mr Hisami was supporting the military effort in Iraq against America's allies. The chair overruled him, but the intervention gave Hisami time to pour a glass of water and compose himself. Anastasia saw his face was ashen and one hand was shaking where it rested on his leg.

'Whether the reports go to the point that Mr Hisami is a man of action,' said Speight, 'he has undeniably donated large sums to humanitarian causes. He has used this as a cover to supply money to buy weapons for the Kurdish forces within the last few months.' He reached down and retrieved some papers. 'I have documentation here, which I enter in the record, that shows in excess of $50 million of transfers to accounts known to be operated by the Kurds. All I ask Mr Hisami now, is where are the medical centres and hospitals? Where are the scores of doctors and nurses? Where is the life-saving equipment which that kind of money buys?'

This is what the reporters had been waiting for. A murmur ran through Room 2172. Photographers jumped up to catch Hisami's expression, but he had his head in his hands and was looking down. Anastasia moved forward, but before she could do anything Stewart Steen made a helpless flapping motion, thrust his legs out and lay back rigid in his chair. His eyes were staring at the ceiling and his mouth foamed at the corners. 'We need help here!' she yelled. 'Get a doctor!'

Then it was Hisami's turn. He pushed his chair back, kicked out his legs and waved his arms about wildly. His eyes searched the room with a total lack of comprehension and then he seemed propelled backwards by some unseen force, which caused him to fall over the back of his chair. His most trusted aide was unable to prevent him falling to the ground, where he lay rigid with a sound of gurgling in his throat.

'Clear the room and get a doctor in here now!' shouted the Chair. 'Call 911. I said clear the room, goddammit.'

But a louder voice, that of Warren Speight, prevailed. 'Don't touch them!' he commanded. Then, leaning forward, he called to Tulliver, who was crouched over Hisami. 'Sir, sir, do not move. They've likely been poisoned. Step away from him now, sir! Do as I say, please.'

The word 'poisoned' was all that was needed to clear the room. Over seventy people filed out instantly, only a few of them daring to look back. Very soon, the periphery of 2172 was swarming with Capitol Police, and not long afterwards came men in biohazard suits, trained for precisely this emergency. Anastasia and Tulliver stood rooted to the spot, looking down at the two men, who, in their agony, were completely unrecognisable.

CHAPTER 5

Bulletin

Samson waited over an hour in his office before he spoke to Macy Harp, time he filled with Cedar's accounts and invoices that needed attention. A text had arrived from Imogen postponing the conference call at Macy's office– clearly everything had been upended by Harland's death. Macy eventually phoned at 8.25 p.m.

'I'm sorry,' said Samson. 'I know what Bobby meant to you, Macy.'

There was a brief silence at the other end. 'He only had a few months left and the fucking bastards robbed him of that.' His voice faltered. 'He had cancer, but kept going.' He stopped, overcome with grief. 'He was a great man and as reliable and brave as hell. I loved him dearly.'

'Of course you did, Macy. I'm sorry – I'm bloody useless at this. Never know what to say.'

'What can anyone say?'

'Any idea who's responsible? I had Nyman round here. He told me about it, but he hadn't got any details.'

'Yes, I guess the Office will be getting worked up, though Bobby thought they were a bunch of clowns latterly. Our conference call – the one I wanted you in on – has been delayed and I don't want to talk about this on the phone. Let's have a bite.'

'Not here. Nyman's having dinner with a woman – probably Sonia Fell – and he said that I am going to be monitored from now on because of that business in Narva. He thinks there's a connection with Bobby.'

'Well, you know how to avoid them. There's an Italian restaurant off Shepherd's Market – Corfinio. I'll see you there in ten minutes.'

Samson put on a clean shirt and changed jackets then left through the kitchen and down an alley where Cedar's bins were lined up. Not many minutes later he found Macy in the restaurant with a bottle of red wine and the menu.

'We'll order then talk,' he said. He was flushed and distraught, and angrier than Samson had ever seen him.

'I met Bobby when I was twenty-seven, you know. I was a lad, just joined MI6 and didn't know shit from sawdust. Bobby was my senior by five years and he taught me everything. We worked on a lot of the same operations. Good judgement! Really had a nose for it. Almost second sight. And he never, ever fucking played games.'

They ordered and were silent for a few minutes. Harp slung back a glass of wine and poured another with a fierce look.

'Did you talk to Ulrike?'

'Not yet – she'll be devastated. Of course, she was preparing for his death. He was in the final stretch. I pray he had the sense to tell her how much he loved her, because he did! She was the love of his life, you know.' He stopped. There were tears in his ears. 'It's absolutely bloody, the whole thing.'

Samson looked down. 'I know.'

'We have to find these fuckers and deal with them.' Macy gripped his hand. 'Deal with them. That's what he would have done. That's what he *did*. He dealt with the people who killed Ulrike's husband. He sorted out some bastards in Bosnia and the Czech Republic. This was a man who was tortured, blown up in a fucking plane, and he never, ever buckled.

He fought the good fight is what he did.' He raised his glass. Samson did likewise and for the second time that evening he drank to the memory of Robert Harland.

Presently, Samson asked, 'What do you think about Nyman's theory? He says it's the Russians avenging the deaths of Chumak and Bukov. All those who were at Narva are now targeted. That's me, Anastasia, Naji Touma, and, I guess, my friend Vuk Divjak.

'The Serb rascal?'

'The same.'

Macy looked away and frowned. 'Why now? Why not a couple of years back? And who were Chumak and Bukov? They were nothing. You don't go assassinating a man like Bobby Harland because of a couple of dead grease monkeys. It doesn't add up.'

'They had a go at me today,' said Samson, and Macy looked up from his glass. 'I thought he was going to attack Zoe Freemantle, but there's no doubt he was after me, though he was about as useless an assassin as ever lived. I believe they put a tracker on my bike.' He told him the whole story.

'Well, that does change things. Did you tell Nyman?'

Samson shook his head.

'Good.'

The food arrived and Macy ordered another bottle of wine.

'I thought we had a conference call later.'

'We do, and it's important but, frankly, I need this.' He stopped, pushed the veal around his plate, ate a potato then put his knife and fork down. 'So Nyman put surveillance on you without knowing about this attack on you. He will have got the security services involved, and they wouldn't be up for that unless they thought there would be success at the end of it. So what's he told them? What does he know that he hasn't told you?' Macy may have been feverishly trying to forget his grief, but what he said made sense.

Samson thought for a few moments. 'My rule with Nyman is that the thing he tells you is usually dead opposite of the truth, so I'm working on the assumption that it has nothing to do with Narva. Oh, by the way, I got sacked from GreenState. Zoe eyeballed me at the Junction and had me fired for stalking her, so I guess that's the end of that job. And another thing, I had to lose the motorbike.'

'You've had a busy day. That's a pity, but it couldn't be avoided. You had to defend yourself.' He paused and considered his uneaten meal. 'Actually, the conference call is all to do with her.' He put his hand up. 'Don't ask! Denis will fill you in.'

'Hisami! What's he got to do with this?'

'He's paying the bills. That's why you were getting two grand a day, Samson.'

'Why's he protecting a young environmentalist in London?'

'You can ask him yourself shortly.' He checked his watch. 'I told him you needed more information and that you were likely to get bored and chuck in the towel unless he told you more.'

As Samson would remember it, Imogen phoned a few moments later. In fact, Macy and he talked for twenty minutes about Berlin and how Harland had extracted firstly an Arab terrorist and, on the night when the Wall came down, brought two agents over, the art historian Rudi Rosenharte and the woman who was known as Kafka – Ulrike Klaar – whom Harland eventually married. Both had been working for Bobby.

When Imogen's call came, Macy listened intently then exclaimed, 'Jesus Christ! Is he alive?' Without looking at Samson, he asked, 'What about his wife, Anastasia? She's okay – good.' He listened a few more seconds, then hung up and searched for a text from Imogen with the link she'd mentioned.

'What the hell's happened?'

'Hisami was poisoned in Congress. He's still alive. A lawyer is dead. It's all on CNN.'

Macy found it on his phone and held it so Samson could see the screen. The clip started with a reporter in the hallway of the Rayburn Building explaining that a Foreign Affairs hearing had been cleared because a

witness and his lawyer had fallen ill at a dramatic moment in the proceedings. The voice of the reporter continued as footage from inside
Room 2172 was shown. The Ranking Member, Congressman Speight,
was seen flourishing evidence of money transfers to Kurd-controlled
accounts. The cameras turned to the lawyer, who was gripped by some
sort of spasm. Samson saw Anastasia jump up and call for help. At that
moment, Denis fell over the back of his chair and collapsed at the feet
of Jim Tulliver. There followed random footage from the media cameras
in the room, as well as from people's phones, which did a better job of
capturing the chaos of the situation. The report cut from a close-up of
Denis Hisami's body on the floor to a shot of the lawyer, who already
looked dead but was said to have survived another thirty minutes, then to
the chair of the committee waving people out of the room and Speight
shouting at someone and gesticulating.

'At this time,' said the reporter to camera, 'the FBI has confirmed that
Mr Hisami and Mr Steen were poisoned, but there is no information as
yet about the substance used. Samples have been taken from Room 2172
where the hearing was taking place and freshman congresswoman Shera
Ricard's office, where a meeting was held before the hearing, attended
by Hisami and Steen. The Agency has confirmed that tests are being
conducted on the others at that meeting. These include Congresswoman
Ricard and Denis Hisami's wife, Anastasia. No trace of the substance has
yet been found in the Cannon Building. It will likely be compared with
those collected when a nerve agent called Novichok was used in the case
of a Russian father and daughter in Salisbury, England, in 2018. In the
past, the FBI has been unwilling to reveal such details. They are examining footage from the media taken immediately before the hearing and the
Bureau is appealing to any members of the public who may have useful
footage on their phones. At the time of the hearing, a group protesting
against climate change were demonstrating in the network of tunnels
under the Capitol. An FBI spokesperson stressed that the Agency does
not believe the protestors had anything to do with the incident, but they

may have recorded valuable evidence in filming the protest. We will bring you updates on Mr Hisami's condition and any further developments as we have them.'

A search of the Web produced no fresh information. Samson sent a text to Jim Tulliver, asking for news, and then one to Naji Touma: 'Naji, we need to talk, soonest. Where are you? Samson.'

By the time they reached Macy's offices at Hendricks Harp two blocks away, Tulliver had replied. Samson read the text out to Macy. 'Anastasia and I are okay. Denis is in a coma – he may not get through the night. Doctors won't say how they are treating him. We are being kept here for "observation". They're worried we'll infect others with the agent. Our clothes have been taken away. You sent a message about Robert Harland. You know that Denis and he had recent business dealings??? How did he die? Why did you warn me?'

'Don't reply to those questions now,' said Macy. 'Tulliver is reliable, but we don't want him telling the FBI and them linking what happened to Bobby with Denis.'

'Nyman will make the connection – he'll tell them. I guess this means his bloody theory is right.' He stopped and sat down in one of the chairs facing Macy. 'What business dealings did Denis have with Harland? They surely never met. He was in New York and confined to his apartment with an ankle monitor during the business at Narva.'

'They did meet. When the Homeland Security investigation was over, Denis flew over to thank Harland for his part in freeing Anastasia. He behaved impeccably, by the way, and didn't ask about you and his wife. Harland was impressed with him, said he was a grown-up. They got on very well indeed.'

Samson absorbed this. 'So, what was their business?'

'I don't know. I simply arranged for you to protect the young woman at GreenState on Denis Hisami's behalf. I have no idea what they were cooking up and didn't ask. You have to remember Bobby was very sick. I doubt he was up to much, apart from painting.'

Samson thought for a moment. 'Nyman said he knew Harland was working on something.'

'Did he now?'

'Yes, I'm sure he said there was evidence he was working on something, and that he and Ulrike were hiding out in a cabin on a "lonely stretch of land" because he knew he was in danger.'

'The only problem Bobby faced was not getting enough work done,' said Macy quickly. 'He had an exhibition in Tallinn in a couple of weeks. I said I'd go. We were going to have dinner after the opening. Like old times.' He pointed to a very small seascape of deep slate greys beyond his desk. 'That's Bobby's from five years ago. You can see his natural talent – it has the freshness of a much younger artist.' He shook his head as the loss struck him with renewed force.

'So where does Zoe Freemantle come in?'

'I told you I've no bloody idea,' Macy snapped.

That didn't seem right to Samson, but he didn't make an issue of it and got up. 'Sorry.'

The older man shook his head sympathetically. 'It's not you. It's the fuckers who took him.'

'You won't mind if I talk to Tulliver? He must know why Denis was paying for Zoe's protection. I'll tell him that Denis was going to speak to us about it this evening. I'll make it plain that he needs to tell us.'

'This can wait until tomorrow.'

Samson nodded and went over and squeezed Macy's shoulder. 'I'm sorry, old friend. It's grim for you. I'll call tomorrow.'

'Righty-ho!' said Macy, stiff upper lip asserting itself. 'Ring me first thing and we'll put our heads together. You know your way out. And, for fuck's sake, take care of yourself!'

CHAPTER 6

The Balsam Tree

He walked from Hendricks Harp to Park Lane and crossed into the park, a good way to lose a tail at night, and one he'd used a couple of times after dining with certain characters from the Middle East in the Edgware Road during his years with SIS. The park also held a romantic memory for him. Four years ago, in the spring, he had come there late one night with Anastasia with a bottle and cigarettes. They had stood under the balsam poplar near the Serpentine, marvelling at the scent of its buds, drained and exhilarated after spending the evening fucking like wildcats, as she had indelicately put it.

He stopped at the memorial to the Reformers' Tree, the oak that was burned to a stump by protestors wanting the vote for all men in the 1860s, and crouched down on the mosaic, looking for pursuing silhouettes against the lights of Park Lane. He saw none but maintained the position and took out his phone to dial Tulliver, who picked up on the second ring.

'Jim, sorry to call – didn't want to bother Anastasia.'

'Good decision, Samson – she's got enough to deal with. We don't know what's happening with Denis, and she's very upset. We may lose him. I know things are complicated, but you have to respect that she's had really serious problems and Denis looked after her.' That speech delivered, he exhaled and his tone softened. 'What happened to Harland?'

'I need you to keep this to yourself. He was shot dead this morning – about ten hours ahead of the attack in Congress. There's been nothing in the news so far and, obviously, we don't want people to make that connection.'

'Why not, if it helps catch the perpetrators?'

Satisfied that no one had followed him, Samson stood up and began to wander round the circular memorial. 'Because they had business together, Jim. Do you want the FBI crawling through that? Denis was going to talk to Macy tonight and he wanted me on the call. He was going to explain what they were doing. It was going to be a long session.'

'I doubt that. He didn't usually speak about such things on the phone.'

'Well, that's what he told Macy. You can say now what they were doing. I mean, why was he paying for me to watch Zoe Freemantle at GreenState? What the hell is this about, Jim?'

'I can't tell you, because I don't know. If Denis was paying you, he didn't tell me – probably didn't tell anyone. That's the way he works.'

'Why Zoe Freemantle?'

'The name means absolutely nothing to me. I've never heard of her.'

'But you knew Denis went to see Harland in Tallinn to thank him personally for his part in rescuing Anastasia. And they got on well and saw each other and were working on something together. People here think it's all about revenge for what happened at the bridge – the two dead Russians.'

'I knew that Denis went to Estonia, but Anastasia doesn't, and I'm sure that Denis would prefer you keep it that way. And to your point about theories – I'm hearing a lot of them right now, and we need to concentrate on what happened, which is that someone walked into Congress with a bunch of papers drenched in nerve agent and handed them to Denis. It's profoundly shocking to the country and, frankly, no one is thinking in straight lines at the moment.'

'Did they ID the man who gave them to Denis?'

'They've got a clear shot of him, but no name as yet. The FBI will track him through the CCTV around the Capitol and they'll get a pretty good idea of his route into the Rayburn and where he came from. But none of that has been made public. Denis had only momentary contact with the agent, but that poor guy Stewart Steen had it all over him.'

'Seems odd, doesn't it? If you're going to attempt to kill someone, the Capitol is the very last place you'd try, unless . . .'

'. . . You were making a point,' said Tulliver.

'Who would want to make that point?' He considered telling Tulliver about his own narrow escape but saw no point. 'Will you let me know what happens, Jim, and if it's appropriate, pass on my concern to Anastasia for both her and Denis.'

'I will. She read your text over my shoulder . . .'

'That's like her . . .'

'Wish I had acted on it, Samson,' Tulliver said quickly. 'Wish I'd shown it to Denis. But she told me not to. She's asked me to find out about Harland. I'll tell her we've talked.'

'Stay in touch, Jim.'

'I'll do that.'

He walked on, crossed the Serpentine and vaulted over the low fence into Kensington Gardens, now locked for the night. He found the balsam poplar, which was at its fragrant best, and after listening to the sounds of the birds out on the water and thinking about that night and all that had passed since, moved to exit the gardens through the turnstile at Lancaster Gate. It took him a further twenty minutes to reach the avenue of tall, mid-nineteenth-century white townhouses in Maida Vale where he owned two flats, the top one now occupied by a composer of distracted nature named David Jericho and his husband, Derek, a set designer, whom Samson met with his dog as he thumbed through his post in the lobby.

'I thought you were in – we heard the TV,' said Derek.

'My friend, I suspect, but thanks for keeping an eye out,' said Samson, heading for the stairs. He had already checked the street thoroughly and seen no sign of any surveillance.

Jo Hayes was waiting for him on his bed with a bottle of white wine. 'I saw what happened in Washington,' she said, after he kissed her right and left. 'That was her?'

He nodded.

'I'd never seen her before. Is she okay?'

'Looks like it, but her husband is in a coma. I spoke to his right-hand man. It's touch and go.'

She eyed him. 'So is this connected – the cross-dressing knifeman and what happened to them?'

He lifted his shoulders and sat down on the bed next to her. 'Different kinds of attacks: one involved weapons-grade nerve agent, the other a kitchen knife. They don't tally.'

'But there's something going on, Samson.'

He thought for a few moments then told her about Harland. 'You are now one of three people who know that there were three separate attacks within 10 hours of each other on individuals who were, in one way or another, associated with the events surrounding Anastasia's kidnap and her subsequent rescue at Narva. The obvious conclusion, which is supported by my former colleagues at SIS, is that Harland's murder was revenge by the Russians.' He took her hand. 'There's a lot to say for the theory, but it doesn't feel right to me.'

'Are you okay?'

'Fine, but I'm worried about Denis and I liked Robert Harland a lot.'

'And Anastasia?'

'She's going to be okay. But thanks for asking.'

'They know who tried to kill you. I don't have a name, but he's a Serb – hit man, people smuggler and enforcer with a lot of aliases. Brought in for the job, apparently.'

'Yet he's not very good at it.'

'He would have killed you! You were saved by one of our officers.'

'True.'

'They still don't know who you are. I'm breaking every rule in the book by not telling them. I could lose my job.'

'You recognised a jacket – that's all.'

'Which I notice you've changed.'

'Yes, for reasons of identification,' he said without skipping a beat. 'Look, if you tell them it was me, my life becomes a lot more difficult. I can't spend the next few days being interviewed by the police.'

'You are, however, going to have to tell me what you were doing at the Junction.' She reached for the glass of wine on the bedside table and gave him a look that was halfway between investigating copper and sexy lover. He waited to see where it would settle, which it did, to the former.

'I was waiting for someone, a young woman I was hired to keep an eye on, make sure she was safe. I thought she might turn up there – that's all.'

'Name?'

He shook his head. 'Client confidentiality.'

'And did she turn up?'

'Maybe. It was a pretty confused situation.'

She looked doubtful. 'If she was there, and I am assuming she was, I hope she had nothing to do with the building opposite where you were attacked.'

'Why?'

'That's an official secret,' she said. 'Let's just say that I heard that particular building holds a lot of interest for the police and security services.'

'What kind of interest?'

'I don't know. But beware, Samson – this is a really serious matter.' She put down the glass. 'Now, I'm going to have a shower. Then you can decide whether you want to make love, or not. I'm easy either way.'

He caught her as she passed him, hooked his arm around her waist and pulled her back on the bed. He looked into her eyes with near-sighted amusement. 'What's the word for this thing we have? We make no demands and we're easy with each other; close yet ignorant about huge areas of each other's lives. We've saved each other in bad times, we cheer each other up and we trust each other.'

She stiffened. 'Whatever gave you that idea? I don't trust you, Samson. Never! You're too devious.'

'But I trust you.'

'You delude yourself.'

He grinned. 'So what is this?'

'Well, we have these things in common – we've both had our hearts broken yet we don't see why we should be denied sex and companionship. We find the same things funny. We like each other, but we give each other a lot of space. I love my place in the country, and I don't want you there.' Jo had bought a cottage outside a Berkshire village and kept a horse in local stables with the legacy from a relative, sang in the choir and had started gardening. 'For a while,' she continued, 'I thought it was like a brother-and-sister thing.'

Samson grimaced.

'But lately it seems more like a gay relationship between opposite sexes.'

'That makes no sense.'

'It does, because we know exactly the way the other works, i.e., like two members of the same sex, or, indeed, a brother and sister. There's a lot less mystery than when you're in love and, of course, there's no rapture, but it's pretty good, and you'll do.' She squeezed his thigh, rose and stood above him with a look of high-spirited, erotic challenge. 'I'm going to wash the Met right out of my hair,' she said, and took off her shoes and untucked her shirt.

'You're magnificent,' he said. 'However, I need to think through things in the next room.'

'You're going to make one of your little diagrams – how exciting!'

'I'm afraid so.'

'Okay,' she said, and moved closer so that her breasts were at eye level, waited for a few seconds then kissed him with a passionate commitment that made Samson reconsider the urgency of going next door.

CHAPTER 7

Cock and Bull

The meeting at Carlton House Terrace to discuss the Harland assassination and the official reaction started at 10 a.m. in the building where Samson was first interviewed before joining SIS several years before. Chaired by Lewis Ott, the deputy head of SIS, the gathering included Peter Nyman and Sonia Fell and two from the security services who gave only their first names – Shriti and Caroline – and appeared to be on good terms with Sonia. Macy Harp and Samson were shown in at ten fifteen after the intelligence services had, as Ott put it, rolled the pitch.

'We're going to be got at,' said Macy in the waiting area, as he lowered the pot of poorly filtered coffee with a look of dismay. 'The only reason we're here is because they want information. You know better than to tell them anything, of course, Samson.'

Ott, tall, with the limitless self-esteem and quiet menace of the mandarin spy, said he was sure he didn't have to remind them that they had all signed the Official Secrets Act, then moved to Harland's murder, describing in detail the events on Bear Island Peninsula. He had been shot four times, three bullets to the chest and one to the leg. His wife was on the scene in minutes, but he was already dead. She saw a man fleeing – the same figure that had aroused her suspicion fifteen minutes before. The gunman seemed in some difficulty and it subsequently became clear that Harland had fought back and managed to set the man alight with a burner and turpentine. At the news that his friend hadn't gone into that good night gently, Macy looked up at the ceiling and smiled.

'The local police understand the importance of all this because Robert Harland was well connected, had advised on the setting up of the foreign intelligence operation and had many friends in the KaPo – the Kaitse-politseiamet. So there's been no lack of urgency and, after examining his phone, they found a photograph of the man in a series of rapidly taken landscape studies. Enhanced and enlarged, the photographs enabled them to track down the suspect in Tallinn, where he was being treated in hospital for burns to his stomach and thighs and, as it happens, a developing case of pneumonia. He's a Ukrainian national who was hired for the job – not your average international hit man, by any means; a thug who was paid €30,000. He's told the police everything but appears to know little about the people who hired him, and he certainly didn't ask them about the target. If Robert Harland hadn't managed to inflict those injuries on the killer in the last minutes of his life, he would never have been caught. Even in death, our former colleague and, if I may say so, the hero of our service, was as effective as ever.' He looked around and his eyes came to rest on Macy. 'Does anyone want to say anything about him now?'

Macy shook his head; Samson didn't lift his eyes from the table.

'The Foreign Secretary,' continued Ott, 'is anxious that Robert Harland is accorded all the honour our country has to offer. He has sent his condolences to the widow. There will be an announcement later today and I gather an obituary is underway for *The Times*.'

'Who's writing that?' asked Macy.

'I'm drafting notes,' said Nyman. 'Their security correspondent will knock them into shape.'

'Peter, what the fuck do you know about Bobby?' Macy said.

Nyman was unfazed. 'A lot of his career is in the archive – the main operations, and so forth. And I did know him, of course, Macy. I worked with him. I respected him greatly.' He pursed his lips in a tiny, round hole, which the French describe as the *cul de canard* – the duck's arse.

'Bollocks, you did! You didn't *know* him. You weren't in Berlin in '89. Were you there with him in Czechoslovakia? Bosnia? New York? No, of course you weren't. You don't have the first bloody clue what he did for our country, Peter.'

Ott intervened. 'Can I suggest you run your notes past Macy before sending them to the paper, Peter? That all right with you, Macy?'

Macy nodded, but the outrage hadn't left his expression. 'And on the funeral, make sure you go along with whatever Ulrike wants. It's likely to be modest.'

'What about a memorial service in London, then? Grosvenor Chapel is a marvellous space. There are a lot of people who would want to attend, you know.'

'Ask Ulrike before you start thinking about arranging that. It's the bloody last thing Bobby would have wanted. Anyway, this is all beside the point. You haven't asked us here to talk about the obituary and the funeral.' Macy wiped a handkerchief around his chin and neck. He looked ill, but then Samson had seen him sink a lot of booze the night before. 'You've got something to say to us, so you might as well get on with it.'

'Thank you, Macy!' Ott bowed to his senior status, which of course was an entirely sarcastic gesture. 'Naturally, we've linked yesterday's two incidents and have concluded that this is blowback from events at Narva, at which Denis Hisami and Robert Harland were key participants, as indeed you were, Paul. And we believe it would be helpful to the Americans if they viewed the events in Congress in that context, rather than as an attack on the American state. We think it's best to downplay things at the moment. The phrase "nerve agent" is not helpful in this regard and in fact the substance used was much less potent than Novichok.'

'Yet it was a nerve agent,' said Samson. 'The symptoms were all there – sweating, loss of body control, muscle paralysis, salivation. The lawyer Steen died within half an hour or so of coming into contact with it.'

'It seems that after he handled the papers he must have touched his lips. He probably ingested quite a large amount,' said Ott. 'But moving on, what interests us are the common denominators, which is why we have asked you in, Paul.'

He signalled to Caroline. She spun a laptop that was primed to show a short video and hit 'play'. It was the film from the Junction. Samson saw himself block the attacker to the left, go to the right, grab his upper arm, start to punch his Adam's apple and chin and aim a kick at his groin. Even when the police officer shouted and Samson turned there was never a clear shot of his face.

'Impressive self-defence,' said Ott. He waited for a reaction but got none. 'We know it was you, Samson, because Shriti here was part of an operation at that intersection and she saw you. But we needed her to see you again in the flesh, which is why I'm so pleased you could make it this morning.'

Samson still didn't react.

'I suppose the immediate interest for us is this character who attacked you. Since we have had the film, our friends at the Security Service have been beavering away to identify him, and they have come up with an ID. He is a famous gangster from Montenegro. He is named Miroslav Rajavic but goes by the name Matador, which you no doubt know also means "killer" or "assassin" in Spanish, and this fellow lives up to his name by using a long knife or even a sword – his *espada*, I suppose. But the interesting part, and this is where I must offer congratulations to the security services team, is that we have tied him to the attack in Congress.'

Caroline brought up more video footage. Macy and Samson, sitting next to each other, had to lean forward to see clearly. It lasted no more than a few seconds. Denis Hisami, seen from the side, was moving through a crowd in a corridor that was patchily lit by TV lights. A man

stepped forward, handed him papers and immediately backed away. Hisami looked down, looked up and passed the papers to Steen on his right.
The film ended but was followed by two freeze frames, which showed
the man's face.

'Caroline, would you take over?'

Caroline was a familiar intelligence services type – late thirties, intense
and with a no-nonsense attitude to clothes and make-up. She had a fringe
and short, fair hair, which she nervously hooked behind each ear before
looking down at an iPad. 'This turns out to be a man named Vladan
Drasko,' she said. 'One of our people had the idea of putting his photograph through a program that allows us to search for known associates
on a database using facial recognition, and we came up with this.' She
turned the iPad and there was Drasko, with longer hair and less weight,
sitting next to the Matador with a pair of Balkan beauties and a row of
shot glasses.

'This was Belgrade three years ago,' said Caroline. 'It comes from the
Facebook page of one of the women in the photograph.'

'Facebook is such a really terrific resource,' said Ott. 'The point that
will not escape you, Paul, is that you and Denis Hisami were targeted
on the same day by two killers who know each other. We're now using
photographs of the Ukrainian assassin, taken in hospital overnight, to
see if we can match him with these two; it would be something like
a royal flush if we did. In short, we'd be able to tell the FBI and CIA
why this attack happened and ID the main suspect. Not bad in less than
twenty-four hours.'

'And Russia?' said Samson.

'No need to blame Russia – that's the beauty of it. None of the perpetrators is Russian.'

'But the entire plot to kidnap Anastasia two years ago was designed to
suppress information about a Russian operation to wash money through
the States to disrupt democracy in Europe.'

'You say *Russian* operation, but that was never clearly established, was it?' said Ott. 'Adam Crane – aka Aleksis Chumak – started out life as Ukrainian. And Nikita Bukov? Well, who's to say he was ever involved? And there were certainly never any direct ties to a Russian agency. They were deniable crooks and, as it turned out, quite expendable.'

Nyman nodded sagely throughout this.

'Then who gave the order to kill Hisami, Harland and me?'

'That doesn't concern us at the moment. This is the settling of some old scores by persons unknown who were undoubtedly annoyed about the disappearance of all those laundered millions. It's all water under the bridge at Narva.' Ott was pleased with that line.

Macy gave Samson a look to say that there wasn't any point – the intelligence services had the solution they wanted. He made a move to leave.

'There are a couple of outstanding matters,' said Ott. 'We're anxious to catch the Matador and, of course, we wish to protect you, Samson.'

Samson gave an audible groan. 'When Peter mentioned this I made it clear that I didn't want any kind of surveillance or protection.'

'He very nearly succeeded in killing you yesterday. You do need some help looking after yourself.'

Samson got up and turned to face Nyman and Sonia Fell, who had barely moved in the last half-hour. 'These two will tell you that I am perfectly capable of looking after myself and, at the same time, clearing up their mess in Macedonia and bungling ineptitude in Estonia. That kind of protection I can do without.'

Macy patted the table and rose. 'I think we have contributed all we can here.'

'There is one other thing,' said Ott. 'We would rather like to know what you were doing at that intersection in north London yesterday.'

'Would you?' said Samson.

'The area is of interest to Caroline and Shriti's colleagues in the Security Service. And they wondered how you came to be in that particular spot.'

'I was hoping to meet someone.'

'Did you meet them?'

'No, things fell apart, as you've just seen in that video.'

'Name of person?'

'That has absolutely nothing to do with your operation, and it is a private matter.'

'So you don't know why the Security Service and the police were there? We are to believe your presence was a coincidence?'

'Yes, I have no interest in the area.'

Shriti looked unconvinced but gave a resigned shrug.

'Then we thank you both for your time,' said Ott.

Outside, Samson found himself groping for a cigarette, although he'd quit many months ago now. 'That,' he said as he and Macy started walking, 'is exactly why I don't work with those people any longer – all that wheels-within-wheels shit and turning tricks for our American friends.'

'Didn't use to be like that. We knew who the enemy was in my day. Now you wonder . . .'

As they walked towards Pall Mall, Macy stopped to admire some almond blossom near the Athenaeum Club, an oddly intense expression on his face. 'You do know that was all cock and bull,' he said. 'The whole purpose was to put us off the scent. However, being rather foolish, they underlined at least one area of interest.'

'The Edgar Building,' said Samson.

'Indeed, but also the fact that they are determined not to blame the Russians. By the way, Ott is not as ahead of the game as he thinks. Vladan Drasko was found dead in a motel room in Virginia. Poisoned himself handling the nerve agent, no doubt.' He stopped to hail a cab. 'What're you going to do now?'

'Talk to Zoe Freemantle.'

'Denis put £20k behind the bar, as it were. So you have no worries about money.'

'There's something else that interested me. Peter Nyman let slip yesterday that Bobby had been working on something. They didn't mention that today – why? That must mean they have an idea what it was, but they didn't want us to pursue it. It would be nice to know how much Denis and Bobby saw each other.'

'Then you may have to talk to Anastasia. Or Ulrike. One of them must know.' He glanced at Samson. 'And by the way, don't think those bastards are going to look after you. If my hunch is right, they'd rather we didn't find out what they're trying to protect, and that means hanging you out to dry won't be a problem. They'll keep tabs on you, but they won't lift a finger to save you.'

'Yes,' said Samson. 'That was precisely my interpretation.'

Macy opened the cab door. 'Can I give you a lift to Cedar?'

'Thanks, but I need some exercise.'

'Okay. Go and find the people who ordered my old friend's death, Samson.'

Samson walked briskly to Jermyn Street and turned right into one of the arcades that led to Piccadilly. As he looked absently into a store selling expensive shaving brushes and creams, thinking of his father's reverence for the finer things of what he supposed to be the English gentleman's life, the call came in from a more recent immigrant. It was from Naji Touma, the Syrian kid who, over five years before, had darted through Greece and Macedonia like the lively bug that supplied his codename – FIREFLY. He was now in London, on a six-month secondment at Imperial College, where, to Samson's mild astonishment, he was thought to have original things to say about dark matter and dark energy.

'Naj, we need to talk.'

'About Mr Harland? I know.'

'How do you know?'

'Mrs Harland. She emailed me.'

'I see. I'm sorry. It's very bad news.' Naji and Harland had formed an unlikely relationship during the days before and after Anastasia's release.

While Samson and Anastasia were debriefed by Estonian intelligence, the pair of them sat at Harland's kitchen table in his seaside cottage, talking for hours. Harland was fascinated by the speed and range of Naji's mind and murmured to Samson that he sometimes felt he was in the presence of one of the great intellects of the day. Samson remembered looking over at Naji's vacant expression and doubting that, but a year later Naji had won a prize for early career astrophysicists with an essay written in English. Harland went to Norway to watch him receive it. It was plain that he had become a substitute for Naji's father, for whom the boy still grieved. 'You okay?' Samson asked after a long silence.

'I am very sad. Mr Harland was a good man to me. A very, very nice man. A very clever man.'

'Yes.'

'I will attend his funeral.'

'Err, yes, so will I. It's going to be next week, we think. But I just wanted to stress something that you and I should both be aware of, Naj. There's a theory that all of us involved in getting Anastasia off that bridge are being targeted by the Russians and, of course, you were crucial to the operation. In fact, we wouldn't have pulled it off without you. Bobby was shot, Denis Hisami was poisoned, and Naj, I have to tell you that someone attacked me in the street on the same day, so the revenge theory could be right, and you need to be extra careful.'

'You are okay, Samson?'

'Yes, but I was lucky and I don't want you exposed to the same risk.'

Naji absorbed this. 'No one knows I was at Narva.'

'That's true, unless there was a leak from the Estonian intelligence service, which is highly unlikely.'

'I will be okay, Samson.'

'Well, just be careful. Do you want to meet up?'

'I cannot. I am busy with my project.' He stopped. Samson could hear him fidgeting. 'How is Anastasia?' Naji asked.

'She wasn't hurt in Washington but she must have been very shocked by what happened. Denis is still in a coma.' He was playing it straight, though he knew exactly what Naji was asking – had he talked to her?

'She will be at Mr Harland's funeral?'

'I can't say. I guess she'll stay in Washington to look after Denis.'

'I must go now. Goodbye, Samson. I will meet you at the funeral.'

'Yes. Naji. Stay safe.'

Samson looked across Piccadilly to the line of exhibition posters on the Royal Academy railings, thinking about Naji. A memory of his time with Anastasia came to him. A late Saturday breakfast before going to the show of American art at the academy, where they stood for twenty minutes in awe of an enormous painting of a glacier. It seemed a long time ago: the scrawny Syrian kid had grown into a man in those years. He was now over six feet and good-looking with it, but he could be remote and also a little eccentric, jumping wildly from subject to subject in his increasingly impressive English. Even taking into account Naji's idiosyncrasies and his obvious sadness at Harland's death, the conversation had definitely been off. It was as though he didn't want to connect at all.

CHAPTER 8

Anastasia

Anastasia was allowed no physical contact with her husband, who lay isolated in a room on the hospital's top floor, surrounded by more medical equipment than she had ever seen concentrated around one person. She peered through an observation window and saw his chest rise and fall and watched the heart and blood pressure monitors. A nurse in protective clothing and wearing a mask and fume hood sat beside him, checking the drips and monitors. Sometimes she held his hand and nodded to Anastasia, as though she were her proxy. He showed no signs of coming out of his coma, which his doctors suggested was maybe a good thing, because he was being saved the pain and distress of incontinence, vomiting and mental disorientation. Denis was fastidious and he would have found it all mortifying.

Unlike the lawyer Stewart Steen, he'd survived the onslaught of the nerve agent, and that was due to relatively low exposure, rapid diagnosis and the speedy application of a drug called atropine, used to counter the sudden decline in the heart rate, the restriction of muscles in the chest and the production of a lot of watery sputum. He was over the worst. She hoped one day to be able to tell him that he had quickly exhausted the hospital's stocks of atropine and was only saved by a trainee nurse who thought of phoning her brother in a veterinarian clinic, where the drug was routinely used in operations on large dogs, and arranged for all the practice's supplies of the drug to be biked across DC. They arrived just in time.

The FBI was a constant presence in the hospital, as were the TV vans outside. When it was clear that Tulliver and she had not been contaminated and were showing no signs of sickness, they were interviewed about all aspects of Denis Hisami's controversial – their word – career. A lot of ground was covered – his past as a commander in the PUK, the business in Macedonia when a squad of IS terrorists was wiped out, the affair that led to her kidnap and the death of two Russians on the border between Estonia and Russia at Narva, to say nothing of the enemies he'd made in business and politics. Special Agent Edward Reiner observed that he would be hard pressed to find another American citizen whose back story included so many people with the means, motive and malice to kill him. The FBI team were as considerate as they could be, but the interviews added to her sense of a siege. Reiner was smart and patient, and his sidekick, Agent Paula Berg, sat like a watchful member of the crow family.

Late in the afternoon of the second day, when she was alone in the room with them and assumed Tulliver was being given the third degree by another team down the hall, Reiner began to tell her the details of the attack. He again showed her the film from the Rayburn Building of a burly man with short black hair and dressed in a dark suit who thrust some papers into Denis's hands then quickly backed away. An enlargement of a still revealed he had been wearing surgical gloves. 'This individual's name was Vladan Drasko,' he said. 'He was a thirty-eight-year-old Serbian national from the district of Novi Grad in Belgrade. You've already said that you didn't recognise him from the film, but given you spent time in the Balkans, I wonder if that name has any meaning for you.'

She shrugged. 'No. Did you say *was* a thirty-eight-year-old Serb? *Was?*'

'He poisoned himself by accident at a motel near Fredericksburg, Virginia. Drasko called the desk clerk to summon help but died before it arrived. The motel is being decontaminated, and the rental car examined, and EMS personnel who attended are under observation.' He paused for a couple of beats. 'How much do you know about nerve agents like this one, Mrs Hisami?'

'Nothing, I'm a psychologist. I don't even know what substance was used to poison my husband, though the TV news says it may be Novichok.'

'Not exactly, but it's related to the group of nerve agents developed by the Soviets in a programme before the fall of the Berlin Wall. Novichok is what is known as a binary agent, which means that it activates after two harmless inert substances are combined. The material that poisoned your husband was an antecedent of Novichok. It's a unitary agent, which means that it becomes lethal the moment it's manufactured. No combination is required – there's just one substance. For obvious reasons, this greatly concerns us. The idea that Mr Drasko brought the material into America in a sealed flask is highly disturbing. Though we're satisfied that we now have that container and the remaining agent, we're treating this very seriously.

'This brings me to information that has come from British intelligence. A few hours before your husband was poisoned, there were two other attacks: Robert Harland, a former senior operative with MI6 – who you knew – was killed by a lone gunman in Estonia, and in London, Paul Samson, who was involved with you and your husband in the Macedonian incident – the CIA has given us a full briefing on that – was attacked by a man with a knife in the street. You know all these individuals: you're close to two and a friend of the third.'

Her stomach turned over. 'Is he all right?'

'He wasn't hurt. He fought off the attacker. Film of the incident has emerged on social media, but he's not identified in it.'

'I knew about Harland but had no idea about Samson.'

'He seems to have made light of it. According to Mr Tulliver, he didn't mention the attack when they spoke last night.'

'That's like him.'

Reiner was silent. He looked from Anastasia to Agent Berg and back again.

Berg glanced at her phone. 'We're about to be joined by our friends from the Agency,' she said, looking up.

'Three men in your life, and they were all targeted. Why? Apart from you, what's the connection, Mrs Hisami?'

She opened her hands incredulously. 'Are you saying I'm somehow responsible?'

'No, no – of course not. Apart from anything else, you could easily have been contaminated, along with Mr Steen and your husband. But you're the link and we need to understand what that means for this investigation.'

'Honestly, I have no idea. I just can't help you.'

There was a knock at the door and two men entered. They nodded to her, but didn't give their names. A middle-aged man with a brush of stiff grey hair and a dark moustache took the only available chair, while the second, who was younger and wore square tinted lenses and a light grey suit, leaned against the wall and folded his arms. Reiner pointed to the two men with his index finger and a cocked thumb. 'These gentlemen are from the CIA.' He waited for the lead CIA agent to put a recorder on the low table in the middle of the room then continued. 'The British have told us that they believe this is a revenge attack by certain parties, maybe Russian, following the death of the two men during your rescue by Paul Samson. What do you say to that?'

'What can I say? Paul Samson and I were both shot. I have very little memory of what happened that night. I can tell you that I was kidnapped in the Italian countryside, saw two migrants murdered and woke up in a container on a ship alongside the bodies of the men who had killed the migrants and abducted me. I was held in an isolated compound in western Russia. I escaped, was recaptured and threatened with execution beside an open grave.' She held Reiner's gaze. 'So, no, I don't remember a lot from that evening except it was even more terrifying than anything I had experienced on the ship, or locked in a box in the freezing cold. Later I developed PTSD and I was in treatment for months. I had little understanding of exactly what my husband was involved in until some weeks after I was freed. Now I know he exposed the laundering of Russian money that was being used by fascist groups in Europe. Seems like he did a really good job, though, naturally, he was never thanked for it and, as requested by you people, he has never spoken of what happened. No one has. It remains a secret.'

'I'm sorry ma'am, but we have to ask these questions. This is a matter of national security.'

'Would you like water, a Diet Coke?' offered Agent Berg.

'No, thanks.'

'May I?' asked the older CIA man. 'Mrs Hisami, it is hard for us to know where to start. Are we dealing with some crazy Russian slash Balkan blowback to the first drama you were all involved in, when it is known your husband wiped out an entire IS unit, or is this about our friends in fur hats reacting to the second drama – the one in Estonia which you've just referred to? The British, for reasons best known to themselves, want to relegate these attacks to the category of gangster revenge. They say it was all about the money that went missing after you were released. Really? Two years on? That sounds like a whole lot of flapdoodle to us.' He looked impatiently around the room. 'There were three attacks in the space of a few hours against people who were connected. All, save the lawyer, had some part in one of the other two incidents. That's why we're asking you.'

'I understand – really, I do. But I'm baffled and I don't know which way to turn. One moment Denis is being criticised and investigated for offering relief to people bombed out of their homes, starving and brutalised. The next he's poisoned and we're locked up in this hospital and he's on the point of dying and you're here asking me questions as if I had the whole damn picture in my head.' She stopped and looked at them in turn. 'Why is it in this country victims are treated as perpetrators? Why is that?'

'Mr Hisami and Mr Harland, did they ever meet?' asked the CIA man who was leaning against the wall.

'My husband flew to Tallinn to thank Mr Harland for all that he did to get me released. At the time, he didn't tell me because, well, I wasn't in great shape. I had a lot of problems, and I guess he didn't want to remind me of that terrible period.'

'That's understandable,' said Agent Berg. 'But we're trying to understand both the criminal aspect to this event as well as the intelligence implications, and you're all we got.' She took a folder out of her bag and flipped it open. 'This here is a photograph taken three years ago of the men who attempted to kill Mr Samson and your husband. They were best buddies and they tried to kill the two men in your life on the same day.'

'That is a remarkable coincidence, is it not?' Reiner said.

After the incident at Narva, and the long debriefing in Estonia, it wasn't surprising they knew about Samson and her, but it made her angry. What possible relevance could it have now? 'Again, it seems like you're accusing me of something,' she said angrily.

'No, ma'am,' said Reiner, smoothing the air with his hand. 'We're just trying to figure it all out and ensure that the American public and their legislators are never exposed to something like this again. It's as simple as that.'

The room was silent. All four investigators looked at her expectantly.

The lead CIA man leaned forward in his chair with his hands on his thighs. 'There's an answer here, and it lies somewhere between three men – your husband, the late Robert Harland and your close friend Paul Samson, who was once also a member of the British intelligence services. Two of them can't speak to us. That leaves Samson, but British intelligence say he knows nothing. Is that likely?'

'We haven't been in touch for nearly two years. I can't tell you anything about him.'

'He seems a difficult character to make out. They describe him as a loser and kind of dismiss him. They say he's got gambling issues and has taken to low-grade security work to pay off his debts. That sound right to you?'

It didn't, but she shrugged noncommittally.

'He's the only other person who can help us. We need to talk to him. Can you fix that for us?'

'You can arrange that for yourselves, surely. He's got a restaurant – Cedar. Just pay him a visit. Paul is not some kind of criminal. He'll help if he can.'

'You see, Mrs Hisami,' continued the older man, 'the Bureau here have already made clear to you the seriousness of the situation. We at the Agency have a responsibility to track down the source of this material that was used against your husband and make sure that the supply line and the people who commissioned this act of terror are neutralised. We've deployed a lot of resources in that endeavour. But you'll appreciate that at the very beginning of that process must come an understanding of motive. Why did someone want to kill your husband in such a dramatic manner – in Congress, in front of the media and all these people? Why? This is, literally, unprecedented. Large numbers of people could have been hurt, including Members of Congress from all over the country. That is a big deal.'

'I saw what it did to Mr Steen and my husband. I do not take this lightly, sir.'

'Let's be frank,' he continued. 'If someone wanted to kill your husband, why not shoot him? A hit on the way to his office?'

'I suppose that's a good question, yes . . .'

'The people who ordered this thing wanted to create a spectacle of your husband collapsing in the middle of the congressional hearing. There's a gigantic message in that, either to your husband and his associates, or to our country. Which do you think it is?'

'How am I meant to answer that? I don't know – I simply don't know.'

He sat back. 'Well, I'll tell you what we think. We believe that this was a message to your husband and his associates, and that would include you.'

'I really can't say.' She looked up. A nurse was signalling through the glass door. 'Excuse me.' Anastasia got up and went to the door.

The nurse looked inside. 'Hope this is okay, but I wanted to tell you that he squeezed my hand a little. He knew I was there. He responded when I spoke to him. He's still very sick, but the doctor told me that I should tell you.'

'Thank you, I'll come now.' Anastasia turned to the room. 'I understand why this is so important and that you have to go over everything, but I don't know how to help. Right now I need to be with my husband. I'm sorry.'

The four agents rose. Reiner said he would be on hand if she thought of anything, or if, pray to God, her husband came round.

Since being detained in New York's Metropolitan Correctional Center by ICE on false charges and, as a result, losing a great part of his fortune, her husband had become an obsessive gatherer of intelligence. He needed to know who his enemies were and what they were saying about him, and never more so than in this current campaign against him by conservative forces in Congress. He watched for their knives, but not the poison. She looked down at him through the observation window – he appeared shrunken and helpless amidst all the drips and wires, and she couldn't believe he'd even summoned the energy to squeeze the gloved hand of the nurse. He seemed all but dead.

She went to talk to Jim Tulliver, who had also been given a hard time by the CIA and the FBI, and what he described as a meathead from Homeland Security. He jerked his thumb upwards and raised his eyebrows and she understood that they should go to the roof, where there was a glass lean-to, a kind of conservatory where mobile patients could read and catch the sun. They went through the conservatory into the warm late afternoon.

'Pretty sure they're listening to us,' he said, handing her a phone. 'I carry this one for Denis. You should use it if you're going to make any sensitive calls. I put Samson's number on it. Maybe you should tell him they want to talk.' He studied her. 'You okay?'

'Of course.' She'd played up her vulnerability with the agencies but, in truth, she was feeling a lot stronger than she had for a long time. She recognised the fight rising in her. It came from her father and she didn't much like the attendant belligerence, but it was preferable to her adored mother's resignation and fatalism and, as her therapist kept telling her, it was what had saved her during the kidnap.

'So how are we on the business?' she asked Tulliver, who looked rather strange in the sportswear the office had sent over to the hospital.

'Everyone is concerned for Denis, of course, but he turned things round in the last couple of years in a quite remarkable way. We're debt-free after the sale of our big stake in TV. To be frank, we're killing it. We're cash-rich and there are no crises.'

'Have you talked to our partners and the banks about the power of attorney?'

'Yeah, they're good. They know you're sound. You have a lot of respect out there. "Resilient" is the word they use for you, Anastasia. I think it's a good one.'

'No doubts whatsoever?'

Tulliver shook his head.

'Obviously, it's for a short time,' she continued, 'and the only thing I give a damn about is who did this. I agree with the CIA – I don't believe this has anything to do with Narva. Do you know what Denis and Bobby Harland were talking about?'

He didn't answer.

'You going to say anything about that?'

'No, because I don't have any idea.'

She didn't believe him. Even if Denis hadn't told him, Tulliver would have made it his business to find out. She looked away to the sun descending over the capital into the blue vastness of America. 'What do you think I should do?'

'The agencies are going to sit on your tail here,' he replied. 'It'll be hard to achieve anything. Samson's your man.' He stopped, realising what he'd just said. 'Sorry, you know what I mean – talk to him, will you?'

Their attention was caught by a large raptor circling over the hospital building. They watched for a few seconds. 'What an amazing bird,' she said.

'It's a red-tailed hawk.'

'Who knew you were a birder?'

'I like to know what I'm looking at,' he said.

'I do, too.' She checked his expression. 'You never let on, do you? But I need you to open up on this. How many times did Denis meet Harland? Where did they meet? I want the flight logs, dates, venues – everything. And I want to hear what actions followed from these meetings, even if you doubt whether they were directly related. Why was Denis paying so much money to protect the woman you told me about? Who the hell is she? What's she doing to warrant that much money? Is Denis paying for anyone else?' She stopped and thought. 'And why Samson? He's not a bodyguard, for fuck's sake. Is it true what they say about his debt? Jesus, what an idiot! I want to talk to Macy Harp, so I'll need his cell number. We have funds, and I know Denis would be happy to spend it on this, so let's make those available to whoever needs it. I want to know absolutely everything, Jim. Every goddamn thing!'

He held out his phone. 'That's Macy's number.'

She copied it into the mobile he'd given her before. 'I'll need that information by tomorrow, Jim. Tonight if you can get it.'

Tulliver nodded and returned to watch the hawk dropping in a glide path towards a park behind the hospital. 'They come into the city to hunt rats,' he said. 'A lot of rats in DC.'

An hour later Dr Michael Lazarus came to her room to tell her that a second round of tests were clear and that there was no chance of her developing any symptoms. She had been lucky, he said. Tulliver more so because there were traces on his suit and the sole of his left shoe, which must have come into contact with Denis's clothing as he tried to help him. A responding member of the United States Capitol Police had some slight exposure and was being treated at a different location. He had asked for his condition not to be made public because of his wife's fragile mental health.

'Which brings me to your husband,' said Lazarus with a reassuring smile. 'Broadly, it's good news. He's stable and is responding to treatment. We're seeing improvements every hour in his general condition. Analysis has shown that this agent was a precursor to Novichok. Basically, it's a concentrated organophosphate, a pesticide, though the chemical structure is new to the toxicologists who have been working on this case, and we wonder if this variation in the structure is responsible for the seizures. He suffered another today, which is disappointing. We've given him a pretty large dose of Diazepam – you probably know it as Valium – which is effective at suppressing seizures, but we really wish he wasn't having them at this stage.' He placed his hands together and put them to his lips.

'The nurse said he squeezed her hand.'

'He did, and mine, also. He's on the edge of consciousness, but we don't want him to come round yet. He needs rest. The first twenty-four hours of nerve-agent attack are unpleasant and traumatic, and really terrifying for the victim. We still don't know the extent of damage to his peripheral nervous system. He may have some problems walking and his sense of touch may be affected. But, look, we're pleased and we are ninety per cent certain that he's going to pull through. He's fit and tough. I gather he's been through some rough times and is used to hardship.'

She nodded. 'What about his mental capacity?'

'A little slow to start with, but it will take time to assess if there's any long-term cognitive impairment. We need to control the seizures that cause that kind of damage and we want to make sure that he isn't going to be left with temporal lobe epilepsy, which is one possibility that I have to warn you about. It's a long road, but I'm hopeful he will make a full recovery.'

'How long?'

'Six to nine months, but a lot of rehabilitation can take place at his home.'

'I'm thinking about his business.'

Lazarus shook his head. 'You can probably forget the next three or four months. He won't have the concentration, or the stamina. Someone is going to have to take his place. Is that a problem?'

'Jesus. The business is all in his head – it's all literally locked up in there.'

'I'm afraid I can't help you with that.' He got up and took her hand. 'We'll keep you in touch with any developments, and I'll see you at the end of the week. Good luck, Mrs Hisami.'

CHAPTER 9

Düppel

There were two employees at GreenState that Samson thought he could tap for information on Zoe. Rob, the volunteer organiser, was one, although the appalling Desmond had almost certainly told him about Samson's 'harassment' of Ingrid Cole. There was also Francis, a bright lad in Digital who had shared the volunteer room with Samson for most of the time he had worked there, using the name Michael Ash; he might not have been told why 'Ash' had been told to go. Francis left work promptly at five thirty every day and walked to St James's Park Tube. On one occasion Samson had accompanied him and they'd had a drink in a noisy pub full of tech people who worked around Whitehall. Many of them were gamers and Francis dropped in most evenings to talk to his gamer pals.

Samson bought himself a pint of lager and took up position near the door. Francis appeared bang on time with his odd, lolloping walk, hands sunk deep in his trouser pockets and a bag slung across his body. 'What's up, Michael? You weren't in today, right?' he said, flicking his forelock back and grinning ambiguously.

'No, couldn't make it. And I've got to admit, I had a problem with Desmond – he didn't like me reading up about GreenState's business structure.' He ordered Francis a pint.

'The guy's an arsehole. Knows fuck all. Total wanker.'

'On that we agree,' said Samson. 'Why are they so sensitive about it all? I mean, it's just like any NGO, right?'

'It's different. It's got a huge membership, which is like three or four times the size of any political party, and it's really, really rich. Members' income has got to be over twenty-five mill' a year, and that's not including all the donations and what have you.'

'Ingrid was saying something similar.'

'You talked to Ingrid? No one talks to Ingrid. She's scary.' He sank half of his pint in one long draught and gave Samson a sideways look. 'But she's really hot,' he concluded, wiping foam from his upper lip.

'You see her today?'

'Nope, she's on compassionate leave. Away for the next couple of weeks – a family bereavement, apparently, which is totally mortifying for the guys in Digital.'

'Someone close?'

'Has to be for that length of time off, right?'

'I'm not sure what she actually does?' Samson wanted Francis's take.

'She's an all-rounder. Totally gets digital. She can code and she's terrific at messaging and video – has a lot of great ideas. She's literally the only senior person who knows what they're talking about in meetings. For example, she can read the MRP results really well.'

'What's that?'

'Multi-level regression and post-stratification polling. That's a survey on attitudes by using very large samples – maybe as many as a hundred thousand. It's all about using demographics to predict the way people are going to feel about certain issues. It's pretty cool. Ingrid is really good at the analysis side – she has that kind of bent.'

Samson thought and looked down at Francis's empty glass. 'Want another?'

'Yep, if you're buying.'

'So this is basically where Ingrid sits – right at the top of that mound of data.'

'Nah, she has input on what GreenState is going to research, but she doesn't have access to the whole database – that's restricted. Nobody does, except maybe the people at the top – the PR guy, some others.'

'Who's the PR guy?'

'Jonathan Mobius. He sold his Mobius Strand for millions. Seventy-five mill', I think. He's part of some big-dick US corporation and he works for them and does GreenState.'

'Does GreenState?'

'Chairs it – and he's still at his own company.'

'None of that is very clear on the Web.'

'There are a lot of fake stories out there, a lot of ghosts and mirages. Düppel!'

'Düppel?'

'Otherwise known as *chaff* – radar-fucking countermeasures, developed in the Berlin suburb of Düppel by the Luftwaffe during the Second World War.'

'Whose radar?'

'Anyone's.' He looked at Samson with amusement from beneath his forelock. 'We couldn't decide whether you were fired because you were stalking Ingrid or because you were some kind of spook. Everyone noticed you getting the jump on Ingrid before she left the office – the water-bottle thing – so we assumed that you were, like, hot for her. People watch each other really closely in a place like GreenState. But then we reasoned that if that fuckwit Desmond was telling everyone that you harassed Ingrid, then it had to be the other thing. The spying thing.'

Samson grinned. 'I'll get that pint.' He waved at the barman. 'What about Mobius?' he went on.

'You didn't say which you were doing – stalking or spying.'

'Neither. Really! Now tell me about Mobius.'

'I don't know anything about him – except Jonathan Mobius is worth a fortune. We never see him except once a year, when he brings in dough-nuts and gets down, dirty and digital, but he hasn't the first fucking clue. You can see him for yourself at the GreenState rally in a couple of weeks. It's free. They need numbers. They'll let anyone in – even a fucking stalker.' Francis snorted into his beer.

'Good speaking to you, Francis,' Samson said, sliding off the stool. 'I gave you my number before – yes? So, if anything occurs to you, dial it.'

'What's that mean?'

Samson placed a hand on his shoulder and spoke to his ear. 'I think you know I'm a good guy. That's why you've talked to me. If you have anything you think a good guy might want to hear, call me, okay?'

Francis gave him a knowing smirk. 'Okay, Mr Spy.'

CHAPTER 10

The Pit

The word 'Düppel' played in his mind as he circled two blocks then went through St James's Park Tube station and exited on the western side to lose any watchers he might have picked up. If GreenState had taken so much trouble to obscure its ownership structure, it had much else to hide, and that was surely what Zoe Freemantle was there to find out. He wondered where the Edgar Building fitted into the picture.

He spent an hour going through his dry-cleaning routines. Certain that he wasn't being followed, he made his way to a backstreet on the Fulham side of Putney Bridge, which was conveniently close to the Tube line, bus station and the river-boat service Zoe often used to travel in to GreenState.

She lived there as Ingrid Cole in a recently converted two-storey building called Sail Maker's Yard, in which there were eight apartments of various sizes used for short-term rentals. She had one of the smaller ones – Number Eight, also called 'Jib'. He'd been there twice before and on one occasion had managed, through the letting agency, to gain access to the building and have a look round Jib. It was coming free at the end of June and Samson said he was looking for somewhere for the Wimbledon fortnight in July. He had no desire to poke around Zoe's things, but he did want to see if she was living there full-time and whether she had a partner, in which case his job of keeping an eye on her security would perhaps be a little easier. A sponge bag and toothbrush, on charge, were in the bathroom, and a little basic make-up sat by the mirror in the bedroom. There were very few personal items other than three small framed photographs on the windowsill, which he guessed were part of Ingrid Cole's backstory and meant nothing to Zoe Freemantle. He was unable to look in the wardrobe, because the letting agent was with him, yet he reckoned that everything in the flat belonging to Ingrid Cole would probably fit into the medium-sized suitcase standing in the corner of the bedroom. Ingrid Cole's residence was only lightly touched by habitation and there was, of course, no sign that this sparse, unbelievable existence was shared with anyone.

He knew she spent some nights at the flat that overlooked the street because he had followed her there, but it appeared she was elsewhere that evening. The curtains weren't drawn and no light came from inside. He moved to the doorway of the bookshop directly opposite the flat, climbed the three steps to the door and stood on tiptoe. It was hard to see, but he was sure that the three photograph frames had vanished from the bedroom windowsill.

His phone went. 'Macy!'

'Where are you?'

'Looking for Zoe. Any news?'

'Tulliver was in touch. Denis is still in a coma. Looks like he won't recover any time soon – it's a long process. A couple of years ago, when Anastasia went home after the kidnap and he was released from detention by the Department of Homeland Security, they put a lot of measures in place. She's got power of attorney and is taking over everything, so I expect to be hearing from her directly . . .'

'Hold on, Macy! There was a sound of the electronic buzzer that opened the double gates that accessed a tiny enclosed garden and all the flats. He saw no one but heard footsteps and some wheels bumping over the paving flags beyond the gates. 'I think this might be her. I'm going.'

Someone had unlocked the iron gates but was waiting to move into the street. A car came round the right-angle bend near the Tube station at the bottom of the street and moved slowly towards him. The driver was looking for an address. He stopped outside Sail Maker's Yard. The gate swung open and Zoe appeared, towing the suitcase he'd seen in the flat; a red bobble was tied to the side handle to make identification at an airport carousel easier.

She shoved the suitcase on to the back seat and followed. As she was exchanging words with the driver, a motorbike rounded the corner. This, too, was moving slowly. Just as Samson saw the blue livery of the bike and a pillion passenger holding the phone in his palm, Zoe's car moved off. The bike roared up the street, drew level with the car and slowed so the pillion passenger could lean down and look inside. The driver sounded his horn, made as if to steer into the bike then accelerated away. The bike shot ahead of the car and turned right at the end of the street. They weren't interested in Zoe, so the only conclusion must be they were searching for him, and he knew exactly how they'd found him, but he couldn't do anything about that now. He left the doorway and sprinted the 150 yards towards the Tube station. As he reached the right-angle bend he heard the bike behind. He ran across the street, vaulted the barrier and tore up the stairs of the Victorian station. A District Line train was standing at the platform. It was going north. He leapt on as the doors closed and looked back to see a figure in a hoodie reach the top of the stairs as the train drew out.

On the train, he turned off the three phones he carried and took the batteries out. The only way they could have found him was to track one of his numbers. He changed lines and went to Victoria, where he used a payphone to call Cedar's reservations number. He got through to Ivan; his maître d' stand faced the entrance to the restaurant and gave him a good view of the street. Having worked at Cedar for twenty years, Ivan knew the street better than anyone and was on good terms with the club doormen, the prostitutes that trawled for Middle Eastern men and the security details of nearby embassies that made up the particular Mayfair ecosystem.

'Notice anyone strange hanging about the place today?' Samson asked. 'Two men on a motorbike; one is large and freakish. Can you put the word out on him?'

'Nothing of that nature so far,' Ivan replied. 'Most of the freaks are in the restaurant.'

Samson laughed. 'What are our numbers like tonight?'

'Good – a hundred and sixty-five-plus covers.'

'Excellent. There's something I need you to do. There's a box in the office beneath my desk. You can't miss it. Can you bring it in a cab and pick me up at Victoria Station, by the Gatwick Express entrance.'

Half an hour later Ivan arrived in a cab with the box. As they travelled back to the restaurant, Samson unlocked it and replaced the two phone sets inside with the three in his pockets. Ivan gave him a quizzical look.

'It's a Faraday box. Blocks all signals. The phones can't be accessed or tracked when they're in it. One of these has been giving away my position. Any news from your street network, Ivan?'

'Maybe some surveillance earlier in the day, but there's always something going on and it's hard to say who the hell the target is.'

'You got that information quickly.'

'We've got a message group to alert each other to problems. The girls started exchanging information on police in the area, men to avoid, high rollers from the clubs – that kind of thing. Our group is called Mayfair Ladies.'

Samson grinned. 'No one's seen the big fellow on a bike yet?' He opened up one of the new phones and found the film of the Matador on social media. He froze it and took a screengrab, which he sent to Ivan's phone. 'Can you circulate that to Mayfair Ladies? He had a go at me with a knife yesterday and followed me this evening.'

'Then we must make sure he doesn't have another opportunity,' said Ivan, seemingly untroubled by the news that someone had tried to murder his boss, which was, after all, not an uncommon event.

At Cedar, Samson took a screen grab of the man who had poisoned Hisami at the Rayburn Building, and sent it together with the one of the Matador to a number belonging to Vuk Divjak. Vuk had helped Samson on the search for Naji and had been at Narva. He was well connected to the Balkan underworld. If there was anyone who'd be able to help Samson find out about the pair it would be him, although the information would undoubtedly arrive scrambled in Vuk's version of English.

He sent his new number to several people, including Macy Harp, his assistant, Imogen, Naji and Jo Hayes and then called Jo, wondering if she was going to spend a second night at the flat. She'd brought a bag with her the night before and he couldn't remember seeing her leave with it. There was no response to the call, or his earlier message. He phoned down to Ivan. The street appeared to be clear, but he left by a side entrance and worked his way north to a mews where he met the cab ordered by Ivan.

The taxi dropped him about a short walk south of the Junction and he approached on foot. He passed through it twice on either side, noting one or two lights springing from different parts of the Edgar Coach and Engineering Works, and by the time he took up position in Cooper's Court – where he'd left the motorbike, which had vanished – he was sure that no one else was watching the building; at least, there was nothing like the operation he'd seen a couple of days before. This seemed odd, given Jo's insistence that the place held a special interest for the security services and the two members of MI5 had more or less confirmed that at the meeting in Carlton House Terrace.

He pulled out the small binoculars from his jacket and scanned the building, but saw nothing. After half an hour, his attention was drawn to a car that issued from a loading bay a little way along Herbert Street, to the east of the Junction. Previously, he'd ignored the loading bay because it was so far from the entrance, but it was conceivable that it served the

Edgar. He crossed the road for a better view and placed himself in a recess between a locksmith and a wine warehouse. Knowing that an encounter with Zoe was extremely unlikely, he decided to give it another half-hour before leaving for his flat.

He waited and watched. As the bars up Herbert Street emptied and the traffic on the pavements thinned, a young homeless woman wearing a large coat over a parka asked him for money. He felt his pockets for change and, finding none, gave her a £20 note. She looked up at him, astonished. Her face was pinched from a winter on the streets and there was a recent cut above her left eye. 'Why are you out here?' he asked. 'Is there nowhere you can go?'

These were questions she wasn't going to answer. 'Thanks for this.' She was shaking. He asked if there was something the matter. She looked away. 'Twenty quid! It's been a while since someone's been that good to me. They think you're going to spend it on drugs, but I'll get food with this and maybe a couple of cans of lager. Thanks, mate.'

'My pleasure,' he said. 'A need is a need – you spend it on what you want.' He hoped she might now leave him, but she leaned against the locksmith's window, produced a bag of tobacco and rolled a cigarette, which she then offered to him.

'I quit,' he said, 'but thanks.'

She had trouble making her lighter work because her hands were cold. He took it and cupped his hand round the flame. The paper flared, she inhaled then spat out bits of tobacco. 'I saw you before. Why are you here?' she asked. The money was being stowed in a pocket somewhere beneath the overcoats. 'My name's Remy,' she said.

'Mine's Paul.'

'Why are you here?'

He looked down at the small pale face and lank brown hair and estimated her age at about twenty. The lights of the passing traffic washed her cheeks and glittered in her dark eyes. 'I'm interested in what goes on in that building over there,' he said. 'Hoping to spot someone I know.'

'Join the queue,' she said.

'What do you mean?'

'They raided that yesterday and took away a fella.' She jerked her chin towards the front entrance of the Edgar Building. 'But they got the wrong place.' She stopped and examined him. 'Are you a cop, Paul?'

'No, Remy, I'm not a cop.'

'I guessed not. Police wouldn't give me twenty quid for nowt.'

'Where are you from?'

'Leeds – my Dad was Belgian.'

'Really! Why're you on the street?'

'I'm not. I've got a place. My stepdad's why I'm down here, if that's what you're asking. He's a cunt.'

Her eyes moved restlessly over the street. In profile, she had a resolute chin and her mouth was clamped determinedly shut. She was far from the victim he'd taken her for at first. 'Which building should they have raided?' he asked.

She gestured with her cigarette to the loading bay in front of them. 'That one. But there're only a few people in now. It's a shame, 'cos they used to pay me and my mate to watch for 'em, tip 'em off, like, if there's anything odd going on.'

'What goes on there?'

'Tons of things – art and shit. There are businesses in there. A recording studio, video stuff, anarchists and the like.'

'Anarchists and the like – what do you mean?'

'I dunno – political people. There's two buildings, see, and they've got the same fire escape at the back. At the top there's a kind of bridge. You can go between the two if the door's not locked. That's what they did the whole time, went in one building an' out the other. So when they raided that place they didn't find anything 'cos everyone'd already buggered off.'

'Do you know what the police were looking for?'

'Nope.'

'So who's left?'

'Some geeks.'

'How do you know all this?'

'Because I live in the effing place! You want to see?'

'That would be great.'

She told him it would cost another twenty pounds, which he gave her. They set off along Herbert Street, with Remy moving at a lick, then turned left and came to a lane, cut through two large buildings, a space wide enough to take a vehicle, but blocked by five large refuse bins and a skip. Glass bulkhead lights illuminated the entrance, but the far end was cast in Victorian gloom. Remy went to a heavy wooden door that appeared to be sealed by two metal bars. But these were easily raised and she scraped it open across a concrete threshold. She looked at him in the dark. 'I can trust you, can't I, Paul? You're not a fucking weirdo, are you?'

'No, I'm not a fucking weirdo. And, by the way, you were the one who approached me out there.'

'True,' she said, and led him into a dark space, flicked her lighter to locate a flight of stone steps that descended to another door, which had been crowbarred from the jamb but still took some opening. It was warm and Samson smelled heating oil. She flipped a switch and three naked lights came on. They were in a long white corridor with a dado line painted in blue and storerooms going off to the left filled with office furniture, old computers and printers. The last room, which was next to an oil-fired boiler, was what she called her 'gaff'. He saw an executive recliner chair with a ripped seat, six flat black sofa cushions arranged to form a mattress, a table on which stood a kettle without a lid, a carton of milk, pots of instant snacks that required only hot water, and a candle in a jar. There were cans of lager, paperbacks and some magazines.

'How long have you been here?' asked Samson.

'Since Christmas, when the caretaker let me in. I pay him when I can, just a few quid. So it's like a real home . . . well, sort of. And he doesn't want anything. Doesn't want to fuck me. I can be here at night and at weekends but never during the working day. And I can't smoke down here. Never!'

'You've made it nice,' said Samson. 'But it must be lonely sometimes.'

She didn't react to that observation and he wished he hadn't said it. As Anastasia used to remind him, loneliness was chronic in the dispossessed and a big cause of mental illness. It was also, oddly, a subject of shame.

They began her tour and Remy explained the owners were waiting to develop the two buildings together because they'd bought the whole site, but there was a campaign against tearing down the Edgar because it was full of artists' studios and the building was regarded as a landmark with some architectural merit, so all the enterprises had only twelve-month leases. The two buildings were still managed separately, but she'd learned about access to the fire escapes and had explored the Edgar at night. She'd found a shower, which she used at the beginning of the weekend when the water was still hot and there was no one around.

'Have you ever come across a woman called Ingrid here?'

'Nope.'

'She's very tall, has brown hair and dresses well. She's actually called Zoe, but she uses the name Ingrid Cole.'

'Maybe in the Pit. Yeah, I've seen her there.'

'What's the Pit?'

'It's like a big room. It feels like it's underground because there's no daylight.'

She led him to a long room where several tables had been pushed together at the centre. On the wall was a large TV screen from which connector leads hung. Leads and cables were everywhere, chairs were pushed back and the waste bins overflowed with disposable white cups, pizza boxes and sandwich packets. He noticed a laptop charger that had been left behind. It was still warm. Beneath a long whiteboard, five cables ran through a hole that had been messily punched in the plasterboard wall. There were no signs of a router of any sort, or a phone line, and Samson assumed that this arrangement was used to disguise their presence. His

eyes came to rest on the whiteboard. The writing had been wiped but
he could make out some column headings. Among them were the words
'PIT' and 'EAR'. Of the other three headings only the letters O R A, R
N and S F R O remained. He photographed the board with his phone
and when his flash went off realised that the board was still damp – it had
only just been wiped.

He began investigating one of the waste bins to see if there were any
discarded notes. It always amazed him what people consigned to the
doubtful security of trash cans, but Remy held up her hand. 'Shut the
fuck up, will you! Someone's in the bay.' She listened with her head to
the side then beckoned him to follow her through a door at the far end
of the Pit. They went along a corridor and climbed a darkened stairway
to an office, where a partner's desk stood by a window overlooking the
loading bay. The only light in the bay came from a small black van, waiting to exit. A figure was standing at the side of a shutter door to operate
the switch that would bring the curtain up, but was evidently having
some difficulty. The winding mechanism kept cutting out so the curtain
would rise a little at a time. The driver joined him and they eventually got
it high enough for the van to clear. The driver returned to the van and
moved it forward so that his lights swept the tall, slender individual who
waited by the controls to lower the shutter. A fraction of a second before
he turned his face, Samson's subconscious prodded him. By the time he
saw the slightly crazy grin and a thumbs-up sign he already knew he was
looking at the young man who'd once been known only by the codename
Firefly – Naji Touma.

CHAPTER 11

Strains of Illyria

Samson didn't call out. No point. Naji wouldn't hear him through the glass as he ducked under the shutter. Besides, nothing would be gained by showing his hand now, although his mind teemed with questions for Naji, and, for that matter, Zoe Freemantle, both of whom, it was now evident, had been set up by Harland in an operation that was paid for by Denis Hisami. What also became plain to him, as he and Remy went down to the loading bay so he could leave the same way as Naji, was that the operation in the Pit was probably the cause of both Harland's death and the poisoning of Denis Hisami. He said goodbye to Remy in the street, gave her a little more money and the phone number for a woman called Rebecca Dunbar, a university friend of Anastasia's who'd set up a shelter for young women. He didn't know if the number still worked, but he hoped Remy would try. Remy shrugged unenthusiastically and went off to look for something to eat. Samson turned west and started looking for a cab. As he walked, he dialled Macy Harp and left instructions to call back as soon as he could.

He always told cabbies to drop him near where the Grand Union and Regent's canals meet at Little Venice so he could walk the few hundred metres to his building. In his street, he came across his tenants, Jericho and Derek, walking their new dog. Derek, who had an obsessive nature, was anxious to discuss the automatic lighting in the hallway, which wasn't working, and the lock of the main door, which appeared to be loose. Samson said he would look into these the following day.

'We thought you were in because we heard some movements,' said Derek. 'We knocked and didn't get an answer so we left a note about the lights.'

'It's my friend,' said Samson.

'Well, there's an invitation to Jericho's premiere attached to the note, which is ultra, ultra polite. Promise!' He looked at Jericho. 'Unlike the note someone sent Mr Samson after a rush of blood to the head, but we won't go into that now, will we, Jericho?' His partner looked down rather hopelessly at the dog, which had wound its lead round his legs.

'I'll get the building manager to sort out the lights,' said Samson, 'but you know it's not strictly my responsibility. You can call him direct. It will come just as well from you as from me.'

'Never! You own most of the building,' said Derek, walking the dog lead round Jericho.

'What breed?' asked Samson, taking in the animal's huge bat ears and under-bite.

'Non-specific dog,' said Jericho.

'Take no notice of him,' said Derek. 'She's a Boston terrier with a twist of pug.' They turned and walked with him towards the door of their building.

'You should start calling the building manager yourselves,' he said. 'I'm away a lot.'

'In the Balkans?' said Jericho absently.

Samson stopped at the door and wheeled round. 'What makes you say that?'

'The strains of Illyria greeted us as we passed your door. Serbo-Croatian of some description, but I couldn't swear to the region. Your friend, perhaps?'

'A man's voice?'

'Yes, one voice, speaking on the phone, possibly, not mellifluous, by any means.'

'Definitely not mellifluous,' said Derek.

Samson glanced up at the first floor. The rooms facing the street were dark and the blinds on to the balcony were up. 'Have you got a phone with you? Good. Call the police. Tell them there's a break-in at this address. Now go over to the other side of the street and wait for them.' The couple looked astonished, but did as they were told.

He unlocked the door and noticed, in the light of the street, fresh gouge marks on the bolts of both locks. They had been forced by a pry bar or a large screwdriver, a crude job that required only brute strength. He hooked the door so that it wouldn't swing shut and send a sound reverberating through the three-storey townhouse. The automatic lighting didn't come on, but that was to his advantage. He listened for a few seconds. No sound came from the basement, or the ground-floor flat. He moved along the hallway, climbed halfway up the first flight of stairs and listened again. He dialled Jo's number. The phone sounded in the flat, but for just two rings before the call was rejected. That was all the confirmation he needed. Jo was in the flat yet hadn't switched the lights on. He sent her a text – 'See you in 30 minutes' – and heard it ping about half a minute later. If the Serb was with her and reading her texts, he'd maybe relax. He crept to his door. Someone was moving inside, heavier than Jo. He put his face to the door. A slight draught bore Jo's scent and something else – the smell of takeaway food.

He could wait until the police arrived, although there was no guarantee they'd get there in time, or he could try to flush the man out. He went to the top floor and used his phone torch to find the fire extinguisher on the landing, lifted it from the stand and returned to the first floor. The noise of someone moving had stopped, but he heard the low rumble of a man speaking. He reached up to the smoke detector and pressed the test button. Alarms sounded through the building for thirty seconds then shut off. He did it again and moved quickly to put his key in the lock and turn it, knowing that the alarm would drown out the click. The door was slightly open. The alarm died. He waited, back pressed against the wall, straining for any new sounds in the flat. No sign of the police. He had to go in. He raised the fire extinguisher with one hand wrapped around the trigger and pushed the door open with his foot. Nothing moved. He peered into the dark of the flat. He saw little, but sensed the man was there and thought he heard him breathing heavily on the far side of the sitting room. He moved a few paces forward, through the opening into the flat's main space. The first police siren entered the street and stopped outside the building; a second followed close behind. Lights pulsed on the ceiling. He became aware of a dark shape on the floor – Jo. At the same moment he saw the blur of a figure moving towards him.

No training; no moves this time – just cold fury. He'd had a vague plan to let the extinguisher off to blind the man but instead he swung it with his right hand and connected with the bulk coming at him. There was a dull ring. He couldn't be certain, but the extinguisher seemed to hit the man's shoulder and glance upwards to the side of his face. He staggered. Samson swung the extinguisher again, and it skidded across the man's back and landed at the base of his cranium. The man lashed out leftwards with a weapon and Samson felt a spark of pain in his leg. This wasn't going to stop him. He turned to his right, seized the edge of the kitchen island, jumped up and toppled the knife block so the knives spilled towards him. He grasped one and hit the light switches on the wall nearby.

What he saw was not the Matador, but a thinner man, reeling as though drunk. There was a knife in his right hand, but it was held loosely and was about to slip from his grasp. The man clutched the side of his head with his left hand. He was in great pain, though there was no sign of any wound, no blood whatsoever. The knife dropped on to the rug. He screamed but not in any language that Samson recognised. Then came pure gibberish. He staggered two paces, froze, his hand still holding his head and rolled over on to the rug.

Police were calling from the stairs. Samson yelled out, flung the knife on to the kitchen surface and went to Jo on the floor. She was bound and gagged and had been stabbed in her upper arm, he guessed some time before, because blood had dried on her jacket. 'Get an ambulance,' he shouted as two male officers rushed in. 'She's a police officer. She's lost blood.' He looked up. They were dithering. 'Now!' he shouted. 'Do it now!'

Jo was conscious and as he untied the gag she looked up and nodded to say she was going to be okay. 'He was going to rape me, the bastard,' she whispered. 'You sent a text and he told me how he was going to fill the thirty minutes, then he told his friend.' She jerked her head. A phone was on the lamp table. The line was open – the creep had been planning to describe what he was doing. Jo's phone lay beside it. He turned her gently to one side so he could undo the tie used to bind her. He kissed her on the forehead and examined the wound, which was still oozing blood. 'Hold on there,' he said.

He retrieved from his store cupboard a small emergency bag he'd taken to Syria, which consisted mostly of gauze and dressings, plus three shots of morphine which he'd bought in Turkey for a trip into ISIS-held territory then brought them back to Britain illegally, forgetting they were in his luggage. He packed the wound and held his thumb over it.

'Why didn't you answer your phone?' she asked.

'I had to change numbers. They were tracking me. That's how they got this address. Are you in pain? I have something for it.'

'No . . . I can do this. But I can't fucking do us, Samson!'

'We'll talk about that later. Need to get you to hospital first.'

A female officer was with them. 'Who are you, love?' she asked Jo.

'Inspector Joanna Hayes. I'm with Met Ops – MO2.'

'Are you on an operation? Someone I should contact?'

'Oddly enough, this is a night off,' she said dryly. 'Tell Assistant Commissioner Steve Raven. There will be someone at MO2 now.'

The officer checked that Samson knew what he was doing, moved away and spoke into her lapel mic.

'There's this fella in my village,' continued Jo. 'Restores furniture. Sings in the choir. Grows special tulips . . .'

'Later,' he said.

Two paramedics were in the room. Others were coming through the door with more police. One used a pen torch to peer into the eyes of the assailant. She spoke to her controller and gave a read-out of vital signs, which were zero in every department. A man came over with a bag to check Jo. 'We'll get you into the ambulance,' he said when he'd looked at the wound beneath Samson's temporary dressing. 'You're going to be fine.' Then he focused on Samson. 'Actually, I'm just as concerned about that leg of yours, sir. You have a nasty cut there and you're still bleeding. Are you aware of that?'

He looked down. His trouser leg was soaked beneath a small tear. The blood on the floor was his, not Jo's.

'We'll need stretchers for you both.' He spoke into a radio. 'And you, sir, stop moving about! You'll lose more blood if you go on like that. Sit down and put your leg up here,' he said, patting the ottoman. He cut the trouser leg off, plugged the wound on the inside of Samson's right thigh and uncoiled a dressing tightly round his leg

'What about that man?' asked Samson.

The paramedic looked over his shoulder at his colleagues going through CPR, and shook his head. 'He's suffered trauma to the head. Severe brain haemorrhage, most likely, but we'll see if they can get him breathing again. He attacked you both, right?'

'That's the one,' said Samson, and reached over to the table where there were two phones and a half-consumed kebab wrapped in pitta bread. Who goes to kill with a takeaway? He looked at the attacker's phone. The call had ended, but he entered the last-dialled number in 'Notes' on his own phone and for one moment considered pocketing the attacker's phone.

'It's a crime scene, Samson,' Jo said wearily. 'Don't be a bloody idiot.'

He put it back on the table.

'I assume the alarm was you,' she said. 'He had his jeans round his ankles when it went off. He was going to have his fun. What the fuck is it with men, by the way? You must tell me some day. He didn't have time to pull them up properly before you got inside the flat. It was his undoing. Once you were in he had to stay quiet. He held the knife to my face to keep me from making a noise. Then he went for you. I heard him stumble and I assume you hit him at that moment. Jesus, what a noise! You must have cracked his skull. But you came exactly at the right moment – neither too soon, nor too late. Perfect timing, as usual. Thank you.' Her eyes glinted.

He tipped his head towards the paramedics working on the unconscious man. 'Fuck him,' she hissed. 'He was going to rape me and kill us both. Fuck him.' She felt her arm gingerly. 'This really aches – how's yours?'

'Hurts,' he said. 'Look, sorry, Jo. Here, in my flat – I'm appalled that you were attacked.'

'You can't help it. People always want to kill you, and someday some bloody idiot will succeed.'

He didn't answer. Suddenly he felt faint, and colder than he could ever remember, and one of the paramedics was by his side shouting for help.

CHAPTER 12

The Gravel Washer

In the afternoon, Anastasia set up an office in a hospital room used for counselling. It had a line of five bonsai trees that she decided to keep. She would stay until Denis had emerged from his coma. There was a lot to do. Lawyers came to formally put in place the power of attorney. Two bankers followed, ostensibly to wish Denis well but in reality to find out whether he was going to be permanently incapacitated. She thanked them, smiled and lied through her teeth. The head of Denis's West Coast office flew in, bringing half a dozen decisions and his own frank concerns about the future of the operation without Denis at the helm. The San Francisco office consisted of sixteen people, and in New York a further eight were employed. Small numbers, but the calibre of employee meant a sizeable payroll, something Denis had always avoided in the past. They paid for themselves in profits, but $450,000 left Denis's accounts each month before he had even settled bills for office space, health care, and all the rest of it. Guided by Tulliver, she gave the go-ahead on two investments, told him to stall on three and cancel one. She had no idea whether she was right, but she was at least decisive.

When the room was eventually clear, Tulliver handed her two pages about Denis's unexplained movements in the last year and a half, together with a handwritten note that read, 'If you've got questions, we'll go to the roof.' He made a circling motion with his hand to indicate that the place might be bugged. She knew that his concerns about surveillance meant that he wouldn't have emailed her the information.

Before she could read them Tulliver looked up from a message on his phone and said, 'Jesus, Martin Reid is in the building! He wants to see you. I'll get rid of him.'

'What does he want?' The billionaire was sometimes Denis's ally; others his enemy.

'Christ knows.'

'I'll see him.'

A few minutes later Reid and an aide appeared in the room. Reid dismissed the aide and, expecting Tulliver to take the hint, glowered when he showed no sign of leaving. 'While Denis is sick,' said Tulliver, 'Mrs Hisami and I are working this ride together. You can take it or leave it. Isn't that right, Anastasia?'

'Absolutely, Jim.'

Reid sat down and considered what to say. Known as the 'gravel washer' for his habit of periodically removing the entire drive of his estate in Wyoming and having it cleaned, Reid was more or less retired from a career of nailing competitors to dry on a washboard in the prairie wind, as he put it. He'd lost his childhood-sweetheart wife to a rapid form of dementia and then a son to a helicopter accident and was seldom seen on the West Coast nowadays. The last time Anastasia met him was at a fundraiser, when he talked unceasingly about the life of Julius Caesar, with whom he was obsessed, and obliquely warned her about Hisami's enemies. He told her Denis should lie low and lay off, whatever that meant. She didn't like Marty Reid. He was opinionated, never listened or suffered the slightest doubt, and his politics were anathema to her. He was terrifying and brutal, yet she felt some sympathy for him that evening. He was lost without his wife and son. All his money and power meant nothing to him and he freely admitted that his life was ending in disappointment and loneliness.

After Reid had progressed, rather awkwardly, through the formalities of asking how Denis was, he said, 'I don't like your politics, Ana, and I don't like Denis's politics either.' He was the only person on the planet who called her Ana, but seemed deaf to frequent correction.

'You've made that clear before,' she said.

'Yes, I imagine I have. But I'm different to the charlatans in this town. I'm a conservative, but I believe in the Constitution, which means that comes first with me and my views about American society come second. That's why I admire your husband, and why I have time for you, Ana. You're principled people and you have beliefs that are guided by values. They're not mine, but I recognise they are values, which is more than you can say for most people.'

'Forgive me for asking, but where's this going, Marty?'

He raised a hand – he wasn't done yet. 'What happened to Denis was an offence to the body politic, not just to his rights and the man who died. It showed contempt for our democratic institutions, and that I will not tolerate.'

'Yes . . .' she started.

'I won't tolerate it,' he repeated, as if she hadn't understood. His face had darkened and seemed to have expanded. She suddenly thought of what Denis had once said: 'The thing with Martin Reid is that he's all granite outside, but twice as hard inside.'

Tulliver came to the rescue. 'What are you proposing we should do?'

'I'm not proposing that you do anything, dammit. I'm telling you now that I'm going to act.'

Tulliver put up a hand, rose and whispered to him. Reid nodded and also got up. They all three walked to a deserted seating area with a water cooler and vending machines where there was no risk of electronic sur- veillance. Tulliver leaned forward with hands clasped together and spoke confidentially. 'The FBI, Homeland Security and CIA are all working on the case. We appreciate your concern, and I know Mrs Hisami is touched that you came, but how can you help? Even you, Mr Reid, what can you do alone?'

'Does anyone understand what actually happened at that goddamn company?' Reid snapped, causing Tulliver to recoil slightly.

'We think so, yes,' Tulliver answered, and gave a well- rehearsed summary about the company TangKi, in which Denis Hisami and Reid had invested. 'TangKi was a front for Adam Crane, a Ukrainian named Chumak who was likely working for a branch of Russian intelligence. Denis uncovered the operation to launder millions of dollars and pass them to far-right terror groups in Europe. Anastasia was kidnapped and held in Russia to prevent Denis revealing what he knew.'

'Where did the money come from?'

'You were on the board,' said Tulliver, slightly exasperated. 'You know it came from investors and the company's regular business. Crane drained the accounts with a lot of fake research and investment projects, then vanished.'

'My people went over the figures. A lot more money was involved – tens of millions of dollars. So where did that come from?'

'A hundred and forty-six million dollars in total,' said Tulliver. 'Over a hundred and twenty shell companies were used. We didn't determine precisely all the sources, but, for example, I recall that a chain of realtors in the Pacific North West was involved.'

'But you don't know where the bulk of the money came from. No one does. Is that correct?'

Tulliver conceded that and said no agency had bothered to investigate and pin down the source of all the money.

'So that's where we're going to start,' said Reid. 'There was never any inquiry, because the authorities had persecuted Denis and they wanted to bury the whole goddamn affair. And Denis was relieved he'd got you back, Ana. Then he needed to focus on his business problems, so he didn't pursue it.' He looked at them in turn, attempting to soften his manner. 'I have an instinct about this. I will use everything I have. Is that all right with you, Ana?'

'What do you think, Jim?' she asked.

'Can't do any harm.'

She levelled her gaze at Reid. 'You think these hearings in Congress are part of the campaign against Denis? Maybe the same people who went after him two and a half years ago?'

'I do.'

'What is your opinion about the allegation that Denis is supplying arms to the Kurds?'

'I am agnostic. I've no evidence either way, but I know you two are involved in humanitarian work and I believe Denis when he says he decided to put the money he's made recently to good use in the land of his birth.'

Did she catch something in Tulliver's eyes? She looked hard then said, 'I don't have a problem with your offer of help.'

They rose together. Reid held out his hand. 'You be sure to give Denis my good wishes for his recovery.' He studied her for a beat. 'I have to say, you've come through this experience very well. You are indomitable Ana, and I admire that in a person.'

She felt as indomitable as someone clinging to a life raft. There were no other options. She nodded her thanks and watched him retreat down the hallway to collect his aide. 'He's got a spring in his step,' she said, turning to the papers Tulliver had handed her earlier.

Denis had flown to Europe ten times since the late autumn of 2019 on his own plane. What interested her was that she had hardly been aware of these trips because most of this had been her dark period, which she didn't now even want to acknowledge, as she sat, so composed, in the hospital and very much in charge of her own and Denis's destiny. She was aware that he had gone to Estonia once to meet with and thank Robert Harland, but not five times. And then there were trips to Vienna and London, which could not be directly related to his business, which was now focused in Asia and the United States. There was no clue as to their purpose, although she assumed he would have met with Macy Harp in London. None of the trips lasted more than two days and most were completed in twenty-four hours. He always travelled alone. Occasionally, there were restaurant bills for two or three people. One in Vienna was for four. Denis usually slept on the plane so it didn't surprise her that he rarely seemed to stay overnight in any of the destinations, except in Tallinn, where he spent the night on two different occasions. The thought of her husband talking to Robert Harland and Ulrike made something snatch at her stomach because it was under their roof that she had renewed her affair with Samson and set in train a disastrous period. But the Harlands were far too discreet to let anything slip and, if Denis suspected anything, he had never let on.

The log of Denis's movements didn't tell her much other than that he had been pursuing a project with his usual determination and secrecy. When she had been through it twice, Tulliver pointed upwards and they went to the roof.

'I didn't want to put it in writing, but he's been paying Macy Harp a lot of money, especially in the last month. This is mostly for the protection of the young woman, but there's also a lot of work on company searches, which has been paid for by Hendricks Harp and reimbursed by Denis.'

'He's using them as a channel?'

'Kind of, but I don't think there's anything sinister in that.'

'What companies?'

'I couldn't get that data from Harp. He says he can only deal with Denis. He was pretty upset when we spoke. He and Robert Harland went back a long way.'

'Call him.'

He dialled and handed her the phone. Macy picked up on the third ring.

'It's me, Anastasia, on Jim's phone.' She reminded him that the power of attorney meant that any confidential arrangements that existed between Macy and her husband were now, perforce, to include her. 'I have to know everything, Macy. What we are committed to; where we are exposed.'

He replied that there was a lot he didn't know.

'How long have you been looking after this woman?' she asked.

'Just a few weeks.'

'Who is she?'

'I cannot say. Denis and our late friend believed she was the very best type of asset. Absolutely vital in their project.'

'And you're not going to tell me what that project is.'

'I have some ideas, but these are for face-to-face conversations.'

'When did this all start?'

'I never spoke to our late friend about this. I dealt only with Denis. I would say it was towards the end of 2019.'

'How much did you know?'

'We began to research some companies in the United States, as well as individuals. The list was in our late friend's handwriting. He didn't do email – didn't trust it. That research didn't seem to go anywhere, but that was the start of it all.'

'So this is a really big operation. Which companies? Which people?'

'Again, I will happily share that in person, or in a more secure manner.'

Macy blew his nose furiously, which gave her time to think. 'So what are the reporting arrangements? Who does she send her information to?'

'Our late friend and Denis. Nothing came through this office. Only they knew.'

'And they talked.'

'Yes, they talked all the time. This was very important to them.'

'And do you think someone tried to kill them on the same day because of this *thing* they were doing?'

'Has to be a possibility.' Then he added: 'Yes, I do think that.'

'Then where does Samson fit in? Why was he attacked in the street?'

'I'm not sure.'

'You must have an idea – you employ him. You're responsible for him. You figured out what he would be doing with my husband.'

'As I say, I'm not sure.'

From old, she knew Macy to be evasive. 'Come on, Macy – tell me. I am running things, don't fuck with me.'

'Not on the phone, Anastasia! How's Denis?'

She shook her head in irritation and said, 'Some improvements.' She'd been to see him three hours before. There were fewer tubes and they had raised him a little to guard against pneumonia. His colour was better, too, and a nurse reported that his eyelashes had fluttered as though he was about to open his eyes. His breathing was good and there seemed to be some response when the soles of his feet were gently rubbed. 'I think we're going to need to talk, Macy,' she said. 'I mean, face to face.'

'Yes, but I can't come to you. It's our friend's funeral.'

'Let me look into it, see what I can do. What about Samson?'

'How do you mean?'

'Does he know I'm running things?'

'I told him.'

'Good,' she said, and hung up.

'I can go to London, if you'd prefer,' said Tulliver.

'No, you stay here, Jim. I need to find out what the hell's going on, and I'm the only one who has the power to do that. He can't tell you anything, but he has to tell me.'

'Are you sure?'

What was he worried about? Her breakdown? Her history with Samson? Either way, she damn well wasn't going to hear him out. She gave him a cool look that not even Jim could ignore.

The FBI returned in the early evening. Special Agent Reiner and Agent Paula Berg were joined by a man named J. P. Kristof, a Deputy Assistant Director at the FBI and in charge of the Bureau's operation, who had also been given the role of coordinating efforts across the agencies. She thought he was there to take a look at her, but after a more or less repeat performance by Reiner and Berg, Kristof nodded to Reiner and said, 'Why don't you show Mrs Hisami the planner?'

Reiner opened the door and was handed an attaché case by an agent posted outside. It was Denis's case, the one that Tulliver had carried from the meeting in Congresswoman Ricard's office to the Rayburn Building and Room 2172. Denis used it for meetings, or on the plane when he needed to bring a lot of papers with him. He had had it with him when she first met him, in a hotel in northern Macedonia.

'This was by Mr Tulliver's chair and was left in the room when the hearing was evacuated,' said Reiner. 'It was retrieved and checked for contamination and, as it was obviously a crime scene, we went through the contents. We realised this was likely to be Mr Hisami's case, not Mr Tulliver's.' He flipped the hasps. 'It all seemed pretty straightforward. The papers are related to the hearing and there are the usual items found in a case like this.' He looked up. 'Why are you smiling, Mrs Hisami?'

'The old calculator – it's his Tandy from the seventies.'

Reiner picked it up. 'Does that have significance?'

'Denis bought it when he was a teenager in Kurdistan. It was a big deal for him. Solar-powered, and it still works! He has it to remind himself how far he's come – something like that.'

'So, he keeps personal stuff in the case as well as papers?' asked Reiner.

'I guess.'

He felt in one of the pockets in the lid of the case and pulled out a small red leather book. 'Do you recognise this, Mrs Hisami? It's a two-year planner – two weeks every page? It's kind of neat. I wish I knew where to get hold of one.'

He handed it to her. 'If you look through it, there are only a few entries and a few numbers. In all, there are exactly forty-eight.' He looked at a sheaf of photocopies. 'We would like to know what it all means. There are just five words in the whole two years – PEARL, BERLIN, PITCH, AURORA, SAFFRON – and a whole lot of entries that we surmise are International Banking numbers with the digits mixed up so that the actual bank account number is hidden. Unless we have the key, it will take a lot of computing power to unravel those. 'We're especially interested in the five words, which would seem to be a code, and we wonder if they mean anything to you at all?'

She shook her head. 'But could you leave the photocopies and I'll put my mind to this mystery later on? I can ask Jim Tulliver.'

'We already have. He doesn't know, and if there is someone who would know, it's Mr Tulliver, right? He said he's never seen the planner before, which is odd, wouldn't you say? Mr Tulliver runs a lot of Mr Hisami's life, and, well, this looks kind of important, with all the coded IBAN numbers.' He paused and studied her. 'Obviously, this is something that has personal meaning only to your husband – like the calculator.'

He handed her the photocopies. 'You'll see that the five words appear against certain dates over the last year and a half. We can't see a pattern, but something may occur to you, and if you recognise one of those numbers, that might be the key to unravelling the others.' He waited for her to respond. 'If you're interested, the words appear with differing frequency. BERLIN appears most often, with PEARL coming second. The others are used less frequently.'

She glanced down and saw the word BERLIN against 2 February of the previous year. She remembered that date from the log of Denis's movements. On 2 February he had flown into Tallinn and on the third flown to London before returning to New York. She said nothing but looked at Reiner and raised her shoulders. 'I'll see what I can do. You think this is going to tell you why my husband, Samson and Mr Harland were all attacked on the same day?'

'Maybe,' said the Deputy Assistant Director, putting his hands together to wrap things up. 'The understanding of motive. Why was your husband attacked? Why were Mr Samson and Mr Harland? And why not you?'

The mild callousness of the question startled her. She turned to him. 'How dare you suggest it's a matter of idle curiosity that I haven't been killed or hurt.'

'I meant no offence,' he said. 'Our British friends believe this was a revenge for Narva. If that were the case, you'd be a natural target. That's all I'm saying, Mrs Hisami.'

But the tiger was out of its cage. Anastasia stood up and looked down at him. 'This isn't just one incident, is it, Mr Deputy Assistant Director? My husband has now been persecuted for three years. That campaign against him included my kidnap and his detention on false charges, and now he's been poisoned while answering questions in a show trial whose only purpose was to humiliate and ruin him. Has anyone else in the United States endured such treatment? No! Yet no official organisation has ever come to his aid. Not once was he offered support! That's extraordinary, given what Denis has done for America – the charities he's funded, the taxes he's paid, the jobs he's created.' Her outstretched arm pointed down the hallway to the area where Denis was being treated. 'This is a man who has built whole industries and invested in collapsing projects where there was no hope. And yet he saved people's livelihoods, their homes! He's an American hero, but he's treated like dirt. Why is that? Is it because his politics set him apart from the heartlessness of our times? Or is it because Denis is an outsider with a Middle Eastern background and dark skin?'

Kristof listened impassively and, when she'd finished, asked her to sit down.

She remained standing. 'Mrs Hisami, please understand we have no agenda other than to find out who tried to kill your husband and why. Period.'

Reiner said, 'We'll be grateful for your attention on the planner, Mrs Hisami. And if you think of anything, call me.' He gave her a card with a cell number. 'We assume that you will remain in DC for the foreseeable period, but if you do travel, we'd certainly like to know where you're headed and to stay in touch with you. I don't need to remind you that this is a national security issue in which the President has taken a close interest. We may need to speak with you at any time.'

They rose and moved to the door. Agent Berg hung back a little and turned to her as her two colleagues exited. She gave a brief, corvine smile then said, 'It's nice to see a wife display such passionate loyalty. Don't see that a lot these days. Good day to you, Mrs Hisami.'

Anastasia had no doubt what she meant and, later, when Tulliver joined her by the window of Denis's room, she said. 'They're plugged into us – they're watching everything.'

'What makes you say that?'

'The bitch from the FBI was having a dig about Samson. She was saying, "We know everything about you and we're watching."'

He nodded. 'Heard you painted the barn door red.'

'Jesus, where did that phrase come from?'

'My Kentuckian forebears.'

'I'm going to email you this evening, and I will ask you to have the plane ready for a morning departure to the West Coast from Dulles. I'll say I need to attend to things at the office on behalf of Denis the following day, okay? Maybe schedule the plane to return to DC two days after. Send out a few emails saying I'm going to be there.'

'What about Denis?'

She shook her head. 'They say he's not coming round anytime soon. They keep on telling me about the time required for *complete rehabilitation*. They're preparing me for some bad outcome, Jim. I feel it.' Her arms were folded and her hands had retreated into the sleeves of her cardigan. She turned to him. 'What if he doesn't get better? How are we going to manage all this?'

'One day at a time,' he said, peering through the window. 'Actually, he looks a lot stronger to me.'

'I'll need a car to Dulles at 2 p.m. That okay?'

'And you're going to London?'

She didn't answer.

'And when are you back?'

'Don't know.' After a long look at Denis, she turned to go to her room.

'There's one other thing,' he said. 'I had a call from Warren Speight's office. He wants to express his sympathy to you personally by coming over to the hospital.'

'Why? He's the reason we were in Room 2172 in the first place.'

'He feels he should.'

'The man's a right-wing asshole. Pure fascist.'

He blew his cheeks out then gave her his regretful look. 'I actually wouldn't mind thanking the congressman myself. He saved me from getting covered with nerve agent when I went to help Denis. If he hadn't yelled at me, I would be in there with Denis. Might be useful to hear what he has to say.'

'Fine. We'll do it early tomorrow morning.'

CHAPTER 13

The Tulip Guy

Jo Hayes was informing on him. The realisation came to Samson in the night as he lay half asleep in the hospital ward with his leg stitched and bound. She had kept her colleagues apprised of his movements during Anastasia's kidnap but had, rather decently, tipped him off about the police's intention to arrest him at Heathrow. So, there were no hard feelings and a year or so later they had dined at Cedar and ended up in bed. She called it a 'consolation screw' just to make sure that he knew she knew he still held a candle for Anastasia.

When she appeared in his ward, shoulder bandaged and arm in a sling but managing to hold two cups of coffee from the franchise café in the hospital foyer, he smiled and without the slightest note of recrimination told her, 'I know what you were doing in the flat.'

'How's the leg?' she said, awkwardly handing him a cup. She sat down beside him. 'A millimetre or two to the left and they say you might have bled out.'

'Fine,' he said, though it ached like hell. 'Jo, I know!'

'That's your trouble, Samson. You're far too smart for your own good.'

'For yours,' he said, and grinned again. 'Just tell me why?'

'Drink your coffee,' she said, unabashed.

'You said you hadn't identified me to your colleagues from that piece of film in the street, but of course you had and they told you to watch me. That's why you were at the flat last night. Jo, you never stay two nights in a row.' He was still smiling but also watching intently for her reaction.

'Fuck it – yes.'

'Well, they damn nearly got you killed, didn't they? I hope you tell them that.'

'I have.' She smiled. 'Thanks for being such a grown-up, Samson.'

'What's a little surveillance between friends?'

'I told you more than I told them.'

'I know you did. Of course, they don't give a damn about my safety, or yours for that matter. If they were worried about me, as they said, they'd have had me covered when they followed me to Putney Bridge. Whoever's after me was tracking my phone, which is why I had to turn it off and swap phones. Hence you couldn't call me.'

She pouted then sipped her coffee.

'So, what do they want?'

She moved closer so she was just a few inches from his face. Their eyes danced with routine intimacy, which made her smile briefly. 'They want to know why you were outside that building.'

'The Edgar? Why?'

'There was something going on there. They raided it and picked up an individual they were looking for, but they didn't find what they wanted. It's all a bit vague, but they want to know what the fuck you were doing there.'

He put the coffee cup down and reached for her hand. 'You can tell them I have absolutely no interest in the building, or whatever goes on there. Will you do that for me? It was coincidence that my work took me there. Nothing more.'

She nodded and withdrew her hand.

'Do they have an ID for the man who tried to kill us?'

'You know he died?'

'I assumed that was the case, yes.'

'His name was Pim Visser. Dutch citizen. Born in Rotterdam thirty-six years ago. Served four years for smuggling ecstasy. Dutch police say he had good connections in the criminal underground in Rotterdam – the penose – and may have been an ad hoc contract killer. He was nicknamed Rossi after the Italian motorcycle champion because he used high speed bikes to deliver drugs to the club scene all over Europe. An addict with a reputation for extreme violence, he was a suspect in the murder of a prostitute in Rotterdam and had two convictions for sexual assault.'

'So was Rossi the driver for Miroslav Rajavic – the Matador?'

'That's assumed to be the case.'

'I don't understand how my neighbour heard Serbian in the flat when this man was Dutch.'

'Visser had a Yugoslav mother. He speaks fluent Serbian. He was the link between the penose and the Balkan crime scene, mostly concerning the MDA market, it is believed. He was part of the delivery chain that fed ecstasy into Slovenia, Croatia and Serbia.'

'So he was talking to the Matador on the phone.'

'Yeah, it seemed that he was summoning help from his partner. Maybe he wasn't sure of himself or was insisting that the other man – your Matador – carried out the contract, as it was his contract. I don't know. But there was some kind of dispute and that was why he was shouting.'

The pattern was now established beyond doubt. Four men had been hired from the criminal underworld in Europe to do contract killings which would require a far higher degree of professionalism than any of them was capable of. Two were dead, one was in custody and the fourth had gone missing. He reminded himself to call Vuk Divjak in Serbia later.

'Thanks for all that,' he said. 'So, you were going to tell me about the tulip guy – the man in the village you're seeing.'

'He's a dear, I like him a lot. I would have spoken about this sooner but, well, you're incredibly sweet, too, Samson. And we do have our good times, don't we?'

'We certainly do.'

She brushed the back of his hand with her fingernails. 'Our time together is, like, halfway to love for me. Do you understand? It's so good in bed that I kind of wonder why the hell we aren't in love, just like anyone else would be. But you aren't available and that has come to really matter to me, despite, or because of our extraordinary sex life.'

'Despite, or because of,' he echoed rather hopelessly. 'So, you are planning to set up with the tulip guy?'

'His name is Leo.'

'I prefer Tulip Guy.'

'We'll see how things go. He's helped me with a problem and I'm grateful to him.'

'What was that?'

She didn't reply and drew back a little. 'I was worried they might give you a hard time about killing that man.'

'Why. It was quite straightforward. They interviewed me last night. They wanted to know how many times I hit him. It was twice – once on the head and maybe a glancing blow which ended up on his head. They said they would wait for the autopsy.'

She looked concerned. 'They could make life difficult for you over the next few weeks. They might cause trouble at the inquest. Not all my colleagues are good people. And there is' – she lowered her voice – 'a real sense that you pose some kind of threat.'

'Have you made a statement?'

'Yes, while you were being stitched up.'

'An unfortunate phrase. How many times did you say I hit him?'

'Once or twice – I wasn't sure, but I did say you reached for a knife, which would certainly indicate a determination to harm him.'

'Right, but you'd been stabbed and you told them he was going to assault you, and he would have killed you afterwards.'

She looked down and nodded.

'Good.' He stopped, pulled the bedclothes back and pointed to the bag brought to the hospital by Derek and Jericho earlier. 'Can you hand me that? I'm going to get dressed. I've got things to do.'

'What about your leg?'

'It'll be fine.'

When he finished dressing, he sat on the bed and smiled at her. 'What was the problem the tulip guy helped you with?'

She bit her lip. 'I got to using a little coke in the clubs when I used to perform. It became a bad habit. This was two years ago, when we weren't seeing each other. I went into rehab and quit really easily. Leo is an ex-addict and he was very supportive. The worst part is that a senior colleague found out about it. Of course, they didn't refer to it when they asked me to watch you a couple of days ago, but you know it's in the background. I could be fired for use of a Class A drug. I'm sorry – it doesn't make me proud – but that's how I came to be in your flat last night. They wanted to know what you're doing.'

'The important thing is this, Jo – I wasn't there for you, but the tulip guy was.' He put his hand up to her face and she pressed her cheek into his palm.

'You had your own addiction, didn't you, Samson? You went gambling crazy.'

'Yes, but I quit too, and paid off my debts.'

They were silent.

'Is this it?' he asked.

'Yes, it is.'

'Were you going to tell me about informing on me?'

'Of course not.' She took his hand, brought it up to her lips and kissed it. 'Goodbye, dear Samson. And for fuck's sake, try to stay alive.' She got up and left with a look of heartfelt regret.

★

An hour later he was told he could leave, but two police officers, an inspector named Glynn Jones and a Sergeant Taylor, arrived with more questions. They were puzzling over the motive of the dead man, who they identified to Samson as Pim Visser, not knowing that he was already familiar with the name. Jones declared himself mystified. What was a face from Rotterdam's underworld doing in Samson's flat? What had Samson done to earn the attention of the people who paid Visser and Miroslav Rajavic? In their questioning, Samson saw an obvious conflict and waited for the moment when Taylor, a short, wheedling individual with a cowlick and not the brightest look in his eye, asked again and again about the blows he'd delivered to the man's head, as though Samson had intended to kill him.

'On the one hand, you're telling me that these two men were extremely dangerous individuals, yet, on the other hand, you seem to be saying that I used excessive force and ask why I couldn't have immobilised Visser, sat him down, offered him a drink and reasoned with him.'

'There's no need for sarcasm, Mr Samson.'

'Tell me what you would have me do in those circumstances. Seriously! I knew Inspector Hayes was in the flat because I heard her phone, yet it was dark and there was no sound from inside. I knew she was in trouble and my only thought was to rescue her. As it turned out, he'd stabbed her and was about to rape her. He had already lowered his trousers – right? So this was not a normal break-in. He would have killed us both, after having raped a senior police officer.'

'But you didn't know this when he came at you, sir,' said Sergeant Taylor.

Samson gazed at him. 'Of course I bloody didn't know that, but it was lucky I hit him with all the force I could muster, or we might both not be here.'

'And you hit him again.'

'Yes, but I was being stabbed at the time, remember?' He looked down at his leg.

'And you grabbed a kitchen knife, which you intended to use.'

'Of course! What's your point? This was a life-or-death situation. I'd have had no problem using that knife. No problem at all!'

'We have to consider that you used unreasonable force.'

'I'd like to see you make that case in court. And, with Inspector Hayes as a witness, forget it. Have you looked into Pim Visser's background? How many people is he suspected of killing?'

'We are simply doing our job, sir.'

'You're doing your job – exactly! So you know the man's movements before he went to my home. You have his phone, so you can find out who he was speaking to from the flat. You can find out when he arrived in this country, because his face will be on CCTV at Harwich or somewhere. You know all this, right, and you don't need me to tell you that this was a murderous psychopath with a lifelong history of violence.'

'We are working on all that.'

'What transport did he use to get to my flat?'

'We assume a motorcycle.'

'But you haven't located that motorcycle. Is that correct? So that might lead you to conclude he was dropped off near my place. But he brought his own supper with him, so maybe there was a stop on the way.'

The officers looked mystified.

'There was a half-eaten kebab in the flat. The only place he could have got that near my flat was at Jimmy's Kebab on Edgware Road. Jimmy's is bound to have CCTV, so you can see what time he got there and whether he was accompanied by anyone, which he must have been, because no one is going to walk from Jimmy's to my flat and wait to eat their takeaway.' He stopped. 'He would eat it on the way, no?'

There was no need to make them look any more foolish, but he continued. 'We know he forced his way into the flat after Inspector Hayes arrived by cab. He held a knife to her throat and compelled her to open the flat door. But how did he know that she was a friend of mine? Maybe they had the place under surveillance the night before. And why wasn't his partner with him? I'll tell you why, because he was outside my restaurant in Mayfair.' He took out his phone and showed them a photograph of a CCTV still provided by Ivan in the early hours of the morning. It showed Rajavic standing in the street with his hands in the chest pockets of a hoodie. A second, from a different angle, was of him on the phone. The front wheel of a bike could be seen in the background 'Maybe he was talking to Visser at that very moment,' he said.

'Where did these come from?' asked Jones.

'Mayfair Ladies, a message group that operates in my street. The casino across the way from my place uploaded them to the group.' He laid the phone on the bedside table. 'Both these men tried to kill me in the last few days, so the idea that I exercised unreasonable force when confronted with Visser in my own home is simply stupid.' He touched his leg. 'If the knife had entered a little to the left, I wouldn't be here.'

'We take your point,' said Jones.

'So, unless there's something else, I am going to pick some things up at my flat, because while this character is at liberty, I obviously can't live there.'

'It's a crime scene,' chirped Taylor.

'I'm sure you have everything you need by now,' said Samson. He stood up and reached for the cane the hospital had provided. He didn't propose to use it for long, but when he put pressure on his foot the pain in his thigh was considerable. He bent down to get his bag. 'There's one other thing, which you should be aware of,' he said, his face popping up. 'Visser's phone may be the crucial lead in several investigations worldwide. You should give it to the security services – they'll know what to do with it, even if you don't.'

Samson made his usual exit from an interview, which is to say that he rose and walked out before he was told he could go. And, as usual, they didn't try to stop him.

CHAPTER 14

Sex, Venice and a Bullet

The door of his flat was open and police tape was stretched across it. He lifted the tape and walked in. A member of the forensic team in a white suit was packing up equipment in the sitting room. She looked embarrassed and called out. Two men, neither of whom were dressed in overalls, nor looked very much like forensic officers, emerged from a spare bedroom, where Samson kept personal accounts and some family records. They had the smell of MI5.

'What are you doing in there?' he demanded. 'Everything happened out here, as you damn well know.'

'We have to make sure that we haven't missed anything, sir,' replied one.

'Well, now you've checked, you can get the hell out.'

'This is a crime scene, sir.'

The forensic officer looked away. She wasn't having anything to do with them.

'I think you'd better leave before you embarrass yourselves,' said Samson, perching on a kitchen stool. 'You know no more about forensics than I do. No suits, no gloves, no shoe covers. Out!'

He shook his head and glanced at the woman.

'We're all done here, sir,' she said to him, with a tiny note of solidarity.

When they'd left, he checked over the rooms at the back of the flat and noticed one or two things out of place but nothing seriously wrong. MI5 were on a fishing expedition. He went to his bedroom and worked quickly, packing clothes he'd need for the next two weeks, which included a dark blue suit and tie, a new pair of hiking shoes, T-shirts, jeans, shirts and a sweater. All this was compressed with skill into a medium-sized bag, which airlines sometimes let him carry on with a rucksack. He was proud of his technique for folding a lightweight, tailored suit, which emerged more or less wearable, and to this he added a slender pair of black brogues, made for him at a time when he had money and cared more about these things than he did now. Into the bag's side pockets he placed the Zeiss binoculars he'd used at the Junction, a head torch and a multi-purpose tool.

He went to the wardrobe and unhooked the leather jacket, his companion in Syria, the Balkans and on the Russian border, where he had been shot, damaging the jacket. This had necessitated a repair by a leather workshop in Brick Lane, which had finally returned the jacket three weeks ago. Samson felt its weight and smiled to himself. The patches where the bullet had entered his shoulder, passed through his body, ripping a much larger hole before slicing into Anastasia's arm, were coloured and aged to match the rest of the jacket and were virtually invisible. He couldn't help but remember the remark made by one of them – he didn't recall whether it was him or Anastasia – to the effect that the only things they had in common were Venice, sex and a bullet. As they watched a figure make his way across the beach in front of Harland's seaside cottage in Estonia nearly three years before, they had realised there was something else they shared – a profound affection for Naji Touma, whom she'd first encountered in a refugee camp on the Greek island of Lesbos.

He took everything and dumped it at the base of the kitchen island, turned on the coffee machine to make an espresso, then thought for a few moments before calling Naji. There was no point in confronting him with his discovery in a phone call, although he urgently needed to find out what Naji was doing at the Junction and the nature of his connection to Zoe Freemantle, and the only way he could do that was to see him in person. Naji answered on the first ring.

'Naji, it turns out that I do need to see you,' he said. 'Can we meet for coffee near Imperial?'

'No,' Naji replied.

'Why not?'

'I'm on a plane. I leave now.'

'In that I case I wonder if you could just explain why you were—'

'I cannot. The plane is leaving now. I have to turn off the phone.' It was true. Samson heard an announcement in the background telling passengers to do precisely that.

'Then when can we speak?'

'At Mr Harland's funeral, maybe.'

'Naji, this is serious, I need to talk to you before next week,' he said, but Naji had gone.

He sipped his coffee, aware of the throbbing pain in his leg, and considered using one of the three shots of morphine that he'd bought in Turkey. He went to retrieve the emergency medical bag from where Jo had lain bleeding, and noted, by the by, that the kebab had gone and the stains from their blood had combined to ruin both the sofa and the Persian hand-knotted rug which had been purchased with Anastasia's encouragement. He examined the 10mg morphine sulphate pen injector, saw that it was just shy of its expiry date but decided that, if he used it, he'd be flying for the rest of the day. He placed the little bag that he'd used to treat Jo in the rucksack.

He left messages for Macy Harp and made another call to Vuk, whose voicemail wasn't working. He took two painkillers with the coffee and waited. A minute later, his phone lit up with an incoming call.

A cackle was followed by a burst of smoker's cough, then finally some speech.

'How is English pussy?' Vuk Divjak asked, before disposing of the phlegm in a way that was all too plain.

'Vuk, how charming. Thank you.'

'I have sickness – like snake 'flu.'

'Vuk, you smoke too much.'

'No point speaking to English pussy because Vuk knew nothing about men.'

'Okay, it's been great to hear from you, Vuk. Shall we talk when you're feeling better? Let's catch up on your latest adventures in the Serbian justice system.'

'Funny fucking English pussy – you joking with poor old Vuk Divjak.'

'Just a little,' said Samson. 'But mostly I mean it.'

'When I know zero, that was in past.'

Samson's mind reeled. 'Sorry, I didn't get that one, Vuk. What are you trying to say?'

'Not *trying* to say. I *am* saying this to you now, idiot.'

'Okay, I'm listening.'

'In past I know nothing. Now I am knowing everything and I am not telling Sonia Fell.'

'MI6 have asked you about these men?' He recalled that Vuk had come to him from the UK's Belgrade embassy, via Sonia. It was natural for her to call him. MI6 and the CIA would be all over the Belgrade criminal community.

'Yes, they ask me, and I did not tell them because I then know zero. Now is different. I know more than zero – a lot more than zero.'

'So what do you know?'

'First we talk business terms.'

'You're selling the information!'

'Yes, this is my lifehood.'

'Your livelihood! "Lifehood" isn't a word.'

'That's what I say.'

'What sort of money do you want?'

'Ten thousand euro.'

Samson coughed. 'Forget it, Vuk. That's way too much.'

There was an uncharacteristic silence at the other end. 'Okay, I sell to Sonia Fell and MI6 Pussies. This is good.'

'MI6 won't pay you €10,000, Vuk.'

'Then CIA.'

'They might do. And by the way, Vuk, I have absolutely no problem with you selling your information to either agency, so don't think I'm going to join a bidding war for it. But I thought you liked Mr Harland and would want us to bring justice to his wife, Ulrike. And Vuk, these people have tried to kill me twice.'

Samson told him about being attacked by the Matador and Visser. 'Look,' he said eventually. 'Why don't you think about it and call me back?'

Vuk grunted and said he would be in touch.

A second conviction born in the middle of the night was that Macy Harp had been stringing him along and knew far more than he'd admitted. That was always the case with Macy, and when you called him on it he ducked and swerved and always managed to avoid telling the whole truth. This time, however, Samson would get it.

He dialled the number again. 'We need to have a conversation, Macy, and during that conversation you will tell me exactly what the hell is going on. Everything you know.'

'Come over later and we'll have a chat,' said Macy, unperturbed. 'By the way, I'm terribly pleased to hear your voice. Sounds like a very nasty business. Well done getting through that. You did a heroic job.'

'We were lucky,' he said, and before hanging up, added, 'And Macy, I really want some bloody answers.'

He moved to the steel splash plate above the stove and prised it from the wall. Beneath it were blue tiles from the old kitchen decoration, which he levered out to reveal a safe. In the past, he'd kept tens of thousands of pounds in it, but now there was an envelope containing just £5,000. Also in the safe were two sets of identities, including passports and driving licences. The passports were less use in the age of frontier biometrics but could be helpful in establishing an identity inside a country, and not every border was equipped with biometric readers. He chose the Lebanese passport for Aymen Malek, a long-standing resident of the 14th arrondissement, in Paris, and the possessor of an indefinite *carte de séjour* linked to an apartment block where a helpful resident forwarded his post for a fee each month. Malek had a liminal presence on professional networking sites as something in banking, a career Samson kept refreshed with posts about minor business triumphs and excruciating messages of thanks to the data, legal or marketing teams in this or that well-known bank. Malek's tendency to sycophancy amused Samson. He stowed Malek's passport and driving licence in his rucksack, together with a wallet that included memberships of the Automobile Club de France, a gun club in Créteil, charge cards in his name and, crucially, up-to-date bills and, finally, the envelope of cash. For good measure, he included the passport of Belgian national Claude Rameau, and the Hungarian identity card he'd used in Estonia in the name of Norbert Soltesz. Neither of these two identities was worked up nearly as well as Malek's.

He rested his leg for a while and looked around the flat. He tended to be practical and unsentimental, but over the years he'd become fond of the building and the neighbourhood. After Anastasia, he'd thought of selling both flats but feared he'd lose the money in his gambling binge, so his home had become an anchor of stability, something he wasn't prepared to lose. Now, while there was a threat to his life, he obviously couldn't live here, but in a more general way it had suddenly soured for him. The man he'd killed had apparently expired in the flat just a few feet from where he now sat. Blood was all over the place; Jo would no longer bring her uncomplicated companionship to Maida Vale; and MI5 had crawled through his possessions, leaving a vague sense of violation. Right then he decided he would sell up. He'd keep the smaller flat until Derek and Jericho, who had, after all, saved his life, wanted to move on.

He rose with the image of Remy in his mind, and dialled Jo. This was breaking some kind of agreement, but his encounter with Remy had prompted a question and no one else could answer it. He recorded a message saying he wouldn't be contacting her unless it was important. Then he left the flat. As he descended to the street, he received a text from Jo. 'They are pressing me to change my statement. You know what that means. If you're going abroad, as you said, leave today. They are going to fucking well tie you up so you can't move. Speak later. X'

CHAPTER 15

Live Frog

It was a warm day in Washington. Across the capital, puffs of white and pink blossom were evidence of an accelerating American spring, the pace of which Anastasia had never quite got used to. The spring of her childhood in the Pindus Mountains in Greece crept slowly across the landscape with several distinct stages. Here, it came and went in one gaudy flash. She was packing, or rather sorting the clothes which had been sent from New York by FedEx, and, like Samson, she included one piece of formal wear in the bag. The rest were practical clothes she used for travel and her work – boots, jeans, sweaters, an olive-green thermal jacket and several versions of a white shirt that allowed the wearer to secure rolled sleeves with a tab. Denis commented that her style increasingly tended towards the military and said he wished she'd sometimes make a concession to femininity, which is why she had worn a plum-coloured shirt and a silver necklace with her suit to the hearing.

It was not yet 7 a.m. For a moment, holding her coffee just below her lips, she watched the joggers in a park. Then Tulliver was beside her, now dressed in a navy jacket, dark grey trousers and button-down blue shirt and looking much more himself. 'Congressman Speight is on his way up. You want me to sit in on this one, too?'

'Absolutely. You have all that thanking to do.'

Speight arrived with a staffer and suggested that they might take breakfast in the main cafeteria. When they got there, the staffer was sent off to get the congressman juice, berries and scrambled eggs, while Tulliver organised coffee. Speight, a lean man with a high parting and a polished, friendly face, waited for Anastasia to take a chair before sitting down himself. Earnestly, he asked how Denis was.

'I hear he's doing fine, and I hope that's the truth, Mrs Hisami,' he said, pouring water into her glass. Her husband's nemesis certainly had manners, but that only served to put her on her guard.

'They're pleased with his progress, but it's a long road,' she said. 'I cannot hide from you that he may suffer permanent impairment.'

'I'm sorry to learn that. We were all very fortunate.'

'You acted quickly, Congressman. You kind of saved the day by shouting at Jim here. How come you knew what was happening?'

Jim added, 'It goes without saying that I'm immensely grateful, Congressman.'

He nodded to Tulliver. 'I was in the military, Mrs Hisami. We underwent basic chemical-weapons training before Desert Storm. People forget that Saddam had deployed nerve agents and mustard gas against his own people at Halabja way before he invaded Kuwait.'

'Actually, it was against Denis's people. Halabja was Kurdish and the people who were killed were all Kurds.'

'I stand corrected, Mrs Hisami.' Speight smiled. 'I know what you were saying when I asked you about your husband – you don't want the committee to recall your husband anytime soon. And I hear you.' He looked around expectantly for the staffer. 'One of my father's rules for life was – if you have to work before breakfast, make sure to eat breakfast first.' He smiled again. 'Shall we wait to do our business until we got some nourishment inside us?'

'Do we have business, Congressman?'

'Maybe we do; maybe we don't.' Tulliver returned with coffee and sat down. Then the staffer appeared with the food.

Speight stirred sweetener into his coffee and chuckled to himself. 'Mark Twain also said something humorous about breakfast – eat a live frog first thing in the morning and nothing worse will happen to you all day.'

'Are you the equivalent of the live frog, Congressman?' she asked, without smiling.

'I sincerely hope not, Mrs Hisami.'

'Why are you here?'

'To express my concern for what happened. Without our inquiries, Denis would not have been there, and Mr Steen would not have been killed.'

'You presumably have your reasons,' said Anastasia.

'I do, and I will not resile from my conviction that your husband supplied military aid to those who wish our country and our allies harm.'

'No, Congressman!' she said, just about controlling herself. 'What I meant was that you must have your reasons for persecuting a man who's trying to bring relief to those who've suffered in his country since way before Halabja. That's politics today, right? The culture wars that say destroying someone on the other side is a win, irrespective of what good they do.'

'Maybe we can park that issue for the moment.' He gestured to the staffer with a fork loaded with egg. 'Matthew here came across an interesting story, which I'm going to share with you in the hope and expectation that you may be able to shed light on it.' Speight popped the egg into his mouth. He liked to take his time. He ate slow and he spoke slow. 'He heard that Mr Steen was carrying evidence in his brief-case that your husband planned to use in the hearing this week, or in a month's time, when he was scheduled to appear in front of the Foreign

Affairs Committee again. This evidence was to be used *in extremis*. In other words, it was a strategy of last resort because it was only half cooked. It was inchoate.'

She began shaking her head several seconds before he landed with such pleasure on the word 'inchoate'.

'Men come here from the FBI, the CIA, business partners of my husband – and they spout theories at me and it means nothing. Mr Steen died and my husband is very sick. Those are the facts. I have no knowledge of what was in Mr Steen's briefcase, still less do I care.'

Speight kept chewing methodically. 'What if the target was the briefcase?' he asked eventually. 'And by that I mean the knowledge held in that briefcase and in the brains of your husband and his lawyer?'

'Look in the briefcase,' she said, exasperated.

With a nod from his boss, Matthew, a tall black man with horn-rimmed spectacles and collar-pin shirt, said, 'It was destroyed because of the high degree of contamination. The film from the hearing at one point shows Mr Steen putting those papers in the case. It had to be incinerated, along with all his clothing.'

'So we shall never know what was inside,' she said.

'Not necessarily,' said Speight. He sucked his cheek to dislodge something from his teeth then wiped his mouth. 'Maybe you have some idea of what was in those papers.'

'I do not,' she said. 'Maybe you should ask Steen's law firm, Lanyado Christie?'

'We already did,' said Matthew. 'But they had no knowledge of any papers other than the regular documents concerning your husband's appearance this week, which the committee also possessed.'

She looked at Tulliver. 'Jim?'

'Nothing like that came my way,' he replied.

Her eyes returned to Speight. 'How do you know there was anything of this nature in the case if the law firm and Denis's chief aide were unaware of it?'

Speight nodded at the logic of this. 'We were all very shocked by the events of two days ago. It was a moment when representatives and their staffs come together. Anyone could have been killed. A nerve agent doesn't distinguish between Democrats and Republicans, and that's made my colleagues recognise how much we have in common. We're in Congress for the American people. We sometimes forget that.'

'You're saying you had help from the Democrats. Who?'

Speight shook his head.

'What was the nature of the question he or she was going to ask?' asked Anastasia.

'Why, the evidence of a conspiracy in the heart of the establishment related to your husband's previous troubles: nothing less! This is standard DC scuttlebutt, but people believe it.'

'Okay, so now you have your story, what do you want with me?'

'There's one other thing. I want us to appear together in front of the news cameras.' Anastasia looked at Tulliver, who scratched his nose and pursed his lips.

'That's for your benefit,' she said, 'because it certainly wouldn't be for mine.'

'I never have any need of publicity, but I want certain individuals to see us together.'

'Who?'

'People. I want them to know that we've been talking,' said Speight.

She thought for a few seconds. 'Okay, I agree. But can I ask you a favour in return? I need to get to the airport because I'm going to the West Coast on business. Can your driver take me? It would save time.'

'Yes, of course, when he's dropped me at the Rayburn. That'll be fine.'

They arranged to meet in the lobby fifteen minutes later. She returned to her room to complete her packing. Tulliver joined her.

'What do you think – friend or foe?' she asked.

He beckoned her into the corridor. 'Foe,' he replied when she was through the door. 'Most definitely foe.'

'Denis says you should never go into an important meeting without a pistol in your back pocket. Even though you aren't going to use it, you know that you can, and that makes all the difference to you and your opponent.'

'Actually, it's a hand grenade. That's the way he usually tells it.'

'So he had his hand grenade in Steen's briefcase – who do you think is most concerned about the hand grenade?'

'Warren Speight.'

'Exactly! Should I appear with him, or is he playing me?'

'He's playing you, but you should go along with it. You've already got a ride to the airport out of him.' Tulliver's eyes danced. 'That was smart of you, Anastasia. The FBI will think you're going to Congress. Have you got your ticket?'

She nodded. 'I hate to ask you, Jim, but could you get my bag into the Congressman's car? I don't want the media reporting that I'm deserting Denis.'

'Of course,' he said. 'By the way, those emails have been sent. I arranged a meeting tomorrow between you and the West Coast staff, which I'll cancel by phone later.'

Before leaving she went to see Denis. His bed had been elevated and she could see much more of him. His colour was better and an expression of contentment had replaced the agonised rictus that froze his features after the attack. A fan in the corner of the bedroom ruffled his hair when it swung round to face him. 'Good luck, dear husband,' she murmured. 'I'll see you in a few days.'

She had to admit Speight was an accomplished media performer. Half a dozen TV crews had gathered at the hospital's main entrance after being tipped off by Matthew, yet he managed to feign surprise that a private visit would attract so much attention. Asked by CNN why he had dropped in on the wife of the man he was in the process of trying to destroy, he replied that his thoughts now were only with the victims and their families. He sent a particular message of condolence to Mr Steen's loved ones and co-workers. Then, gesturing to Anastasia, who stood a little distance from him, he said he'd been pleased to be able to deliver a message to Mrs Hisami in person and was, he confessed with a warm smile in her direction, honoured that she had received him during her painful vigil. On the larger scale, he said, this shocking attack was an outrage against American democracy and intended to thwart all those who were engaged in the sacred conduct thereof. 'An act like this reminds us that we must answer hatred, division and violence by reigniting the spirit of common purpose. And that's what I am doing here, expressing solidarity with Mr and Mrs Hisami.'

Anastasia briefly answered questions about Denis's condition and her own experience of watching Stewart Steen and her husband collapse. She thanked the hospital for saving her husband's life and those in Congress who had acted so promptly to contain the effects of the attack and to help her husband. She glanced at Speight and added that everyone in Congress had reason to be grateful to the Ranking Member, whose chemical warfare training had allowed him to correctly identify the symptoms as being those caused by a nerve agent. This had undoubtedly saved her and her husband's colleagues from contamination, as well as many others. Warren Speight was, she said, the true hero of the hour.

'That was gracious of you, Mrs Hisami, and I thank you for it,' he said to her as they moved to his car.

Reporters shouted out, 'Where are you going now?' Speight waved and smiled and said that he and Mrs Hisami had busy schedules and he hoped they'd forgive the brevity of the interview.

The congressman's driver dropped her at the entrance of the Signature Flight Support Center, the reception for those using private aircraft, about ten minutes' walk from the main terminal building of Dulles International. The Ford hybrid SUV that had followed them from the hospital to the Capitol then the airport, and made no bones about it, pulled up just after Speight's Lexus. The driver and her male companion, both wearing sunglasses, watched her take her bag from Speight's driver and go inside. Then they parked just twenty metres from the door. At the very most, she had half an hour to reach the main terminal, check in and pass through security before the flight closed, but there was only one door and she couldn't leave the private-jet terminal without being seen. She went to the reception to say that she had arrived then passed through to the lounge and at the snack bar poured herself a coffee, which she had no intention of drinking, then mimed forgetfulness and returned to the lobby to see if the car had gone. It had not. One of the agents was standing beside it on his cellphone, looking in the direction of the building. She glanced at the time on her cellphone. Unless she went now, she would miss the plane.

But then a voice called the name she never ever used. 'Ana! My, what a surprise!' She hadn't noticed Marty Reid come through the door, accompanied by a man carrying his bags.

'Marty! What a pleasure!'

'Well, I've already seen you once today.'

'That was yesterday.'

'No. I saw you on Fox with Speight. You're keeping some strange company if you mean to protect your husband. Warren Speight is not – most definitely not – a good man. He's the guy who wants to cut Denis into pieces and feed him to the dogs.'

'He came to see how Denis was and say how sorry he was.'

'What else did he want? Speight never does anything without a reason. I hear he's running around with a theory that Denis had something he was going to reveal to the committee.'

'Really,' said Anastasia. 'Where did you get that from?'

'I keep my ear close to the ground. Always have done.'

'And according to your source, what was he about to reveal?'

'I don't know, but maybe it has something to do with the money I was talking about. No one ever got to the bottom of where it came from. Maybe he was going to name names to demonstrate that people were conspiring against him and the allegations made by Speight and his associates were all false.'

'Maybe,' she said, wondering why the old buzzard was still banging on about the money, and now reconciled to missing her flight. 'Yet I was in a meeting before the hearing with my husband and Mr Steen, and nothing of that nature was discussed.'

'That was with Congresswoman Ricard, right?'

'Yes.' How did Reid know about that meeting? 'I thought you were helping us, Marty, not investigating us.'

'It would just be helpful to know what your husband was going to reveal, if indeed he was planning to reveal something. Has the FBI asked any questions along these lines?'

'No, Marty, they haven't. The Bureau is interested in finding the people who organised and paid for the attack. What Denis might or might not have said in the hearing now seems beside the point, does it not?'

'Where are you going?' he asked abruptly.

'California.'

'Then why are you out here? Why aren't you with your plane?'

'Marty, I'm waiting for someone! Why are you asking these questions? Where the fuck are you going?'

Reid wasn't used to people talking like that to him. Anger flashed in his eyes, but he controlled himself. 'Jackson Hole. It's the nearest airport to my place.'

'Last time we really talked – before all this – we were at an environmental fundraiser, and yet here we are, taking private planes. Strike you as hypocritical?'

He shrugged.

'What do you want?' she asked. 'Why does this mean so much to you?'

'I told you. I believe that some evil forces are at work and I'm one of the few people who can help you and Denis. Good to see you, Ana. I'll be in touch. In the meantime, I strongly advise you to stay away from

Warren Speight. I believe he's at the very heart of this affair. Have a good flight.'

The FBI vehicle had gone. She left the flight centre and walked a short distance along a road called Wind Sock Drive, turned right at the end towards the main Dulles terminal and took a path leading to a grassy bank, which she climbed, relishing the air and the tiny amount of exercise she was getting after being cooped up in the hospital. Resigned to a long wait in one of the lounges, she went to the airline desk to book the next flight to Vienna, where she would transfer to Athens. Overnight, she had arranged to meet in the Greek capital with key members of the Ayshel Hisami Foundation who were working with newly arrived refugees in the Aegean and along Turkey's land borders with Greece and Bulgaria, where people were being gassed, stripped of their clothing, and sometimes shot. As she reminded Tulliver, there was more than one crisis in her life. The teams were in need of money and support, and she could give them both.

She missed her original flight and bought a ticket for the next, which meant a two-hour wait in the airport. At length, she presented her Greek passport in the name of Anastasia Niklaou Christakos to the automatic reader, retrieved a boarding card and headed for Security, all the time dreading that she would be stopped. But she reached the gate and boarded the flight without a hitch. A text message came from Tulliver as she settled into her seat. 'Call me soonest.' She dialled his number.

'I have to tell you that Paul Samson was attacked in his apartment,' he said. 'His friend was also hurt. Samson had to kill the man. He was very, very lucky.'

'Jesus. Are they going to be okay?'

'Macy says yes. But the main point is that you have to be very careful, Anastasia. These people aren't going to give up, and if they think you know what Denis was going to reveal at the hearing, they will try to kill you, too.'

CHAPTER 16

Bubble Wrap

'What's your question?' snapped Jo Hayes when she answered Samson's call. 'I've got about two minutes before I see my boss.'

'I'm sorry,' he said.

'Well, it's not fucking ideal. I only dumped you this morning.'

'It was about the Edgar Building. It was raided and someone was arrested. I hoped you might tell me about them.'

'No, I bloody can't.'

He didn't persist. There was no point with Jo. 'How's your arm?'

'Shit. How's your leg?'

'Fine.' It wasn't. A doctor called from the hospital and said he shouldn't have been discharged because he thought the knife might have cut into the muscular branch of the sciatic nerve as well as grazing the femoral artery. That would account for the shooting pain Samson was experiencing.

'You looked terrible this morning.' She stopped and exhaled badtemperedly. 'Oh, fuck it! I guess you did save my life. The people they picked up weren't the ones they were looking for. They got the wrong building.'

'How so?'

'I don't flaming know.'

But she did, and she had much more time than she'd made out. He talked it out of her over the next ten minutes, and used some guile in the process by deliberately stating things that he knew were wrong, such as the number of people taken away for questioning after the police raided the building – he said six were arrested – and the reason for the raid, which he suggested was suspected terrorist activity. No, she said, succumbing to the natural instinct of human beings, especially current and former lovers, to correct each other – just two people had been questioned and only one was taken away from the Edgar. As for the motive of the police and Security Service, he was completely wrong. It had nothing to do with terrorism and everything to do with some highly unusual encrypted communications coming from the area, which had piqued the interest of GCHQ, Cheltenham, who prompted the security services to look into the source at the Edgar Building; they in turn had involved the police. Some of this traffic had been decoded and found to contain establishment names in Britain and the United States – politicians and well-known businesspeople. But that was all they had extracted from the messages.

Given the prominence of the people and the novelty of the cryptographic techniques, it was decided to watch the building and see who was sending these communications. One of the organisations that came under suspicion was a porn site called Secorum, which attempted to disguise the ugliness of its product with good lighting and tasteful surroundings; Jo called it the *House & Garden* of porn. Filming was done on sets constructed in a suite of rooms rented by a man named Harry Diamond. Above the porn site's studio was the office of reactt.org.uk, one of the many inflammatory racist organisations the security services monitored as a matter of course. Run by an individual named Toby Fawcett and three others, all of them known to MI5, ReacTT seemed to be the likely culprit. However, GCHQ technicians realised the infrequent bursts of communication came from both organisations, plus another site that was engaged in the illegal sale of hard-to-find medications. And this struck them as very odd indeed.

The Edgar was raided. Harry Diamond was invited to explain himself, as was Mr Fawcett, who was picked up at home, and after several hours it became clear that both organisations' websites and broadband had been hacked to provide someone else cover. In the case of Secorum there was an actual Ethernet cable plugged into the office router, and that cable was found to run into the roof of an adjacent building, 209 Herbert Street. The other end had yet to be traced, though Samson was certain that he himself had seen it, together with many other cables, running through a hole punched in the wall of the Pit, about a hundred and fifty metres away from the front of the Edgar Building. He wondered if this was Naji's idea, too, for he was damned sure that Naji was the author of the new encryption. Aged twelve, Naji had buried information about Islamic State in a game where kids built fantasy structures in the virtual world. He had made one that was also a kind of archive that only he could open.

'That's all I have,' Jo said eventually. 'They never found the source of the signals and won't now, because they've stopped.'

'I owe you, Jo. Thanks.'

'You don't – we're quits. Our paths go different directions from now on, Samson.'

'I won't trouble you again, Jo.'

'Don't,' she said, and hung up. He'd never heard that tone in her voice before.

He phoned Macy and left another message. 'I'm at Cedar and I'm coming round now.' He got up and stood, grimacing for a second or two as the pain ran up and down his leg and into his buttocks. Then he moved towards the stairs and hobbled down, using his stick to break the force on his leg. At the bottom of the stairs was a short passage that led to a door with a transom light above it. If there was sunlight in the street the shadows were sometimes projected upwards and played on the surface of the glass. He could make out two distinct shapes, which he estimated were standing about six feet away from the door. He heard the rumble of Ivan's voice making excuses. They must be police. He cursed to himself.

By now he knew the routine. An unmarked Range Rover or some other SUV would take him to a police station, most likely West End Central in Savile Row. An MI5 officer would be waiting in the vehicle and he or she would say nothing. It wasn't an arrest, of course, but an invitation to speak about matters of common interest, an update, or 'sharing of perspectives', as Peter Nyman liked to put it, though the needs of the state and attendant menace loomed in the background. Nyman usually had something to do with setting up these sessions, which he amused himself by calling 'tea and chat'.

Samson opened the door and was confronted by two men looking straight at him. The cut of their suits, the polished shoes and general care taken with their grooming told him that they were American intelligence officers, who, on the whole, are more crisply turned out than their British counterparts.

'We're from the US Embassy,' said a man in his late forties with a dark moustache. 'And we'd very much like to speak with you. We have a car outside.'

Samson frowned and shook his head. Ivan looked as though he might retrieve, for the first time, a baseball bat that he insisted on keeping hidden under the maître d's desk. 'I'm sure you're kosher,' said Samson. 'It's just that I've had a difficult few days. People keep trying to kill me.'

'Let me introduce us. I'm Frank Toombs from the Central Intelligence Agency and this is Special Agent Edward Reiner from the FBI.' Reiner showed him ID. 'We're kind of here unofficially.'

'You don't want the security services and SIS knowing what you're doing.'

'Oh, they know we're here, for sure. But we just want to hold some conversations without them in the room. Does that seem strange to you?'

Samson looked at Toombs. 'There's a famous expert on tradecraft in the Agency who retired a few years ago,' he said. 'Can you give me their name and tell me which office they worked in?'

Toombs grinned. 'You're testing me! Sure! Okay! That was Mavis Hoyle, and her last post was in the Office of Mission Resources, though that's classified information, Mr Samson.'

'What's her passion?'

'Some kind of dog – she shows them all over the country now.'

'Weimaraners,' said Samson.

'So you knew Mavis? The best-looking fifty-five-year-old on the planet, and certainly the smartest.'

'Yes, I spent three months on attachment in Virginia and I attended classes with Mavis. When do you want to do this?'

'We would appreciate just an hour or so of your time now,' said Reiner. 'It really is important.'

Toombs put on sunglasses and, gesturing to the door, said, 'Shall we, Mr Samson? It's a short ride.'

They drove to an office building near the new US embassy, south of the Thames, and entered a loading bay very much like the one where Samson had glimpsed Naji. A young woman met them and showed them to a room, with which Toombs and Reiner were evidently unfamiliar. Reiner explained, by the by, that they had only just flown into Northolt. Two younger men joined them. Samson assumed they were CIA because they deferred to Toombs. They all sat down.

'So,' said Reiner, pinching his lower lip. 'We have two missions. The first is to establish who is behind the attack in Congress and understand their motive. The second, which is more Mr Toombs's area of interest, is to eliminate the threat that brought nerve agent into the heart of our democracy and to make sure that it never occurs again. That means identifying the person or persons who ordered this attack, the chain of command and supply line for the material. We make the assumption that you cannot help us with the second but that you are crucial to the first part. You have much in common with the victims in that you are one of the assassination targets and you have worked with both of them closely at different times. We know all about what happened in Macedonia, we know about Hisami's role, and we are fully aware of what occurred in Narva, Estonia. By the way, I think I should mention that we don't – repeat: *don't* – think this has anything to do with that incident, but do you?'

'No.'

'Then why are your people pushing it?' asked Toombs.

'I've no idea.'

'The thing I'm having a problem with is this,' continued Toombs, now altogether less friendly. 'Our people here have been watching closely and it's like your guys don't give a fuck. A paid assassin murders one of the greatest spies in the last fifty years, and what do they say? "Oh dear me, where shall we have the memorial event, and will there be cake and tea?"' For this he attempted a British accent. 'Seems like they just want to shove the whole thing into the office incinerator and move on – right?'

'I can't say,' said Samson. 'I'm out of the loop.'

'But you aren't. You're the main man – the guy everyone wants to off. And I ask myself, where's the fucking bubble wrap? They've done nothing to protect you. Why?'

'I don't want protection.'

'Sorry, I gotta tell you this – right now, it looks like they actually want you dead. And that really interests us. Because it means you know something that a lot of people don't want the world to hear – maybe even your own frigging MI6. You were a serving British Intelligence officer, and a good one. You've done them a lot of favours since they let you go – big, important stuff like tracking down the Syrian boy with that mother lode of IS intelligence. They owe you, right? So why don't they give a shit if you're dead? And you have to ask yourself – do they really care that Robert Harland was murdered? Maybe they think he deserved it.'

He looked at Toombs and Reiner and told them he had no idea what MI6 suspected because, humiliatingly enough, he didn't know anything.

'That's exactly what your girlfriend said,' said Toombs. 'Yet you're the only people in the world who can help us.'

'Mrs Hisami is not my girlfriend and we haven't been in touch for over two years, so that's completely irrelevant. Look, just accept that I happen to agree with you about the British end of this investigation. I think it stinks, but I don't know why that is.'

'A smart guy like you, and you *don't know*!' said Toombs. 'I don't buy that. You know that you know something they don't want you to know.'

'That's getting into the territory of known unknowns.'

'What would you do if you were us?' Reiner asked.

'Focus on what Harland and Hisami were doing. They were on to something and it was big. Then, using the four hit men, I'd triangulate to find the person who paid them. At least three of those men knew each other, and the Ukrainian who killed Harland has the exact same profile, so there has to be someone who's plugged into that network, or already knew them. What about the Ukrainian? Have you interviewed him?'

'He's sick, pneumonia,' said Toombs. 'But you're right about the rest of it.' He studied him. 'But this is not just a gangster who hires a few shooters. We're dealing with an individual who has access to an experimental nerve agent.'

'Experimental?'

'It was an early version of the binary agent used by the Russians in Salisbury. The agent used in Congress was unitary, which means—'

'I know what that means,' said Samson testily, and shifted his leg. 'It's crude, difficult to transport and very awkward to handle. So you're wondering where the heck that came from. If this is not a sophisticated binary agent favoured by the Russians, there may be more of this cheap moonshine on the market.'

'Exactly,' said Toombs.

'Ukraine,' said Samson. 'In 2018, Russia was about to deploy chemical weapons in the east of the country. Maybe some of that material found its way to the US. Plus, Ukraine is a really good conduit. I guess the fact that the nerve agent was crude could be a sign that someone is covering their tracks, which would be the same tactic as using a bunch of amateur gunmen instead of professionals.' He glanced at the two younger officers, who had said nothing. One was making a note on his phone. 'Look, there's not a lot I can tell you, but when I learn something, I will. I want to help.'

Toombs raised his eyebrows at Reiner. Reiner nodded, thought for a few moments and looked at Samson. 'This is a story of two briefcases,' he started. 'One briefcase, belonging to the lawyer, was destroyed, and that is a dreadful shame because in it we believe was some material, a dossier – call it what you will – which we think Mr Hisami was going to use if things got rough in the hearing. But the briefcase was pretty much marinated in the nerve agent and it was the first thing to be burned. We don't know the nature of the material, and Mr Steen's office can't help. We have copies of all the documents that his assistant gave him that morning and there's nothing unusual among them. The second briefcase belonged to Mr His-ami, and that contained a mystery in the shape of a two-year calendar with entries that we don't understand. What's so strange about this is that Mr Hisami's assistant and Jim Tulliver kept his calendar electronically, so there was no need for a physical one unless it was a record of activities that he wished to keep secret. Neither Mr Tulliver nor Mrs Hisami were able to tell us what was in the first briefcase, which isn't surprising, and they *insist* they have no understanding of the entries in the calendar.'

'You don't believe them.'

'We don't know who or what to believe. But we wanted to share some of it with you.' He nodded to one of the young men, who worked a laptop. Five words appeared on the television screen: PEARL, BERLIN, PITCH, AURORA and SAFFRON. 'These mean anything to you?'

'No.'

'They're code words for operations or individuals, and they some-times appear in the calendar alongside numbers which we believe are encrypted IBAN numbers. The National Security Agency is working on these and we'll have them pretty soon, unless they've been really scrambled.' Samson thought of Naji. If these numbers had been through

Naji's hands, he doubted anyone would get the right result: Naji had his own approach to encryption. Reiner continued: 'The words appear with varying frequency. BERLIN is the most common, with forty-four mentions. PEARL gets twenty-nine, SAFFRON fourteen, PITCH thirteen and AURORA eleven. Over the last couple of months all five words make more appearances than they did in the two previous months, so, obviously, this signals increased activity of some sort, which we think may have been focused on the hearing in Congress this week.'

Samson had stopped listening. The image in his mind was the poorly cleaned whiteboard in the room known as the Pit in 209 Herbert Street. He wanted to consult the photographs on his phone, but there was really no need because he recalled the remaining letters in at least two of the column headings, which had not quite been wiped clean. PIT did not refer to the room of that name, which was his original supposition, but consisted of the first three letters of the word PITCH. Likewise, EAR was part of the word PEARL. He considered this for a few seconds before deciding that he would tell Reiner and Toombs about this once he had reached either Naji or Zoe Freemantle to ask them what they meant.

Reiner noticed he'd tuned out. 'Is there something on your mind?'

'My leg's giving me gyp – sorry.'

'Are you able to help us with any of this?'

He shook his head. 'Can I make a note of some of these words, or take a photograph?'

'We don't allow photography in the facility, sir,' piped one of the young agents.

'Have you got a photocopy?'

Toombs looked sceptical, but Reiner handed him a printed sheet with the numbers and the five words.

'What about the dates in the calendar where the words appear?'

Reiner shook his head. 'See if you can help with these and then we'll talk about the dates. You may figure something out. And if you do, we would like to hear from you.' He flicked a card across the table.

Toombs got up, tucked his thumbs into the front of his waistband and walked around the room. 'I'll give you my number momentarily, but you may not have time to use it. The reason we came to your restaurant is that Special Agent Reiner heard through his sources that the police are going to use the death of the man you killed in self-defence as an excuse to arrest and detain you. We wanted to speak with you before that happened. I know things are fucked up in this country, but why would they arrest you? To stop you talking? About what, for Chrissake? You don't know anything.' He paused, removed his thumbs from his trousers and clapped his hands together. 'I got it. They know you're going to find out their big secret.' He put air quotes around that. 'And why would that be? Because they know the secret is headed towards you.'

'I'm not sure I understand you,' said Samson.

'Sure you do. You're still in the game. So you know that sometimes you go and find the secret, but other times the secret comes to you, and that's usually when you don't want it. Make no mistake: this secret is coming your way, pal, which means you will be in a position to harm them, just as Mr Hisami and Mr Harland were. That's why they wound up dead and in a coma. And they want you dead. I don't think they'll be bothering with amateurs like Visser and Rajavic any longer. They'll set someone really good on you.'

'Thanks for the reassurance.'

'We want to make friends with you for the time when the secret comes to you. We want to be the guys you share it with because you know we will do the right thing. Does that make sense?' He offered his business card in the palms of both hands.

'You keep saying "them"', said Samson, taking the card. 'Who do you think is them?'

'I guess the *them* is a big part of the secret. Maybe that's the whole goddamn secret, eh? It feels like that to me.' He returned to his chair and leaned back with his hands clasped behind his head. 'There's one thing you need to do and that's get the hell out of this shitty country. Go travel.

It's not good for you here. They have your entire life mapped out and someone high up here wants to nail you.'

Reiner rose and moved to the door. 'I believe you were on your way to a meeting. Can we give you a ride?'

'Yes, Mayfair,' said Samson.

Toombs gave him a pitying look from his chair. 'Myself, I don't think you're going to make it, but the number on the card is good for these two guys, also,' he said, gesturing to the two young agents. 'If you need protection, they're the bubblewrap.'

CHAPTER 17

The Bird

Samson returned to Cedar and went to eat at the table he sometimes used at the rear of the restaurant by the kitchen entrance. It was still early and the surrounding tables were empty. Ivan reported no sightings of the Matador, but a police presence in the street had been noted earlier, although it was not clear whether it had been focused on Cedar. Samson could have gone round to Macy's office immediately, but he needed to eat and ponder things. He'd reached a conclusion about Macy's behaviour and that of his client, Denis Hisami, but the appearance of the FBI and the CIA in town and the odd nature of the meeting with them convinced him that they knew much more than they had let on. Toombs was right. He was still in the game, which is why he recognised that, as well as apparently bringing him into their investigation by sharing some of the mystery contained in Denis Hisami's briefcase, they had tagged him and were basically waiting to see what happened. Toombs offered protection but, in reality, that was also surveillance.

He brought out his phone and texted Vuk Divjak with an offer of €7,500 for his information, then copied the text, along with Vuk's bank details, which he had from a previous job, to Imogen. Vuk was a rogue, but in all the dealings Samson had had with him, he'd never lied. If he said he had information, it was worth having. Macy would kick up, but it was Hisami's money and, besides, Samson was in no mood to spend carefully or, for that matter, to oblige bloody Macy Harp.

Then he brought up the photographs he'd taken in the Pit and was unsurprised to see that all traces of the words on the whiteboard exactly fitted the five words found in Hisami's calendar. PIT was part of PITCH; EAR was what was left of PEARL; ORA of AURORA; R N of BER-LIN; and S FRO of SAFFRON. He asked Ivan to fetch the laptop from his bags, now stowed in the restaurant's cloakroom, ready for him to leave. He entered all five words in the search engine and found a link to something called *Werner's Nomenclature of Colours*. Of course! They were all colours – pitch black; pearl grey; aurora red; Berlin blue and saffron yellow. He found the online version of the nomenclature. The first attempt at classifying colour had subsequently been refined by an Englishman, Patrick Syme, in 1814; the nomenclature was used by Charles Darwin in his scientific observations. Each colour was defined through references to nature, which Samson thought ingenious and also charming. Pearl grey was found on the backs of black-headed and kittiwake gulls and in a mineral called porcelain jasper; pitch black can be seen on the guillemot and in yenite mica; Berlin blue on the wing feathers of a jay; and saffron yellow in the tail coverts of the golden pheasant.

This was Harland all over. But the origin of the code was no great puzzle. Anyone wanting to know the relationship between them would simply put the words in a search engine and locate *Werner's Nomenclature of Colours*. Odd that Toombs and Reiner hadn't mentioned that. Maybe they were testing him, although there seemed no earthly point. The question, of course, was what did the five colours stand for? Having seen the board, Samson was sure that each represented a project and that progress on those five projects was logged in the room where Naji and Zoe Freemantle worked, the operations centre of the whole enterprise.

The phone rang. It was Vuk.

'English pussy, I take deal – €8,000.'

'I said €7,500,' said Samson. 'It's on the way to your account.'

'Vuk needs eight. Big expenses.'

'I'll see what I can do.'

'Money first. Talk later. This clear for you?'

Samson leaned into the phone. 'Vuk, unless you tell me now, you won't get any fucking money. There's time for me to stop the transfer.'

'Okay, I tell you English pussy first thing I know and this only. Name of man who kill Mr Bobby Harland is Nikolai Horobets. He is Ukrajinski.'

The name of the Ukrainian hadn't been released to the media and there was no way Vuk could have read it anywhere. 'Okay, so we're on,' said Samson. 'What else can you tell me?'

'Rajavic, Drasko and Dutch cunt Rossi, they work for Ukrajinski from Vojvodina. Ukrajinski drug lord.'

'So, all three worked for one man. What is the drug lord's name?'

'Oret, but he is now not important. Oret is dead. He killed yesterday with wife.'

'So, the link between them all and the man most likely to have hired them was murdered yesterday?' Samson grabbed an order pad from one of his waiters and wrote down the name Oret.

'Yes, I just say that.'

'How?'

'Shot in car by home.'

'So who paid Oret?'

'Man who is lion killer.'

Samson inhaled. 'Vuk, what do you mean by "lion killer"?' Then he understood. 'Is he a big-game hunter?'

'Yes, of course, very big game-hunter. Ruski. Maybe living in Kipar.'

'Kipar? Ah yes, Cyprus. So, this individual you've heard about could be a Russian national based in Cyprus. Is he the person who arranged for the supply of the nerve agent?'

'I do not know this. His name Anatoly Stepurin. Maybe he is GRU or maybe FSB.'

Samson made a note. 'What makes you think this?'

'His name in newspaper.'

'Hold on a moment, Vuk. I'm just going to look this character up.' He entered the name into the search engine and without too much trouble found Stepurin exposed in the French press as someone with a background in military intelligence and now an organiser of illegal big-game hunting. A French investigative journalism unit named Rochet had managed to trace his phone to dark facilities in and around Moscow that were particularly associated with 'foreign actions', which invariably meant assassinations.

'This man is practically famous,' said Samson. 'Can you tie him to Oret?'

'I have zero more information. But this is good for English pussy, no?'

'Yes, it looks very good – thank you, Vuk.'

'I go now to drink and fuck my girl. Cheerio, English pussy.'

Samson hung up and at that moment saw Ivan look round, hand Samson's bags to a waiter to bring them over and then make urgent flapping motions with his hand below the desk. Samson got up and, without looking back, entered the kitchen, walked past the half-dozen cooks, who took no notice of him, and moved to the side door. At the far end of the narrow passage between the two buildings he saw the blue and yellow of a police vehicle parked at the front of the restaurant. He turned left, squeezed past the bins and moved to the northern end of the passage, which opened into a mews, where he waited for the cab that he knew Ivan would send on the restaurant account. Fifteen minutes later, after a journey that took him a long route around Mayfair, he was standing in Macy Harp's suite of offices, confronted by a man in his seventies who rose from one of the armchairs to greet him.

He had once been very tall. Even with the stoop of old age, he had a few centimetres on Samson and now looked down at him with watery blue eyes that had the playful, lunatic energy of a gun dog. His nose was long and bony; his cheeks were hollow and creased from a lifetime of manic grinning. On his scalp there was a light covering of sandy-grey hair that received no attention whatsoever. He was deeply tanned with liver spots on his hands and wrists, and on his forehead was evidence of the removal, by surgery, of at least one troubling lesion. He took Samson's hand in an iron grip and, for a moment, his eyes stopped moving and he studied him with professional interest. Then he made a noise that was halfway between a bark and a laugh and managed to convey both pleasure and warmth.

This turned out to be Cuth Avocet, a contemporary of Robert Harland and Macy Harp's in SIS and an early partner in Hendricks Harp, though, for one reason or another, he had found it necessary to remove himself to a ranch fifty miles from the town of Broom in Western Australia, where he'd remained for three decades, building a nature reserve and bringing up a second family. He was known as the Bird. Most people assumed that the Bird was dead, and that was the way he liked it. Looking at this SIS dinosaur, with his bush jacket, silver snake bangle, and enormous feet shod in giant-sized trainers, Samson decided he was one of the upper class's natural killers, a man who'd blow up a bridge or slit a throat with the same ease as casting a trout line on some posh friend's stretch of water.

Before they sat down, he told them that the police were about to arrest him and he had very little time. 'Won't your friend be bored by all this? It's going to be detailed, I'm afraid,' he said to Macy.

'Cuth is up to speed and has some things to tell you,' said Macy.

'I want more on Zoe Freemantle, Macy, and no bullshit. My assumption is that she was hacking GreenState's system. She never left the office without her laptop, always took it with her to the washroom or a meeting. It was never out of her sight. Do you know whether she had any help on the inside?'

'No.'

'You weren't protecting anyone else and you're not aware of any other part of operation Harland and Hisami?'

'No, though I was aware that Denis and Bobby were working on a broad canvas.'

'But you know nothing of that.'

'No.'

'Who was Zoe reporting to?'

'Ultimately, Denis. But there must have been an intermediary.'

'And you didn't know who that was?'

Macy shook his head.

Samson didn't believe him. 'But we can assume,' he continued, 'that GreenState is the vital part of this investigation and that there was reason to believe Zoe was at increased risk, which is why I was employed. But instead of pursuing Zoe, who was, after all, working for Denis and Bobby, they twice tried to kill me. How does that make sense?'

'I think it may simply be a mistake. Your connection with Bobby and Denis is known. When you showed up at GreenState, it was assumed that you were the person they had to fear.'

The Bird's leg was jigging. He cleared his throat and looked at Macy mischievously. He had already got there.

'You put me in as a decoy,' said Samson.

'That may have been their plan,' said Macy, 'but I had no idea. They assumed you could look after yourself, and it was for a very short period of time. And let's not forget, you were being handsomely rewarded.'

'You put me in as a bloody decoy,' Samson repeated, only just keeping his temper, 'and ever since I have been taking the heat. Two attempts on my life, my friend was nearly killed, and now the police and both the Bureau and the Agency are on my case, while Zoe Freemantle freely flits here and there without the slightest problem. I have to admit, it worked very well.' He stopped and examined them both with some irritation, then, to Macy, he said, 'Are you going to give me a drink?' The wine he'd had with his meal had eased the pain in his leg, but it was now returning.

Macy got up and poured them each a whisky, which in the Bird's case was downed in one.

'Then there is Naji,' said Samson, studying Macy closely for a reaction. 'What do you know about his involvement?'

'The boy you chased around Macedonia? I know nothing of his involvement. Is he here, in London?'

'He was working in the place that Zoe visited in east London. They've cleared it out now, but I saw him there, and that would fit with the level of sophisticated communications that GCHQ had traced coming from the area. Harland and Naji got on well. He spotted the talent and bloody well groomed him for the job.'

The Bird nodded. That evidently sounded like his old friend. A silence ensued as Samson thought. The two older men watched him. 'Maybe,' he said at length, 'we're looking at something that's a rushed job. Maybe the person who ordered these killings was moving very rapidly because they were trying to stop something from happening. The best way of doing that was immediately killing the people they considered were the principals. Is that a fair conclusion?'

Macy nodded.

'So,' continued Samson, 'they were trying to protect someone or something from an imminent threat that stemmed from the investigation at GreenState. And GreenState is vital; otherwise I wouldn't have been used as a decoy. Have you learned anything more about Zoe Freemantle, Macy?'

'No.'

'I watched her leave her apartment last night. The place was part of her backstory – not her real home. She knows what happened to Bobby and Denis and she was in the street when I was attacked the first time, so we can assume that she's either gone to ground or has skipped the country because she's in great danger.'

The Bird made a snorting noise and looked up good-naturedly at Samson.

'Cuth has a theory, but he also has some information,' said Macy. 'Tell Samson, Cuth.'

The Bird's gaze locked on to a vase of flowers on the coffee table in front of him. 'I talked to Bobby a couple of weeks ago. We were friends from a long time back, like Macy here.' He looked up and offered him a comradely smile, which was reciprocated. 'When he got cancer, I rang quite a bit. These last few weeks, he knew he was out of time, and that makes me think that Bobby wanted to see some results from what he and your friend Mr Hisami were doing. So, I believe you're spot on when you say it was a rushed job. Rushed on both sides – these Balkan cut-throats were obviously recruited in a blind panic.'

Macy interrupted. 'Stop waffling, Cuth, and tell him your bloody information.'

The Bird's great hands came together and he rubbed his knuckles as though trying to restore the circulation. 'It all goes back to Berlin. You know that the three of us – Bobby, Macy and me – were part of the operation to extract an Arab terrorist named Abu Jemal in '89 and, subsequently, we helped Bobby exfiltrate his two agents on the night the Wall came down. Their names were Rudi Rosenharte and Ulrike Klaar. You probably know that they married and then Rudi was murdered by ex-Stasi assassins and Ulrike ended up marrying Bobby.'

'Yes, she told me the story.'

'Well, they were both invited back to Berlin for the thirtieth-anniversary celebrations. Very discreet, very low key, no bloody journalists – a lunch with some old faces, a few veterans from the GDR networks, heads of the German intelligence services, station chiefs, the mayor of the city, and so forth. I gather the German Chancellor looked in and was very sweet to one and all. Of course, she was from the East, as you know.'

'They told me about it,' said Samson. 'He asked me there for the an-niversary and I had dinner with Bobby, Ulrike and her son that evening.'

'Really! Anyway, sometime during that weekend he laid eyes on an individual he thought was dead. He called this person the "Ghost from the East". Ulrike may know who it was, but he certainly wouldn't tell me. He never spoke about this again to me, but I knew it was terribly important to him.'

Macy got up from his desk, moved to the drinks cabinet and waggled the decanter at them. Samson shook his head. 'This all may seem like history to you,' continued the Bird, 'but very soon after that weekend in Berlin, Denis and Bobby, who had already met, came together and started cooking up something. Denis funded it and Bobby acted as director.'

'Good of you to bloody well tell me all this,' said Samson to Macy.

'It wasn't in my power to do so. It was Denis's decision, and he would have told you everything in the call he'd arranged.' He looked embarrassed, swirled the whisky in his glass before knocking it back in one. 'What're you going to do?'

'I'm going to have to talk with Nikolai Horobets, the man who killed Harland.'

'They've got him locked down in that hospital.'

'Not for me he isn't.' He stopped. 'I will need money – a lot of it. You have the bank details for Aymen Malek and Claude Rameau. Tell Tulliver this is for my expenses. I'll need 10k initially. More later.'

'Anastasia is running the show now. We'll have to ask her.'

'Fine, you talk to her.'

'I'll give her your new number. How are you planning to get out of the country? Imogen said the police were here three hours ago. They told her they'd be back.'

'Ferry to Belfast, drive to Dublin then ferry to France. I'll use the Belgian ID.'

'There'll be a biometric check at the ferry terminal.'

'Never been a problem before.'

At this the Bird woke from a reverie. He had a better idea. He'd need to make a call, because he wasn't sure his contact was still in business. He pulled out a surprisingly sophisticated smartphone, dialled and waited, looking up at the ceiling with an absolutely insane expression on his face. Samson shook his head and began to make moves to collect his bags, which had been brought round from Cedar by a waiter. Macy raised a hand to him to say, hold on. At length, the Bird's face lit up and after several barks of pleasure he said, 'I have a friend who needs a ride.'

They waited until first light the next day for the spring tide to float *Silent Flight*, the forty-eight-foot sloop skippered by Gus Grinnel, an old MI6 hand who had come close to qualifying for the Olympics as helm in the Flying Dutchman Dinghy Class but instead ended up representing his country in the year-round Cold War regatta in the Southern Baltic. The yacht crept along a channel between the mudflats to the north of the Kent town of Faversham and took about half an hour to reach open water, whereupon Samson was stood down from his duty of buoy spotting.

Gus was cantankerous and almost certainly a drunk. Samson saw that relations between him and his Belgian crew, Fleur – thirty years his junior – were more or less broken. They snapped at each other constantly and disagreed about everything. They were proficient sailors, however, and Samson decided to let them get on with it. He went down below to rest his leg and read the *Times* obituary for Harland which Macy had cut and pasted into an email. He'd added a note: 'Needless to say, Nyman didn't show his notes to me before submitting them. I won't bother sending the news story. Suffice to say that it was inaccurate in almost every detail and identified the killer as a man with known mental-health problems, without giving his nationality. But the obit is okay, as far as it goes.'

Robert Harland

The spy's spy and hero of the Cold War

Born into a Scottish family with a history of colonial adventure, particularly on his mother's side, Robert Harland seemed destined to find a role for himself in MI6, the British Secret Intelligence Service, and to become one of its key operatives in the final decade of the

Cold War. Many of his exploits remain subject to the Official Secrets Act because the ideas and tradecraft he developed are still used by a younger generation of spies today, but what is known of his career amply confirms Harland's reputation as the 'Spy's spy'.

Although bright and athletic, Harland was not a success at school and was twice expelled for flouting regulations and for youthful pranks. His mother died when he was sixteen and his father, with whom Harland had a distant relationship, despaired of his son and put him to work on a local farm in Argyll. The tough life of a hill farmer suited the young man, but Harland made arrangements on his own to prepare for and sit the Oxbridge entrance exams. He went up to Oxford to study modern languages, where he gained a hockey blue and was spotted by MI6. After coming down he joined the army and the Black Watch. He was stationed in Germany and later in Northern Ireland, where he saw first hand what he regarded as the inept and brutal treatment of Catholics at the beginning of the Troubles. He held a lifelong belief that the North and South of Ireland should be united.

He joined MI6 in 1976 and after a routine posting to an embassy – in his case, New Delhi – he was sent to Berlin Station, then housed in the city's old Olympic Stadium. Harland's exceptional linguistic skill and attuned ear came into play: he was capable not only of speaking a language idiomatically but shifting from one regional accent to another, a talent that proved a great advantage when operating behind the Iron Curtain. He soon showed himself to be one of the more resourceful operatives, and by 1980 was running the Green Glass network across three Warsaw Pact countries.

The Green Glass network was based on the agricultural salesmen and suppliers who travelled extensively in the Warsaw Pact countries and had frequent contact with the West because of the Communists' desperate need for foreign currency. When the Stasi uncovered the GDR part of the network three years later, it was felt that Harland had nothing more to offer in that particular theatre of the Cold War, and he moved to take up postings in Ankara and Cairo, neither of which he enjoyed as much as Berlin. By the end of the 1980s, however, he was back in Europe, preparing for one of the great intelligence operations of the era – extracting the Stasi-sponsored Arab terrorist Abu Jemal from a safe house in Leipzig, where the terrorist enjoyed the company of mistresses laid on by the GDR. The planning and execution were all Harland's, and on the night the Wall came down he was responsible for springing his agent Kafka from the Stasi interrogation centre in Hohenschönhausen and, after a dash across East Berlin, he, Kafka and a double agent named Rudi Rosenharte reached the Wall at the moment it became possible to cross to the West without papers.

He always said that luck and good timing were as important as preparation and tradecraft, although he excelled at both. In Turkey, he happened upon the lynchpin figure – a Russian pilot – in the plot to flood Western Europe and America with Afghani heroin. In Egypt he was responsible for identifying key Libyan agents supplying arms to Western terrorists, as well as the man providing mortars and anti-personnel mines to civil wars across the continent, who also happened to be Russian.

A good-looking man with a commanding presence, Robert Harland was also famously taciturn, and he did not suffer fools, particularly in the upper echelons of SIS. But he could wear a suit and tie with the best of them. In New York, he worked undercover in the UK mission to the UN and was an impressive and convincing figure. Yet even there he could not escape drama and was one of the few passengers to survive an air crash at La Guardia.

Harland suffered for his country, at one stage being held and tortured by the feared Czechoslovak State Security, the StB. He never spoke of this ordeal and refused all honours. It is believed that he became disenchanted with MI6 and with his own country, especially after Brexit, which he deplored. Having helped the Estonians establish an intelligence service to defend the country against the Russian threat, he took out Estonian citizenship and made a new life with his wife, Ulrike, in Tallinn.

He leaves his wife, Ulrike, and a stepson – the German filmmaker Rudi Rosenharte, the son of his wife's first husband and the man who Harland rescued from East Berlin.

Forty miles out from Zeebrugge, the wind swung round to the east and increased. Samson went up on deck. Gus, who had been taking regular pulls from a flask for most of the voyage, darted a black look at Fleur, handed over to her and went to sleep it off below. There were still five hours to port. Fleur amused herself by showing Samson the basics of sailing, teaching him to keep his eye on the luff of the sail, in the angle between the mast and the boom, as they steered as close as he could into the wind. He found himself enjoying the feel of the yacht surging forward in a force five and suddenly understood why Anastasia, a lifelong sailor, went on about it.

Fleur made them coffee and, as she handed him the mug, said, 'I'm leaving him when we get there. I've had enough.'

Samson gave her an understanding nod but said nothing.

'He was once a hero, but now he's just a sad old drunk. Sometimes he hits me,' she added casually.

'Then you should probably leave.'

'But of course I hit him back, and he always comes off worse. Have you got anyone special?' she asked, with some interest in her eye.

He shook his head.

Later on, as they approached port and came within range of cellphone masts, his phone began to ping with messages, then it rang and Anastasia said hello for the first time in two years.

He was taken aback, and she was also unsettled, it seemed, and blurted, 'Hi. Where are you?' then corrected herself before Samson had time to respond. 'I meant to say, how are you? Macy told me what happened. I was shocked. I would have called before but I was on a plane. Are you okay?'

'It's good to hear you, but we can't talk on an open phone. I'll send you a link to an encryption package, plus another number. Call me in two or three hours.'

He hung up.

Fleur gave him a knowing smile. 'So you *do* have someone special. I can tell by your expression. That was her, no?'

PART TWO

CHAPTER 18

Leverkusen-Opladen Intersection

Anastasia tried, but in vain, to reach Samson over the next few hours, so she went to the terrace overlooking the Acropolis, drank wine and occupied herself with administrative emails for the foundation. She completed all she had to do then dialled Naji's number. It rang out once and there was no voicemail message, but a second call was answered.

She heard a dog barking in the background and a man shouting, then an older woman's voice close by.

'Naji?' she said.

'Who is this?'

'It's me – Anastasia. I'm using a different phone.'

'Hi,' he said, rather tentatively.

'Everyone's been trying to get you.'

'Not everyone – just Samson.'

'Well, I have also. Samson is very concerned about you, and I think you know why, Naj.'

He didn't respond.

'I was there when they tried to kill Denis. A lot of people might have died.'

'Yes, I saw this on the news. I saw you, and I was concerned, but then I heard you were okay.'

'They tried to kill Samson. He desperately needs to speak to you. Will you do that for me? It's really, really important.'

'We have talked already. I will see him at the funeral for Mr Harland. Maybe you, too.'

'Ah, he didn't tell me that you'd spoken. Yes, I will be there at the funeral.'

'It was a short conversation. I was on an airplane.'

She heard the dog barking again and a young man call out. 'Where are you? Is that your dog?'

'Friend's dog,' he said.

Then she suddenly knew. 'That's Moon!' she exclaimed. 'You're at that farm with the family. With Ifkar! That's where you're hiding . . . Naji? Naji?' He had hung up.

Having installed the encryption package, she phoned Samson. Again, she was alert to the background noise in the call. She heard people speaking around him and the French public address system. 'Where are you?'

'Brussels. I'm waiting for a train to take me to our favourite city. I've been told they're checking airports in Europe, and this seemed more discreet. And where are you?'

'Athens, I needed to see the team before going to the funeral.'

'Really?'

'Yes, really! I have a job to do. Decisions that can't be delayed.'

'I understand.' His tone softened. 'It's good to hear your voice – really good! How's Denis?'

'I spoke to the hospital. He's no better, no worse. It's just going to take a lot of time. I'm seeing the foundation people in Athens again tomorrow, then I'll be travelling to the funeral.' She paused and looked across the city to the illuminated Parthenon. 'I spoke to Naji. Did you know he'd gone to the farm and is with Ifkar and the old couple?'

'No, I had no idea.'

'He sounded strange. He hung up on me. Is he in danger?'

'Very much so. They are trying to eliminate anyone who might have knowledge of what Denis knew. From their point of view, that includes me, maybe you and maybe Naji.' He told her about spotting Naji leaving the Herbert Street building, and concluded, 'I don't know what the hell Bobby was doing embroiling Naji in all this, but it seems irresponsible of him.'

'What should I do?'

'Let me think about it,' said Samson. 'The nearer we get to solving this, the more dangerous things are going to become for all of us. Denis was preparing to reveal something. Do you know what that was?'

'No. And nor does Jim Tulliver.'

'What about the calendar in his briefcase?'

'The Bureau asked me about that. It means nothing to me. Those codewords and the scrambled numbers.'

'Well, I can help with the codewords. They are all colours: *pitch* black, *pearl* grey, *Berlin* blue, *saffron* yellow, *red* aurora – the choice of an artist. Does that ring any bells? What about the bank accounts? Mean anything to you?'

'No.'

'You haven't got the calendar with you?'

'They gave me photocopies and kept everything else.'

'Look, I think you should call Naji again and try to make him understand the danger he's in.'

'He won't pick up. In any case, he'll just ignore a warning from me.'

'I have the sense there are a lot of young people in this thing. Denis was paying me to watch over a young woman named Zoe Freemantle who was working at an outfit called GreenState, which is important to the whole story, although only Denis and Bobby were in a position to tell us why.'

'GreenState? Denis and I went to a fundraising evening with Green-State in LA last year. And I sat next to someone who is showing a very close interest in all this – Martin Reid, a right-wing billionaire. He's offered to help.'

'Yeah, I know who he is. I'm also interested in a character called Jonathan Mobius, who runs it, but I haven't got on to that yet.'

'That's what we're paying you for, isn't it, Samson?' It was out before she could stop herself.

He waited a few seconds before replying. A familiar coolness ensued. 'I was employed to see no harm came to Zoe Freemantle, but the real reason I was put in there by your husband and Harland was to act as a decoy. As a result, my friend Jo and I were stabbed. Denis wasn't paying me to investigate anything and, by the way, he wasn't compensating me for the risk either.'

'Your friend – how is she?' she asked.

'She's okay, but badly shaken. It was unpleasant – a sexual aspect to it.'

'As to what Denis was doing, I am as much in the dark as you.'

He grunted and said, 'Perhaps we should wait until we meet for this conversation. I'll be travelling for a day or so. You can phone, but I won't have anything new.'

'I'm going to be busy. I have meetings here.'

'Okay, my train has been called. I need to go,' he said.

The call had not gone well, and she had to admit that was probably her fault. She should have had more sense than to needle him, yet, there again, he knew nothing of what she'd been through in the past two years, because he hadn't made the effort to find out. He could have called when she crashed, but he didn't. He assumed that she had rejected him when, in fact, she simply wasn't in any state to talk to him, though desperate to do so. Like every man she knew, he thought it was about him. And the mention of the friend who'd been stabbed, the woman he'd had an affair with before, that didn't help matters.

And apart from telling her to call Naji again, he hadn't given any proper help. Naji was now her first concern.

The call went on playing in her head and half an hour later she realised that Samson had sounded strained and tired. She texted him with 'Sorry – XX.'

Samson boarded the night train to Düsseldorf, where he would change for Berlin and catch the service to Warsaw. He was among the first passengers but, instead of finding his seat straight away, he waited at the door, looking down the platform at the forty or so people making their way to the train. It would be surprising if he'd picked up a tail on the journey from Zeebrugge to Brussels, but he wanted to be sure. The only likely candidates were two men, apparently travelling separately, who boarded the carriage next to his. One, wearing a flat cap and a quilted vest under a dark jacket, stepped aside to allow two women in hijabs on to the train, glanced at Samson then looked away. The other, in a black skiing anorak and with a rucksack hanging from one shoulder, climbed on without looking in Samson's direction but made his way through the carriage and sat a few seats away from the connecting door. The first man went to a seat three rows behind him and began to study his phone. There was absolutely nothing to say they were following him. Samson reminded himself that he hadn't slept properly for two nights and that the pain of his leg might be making him jumpier than usual. Nevertheless, at the moment the doors began to close, he stepped down on to the platform and moved away. The man in the cap looked up as the train drew out of the station. Samson couldn't tell if there was anything more than indifference in his expression.

He bought a ticket for Amsterdam, where he would connect with Deutsche Bahn's intercity service to Cologne and Berlin. The whole journey would take about eight hours, during which time he could rest and put his leg up. He went through the same checks as the train prepared to leave Brussels for the Dutch capital, then again when he was leaving Amsterdam Centraal in the early hours, and both times satisfied himself that he was alone.

Once on the almost-empty train for Berlin, he ate a baguette and drank one of two half-bottles of red wine he'd bought. He lifted the leg with both hands to rest it on the opposite seat, but this seemed to make it worse. He looked around. No more than half a dozen people were in the carriage. He dived into his bag and took out one of the three morphine pen injectors and, as per the instructions, placed the blunt purple end to his good thigh and pressed as firmly as he could. He winced at the pain. Nothing much happened so he distracted himself by making a list.

His lists were the subject of mockery by Jo and Anastasia, yet they worked to reduce a tangle of facts and ideas in his mind to a few simple statements.

He wrote:

1. Nov. 2019 Harland saw someone in Berlin – the 'Ghost from the East'.

    The Ghost is German (?)

2. Harland collaborates with Denis Hisami. That means the Ghost must have relevance, or live in the US.

3. Hisami pays for team of young investigators. They are hacking GreenState. Is Ghost part of GreenState? Maybe owner? Who is Jonathan Mobius? Originally German?

4. Five colour code names. Are the colours targets, or operatives?

5. Hisami to reveal in Congress part or all of what they have found out to show who is behind attacks on him in the US.

6. The Ghost gets wind of this and orders pre-emptive hits on Harland, Hisami and me.

7. A Serb named Oret who may have hired three killers is murdered.

8. Anatoly Stepurin, Russian operative ultimate boss and behind Oret's murder? Kremlin?

His leg began to feel better. He sat back and watched little towns flash by in the vast black night of northern Europe. Toombs was right: there was only one question – who? And plainly that was no mystery, because Naji and Zoe Freemantle knew whom they were investigating. And almost certainly Ulrike knew, because it was inconceivable that Harland had not told her about the individual he'd seen in Berlin.

So, he needn't concern himself with the details of the killers, who paid for them, who snuffed out the man called Oret, or where the chemical warfare agent came from. These things were not his business. But they were the CIA's, and there was no point in keeping what knowledge he had to himself. He did two things. He texted Anastasia to underline how important it was to find Naji. Not only was he in danger, but he was currently the only person who could help them. 'As your humble employee, can I ask you to make this a priority and get hold of him as soon as possible? XX,' he wrote. Then he withdrew Toombs's card from his wallet and called him. Toombs answered immediately.

'I may lose you,' said Samson.

'You already did! Why the hell did you get off that train?'

'Those two men were yours?'

'There were no two *men*.'

'The only women I saw were in hijab.'

'Right. They were there to protect you. Look, Mr Samson, if we can find you, so can the people who want to kill you before you get to Estonia – that's where you're headed, right?'

'I have information for you.'

'Save it,' Toombs snapped. 'I'll send you instructions for the Company encryption, then sit on your goddamn phone and stop the signal.' He was told to download an app from a website and enter a series of passcodes into the app, which he did. The app promptly vanished from his screen.

'The five words,' began Samson. 'Berlin, pitch, pearl, etcetera – are all colours, but of course you knew that. I can't help you with the numbers, but I guess you've figured that out, unless the NSA computers are finding it hard to crack encryption that they haven't seen before.' He let that hang in the air, but Toombs didn't bite. 'Then there was a man named Oret, who seems likely to have hired at least three of the killers, but he was murdered.'

'We know about Oret.'

'And you know who killed him and his wife?'

'Go on.'

'Try a man called Anatoly Stepurin. Russian. Cyprus-based. Profile looks right: semi-official hood, career killer, and deniable. Résumé includes Special Forces, activity in Ukraine and connections to GRU military intelligence. He's now into illegal big-game hunting. Pay this arsehole £200,000 and you can shoot a lion. Pay him a fraction of that and he will kill a man for you. Most of this is on an investigative French website called Rochet. Looks like the reporters have good contacts with French and German intelligence.'

Toombs exhaled heavily.

'Was that a thank you?'

'Yeah, sure – thanks.'

'Stepurin could be the supplier of the nerve agent.'

'I realise that.'

'Have you got to Nikolai Horobets, the Ukrainian national who killed Harland?'

Toombs didn't reply.

'So, you haven't. Maybe I can do something about that. I have contacts there.'

'That might be useful. Yes, let us know.'

'What are you going to do for me?'

'Aside from trying to keep you alive, although that's going to be really hard, seeing as you are on a different train to the people who were sent to protect you. What more do you need?'

The morphine induced a kind of sweet, lackadaisical wooziness, but also made things clearer. 'Who are Nyman and SIS trying to protect?'

Toombs was walking and Samson assumed he was moving so he could talk more freely. 'You've been straight with us, so I'll help you with this. We don't think they want to protect anyone. We believe they're aware of penetration at the very highest level and want to deal with that in their own time. That's just our theory, which gives your former bosses the benefit of the doubt, and that kind of sticks in my craw. But we think the theory works.' He paused. 'And they don't want you screwing up their plan to deal with the situation quietly. That's why they won't give one airborne fuck if you're killed.'

'Who are we talking about? You got a name?'

'Cabinet-level minister, or government official, but I don't have a name to share with you.'

'Penetration means Russia, right?'

'Yes.'

'And the same thing in the States? Is that what Denis Hisami was going to reveal?'

'You'll have to talk to Reiner, that's his beat. Look, I should go. We'll be in touch. Stay safe.'

Samson fell asleep almost immediately and did not wake up until they pulled into Cologne station, where he had to change trains. He struggled up, feeling like death but noticing that the pain in his leg had disappeared, and walked the few metres to the Berlin train on the adjacent platform. It was early, but already crowds of passengers were waiting for the doors to open. Without knowing why, he moved to the trickle of people who had reached their destination and were making for the concourse. Something told him he had to leave the station as quickly as possible. As he walked, he noticed on the departure board that a train to Frankfurt Airport was due to depart at 6.55 a.m. This gave him an idea. He exited and found a cab. The driver unplugged his earphones and began to move off. Samson turned. A man dashed from the station, looked around and went to the line of waiting Mercedes cabs. He was big, wearing a suit and a short overcoat and was carrying no luggage.

The cab driver's ID was visible. His name was Mohammed. 'Where are you from?' Samson asked in Arabic as they moved off.

The driver looked in the mirror. 'Aleppo – you?'

'Lebanon. A man got in the cab behind and he will attempt to follow us. I need to lose him.' He leaned forward and placed two folded €20 notes on to the passenger seat. 'Can you help me do that, Mohammed?'

'Of course.' He grinned in the mirror. 'That driver is my cousin Saaf. We start work together because we talk on the cab line. He just flashed his lights. You may be right about his passenger.'

Samson thought for a few seconds. 'Can you call Saaf and tell him you've got a good fare to Düsseldorf airport and we're late for a plane? Say it in German so his passenger understands. Make it all sound normal.' That made sense – he had originally been on the Düsseldorf train.

They weaved through the traffic. 'Where do you really want to go?' asked Mohammed.

'Frankfurt Airport.'

They took Autobahn 3 north from Cologne. Mohammed's cousin shared his taste for speed, but at junction 22 – the Leverkusen-Opladen intersection – Mohammed left it until the very last moment before shooting down the slip road off the autobahn. Saaf was going too fast to follow and missed the turning. Mohammed gleefully hooked the air in front of him with a punch. Saaf would now have to travel all the way to junction 21 – the Dreieck-Lagendfeld intersection – before he could turn round and, besides, 21 was more complicated than 22 and they'd be forced to make a detour of a couple of kilometres before they could drive south. Saaf came on the phone and demanded to know what Mohammed was doing. 'Gentleman left his wallet at the station,' Mohammed replied, without skipping a beat.

It would be a two-hour journey to Frankfurt. Samson sent another text to Anastasia. Using the occasional nickname of their times together, he wrote, 'Nas. I am going to be out of range. I really mean it about Firefly. Can you try to get hold of him? I believe he's in great danger.'

On his phone, Samson bought a ticket on the only flight to Tallinn from Frankfurt that week, which left at 9.50 a.m.– tight, but it should work. Occasionally, things fall the right way, he reflected, before placing all his phones in the metalised Faraday envelope and stretching out on the back seat of the cab.

CHAPTER 19

Firefly

Anastasia couldn't fathom how to work the remote for the air conditioning and, on this hot spring night in Athens, found sleep impossible. She got up and sat by the open window and looked through her messages and emails, then texted Naji. 'I'm sorry, but we really need to speak again. Things are becoming dangerous. XXA.'

It was 5 a.m., but the reply came immediately: 'See you at the funeral.'

'Before then! I am going to call you now.'

No response came. She rang his number, but the calls were declined. She cursed and paced around the room, picking at a tub of cheese biscuits from the mini-bar. She dialled Samson. No answer. She left a message for Tulliver asking about Denis and lay down on the bed. It was then that the front desk phoned.

Kyros was the night porter, whom she'd known from a previous post in a larger hotel. There had been some connection with her roguish father, but she wasn't sure what. He asked how she was and said what a pleasure it was to see her name on the hotel registry, then eventually got round to the three men who had asked about her at the front desk. He thought they were police, but two looked like foreigners and didn't say anything.

They would neither confirm nor deny that they were police officers. And they had specifically told him not to inform her of their visit. He didn't like the smell of them one bit. He hesitated to say this, but possibly they were from the Greek National Intelligence Service.

'Can you take my payment on the phone now?' she asked.

'That will not be a problem,' he said. 'We have all your details and we can deal with the mini-bar later.'

'And Kyros, could you charge me for two nights, so my room seems occupied tomorrow and I remain on the registry?'

'Naturally, I will take the payment now and forget to mention that you are checking out to the day shift.'

She booked the first flight to Skopje, the capital of what is now known as northern Macedonia, a little over an hour away – and raised the head of Mediterranean operations for the foundation, George Ciccone, to explain that she must depart sooner than she'd expected. She asked him to find a driver to meet her at Skopje Airport.

She arrived at Skopje mid-morning, but the driver was nowhere to be found. She sat simmering at a café in Arrivals, wondering if she had made the right decision. Making decisions in the early morning was never a good course for her; she tended to get things out of proportion. Now she wondered if Naji was really in as much danger as Samson had suggested. But, naturally, she got no response from him or Samson.

Just as a large man in his forties presented himself, holding a sign for the Aysel Hisami Foundation and introducing himself as Luka, her phone vibrated on the table. There was an American number on the screen. She snatched it up, thinking it would be the hospital, but heard the voice of Special Agent Reiner. 'Where are you, Mrs Hisami? We're wondering why you went to such lengths to deceive us about leaving the US and then ended up in the Balkans.'

'I had meetings. I have a job, responsibilities, and since when did I have to tell the FBI my plans?'

'I asked you to keep us informed of your movements, and now I find you in the Balkans, a hundred kilometres south of the Serbian border. I have one question for you; why are you going north towards Serbia, the country where those two buddies, Vladan Drasko and Miroslav Rajavic, came from?'

'I'm on the way to see old friends – people I've worked with. Macedonia! Different country! You're tracking my phone, right?'

He didn't respond to this. 'Seems like a really strange thing to be doing with your husband in the ICU in Washington. Couldn't your friends wait? Why did you leave the hotel in Athens so early? I was hoping to catch you.'

'That was you? Why didn't you call instead of arriving like secret police at the dead of night? What do you want to say to me?'

'We've been in touch with Mr Samson, as I believe you have. I wanted to warn you that we're certain he's being followed by persons that wish to kill him. There may be others who have the same intention towards you. Samson knows how to look after himself, but you don't. So it seems odd – not to say, extremely dangerous – for you to be headed towards the country that provided two of the four suspects in this affair, indeed the two men who tried to kill your husband and your former lover.'

'Don't be ridiculous. You don't think . . .'

'I don't think anything. I just want to know what you're doing. We're trying to keep you and Samson alive. I suggest you take the first flight back to the States.'

'I'll be returning as soon as I can.'

'Make that tomorrow! Your husband needs you. I'll remind you that this investigation is undoubtedly the most important thing going on in America right now. We need to be able to speak to you in person. Tomorrow, I want to hear you're on your way back to DC. Tomorrow, Mrs Hisami!' He rang off.

She accompanied Luka to the nearly empty car park but stopped short of his Toyota and asked for a cigarette from the packet she'd

spotted in the top pocket of his bush jacket. She moved away to smoke
and think about the call. Why would the FBI track her to Athens then
Skopje and, when they found her, have almost nothing meaningful to
say, except to warn her of the dangers she faced, which were, in any
case, obvious, because they had tried to kill Samson twice and she'd
been beside her husband in Congress? The FBI were keeping tabs on
her and letting her know about it, and that, apparently, was an end in
itself. It was bizarre. She took out her phone and left a message for
Tulliver that she would be out of reach for a while, then turned it off.
Samson would know what to do about a phone that was being tracked,
but she hoped switching hers off and burying it in the bottom of her
bag would be enough.

The farm was exactly as she remembered, though a brand-new barn had
replaced the one where Almunjil's gang of IS killers had held her, Naji and
Samson captive. The collection of stables, the broken stone courtyard, the
bent rails and crooked fencing around the pens were all as they had been,
but the old tractor and trailer had gone and new machinery glinted in the
sunlight. As the car pulled up in the yard, Moon appeared, barking, and
in her wake came three puppies, two white and one cappuccino-coloured.
Anastasia got out and crouched down and was immediately surrounded
by the puppies, while Moon stood back, not letting up with the barking.
Above her, Naji appeared on the old wooden walkway and folded his arms
with an exasperated look. She called out hello, and he shook his head then
ran down the steps to shake her hand and, finally, let her embrace him
and look him over. 'I had no idea how tall you were,' she said. 'You're a
man now!'

'Yes,' he said, and a rueful look darted from beneath his brow, which
she remembered from when she had first encountered him as a boy. 'Why
are you here?' he asked.

'I wanted to see that you were all right and to tell you that you should
have the conversation with Samson. There's a lot going on, and no

one – not the intelligence agencies, the FBI, nor even Samson – can figure it out. He says you know everything?'

He shrugged and looked up at the hill. 'Some things, not everything.' At this, Ifkar came out with a sports bag hooked over his shoulder. He tore down the steps to join them and shake hands with Anastasia and Luka, then kissed her awkwardly on both cheeks. He was larger than she remembered, broad and as strong as a bull. When she saw him last, he had been recovering from an infected bullet wound and, before that, he'd been on the road for months, wandering the mountains alone with Moon until they teamed up with Naji.

The old couple followed. Darko had aged and was now using a stick. He descended the steps arthritically and was shooed forward by Irina, who was impatient to greet Anastasia. She beat her husband to the clinch and gave Anastasia a floury hug, which left hand imprints on her jacket. The ritual was repeated with Darko, who then stepped back and kept slapping his thigh, looking round and laughing with tears in his eyes.

'How long will you stay with us?' asked Irina in the Macedonian language, which Anastasia just about understood. She replied in a combination of Macedonian and Greek that she wasn't planning on staying. The couple weren't having that. Why would she travel all this way just to say hello? She must stay. There was lamb stew and a pastry filled with summer cherries, preserved in the finest home-made brandy, all prepared in Naji's honour. There would be plenty for Luka, too, though she wasn't sure of a bed for him. It would be a feast, and they would drink a beautiful light red wine that came from her people's vineyard in the south. There was no question of Anastasia returning to Skopje to stay in a hotel. She would sleep at the farm and Luka would go to Pudnik, where there was a decent little place run by a young woman, who had recently inherited it from her parents.

Anastasia was moved. Things had worked out well at the farm, where there had been so much terror and slaughter. For the first time in his life,

Ifkar knew what it was to have loving parents, while Darko and Irina had found a son to make up for the loss of their boy and only child in a motorbike accident. And fortune had smiled materially on the poor mountain farmers in the shape of a new barn, tractor and trailer. She wondered if Denis had had anything to do with that. Generous gifts indeed, but ones that also ensured their silence about his presence at the farm that night when he'd saved all their lives and killed three terrorists. That was the way Denis worked.

They dined on Irina's stew and drank her family's wine. Luka decided to remain in Pudnik, so it was the five of them, each one of whom must, in some way, be remembering when they were all together before. But no one brought it up, and Naji and she were certainly not anxious to discuss the other drama in their shared history – Narva Bridge.

She watched Naji closely, remembering his ability as a boy to lie and deceive. He'd look you in the face and say he wouldn't dream of breaking out of the camp and straight away go and do precisely that. From his time being driven round in the back of a pickup by some of the most depraved individuals in ISIS, he had learned to shut down, suspend all scruples and judgement. He survived by denial and by internalising the most dreadful things any human, let alone a young boy, could witness. If Naji didn't want to tell you something, there was never a way of getting it out of him. But she had to make him talk. Their survival depended on it.

After dinner they went to sit on the narrow sheltered walkway outside, and Anastasia accepted one of Darko's cigarettes, much to Naji's disgust. Darko hobbled off to get slivovitz and Ifkar went down to feed the puppies.

She smoked and looked at him without saying anything. He shifted uncomfortably, but she kept silent. She finished the cigarette and took her time stubbing it out, all the while looking at him. Then she smiled. 'Berlin Blue Pitch Black, Pearl Grey Saffron . . . do you want me to go on?'

He said nothing.

'Oh, come on, Naj! Samson found these names on a whiteboard in London. They were in Denis's briefcase, too. Samson saw you in the building, for fuck's sake!'

This surprised him, but he didn't react. 'Naji, I was there when they tried to kill Denis and murdered his lawyer. Denis was probably about to tell the committee something, and you know what it is. Come on, spit it out.'

'I cannot speak about it now.'

She was angry and let him see it. 'This is no game. I need to know what you've been doing. Do you want me killed? Samson, too?'

'Of course not.'

'I have to know. Will you come with me to Estonia tomorrow?'

He gave her one of his withering looks. 'I am going for Mr Harland's funeral – yes. I have a ticket.'

'To Tallinn from Skopje via Belgrade tomorrow?'

'Of course – this is only way.'

'Good, then we will travel together.' Naji gave her a look that suggested he had been asked to escort an elderly maiden aunt. She ignored his reaction, because something had just occurred to her. 'Was Denis giving you money?'

'Of course, I have to pay for my family.' Naji was an entrepreneur. He had started several businesses – mending telephones and selling vegetables and second-hand trainers from a cart in Syria – all to help his family. He would have driven a hard bargain for his services, and Denis would have approved of that and the way he'd kept everything going for the Toumas after his father had been effectively disabled by the Syrian-government torturers. 'Did you meet my husband?' she said suddenly.

A sly little look entered his eyes. 'Yes, down there,' he said, pointing to where the old barn had stood.

'Stop it! Stop thinking you can play me, Naj. Did you meet Denis when he visited Robert Harland in Tallinn? Were you there?'

'Yes.'

'So you three made the plans together, but you were the one who was finding the evidence for them. You were their main investigator. What were you doing, hacking someone's system?' It was as if she wasn't even talking. 'You know, you can be pretty rude, Naji. You have quite an attitude there.'

'I do not mean to offend,' he said, more as a matter of fact than an apology. His attention had gone to the yard, where the puppies were being exercised before being shut up for the night. 'You lead such different lives now, you at the university and Ifkar here on the farm with all the animals.'

He turned to face her. 'Our lives are not so different. He lives under the stars. I live amongst them.'

'It's corny, but I like it,' she said. His gaze returned to Ifkar, who had run into the centre of the yard and stood with his hands on his hips, looking north towards the distant glow of Pudnik. On one of the tracks that led to the farm, the lights from a single vehicle were moving slowly and gingerly, as if the driver didn't know the way, or was worried about the ruts. It wasn't Luka, because he'd phoned earlier to say he would eat in town and see Anastasia at seven the next morning. Ifkar backed towards the steps and came up to where they were sitting, never losing sight of the lights. He spoke rapidly to Naji, who said, 'Ifkar thinks you've been followed here. He knows you are in danger. I told him.'

'Maybe you, too, Naji.'

'Not possible. They do not know about Naji Touma.'

Ifkar brushed past them and seconds later returned with a new hunting rifle that was fitted with a telescopic sight and a small magazine. He raised it to watch the vehicle through the scope and muttered to himself. Now Darko was on the walkway, brandishing an older rifle and a handgun. Irina emerged with a fierce look on her face and, although she was the worse for wear after dinner, he handed her the pistol. They waited for

Ifkar to speak, which, presently, he did. He thought there were other people than the driver in the car but couldn't be sure. He consulted Darko and
it was agreed that he would go and take a closer look. He moved down
the steps, pocketing a second magazine, told Moon to stay and crossed
the yard to vanish into the darkness behind the stables. Darko began
turning off lights while Irina descended to the yard and also disappeared.
Anastasia wondered if they had worked out a drill; they all seem to know
what they were doing. A few minutes passed, then three shots rang out
in the distance. Darko murmured that they came from Ifkar's rifle. That
was the way he always fired: bang, bang – pause – bang. He had killed
three wild boar last autumn, always the same pattern to his shooting. An
incredible shot, an absolute natural, said Darko, and relit the cigarette that
rested on the railing in front of him. They waited: more shots and the
car's lights went out. Then there was some wild shooting, with as many
as thirty rounds loosed off, but not from Ifkar's rifle, Darko stated. He
would conserve his ammunition.

They waited for a further twenty minutes, then there was shouting and
a single shot. Irina appeared in the yard, still illuminated by one light on
the end of the new barn. She was in a state of considerable excitement.
'Ifkar has prisoners!' she shouted up to her husband. Then Ifkar appeared,
his face and hands blackened with mud, prodding two burly men at the
end of his rifle.

'Srbijci,' he told them. Serbians. He dropped two handguns, one
equipped with a silencer, on to the broken stone of the yard, and Irena
picked them up and waved them in the faces of the two men with a
bloodthirsty yell. At that moment there was a distant *crump* as their vehicle blew up. Ifkar had stuffed the petrol tank with a piece of cloth and
lit it, Darko deduced with enormous pride. Naji caught the drift of what
he was saying and applauded his friend.

'We need to find out who they are and why they're here,' Anastasia said.
The two men reminded her of the pair that had kidnapped her on a country
road in southern Italy – street thugs who would turn their hand to anything

for not much money. They were nothing like a professional hit team. They had announced their arrival, botched the approach to the farm, and then the driver, who must also have been armed, had fled when Ifkar shot out his tyres. And yet there was no doubt in Anastasia's mind that they would have killed everyone at the farm without the slightest hesitation.

The men were pushed into the barn. Anastasia was concerned that the old lady, now moving the pistol casually from one hand to the other, could be enjoying herself rather too much and might get carried away with the two Serbs. She went down with Naji. As they crossed the yard, she said, 'Maybe you should hold back. I don't want them to see you.'

She went into the barn, followed by Irina, to find Ifkar holding the gun to the belly of one of the men and cuffing him about the head. She and Ifkar had no common language, but she said in Greek to Irina, 'Are we going to do this? Here, on the very spot where Ifkar himself was tortured? Really! Is that what we do now?' Ifkar understood and stepped back. 'Let's ask these gentlemen in their own language why they are here,' she said to Darko, who spoke Serbian.

He tried a few questions, but nothing was forthcoming, until Moon, who had pursued her master into the darkness after Ifkar had left, bounded into the barn and started barking at the men. The dog's docile nature made you forget what a big, powerful animal she was, and both men concluded that she was about to be set on them. The smaller of the two, who had ear studs and wore a training jacket with stripes up the arms, said he would tell them all he knew, which wasn't very much, as long as the dog was removed.

Moon was locked up with her puppies by Irina, but before Darko recommenced with his questions Anastasia asked him to wait a few moments while she went outside. On the incline at the top end of the yard, where there was good reception, she dialled a number. 'Sorry,' she said to Samson when he answered. 'I know it's late, but I need your advice. I have two Serb gunmen here who were on the way to the farm – yes, that farm – to kill me, or Naji, or both of us. Ifkar, who turns out to be quite the dab hand with a rifle, captured them, but one escaped. Before we hand them over to the police in Pudnik, are there any questions I should ask them?'

'You're with Naji at the farm! How the hell did you wind up there? Frankly, I'd rather you ask Naji what his involvement is.'

'I have – he won't say. I'll get it out of him, though. What do we want to know from these men?'

'You've got limited time, because their partner will raise the alarm.' Samson was coming to and focusing. 'Mention a man named Oret. He's dead, but it will surprise them that you know about him. Then drop the name Stepurin into the conversation. Ask them if they were hired by Anatoly Stepurin.' He told her what he knew of Stepurin then said, 'Of course, the million-dollar question, which you rightly put your finger on, is are they there to kill you or Naji?'

'Anything else?'

'Yeah. The CIA would really like to talk to them before you hand them over to the local police. I'll fix that for you and give them the coordinates of the farm. But you need to get out of there long before Toombs arrives. I don't think they know about Naji. Let's keep it that way, even if the other side does know about him.'

'Toombs – so that's the name of the man who came to see me in the hospital.'

'Grey hair, dark moustache, rude manner?'

'The same.'

'How's Denis?'

'No change,' she said, dissembling. She hadn't called in a day.

'Sorry to hear that. I can't stress too much that you are both in danger. You need to leave the farm now. Send me a text if you get anything interesting and call if you need to.'

She heard him drop his phone and curse before the line went dead.

The smaller man spoke. Darko translated. They had been hired thirty-six hours before in Belgrade and told to find out if a young Arab man was staying at the farm. If he was there, they were to phone a number for further instructions. They didn't know his name or what he looked like. They were paid well – €4,000 each. Did this include a fee for a murder? Was this a wet job? Both of them shook their heads vigorously. They were scouting things out – that was all.

Both men were now looking at her; they had judged, correctly, that their fate lay in her hands. 'We know about Mr Oret because he employed your friends Drasko and Rajavic,' said Anastasia.

This really surprised them, and they exchanged looks. 'And we know that Mr Oret was killed, probably by the man who hired you.' She waited for Darko to translate this and moved a few paces towards them. 'Anatoly Stepurin,' she said to the barn, 'the big man from Cyprus, the Russian who paid you to come here and kill everyone.'

The taller of the two, whose eyebrows met in the middle, shook his head and said in English, 'No killing, just looking.' He pointed to his eyes with two fingers.

'Then why bring guns?'

'For protection.'

'You don't need a silencer for protection. A silencer is for killing.'

They had no answer to this. 'Thank you for confirming that Mr Stepurin hired you. By the way, do you know who I am?'

They looked blank and shook their heads.

'I'm the person who just saved you arses. These good people wanted to kill you and bury your bodies in the woods, where they'll never be found.' Darko translated and signalled his enthusiastic endorsement. 'But, instead, some Americans are coming to talk to you. If you answer their questions, they may let you live.'

She nodded to Darko and went to the top of the yard and texted Samson. 'You scored a bull's eye with Anatoly,' she wrote.

He replied, 'Will tell US friends now. They will come by chopper within 1 hr. Make yourself scarce.'

She wrote, 'They were going to kill N!'

'GO NOW!'

She turned to Naji. 'Samson says we need to leave now. I'll get Luka up here.'

By the time the helicopter's lights appeared from the north, they were making their way down to Pudnik, where they would take the road to the Bulgarian border.

CHAPTER 20

The Peacock

Sometime in the early hours, Harland's widow, Ulrike, left an envelope containing the key to their cabin on Karu Saar – Bear Island – and a map reference at Samson's hotel in Tallinn. She'd said nothing on the phone but simply asked where he was staying. He told her, 'the usual place', which was a discreet little establishment near the Maritime Museum in the old town, and under the usual name, Norbert Soltesz, a name belonging to a deceased Hungarian national. This was one of Samson's least developed identities, but consistency was necessary and, recognising the name and face from his visits over the last two and a half years, the manager awarded him an upgrade.

At 8 a.m. he picked up the envelope and walked through the back streets, thinking about Harland. It was odd to be in Tallinn without him. He was immediately drawn to the old spy, though he was remote and as dry as dust and didn't give a damn whether you liked him or not; he was never interested in saying what he felt, or hearing what others felt. He cherished facts and rigour, not opinion. Only later, as Harland began to trust him, did Samson see the wisdom and humour, but they were never on show, his most pronounced quality being reserve.

At the car-hire outlet in the modern suburbs Samson used the Malek identity and gave the name of another hotel – they'd never check – to acquire a fast little hatchback. He drove west for three hours through forests, huge fields sown with cereal crops and marshlands drained for agriculture that nature was reclaiming. Realising he hadn't eaten a solid hot meal for a while, he stopped at the only roadside café he saw and ordered sausage with an onion, cabbage and potato mash that had been lightly fried. It was a dish of the cook's own devising, she told him, and it was the paprika that made the difference. She recommended he wash it down with a particular brand of beer, which he did. He began to feel much better – Samson wasn't good without food – and found himself in the mood for a cigarette. The cook provided one from a pack of Prima, a Russian brand, left by a couple of gentlemen two days before. He handed the red packet back and asked if there were many Russians still living in the west of Estonia. No, she said, it was just five to ten per cent now, and even less on the islands. These gentlemen were on a fishing expedition; she assumed they were from the east of the country. She told him to keep the pack, but after a moment's hesitation he declined, paid and bade her goodbye.

The spring weather was glorious and he enjoyed being on the road. He thought about Ulrike and her manner in the short phone call of the previous evening. It hadn't even been necessary for him to ask about the cabin. She had immediately understood what he wanted. That could only mean she believed there was something there that might help him, something that she was unable to retrieve for herself, or, more likely in his view, something she wasn't entirely sure existed. He'd wanted to see her before he left, but she said she was busy with the funeral and arrangements for the exhibition of Bobby's work that would open that same day, at a private reception for all those who could not make the service in the tiny church.

He reached Bear Island, not an island but a long peninsula that may once have been an island, and was struck by the emptiness. The coordinates entered into his phone guided him to a spot beyond a ribbon of silver birch trees just coming into leaf. He stopped the car, got out and was immediately aware of the vastness of the sky and a chilly north wind. There was a path about the width of a wheelbarrow, and there was one, upended and chained with a combination lock to an iron post. He assumed it was used to transfer bags and supplies to the cabin from the Harlands' car. He swept the rocky grassland with his binoculars for any sign of the cabin, but saw nothing. He continued along the path for fifteen minutes before he caught sight of a silver chimney pipe rising behind an area of exposed rock. Circling round, he saw the whole cabin, as well as the remarkable views east and west. The cabin seemed run-down at first glance – a shack – but on closer inspection he saw that everything was in order and what he'd thought was driftwood had been ingeniously used to make outside benches and tables. The bleached wood of an old tree root provided pegs, from which hung fishing nets, a pair of barbecue tongs, a small anchor and coils of rope, presumably picked up on the shore. A weathervane fidgeted and squeaked on a pole fixed to the side of the cabin and, apart from the wind in the grass, there was no other sound.

Remembering what the woman in the roadside café had said about the two Russians on a fishing trip, he waited and watched through his binoculars. He focused on the area to the north, where Harland had been targeted, and worked out the route that the killer must have taken if Ulrike had spotted him from the cabin. He decided to follow the same way up the peninsula and see for himself the place where Harland was killed – as he painted the landscape, for God's sake!

The beauty of the place that Harland loved so much was striking, but also its desolation and abandonment: a hulk rusting in the sea, the lighthouse that no longer shone and the mangled evidence of coastal defences from a period of war or paranoia that he could not determine. He found the place without much difficulty. Police tape flapped in the wind and emergency vehicles had left tyre marks and thrown up patches of moss. Oil paint, still wet, was smeared on the ground; scorch marks and traces of blood in the grass told the whole story. He thought of Harland, and of Ulrike coming on the scene and finding her husband dead, her worst fears realised. He hadn't gone without a fight, however, and as a result the killer had been caught. Had he tried to communicate a last message as the killings were set in train in London and Washington DC?

He went a full circle, realising how isolated the spot was, even for this forsaken strip of land, then walked to the cabin. It was several minutes before it came into view. He stopped in his tracks and raised his binoculars – a woman was standing by the door, a big bag over her shoulder and a black scarf wrapped around her neck and over her head. A man came out – tall, young, very thin – wearing a beanie and carrying a small rucksack. Smoke trickled from the metal chimney pipe. They had burned something before leaving– there had been no smoke twenty minutes earlier. The couple set off, but instead of heading for the place where Samson had parked, they followed a path due west and soon disappeared from sight. He lowered his binoculars and continued. He was too far away to see the couple's faces, but he'd recognise the woman's big, confident stride anywhere. Zoe Freemantle.

He went closer and scanned the windows to see if there was any movement inside and, satisfied there was no one else about, approached and tried the door. It was locked. Zoe and her man friend had a key. But so did he, from Ulrike. He opened the door and locked it again once inside. Paper ash glowed in the wood burner. There was a smell of cannabis in the air. On the ashtray a sticky brown mark indicated that a cigarette or joint had recently been left to smoulder there. In the tiny kitchen, he put his hand on the kettle. It was warm. Empty cans of beans and chopped tomatoes and a spent bottle of wine were in the waste bin, and pieces of pasta lodged in the drain of the sink. An inspection of the shower room produced a piece of wet soap in the soap tray and a damp toothbrush. Zoe and her friend had been sleeping and eating there, though not for any length of time, he thought. They hadn't turned over the place. The main room, which served as eating area, sitting room and studio, looked to him undisturbed. Some papers had been destroyed in the wood burner – that was all. He opened the doors of the burner and gently lifted the ashes with a poker to see if there was any residue of writing or print. Nothing.

He felt he was trespassing in the Harlands' snug little retreat but reminded himself that he was there at Ulrike's invitation. He wondered if Ulrike knew Zoe would be there and meant him to find her, but somehow he doubted that. She would have put a note in with the map reference if she had. But Zoe had gone there for a reason and that, surely, was to find something. He began a thorough search of the main room, where Harland and Ulrike had lived those last months. He opened the drawers, felt along the tops of shelves and under the table, chairs and sofa. He pulled back the old kelim rug, tested the floorboards and felt the wooden panels of the walls to see if there was any give or movement. In the bedroom he conducted a similar search, noticing black marks made by oil lamps and candles on the ceiling and above the bed. There were clothes in the wardrobe, a few books on the bedside table, but very little else.

He returned to the main room and sat down at the table where Harland had worked and scraped his chair round and stared out to sea with a drink – the table's surface was patterned by ring marks. The Harlands' presence was very strong, their happiness and love, too. He began to look at the art materials. There were books full of sketches in charcoal and watercolour, quick and vivid. Samson thought he'd love to own one.

He moved the chair and saw that a canvas had been propped against the wall beside a pile of stuff covered with a cloth. He lifted the cloth – an open box of oil paints, tubes without their tops, a couple of sketchpads, a collapsible easel and chair, rags, bottles of drying medium. The whole lot just dumped, and Samson knew why. These had been retrieved from the murder scene and probably handed to Ulrike by the police. Or perhaps she had gathered them together herself and covered them up so she wouldn't have to look. He turned the oil canvas – still wet to the touch – and put it on the table leaning against the wall, stepped back, and knew its significance immediately. The rapid summary in greys and dull greens of a fleeting burst of light out to sea was what Harland had been working on when he was killed. It was dazzling. He must have been pleased with it.

One of two sketchpads in the pile became dislodged and slid to the floor near his feet. Samson's eyes came to rest on the words 'Berlin blue' written on the back. He snatched it up. Close by, in the same desperate scrawl, but in capitals, was 'LOVE YOU'. He leafed through the pages but found nothing else. Harland's last moments had been spent identifying his killer, or the person who ordered his murder, and conveying his love to Ulrike, but she hadn't noticed and had left the sketchbook with the other things. And the police, if they had been struck by the words 'Berlin blue', must have assumed that it simply had something to do with his art. And clearly Zoe, who knew what 'Berlin blue' stood for, hadn't seen it either. He took a photograph and sent it to Ulrike's phone with the caption, 'Did you see this on the back of his sketchbook?'

Her response came quickly: 'No, bring it to me, please.'

'And the painting?'

'Yes.'

'Will do. Can you talk?'

Pause.

'I'm with someone. Later.'

'Who is Berlin Blue?'

No answer came.

Then, quite a while after he'd assumed the exchange was over, came the message: 'Will you cook with Mother's recipe?'

He sent three question marks, and wondered if it had been meant for someone else. He went through to the kitchen, where he noticed that Zoe had left the best part of a litre of milk, together with an unopened pot of yogurt. It might indicate that they were coming back – he hoped they would, because he had a lot of questions for Zoe – but it also meant that he could make tea. He put the kettle on the gas ring and found an old enamel cup with a dried thumbprint on the handle – Harland's cup – located some tea bags and sat down on a wicker chair to wait. The sun had swung round to the west, filling the cabin with afternoon light. His gaze wandered to an enclosed space below the kitchen counter, to four volumes of recipe books, one German, two Estonian and a large old burgundy-coloured book entitled *Mrs Beeton's Book of Household Management*. He was familiar with this book, because his mother always cited the Victorian household goddess as the reason the English didn't know how to eat well. He pulled it from the shelf and felt its weight. On the title page was a name and a date – Mary Harland, Christmas 1948. Harland's mother, presumably.

'Will you cook Mother's recipe?' Ulrike had texted. He turned the pages, wondering at the illustrations of flans and jelly moulds, which his own mother would certainly have mocked, but what about Harland's? This post-war edition of the book had 1,700 pages and he was sure Ulrike didn't mean him to go through all of it. He removed the remaining cookery books and leafed through them, but found nothing. He felt inside the space where the books were stored, tapping the sides and bottom with his fingertips. It all seemed solid enough, until he reached the part where *Mrs Beeton* had stood alone in her dust. He drew back and saw that the plywood base would slide forward. Working a kitchen knife into the crack at the far end, he pulled with the flat of his hand and the section of plywood came out smoothly, revealing a shallow cavity where another book was lying flat. He lifted out the turquoise-bound modern edition of *Werner's Nomenclature of Colours*, the online version of which he'd already studied.

The kettle boiled. He made tea and sat down with Harland's book and his mug. The book was organised simply, from whites, greys, blacks and blues through to browns. Under the entry 'Berlin Blue' was written a name, Mila Daus, and an IBAN number – not scrambled, he suspected. He went back to the blacks. Under 'pitch black' was the name Erik Kukorin. Pearl Grey was marked as Jonathan Mobius; Saffron Yellow was Elliot Jeffreys; and Aurora Red was Chester Abelman. All had IBAN numbers. Mobius was the only name he recognised.

He slotted home the piece of plywood and returned the four cookery books to the space beneath the counter. He went to fetch the sketchpad with Harland's final message and picked up the painting using the wet canvas clips attached to the top, brought both into the kitchen area and put the sketchpad and *Werner's Nomenclature* into his backpack. He made himself another cup of tea. He stirred some sugar into it, unusually for him, and sat down to think things through in a pool of sunlight that came from the skylight at the back of the kitchen. He had the names and the five IBAN numbers, which he guessed were the account numbers used to finance five separate investigations, a good haul for a day's work.

His attention went to a peacock butterfly fluttering at the window of the back door. He remembered Anastasia moving a table in his flat and standing on it with a jar to capture a butterfly and nearly breaking her neck in the process. He smiled to himself and reached to release the catch on the door. At that moment, the panelling to the right of the door exploded. He heard shattered glass falling into the sitting room. Someone had fired from the front of the cabin at his silhouette and missed because he had moved to get the door. He fell to the floor, grabbed the backpack and waited. The door catch was already released – the door would open with a shove. He looked up and saw no one and concluded that the gunman was some distance away – a sniper. He lunged at the door handle and threw his weight at the door. Another shot. There was no report, just the sound of splintering wood to his right as he tumbled across the threshold on to the gravel. He crab-crawled up to the rock behind the house to gain cover and a better view. When he got there, he took the binoculars from the side pocket of the backpack and moved to a gap in the rock where he could search the land in front of the house. Nothing moved. There was no glint of metal or glass in the sunlight, and no sound. He waited. It was vital to know the shooter's position before deciding which way to escape. His leg was giving him less trouble, but running was still out of the question, so he bloody well needed to make the right choice. A killer would expect his quarry to try to escape, whatever the chances. Samson wasn't going to oblige by making a panicky move – another lesson he'd learned in Syria when a sniper pinned him and two guides in a building just over the Turkish border. The guides had sat down with their backs against the wall, propped the guns beside them and closed their eyes. Samson had smoked a lot in those days, and he'd offered them cigarettes. They'd shaken their heads. Smoke could be seen through a telescopic sight and they needed to make the gunman think they had gone. It was very hot. They had no water. They had waited twelve hours and, when they'd eventually moved, they took the hardest, least obvious route, climbing up the side of the building and working their way across roofs pitted by mortar shells. So, now, he waited and watched. But he also texted Ulrike: 'Under fire and pinned down at cabin. Can you call local police?' A reply came a few minutes later. 'Have done. Neighbour coming armed.'

The neighbour was probably a long way off, as were the police, in this empty part of Estonia, but it was better than nothing. Samson waited, certain that between the moment the shooter had fired three shots in quick succession and his own scramble to the rocks there had been very little time for the man to change position. Two other things were in his favour. Unlike a sniper on a battlefield, sooner or later this character would have to check whether he'd killed, wounded or missed his target. The reason he hadn't already done so was because he didn't know whether Samson was armed and lying in wait for him in the cabin. Again, there was a feeling of amateurishness about it all. A professional hit man would have made sure of the shot and kept on coming until he saw the target's body lying at his feet.

Also in Samson's favour was that night would come, though not for another few hours. He passed the time by conducting a minute survey of the terrain to the east of the cabin, where he paused at every tussock and ambivalent shape or shadow. He found the sniper after half an hour in a slight dip in the land, the gun poking through a tussock of marsh grass. The shooter had come prepared for the particular hue of the landscape and was wearing a very effective pale camouflage. Now that Samson knew where he was, he could work out his best route of escape. The trouble was that the land to the south of him – the direction of his car – was very exposed. He waited some more and it dawned on him that he might not necessarily be the target. If the gunman had been after Zoe and her friend, then he would expect a second person in the cabin, who might, of course, be armed.

He had been there well over an hour when he decided to make a move. He tightened the straps on his pack and stumbled as fast as he could towards the shore. There was one area where he would be vulnerable, a rise in the land, which he had to take before descending to the shore. He took it as fast as he could, but that wasn't very fast. The shooter spotted him. Two bullets kicked up earth and grit in front of him. But he was over the summit and moving down. Now that he saw how well hidden it was from the gunman's position, he opted to take the shoreline south. Even if the man pursued him, he had a head start and would make it to his car.

His phone vibrated with a text from Ulrike: 'They are with you now.' He looked around and saw no one, then spied a white bow wave rounding the lighthouse to the north. A rigid inflatable hoved into view with several men on board. The boat was moving very fast then swerved left towards an old concrete jetty, where it rapidly deposited four men. They were armed with wildfowling guns and quickly went to take up positions across the peninsula, two hundred metres apart, as though they were preparing to drive game down the peninsula. Samson moved to see what was happening and was astonished as the line of men started towards the south, letting off volleys from their shotguns as they walked. He ran to the top of the rise to see what the effect would be on the shooter. It was immediate. He snaked backwards then crouched with binoculars to look at the line of men advancing in his direction. He didn't linger further. He shouldered the gun, jogged to the cover of some wind-blasted bushes and vanished.

Samson texted thanks to Ulrike. She replied: 'Police are waiting for him. They've located his vehicle. Can you bring Bobby's painting to the house?'

He entered the cabin and retrieved the painting from the floor. It was lying face up. A bullet had passed clean through the bottom of the canvas where there were a few strokes of translucent colour.

CHAPTER 21

KaPo

He was in Tallinn by 9 p.m. – too late to return the car. He parked outside
the old town walls, quite near to the hotel, and passed through the gates
at the Fat Margaret Tower. As he turned into the narrow street leading
to the Cloister Hotel, a voice called his name. He turned to see Tomas
Sikula, one of his contacts in the KaPo – a senior officer who he'd met in
the debriefing after Narva and who, it turned out, was a good friend and
protégé of Harland's.

He approached with his usual dazzling grin, grasped Samson by the
hand and elbow. 'Paul, you must be losing it – using the same crappy ID
at the same hotel!'

'Ah!' said Samson. 'Thought I'd make things easy for you.' The Hungarian ID he'd used on the registration form had no doubt triggered an
alert at KaPo's offices, not that it mattered.

'It's good to see you, Paul. I gather you had some trouble this afternoon,
but that conforms to recent patterns, no?' His eyes danced with mischief.
'What are your plans for this evening? I know a bar where we can have
dinner.' He looked down. 'What is this here – a painting by Bobby?' He
peered at it. 'What have you done to it – used it for target practice?'

'You mentioned dinner,' said Samson. 'I need a wash and, anyway, I want to put the painting in a safe place at the hotel.'

'Okay, there's a bar at the end of the street. KandaBaar.'

'I know it.' It was the bar where he'd met Harland the first time. 'I'll see you there in fifteen minutes.'

He arrived at the bar, having photographed the pages from the *Werner Nomenclature*. The book was tucked into the inside pocket of his old, scarred leather jacket.

'Beer or wine?' asked Tomas. 'You may need something stronger after being shot at.' Another grin. 'We know all about it – the police informed us immediately. It could only have been you. What were you doing out there, Paul?'

'Picking up a painting and a sketchbook Bobby's widow wanted.'

'A likely story.'

'You saw the painting in my hand.'

'With a bullet hole through it! A good summary of Bobby's life, no?' The waitress came, and Tomas went through his usual routine of flirtation. A strikingly good-looking man, he seemed to need to seduce everyone, even though he was openly gay for what he described as *most of the time*. At length, he let her go with an order for steak, fries and beer. 'So what were you looking for out there? What else were you retrieving for Mrs Harland?'

'Nothing.'

'Please, Paul, don't offend my intelligence. You are a prime target of the people who killed Bobby and tried to poison the whole of Congress.'

Samson shrugged.

'That latest was the third attempt on your life, or have I missed one?'

He nodded.

'Well, I'm glad I caught up with you tonight – who knows whether you'll be here tomorrow. By the way, they didn't catch the man who tried to kill you this afternoon.' He studied Samson. 'You left a message on my phone this morning saying you wanted some help. Hit me! What do you need?'

'I wanted to see the man who killed Bobby – Nikolai Horobets, but . . .'

'Well, I am sorry to inform you that Nikolai passed.'

'Pneumonia? I didn't realise he was so sick.'

'No, VX nerve agent. Ring any bells?'

'Jesus – in the hospital?'

'You know what VX stands for? Extremely fucking venomous. An individual wearing full protective equipment gained access to the secure section where he was being treated, removed his oxygen mask and sprayed his face with the nerve agent. He died a few minutes later. There was no trace of the assassin. But this now conforms to a pattern. Vladan Drasko died in the Virginian motel. The FBI must know that that was no accident, and today we received good information that Miroslav Rajavic, the man who attempted to kill you, was found dead in Belgrade yesterday. Yes, the Matador is no longer with us! That means that all the assassins are dead, including the one that you killed in self-defence.' He placed air quotes around 'self-defence' with a wicked smile.

'Did you get anything out of him before he died?'

'We did. But that's a secret, Paul.'

'Have you told the Americans about him?'

'They'll learn in due course. No need to talk to them.'

Samson asked himself why he said that. 'So, what do you want?'

Tomas smiled regretfully, as though he had left his wallet at home and needed Samson to pick up the tab. He was asking a favour, yet not a very large one. 'We want to know everything, but before you start telling me, there is someone I want you to meet.' He brought his hands together in a gentle clap. A slim man who'd been at the far end of the bar with a newspaper swivelled on the bar stool and slid off. He looked like an architect or a designer, with his cropped blond hair, navy blue spectacle frames, white shirt and knitted black tie. He sat down on the chair at the end of the booth table. He seemed familiar to Samson.

'This is our director, Mr Sollen,' said Tomas. The man offered his hand, palm facing down. 'Aaro Sollen,' he said and tipped his head towards Tomas.

'We know that Bobby and Mr Hisami were collaborating,' began Tomas. 'We became curious when Mr Hisami's plane began appearing at the airport and we concluded they were involved in a project. But we wondered who, what and why they were investigating, and why they needed the help of the young Syrian genius, who was also often in Tallinn.' He looked at Samson hard before saying, 'The boy who so impressed us all two years ago. What was he doing in Tallinn again? We realised that his role was probably technical, so we wondered exactly who they were damn well hacking.'

'I don't know who they were targeting, but I think this all started in Berlin,' said Samson, and went on to explain the Ghost from the East theory – Harland spotting an individual from the old Soviet bloc.

'A Russian?' asked Tomas.

'No, East German, and I heard something about a man called Anatoly Stepurin.' He let Tomas winkle out the connection about a Russian special forces veteran who may or may not have been the paymaster for a man named Oret, who'd turned to the Balkan, Ukrainian and Dutch underworlds for an impromptu team of hit men. Tomas didn't know about Oret, or his death, but KaPo knew of Stepurin. 'That sounds right,' he said. 'Who's he working for – American or Russian interests, do you think?'

'Maybe it's both.'

Tomas caught on quickly. 'You mean Americans that are Russian assets, and these assets may also include Britons.' He stopped. 'So we're talking about long-term, high-level penetration by the old enemy.'

'The old enemy,' repeated Samson.

'But now this is all about power and influence, not ideology.'

'That's always true these days, isn't it?'

'And your own people at SIS?'

'They're not my people, Tomas, but I will say their reaction is pretty fucking weird. They want to explain all this as blowback from Narva – gangsters settling scores for the deaths of Chumak and Bukov – and so keep it well away from the Russian state. But that doesn't stop them wetting their pants about what was going on in some run-down buildings in east London.'

'East London – that's where this whole operation was based?'

'Yes.'

'And financed by Hisami. He was paying you as well?'

Samson nodded.

'Something puzzles us,' said Tomas. 'Why was your and my friend Robert Harland killed when we believe he had ceased working with Mr Hisami because he had just weeks to live?'

'The people who ordered the hit didn't know Harland was ill, nor that they'd stopped collaborating.'

'We think they were attempting to eliminate his knowledge – same with Hisami. That makes us ask why they tried to kill you.' He looked up as the waitress appeared with their dinner.

Sollen smiled and said, 'Why did they try to kill you? You knew nothing. We understand that because the first thing you did when you arrived in Estonia was to go out to Karu Saar in search of whatever you could find. You had a relatively minor role. Why you?' He waited for Samson to respond, but got nothing. 'But you know what you're looking for, because the moment you arrive in Estonia, you choose to go out to the cabin and conduct a search. What did you find?'

'A man with a sniper rifle – I had to get out of there fast.'

'You found something,' said Tomas. 'I can feel it.' He waved his fork at him. 'You're a very determined person.'

'Don't pretend you haven't searched the place,' Samson said. 'You know there's nothing there, Tomas.'

'Ulrike didn't come back to Tallinn after Bobby was murdered. She wanted to grieve alone without people fussing over her. We didn't search the place.'

Samson didn't believe him. Ulrike had returned to Tallinn. If they had been spying on Harland's meeting with Denis Hisami, they wouldn't be averse to poking around his hideout. But he nodded understandingly.

'How did you find the cabin?' asked Sollen.

'Ulrike gave me instructions.'

'By phone?'

'She got a message to me.'

'How?'

'She sent a note to my hotel with a key.'

'Why didn't you go to see her?'

'She didn't want me to. Maybe she's being watched.'

'Yes, the people who killed her husband are here, and they are no doubt watching. Presumably, there was an intermediary who left the note at your hotel. Someone she could trust.'

'I don't know. I was asleep.'

'Such a lot of trouble to take to get a painting and a sketchbook: she could've sent someone from the gallery – they'll do anything to help her right now. But she wanted you to go because she knew that with her help you would find all the data that Bobby accumulated. Was she waiting for you to come to Estonia for the funeral so that you could retrieve those secrets from their hiding place? Perhaps that's why she stayed at the cabin for as long as she did.'

Samson began shaking his head before Sollen finished. 'Why don't you ask her?' he said. 'And while you're about it, you should talk to her about Berlin. I was there, but Bobby didn't tell me about the individual he spotted. He must have told Ulrike.'

Tomas said simply. 'We know you have what you went looking for, Paul, so there's no point talking about Berlin.'

Sollen studied him. 'Can I ask where you were in the cabin when the man shot at you?'

'In the kitchen, near the back door.'

'And he shot at you from the front of the house, through the window of the main room – that's what the police say. How long were you there before he shot?'

'I'm not sure.'

Sollen smiled. He knew Samson couldn't admit to being there much longer than it took to pick up the painting and the sketchbook.

'Does it occur to you that he was watching what you were doing through binoculars and only shot when he was certain you'd found what you were looking for? The fact that he took the shot tells me he thought you had.' He raised a hand. 'Please don't embarrass yourself or us by denying it. The question is, what are we going to do now? Obviously, you're at great risk, but if they think you have shared the information, they may wait to decide what to do next.' His hand now dropped to lie across Samson's, where it remained. 'In Estonia we are on the frontline. Every moment of our professional lives is dedicated to preserving the freedom that we won thirty years ago. That means we have to concentrate very hard on what they're up to in Moscow and how they're trying – and in most cases succeeding – to disrupt Western democracy. I don't need to tell you that these people are very bad. They work through proxies like Stepurin, but the source of the evil resides in those ex-KGB men who run things. These people never went away. They're exactly the same, but now they believe only in money and their own power.' He removed his hand and turned to the waitress to order a cognac, evidently a rare event, from the look on Tomas's face. Nothing was said until the drink arrived. He held the glass up, admired the colour of the liquid and said, 'To the memory of Robert Harland – a friend to liberty and Estonia.' Samson again drank to Harland's memory,

'What would Bobby advise you to do now?' continued Sollen. 'I believe he would tell you to share his information with us. First, this course makes it less likely that you'll be targeted. Second, if anything does happen to you, the information can still be used. We would make sure that it was used to good effect.'

Samson looked around the bar, which was now nearly empty. He had no objection in principle to sharing information with them, but only at the right moment. He was under no illusions about these two. While he dined with Tomas and his boss, his room would have been searched and fitted with bugs and possibly a camera over the desk, the place where he was likely to research the five names he now had.

He drank the remainder of his wine. 'If there were such a cache of secrets, wouldn't it be wise to share it with the CIA and FBI?' he said. 'They've already made big advances, based on material found in Hisami's briefcase.'

Sollen swivelled to him. 'You must not share with the Americans. You have to consider whether the Americans are as corrupted as your own intelligence service appears to be. When penetration has taken place at the highest level, the instinct to cover up and hide the weakness in the system is even greater. These secrets should be used appropriately, and in some cases made public so people understand what the other side is capable of.'

Samson wondered about the vehemence of Sollen's reaction. In the great intelligence bazaar, information was never disclosed without profit, but rather used to gain influence and leverage. Information was the reserve currency – the only thing that actually mattered.

Samson began to make his excuses, but before he could leave two men appeared and waited a little distance from the table. Sollen got up, nodded to Tomas. 'I will see you at the funeral, Mr Samson. Good night.'

Tomas watched the three men move towards the back entrance of KandaBaar. 'Someone tried to poison him with ricin just a few weeks ago. He's too good for them, and they know it.' He paused to deliver one of his winning smiles. 'The deal is this – we will protect you here and make sure that Ulrike is safe, but we need to know everything.'

'Then you will have to find someone who can tell you, because I don't know everything.'

They had reached the end of the road. KaPo wanted everything, but for precisely what purpose wasn't clear, and Samson needed to know.

CHAPTER 22

Ulrike's Story

At the hotel, he gave the desk clerk a €50 note and asked to change rooms because of the likelihood that his room had been bugged while he was at dinner. He moved his things but decided that he wouldn't conduct internet searches of the five names using the hotel's wifi for the reason that Tomas might have compromised that, too. He sent a text to Ulrike. It was eleven o'clock, but he knew she would be up and wasn't surprised when he received a message with instructions to use the garden entrance to her home. He arrived at the door in the mediaeval wall at the back of the Harlands' house. It couldn't be opened from the street without a key. He pushed at it without success then heard it being unlocked from the inside. As the door opened, a match flared and he saw Ulrike briefly. She took his hand and led him through the rambling roses that had got out of control over the last year. 'Be careful, they will cut you to pieces,' she said. They reached the conservatory. The door was open. A cigarette smouldered in an ashtray that rested in a large flower tub by the door. She turned and embraced him and brushed his cheek with the back of her hand. 'How good of you to come, dear Samson. In the few years Bobby knew you, he came to like and admire you. That was rare for him. He would be pleased you're here.'

She picked up the cigarette and took a last drag before extinguishing it, shaking her head. 'I gave up for Bobby, though I knew he was smoking when he was out there. But now, well, I think there is no point, so I smoke.'

'I'm so sorry.'

'I know you are, Samson. I know.' She studied him. 'It's odd – you're like him in so many ways.'

They moved inside. She offered him a whisky, which he accepted to keep her company, and they sat down opposite each other on a pair of wicker sofas. 'I'm glad you came, but you didn't bring the painting and the sketchbook!'

'Didn't want everyone to know where I was going. I've just had dinner with the KaPo.'

'And they want to know everything. They came to see me – Tomas and his boss. I stalled, but, well, I rely on them for my security.'

'You didn't tell them about this,' he said, taking out the *Nomenclature of Colours* and laying it on the table. 'Do you know what's inside?'

'Bobby never let me look at it and he changed his hiding places. Of course, I guessed it was near his mother's cookbook because I caught him with the book in his hands two weeks ago. He never showed the slightest interest in cooking. Never! It was there only to remind him of her.' There was something heroic in her grief. She was still beautifully turned out in her usual colours of grey and beige. Mourning made no difference to the care she had taken over her hair, held in a clip at the back and still quite dark.

'Does anyone else know? Naji?'

She shook her head. 'I was against Bobby using Naji. It was too much of a risk after what that boy had been through. But they needed him and he wanted to do it. There was no question of pressure. I would not have allowed that. But, yes, Naji knows everything.'

'He knows about all the names in this book?'

She nodded and reached into a bowl of sugared almonds. 'I don't cook now. There's no need, so I graze. That is the English expression, isn't it? I like to graze.'

'When I was out at the cabin, I saw a young couple there. There were signs they'd stayed the night. I'm certain one of them was Zoe Freemantle, the woman I was paid to protect in London. Did you know they were there? Were they looking for this?' He tapped the book.

'Ach! They didn't tell me they were going.' She gave him a frustrated look. 'I'll tell you about them later. There are things I have to explain to you. It's complicated.'

It seemed odd but he let it go. 'They were lucky not to be killed.'

'I think the gunman was waiting for you. They can't know about Zoe's involvement. That was an important part of the whole operation. They never knew about her.'

'And the young man?'

She clasped her hands. 'That was my son, Rudi Rosenharte the second.'

Samson's head spun. He'd met Rudi in Berlin but hadn't recognised him at the cabin. He sat back. 'They're a couple?'

'Yes, they are.' She sighed. 'It's very, very complicated, but there's plenty of time for that later.' She topped up the whisky with water and looked at him, gently nodding, as though encouraging herself. 'This story begins in 1989, when I was held for a brief time in Hohenschönhausen prison in East Berlin. But do you want to hear this now? Maybe wait until tomorrow.'

He shook his head.

'I don't sleep, so it makes no difference to me.' She stopped. 'I miss him beside me, you see.'

Samson leaned over and touched her arm. 'We don't have to speak about it now. We can sit here and get drunk on Bobby's whisky.'

'But you have brought the book and you risked your life to get it! I don't think we can ignore that. Bobby was killed for it, and Macy told me that they tried to kill you in London, twice. You and your friend were stabbed, and now they want to arrest you.'

'We're both okay now,' he said, opening the book and handing it to her. 'Who is Mila Daus?'

Ulrike was silent for a few moments as she looked at one of Bobby's early paintings – a study of grass bent in the wind. She glanced at him. Fury had replaced hurt in her eyes. 'Mila Daus is the most evil person I have ever met. You read about those female guards in the camps – that is Mila Daus. There is nothing else to be said. She is everything beyond the gates of Hell. I saw her for a few minutes when she prescribed for me a regime to break my spirit. Because I was suspected of spying against the state, I was to be crushed before the trial. That was the word she used to me – crushed. She said she would see me again in six months, when I wouldn't recognise myself.

'She was well known among dissidents at the time, although, naturally, no one knew her name. She was quite young then – in her thirties – but she had a reputation among those who were held by the Stasi for unusual cruelty. She came from the Stasi College of Law. Yes, they believed in doing everything legally! Mila Daus rose fast and became a leading ex-pert in *Zersetzung*, which translates as "decomposition". They destroyed people's psychology – what the Party called "hostile and negative aspects of a person's dispositions and beliefs" – and they did it from the inside of their mind. They gas-lighted them, smashed their dreams and hopes, their faith, their love, their loyalties. The Stasi tunnelled into a person's soul and hollowed out their being over months and months – maybe years – of twelve-hour interrogations, sleep deprivation, isolation and physical abuse. They turned people's loved ones and friends against them and spread false rumours about infidelities and their sexuality – sometimes even about paedophilia and bestiality, can you believe? Hundreds of thousands of human spirits were broken in that place, in Hohenschön-hausen, and when they were let out, they were shunned.' She reached for her cigarettes. 'I will smoke in here, against my own rules!' she said, breaking off the filter and shaking her head. She lit up, puffed without inhaling. 'No one was punished for the assault on the psychology of an entire nation. They got away with it.

'Mila Daus was the worst of them all. She was very beautiful – of an athletic build – and she was highly intelligent. Such blessings, but such profound evil! She could do what she wanted because she got around her bosses. They all wanted to sleep with her, you see. But she had no time for such frivolity. Her life was devoted to the destruction of men and women who defied the State by such crimes as applying for a travel visa, not joining the Party, making a joke about the Party leaders. She kept a close eye on every case and had an incredible memory for the detail of each person's life. She had a taste for data, and they said that she kept her own files. When a person was broken, she would come to watch the wreckage of a human being in their final interrogations. Sometimes she would recommend another year of punishment to watch as it registered in their faces. She rejoiced in destroying people.' Ulrike took a last drag and stubbed out the cigarette vehemently. 'Mila Daus was the person Bobby saw in Berlin, on the thirtieth-anniversary weekend.'

'What on earth was she doing there? It was surely the last place for a former Stasi officer?'

'I have to give you some more background. Remember, I told you my husband Rudi was murdered when we returned from Spain.' He nodded. 'He was an art historian, a very good one, and we had been to the Prado to view all the paintings that he had studied but never seen. I was pregnant with my son – the handsome man you saw. They attacked our VW camper van as we drove through the Pyrenees. The van crashed and Rudi was killed instantly. I was injured and it looked like I might lose our baby, but I was saved by a farmer and his wife. We were in a deserted part of the mountains – I was lucky the woman knew what she was doing.'

'Yes, you told me the story a while back.'

'Did I go into the aftermath?'

'You said Bobby created a new identity for you and found a place for you and your baby in Berlin.'

'Bobby also tracked down the man who killed Rudi and, before that, his twin brother in Hohenschönhausen.'

'I remember your phrase. You said he *settled the account*.'

'Yes, Bobby and a man named Cuth Avocet found the three killers and made sure they wouldn't come after me and Rudi's baby. Zank died; the other two were incapacitated. I never asked what that meant, but there was never any trouble from them again. That is what settling the account meant.'

'I met Avocet in London a few days ago.'

'Bobby loved him, but of course he's a very dangerous individual, as I expect you saw. They freed me from Hohenschönhausen and later they made sure me and my baby were safe. For that I was very grateful and, in due course, I fell in love with Bobby.' She looked away, suddenly overcome with grief.

'Please! If this upsets you . . .'

'I must continue, because this business is not finished. Bobby is dead before his time.' She clasped her hands in anguish. 'I know he would have willed himself to live to see the exhibition, despite the cancer. He would have loved watching people look at the paintings he worked so hard on. He was so looking forward to it, though of course he never admitted that to me.'

'And Mila Daus?' prompted Samson gently.

'Mila Daus organised and inspired the murder of my first husband, and now she has killed my second husband. That's who Mila Daus is.'

'Before he died, Bobby wrote "Berlin Blue" as well as his message of love for you on the sketchbook, so he knew it was her.'

'Did he? I didn't know her code name.' She smiled. 'But then we didn't know her real name for a long time. Mila Daus was known only as *der Teufel von Hohenschönhausen* – the devil of Hohenschönhausen, or a much ruder word that you probably know, *die Fotze*.' Samson nodded, he did – cunt. 'But Bobby knew her face because for eighteen months he had searched for her and he'd got hold of several photographs of her from the Stasi archive, but these were group shots and she wasn't identified on the back. As I say, she was strikingly beautiful, and people recognised her and he established her involvement in the planning of Rudi's murder. And of course, anyone who had been in Hohenschönhausen knew who she was, but the name eluded him.'

'Why didn't you know her name?'

'She was very clever – she altered the Stasi records so that Mila Daus was described as a social worker. Can you believe that? According to her file, her responsibilities were to help pregnant women who were held by the Stasi and liaise with families of prisoners, giving them psychological support. Investigators overlooked her for a time and, when they finally suspected that her role was much more important, she had vanished – to America, where she married a very, very wealthy man named Heini Muller, a third-generation German, owner of an engineering company. She dry-cleaned her backstory and created a whole new life for herself. But she didn't sit back and live off Muller's money. Not Mila Daus! She went to business school, got herself an MBA and created her own data company. Evidently, she understood what was happening in technology in the nineties and the importance of people's personal information, a lesson she learned in the Stasi. Muller died, leaving a lot of money. His family disputed the will, but she won the court case, and then her career really began to take off because she was very rich as well as being a shrewd investor and businesswoman. She married twice more. The second husband died. His name was Mobius. The third husband is a foot doctor – a podiatrist, I believe it is called. His name is Dr John Gaspar, Italian and German parentage.'

'Who is Jonathan Mobius?'

'Her stepson, I believe. Bobby told me she had an affair with the boy, though he's twenty years younger than her.'

'What was she doing in Berlin that weekend?'

'Can you believe it? One of her companies sponsored some kind of an event to do with anniversary of the fall of the Wall. She owns a German company and they gave money and entertained their clients at the Adlon Hotel.'

'Surely, she might have been recognised a hundred times over that weekend when so many dissidents were celebrating?'

'In the Adlon? I don't think so. Those people have probably never been to such a place. Mila was safe, except Bobby saw her, because he was meeting an old source from the East and he wanted to give the man a good dinner. The man was his best agent.'

'I thought you were.'

'No, we worked together for a very short time and he didn't even know my name. I called myself Kafka – very pretentious.' She smiled at the memory and poured herself another whisky. 'It helps talking and getting a little bit drunk with you here, Samson. Thank you for coming.'

'My pleasure,' he said. 'You know how much . . .'

'Yes, I do – really!' She patted his knee, then sat back and toyed with her necklace. 'Bobby might have forgotten all about Mila Daus, but the man with him knew of her reputation and took photographs with his phone. He checked with the people who had seen her in the prison all those years ago and they all made a positive identification, Bobby showed them to me and of course I knew immediately. *Der Teufel von Hohenschön-hausen.* That was the woman who told me that she would enjoy breaking me and requested Colonel Zank to place me in the U-boat. This was the underground prison, part of the old Nazi building, and it's where Bobby and Rudi found me, although I cannot remember much of that part.'

'Do you have those photographs taken in 2019?'

'Of course. Do you want to see them now?'

'If it's not too much trouble.'

She got up and went to detach her phone from a charger. She came back with glasses on the end of her nose, swiping through the album on her phone.

'You had a long day today,' said Samson.

'You're fishing, Samson.'

'I suppose I am – yes.'

'The CIA were here – a stern individual called Toombs. And that man from SIS that Bobby called the Tick, but I can't remember what his real name is. You know – the man who was shot a little bit in the street outside the club.'

'A little bit shot – that was Nyman.'

'What does it mean – Tick?'

'A tick is an insect that clings to you and sucks your blood.'

'That makes sense. He insinuated his way into the meeting by telling the CIA that I would not see them without him, which was untrue. When they'd gone, Mr Toombs returned without him. I wanted to be helpful because Denis is so ill and to put that poison in Congress and risk so many lives was a disgusting thing to do. But I didn't tell them anything about Mila Daus because I felt we should know what was in the book before we did that and I knew you would find it.' She handed him the phone. 'This is Mila Daus.'

Samson took the phone. He saw a woman in a dark trouser suit surrounded by four men. She was holding a drink in her left hand and wore a shoulder bag on her right side. The men were gesticulating, laughing, seemingly trying to impress. Her face was still beautiful, though her lips were thin and unexpressive. In the five frames, which he guessed were taken over a period of a minute, her countenance did not vary in the least. She looked towards the camera in the penultimate picture – focused, interested, alert to the possibility of being photographed – but in the last she turned away to show a well-proportioned head and face in profile. In this one, the body language and position of the men relative to her revealed who owned the power in the room. Beyond her group, there were several round tables with guests – mostly men – standing by their seats, waiting for Mila Daus to take hers, no doubt. Two waiters were in the process of closing the double doors to the private party. His clandestine skill had not deserted Harland's agent: he had done well to get off so many clear shots in such a short time and without changing his position.

'She has hardly changed,' said Ulrike. 'She's carrying one or two extra kilos around her stomach and hips and her hair is darker, but she is the same woman that I saw in the interrogation room. She didn't bother to alter her appearance to come to Berlin thirty years later. Such arrogance!'

'Why did Bobby think she took that risk?'

'He could only find one answer to that question.'

'She was seeing her handler from Moscow,' said Samson.

Ulrike nodded slowly. 'She's much too powerful to have a handler but, yes, Bobby thought she was talking to someone. The anniversary was possibly used by the Russians to meet up and see some old faces. Quite an irony, but it would delight them after the humiliation of 9 November 1989. Some sort of closure, perhaps. That's why she took the risk.' She picked up the book. 'May I?'

'It's yours now, Ulrike.'

'No, Bobby would have liked you to have it: his legacy to you, Samson,' she said with a very slight smile. 'Shall we look at it together? Why don't you bring your computer over here and we can research the names together?'

'That's going to take some time,' he said.

'"I'm not sleepy and there is no place I'm going to."' She sang the line and glanced at him a little ruefully, as if she really knew she'd had too much to drink. 'Bob Dylan – "Mr Tambourine" Man. Bobby loved his namesake's music – we're going to use him in the service. It's for our generation, of course,' she explained. 'Come over. I want to see what my husband was hiding from me.'

'It's a network – Mila Daus's network. All the people in the Berlin Blue Network,' he said.

CHAPTER 23

The Sargasso Sea

Luka drove Anastasia and Naji across the Bulgarian border to Sofia, where they took a plane to Warsaw then to Vilnius, the capital of Lithuania, and just missed a connecting flight to Tallinn. At Naji's insistence, they kept their distance during the day, but now faced a night in Vilnius airport hotel together before catching the early flight the next day. He had barely spoken to her in the preceding twenty hours and showed no sign of doing so now. When he wasn't looking into the distance, he had his head in his phone and sat with his legs crossed, one foot jigging. He'd removed himself in the way he did as a boy in the camp on Lesbos where she first came across him. When she'd asked him about his parents, or pointed out the impracticality of his plan to walk across Europe to Germany, he simply shut down.

It was late and the hotel restaurant was closed. She insisted that he needed to eat and went to the bar, where the barman assembled a scratch meal of starters, breads, smoked eel and salmon, which Naji delighted in. She wasn't going to ask him anything, but as she handed him the Diet Coke she'd brought with her glass of wine from the bar, she said, 'I want you to know something, Naj. Me and Samson, we think you're the best.

We love you like family. You're very, very special to us. You know that, don't you?'

He looked up, tugged the ring pull and grinned awkwardly.

'That's all right,' she said. 'I know how you feel. I just wanted to make sure that you knew we felt the same way.' She smiled. 'In my line of work, I realise life would be a lot easier for everyone if we took our courage in both hands and said the things that we all need to say but don't know how.'

He nodded. 'It is the same for me, Anastasia. Of course.' Then the foot started jigging again and he took rapid sips of Coke. 'I like eels. They come from the Sargasso Sea, which spins like a black hole, though it isn't like a black hole because nothing disappears there except eels. That's where they go to mate and die. Did you know that?'

'I did. I know two other things about the Sargasso Sea,' she said. 'It has very clear water and it spins clockwise.'

'Not if you are an eel. If you're an eel, it spins counter-clockwise.' He caught her puzzled expression and shook his head in exasperation. He took a piece of paper from his backpack and drew a clockwise arrow. 'Hold the paper above your head against the light. Now you are the eel.'

'Right, it's counter-clockwise,' she said. 'I knew that!'

He shook his head. 'You did not.'

She smiled. 'How do you know about eels?'

'Ifkar catches eels. He tells me about them. We eat them together. We like to go to catch fish together. It is the activity that I like best in my life to go fishing with my friend and Moon.'

'He's a good friend.'

'Best friend – we saved each other's life.' He brought his phone up to his face. Evidently, the conversation was over.

She watched him closely for a few moments, some understanding beginning to dawn. She might have asked the question then, but her own phone sprang into life with a call from Jim Tulliver, who she had been trying to reach between flights. 'How is he?' she asked, getting up to walk away.

'You talked to the doctor?'

'I've had coverage problems and I've been on planes.'

'They won't tell me everything, but I know the guy well enough now and he said Denis is not progressing as they would hope.'

'What does that mean?'

'I think there're some heart issues and maybe something neurological. I don't know. I think you should speak with him as soon as—'

'I will. Have you seen Denis?'

'Yeah, he looks pretty good, though he's still in a coma. Talk to the doc. I told him you were in a different time zone. Where are you, by the way?'

'The Baltic. What about Denis's business?'

'All good, no problems that I can see. You know the FBI were really pissed that you skipped the country like that. I mean, *really* pissed. Reiner called me.'

'Yeah . . . They're in Europe. I had Reiner calling the hotel in Athens.' That seemed a long time ago.

'And your fan club has been in touch. Warren Speight wants to talk urgently and Marty Reid says he has information. They've both been trying to reach you. Reid is on the phone all the time, wanting to know what you're doing, where you are.'

'I'm not really interested in Reid. Speight, what did he want?'

'They're making some move in Congress. I'll try to find out more. I'll talk to the aide again and to Shera Ricard's people. They'll know if something is afoot.'

'Am I hearing this right? Are they thinking of pursuing the investigation of Denis when he's in a coma, for Christ's sake?'

'That's not my impression.'

'I sure hope you're right. I'll call the doctor.'

She rang off and looked across the lobby. Naji was turned away and still had his phone close to his face. She found a chair at the far end and dialled the doctor's assistant. He was busy. She waited, aware of the disconcerting thought that she had buried the real possibility that Denis might not recover. She dialled again and was put straight through to the usually upbeat Dr Jamie Carrew. But his voice was grave and there were no pleasantries. 'I know you are out of DC, Mrs Hisami, so I wanted to bring you up to date with some concerns of mine. Are you aware of any history of breathlessness in Denis?'

'No, he's pretty fit. He plays tennis and exercises in the gym maybe five times a week.'

'I looked at the notes sent to me by his doctor in San Francisco, and there was nothing to explain his arrhythmia, in his case a sometimes dangerously slow heartbeat. His fitness would explain an efficiently low heartbeat, but this is out of the ordinary. I just wanted to establish if this was an underlying condition. So, he hasn't experienced shortness of breath?'

'No.'

'Any chest pains?'

'No, not as far as I'm aware.'

'A fluttering in his chest? Unusual fatigue?'

'No, Denis has exceptional energy.'

'And no blackouts?'

'No.'

'But as you told me, he has a very stressful life. He drinks maybe a little too much and he smokes cigars occasionally. Neither of those is helpful, but I don't believe that they're the cause. So we're going to put him on some medication that should increase his heart rate, but if that doesn't work we may be considering other options. Possibly a surgical intervention, but that has to be balanced with the needs of recovery from the nerve agent. I'll be consulting with other specialists to see what's the best course.'

'This doesn't sound good,' she said. 'Without the heart issue, how's he doing?'

'Better than expected, but he's still in the coma and we won't know what kind of neurological impact he has suffered.'

'God, I wish I hadn't left now.'

'Well, he is comatose, so it wouldn't make a heap of difference. I believe he will recover, but I want to keep an eye on his heart. I'll let you know if there's any change in his condition or in our plans for him. When do you expect to be back in Washington?'

'In two or three days.'

'Good, I look forward to seeing you then. We've got your cell number and will call you with any developments.'

She hung up and walked over to Naji, feeling lousy and wondering why she'd left the States. She communicated some of this to Naji, who looked up and for the first time properly engaged with her. 'You are in charge of Denis's money. You have to be here and you have to be at Mr Harland's funeral because you and Denis owe him.' He gestured the plain truth of his logic. 'You are the boss of this, Anastasia.'

'Then why won't you talk to me about it?'

'I can't. We must wait. Others know things.'

'Who?'

'Zoe.'

'Who is she?'

'The person Samson was protecting. Very beautiful,' he concluded. He snapped up his phone and peered myopically at the screen again.

'What are you doing?'

He jerked his head towards two men at the reception desk. He was using his back camera to watch them. 'No bags,' he said.

Anastasia moved a little to see round a palm plant. Without warning, Naji got up, then, dragging his foot and hooking his arm in front of him, as though he had impaired movement on his right side, he set off towards the reception. He revolved his head and spoke in Arabic to a non-existent caller, smiled goofily at the two men and lunged for the complimentary bowl of sweets on the reception desk, where he spent a little time making his choice. Anastasia held her breath. She had seen him do something like this in the camp when he jumped a food line, and he'd told her that he had put on an act to get past ticket inspection on the ferry to Piraeus. The two men stepped back. Naji wheeled round chaotically and, laughing manically, fell into one of them, then, by way of apology, offered the sweets in his hand to the man. The man stepped back with a look of horror and Naji continued on his way towards the dining area.

A moment later a text came to Anastasia's phone. 'Russians.'

She called him. 'What do we do?'

'You must leave now. They don't know what I look like, but your face is everywhere on the internet. I've got the room key. I will get your bag. Go to the car park. I'll meet you there.'

She felt he was being paranoid, but watched closely from her cover of the palm and a pillar. One of the men casually wandered off in the direction Naji had gone. The second waited for the receptionist to process their bookings and was looking around at the other guests with a keen interest. She got up and backed away to a side door that led to a covered area where some rustic wooden tables and chairs had been pushed together because of the rain. She headed for a strip of wet grass to her left and followed the line of the building into the darkness. At the end she saw a small car park. Naji was nowhere. She moved to the lines of cars, crouched down and dialled Naji's number, but got no reply. She texted: 'I'm in car park. Where are you?' She heard a car's lock operate and saw its lights flash in response. She remained in a crouching position, waiting for the car to start up and leave. Nothing happened. Then she heard Naji call out. She stood up and saw him standing triumphantly by the open door of an Audi. 'Come, we must leave now,' he said.

'You can't just steal a car like that.'

'Rentals are shut.'

'I know, but we have a flight in six hours. Anyway, whose car is it?'

'Russians. They are looking for us. We must go.' That was Naji – nothing superfluous.

She went towards him. 'You took their car key!'

'It was on the desk.'

'What if they are perfectly innocent businessmen?'

'I don't think so,' he said, with absolute certainty. 'I know a killer when I see one.'

He did, too. She shook her damp hair, brushed the rainwater from her jacket and climbed in on the passenger side. Naji groped for the lever to adjust the driver's seat, exclaimed in Arabic and pulled out a small handgun. 'Businessmen with no bags and plenty of guns.'

'Okay, you're right. Should I drive?'

'You have been drinking. Two glasses of wine.'

'One!'

'Two! Mini-bar!' It was true. She'd forgotten the quarter bottle she opened while trying to get hold of Tulliver and Dr Carrew.

'Do you drive? I mean, do you have any experience?'

'Yes, I am the most excellent driver.'

'You stole a policeman's car when you were a kid and crashed it. I know that. Have you done any driving since then?'

'Of course.'

'Where?'

'All over.'

'What are we going to do with the car?'

'Drive to Riga in Latvia and burn it. Then my sister Munira will bring us to Tallinn. She will enjoy that.'

'Why would we burn a perfectly good car?'

'Those men came to murder us, and I do not want the car to be found in Riga. Seat belt, please.'

'Then you should not stop in Riga. We should go straight to Tallinn. We have to think of the two borders between here and Tallinn.'

'Not a problem. Our car has Latvian registration and I know driver's name. I saw it on registration card.' He started the engine, moved sedately towards the exit and fed the ticket he'd found in the sun-visor clip into the machine. They thought they heard a shout before the barrier rose, but they couldn't be sure because of the noise of the rain. Naji didn't hang around. In the first few seconds of the journey, Anastasia decided she would never let him drive her again. Her phone told her that it was exactly six hundred kilometres to Tallinn. They'd be there by morning if Naji didn't kill them first.

'I like this car,' shouted Naji, 'Audi Q7 has good economy and great driver engagement. Mr Stepurin has good taste.' He winked at her.

'Stepurin!'

'Name on the hotel registration card with car registration. That is why I know we should leave.'

CHAPTER 24

Wet Grass

Ulrike handled the book with a kind of reverence; it was intensely important to her husband and therefore almost sacred to her. She moved through it, brushing its pages with the flat of her hands and smiling. 'It really is a work of art, the way it's laid out and with the references to colour found in nature,' she said. 'Poetic, in its way.'

She let it rest open in her lap and laid her hands on the end papers, then glanced down with a look of enquiry. 'What is this?' she said, picking up the book and examining the endpaper pasted to the back cover. 'Aha! Bobby has left something for us. Can you get me a knife from the kitchen, dear Samson?'

She slipped the knife into the almost invisible slit between the endpaper and the hard cover and retrieved a single sheet of thin marker paper, looked at it and handed it to Samson. 'Here are some more names for you.'

There were another twelve, each of them filed under one of the colours. These were the people working for, or associated with Jonathan Mobius, Erik Kukorin, Chester Abelman and Elliot Jeffreys. Apart from Mobius, none of the four original names or the dozen hidden in the back of the book meant anything to them.

'This is Mila Daus's network,' said Ulrike, taking back the paper. 'And you see Bobby has dated each addition, and the last one was made three months ago, which is when I believe he decided that he had done enough and he was going to concentrate on the show.'

'Let's start at the top,' said Samson, reaching for his computer. 'With Mila Daus.'

There was very little on the Web about her under any of her three married names – Muller, Mobius and Gaspar. A legal dispute with her first husband Muller's children over a $30 million fortune in 1996 was almost expunged, and the lone court document they found was buried with numerous similar references that led to '404 Page Not Found' or 'DNS error' notices. This was Düppel, the chaff that Francis, the young member of the tech team at GreenState, had spoken about. Anyone researching the court case would have given up. It was even a challenge to find the names of Muller's two children, Karen and George, because they too had been more or less airbrushed from the internet. Mila Daus did not exist, and, when they went back to 1989 and accounts of the Stasi, they found nothing that would link her to the programme of mass psychological torture – nothing that would impede the progress in American society of the icy young beauty from the GDR.

'It's going to be tough to prove that this woman is the same person you saw in prison,' said Samson. 'Identification at thirty years' distance won't be accepted.'

'It was for Nazi war criminals,' said Ulrike sharply.

'But we will need ways of connecting her to that past.'

'If she's running a Russian spy ring, which is what Bobby knew this to be, does it really matter if we don't link her to the Stasi?'

'Still, we have to prove the purpose of the network,' said Samson. 'There's nothing in the book to say what these seventeen individuals are actually doing.'

'The proof exists. Bobby had it; Denis had it.'

'And this is what Denis was going to reveal in Congress.'

She frowned, searched frantically for her cigarettes. 'Bobby didn't know about that. I'm sure Denis didn't tell him, and in fact I'm certain that he would have informed Bobby because they worked so closely together. They were very fond of each other, respected each other's life experience.' The packet revealed itself when she shifted on the sofa. She took out a cigarette but did not light it. 'I believe Mila Daus struck early. She knew what was coming and moved to stop it.' Samson sat back and waited. She lit up and inhaled. 'The funeral is a target. There will be security. So many of Bobby's friends and old colleagues are determined to come. The police are going to shut off some streets and they'll have armed guards at the church and the gallery afterwards. Not everyone is invited to the reception – just family and a few trusted friends, but we will need protection.' She gave him an odd look. 'But we have to pay for that. You understand what I'm saying, don't you, Samson?'

'With this?' He waved his hand at the laptops on the table. 'Tomas already mentioned that to me.'

'He phoned after he saw you,' she said. 'He knew you were hiding something, so they made the security conditional on receiving what we have. I had to say yes.'

'Do you know what Naji and Zoe and the others found out about Daus's networks?'

'No.'

'So, you give KaPo what you know and leave it at that.'

She nodded, and they moved on to the only other name they recognised – Jonathan Mobius. Mobius was forty-seven, a multimillionaire who had sold his communications and PR company but remained on the board and was the chair of GreenState. He was the son of Arthur Mobius, whom Mila Daus had married in late 1996, a few months after the court case with the Muller family was concluded and her fortune assured. Arthur Mobius was also rich, and he died in circumstances that were never fully explained. Samson looked up the week of his death in the local newspaper in New York state, the *Wyoming County Star*, and found that the paper's archive wasn't digitised. But each edition of the newspaper had been photographed and, with the help of a magnification tool, you could read the entire paper. The headline at the top of page three of the old-time broadsheet from Thursday 7 October 1999 read 'Notable Businessman Dies in Power Line Tragedy'. Below this was a picture of Arthur Mobius on his wedding day, a solid man – comb-over, late fifties – with his bride in sunglasses lightly hanging on his arm. She wore high heels and a cream two-piece suit. It showed her figure to good effect – she was still trim for her early forties. In the background were a party of stout, beaming relatives and to Arthur's left was his only child, Jonathan, who seemed somehow detached from the occasion.

Samson read the first paragraphs of the story. "'Mystery surrounds the death of computer pioneer and benefactor Arthur Mobius II, aged 62, after his body was found lying near a live power line at Allan's Farm Estate, near Silver Lake.

"'Mr Mobius, a mathematician and inventor of early software for hand-held organisers, was found near a group of beehives, where a power line came down. One theory is that Mr Mobius, a lifelong beekeeper, was trying to remove the line from the beehives, one of which was burnt out. However, power-company engineers said that the hive might have caught light after Mr Mobius had been electrocuted. They believe the line was hidden in wet grass and Mr Mobius likely did not see it and stumbled on it. He is thought to have died instantly.

"'The Wyoming County Sheriff's Department and the Fire Department attended the scene. Investigation is now underway to determine how the power line, which was part of the property's internal power arrangements, not the distribution grid, came down. Early examination of the line indicates that it may have been cut.

"'Mr Mobius's widow, Mila, who is a director of his company, A. J. Mobius Data, was away on business at the time of the accident. The Sheriff's Department interviewed Jonathan Mobius, 27, his heir, who is also a director of his late father's company, at Allan's Farm. Mr Mobius discovered his father's body late Tuesday evening and is said to be in a state of shock.'"

Samson looked up. 'So they arranged his death.'

Ulrike nodded and leaned over to look at the photograph. 'She seduces the young man then they decide to get rid of Arthur when she's away and so speed up the business of inheriting. I wonder if she slept with him before the wedding.' She raised her reading glasses from the end of her nose to her forehead and Samson momentarily saw the grief in her eyes. 'What did she want? She was already wealthy, and we can assume she would have inherited anyway. It wasn't for love, because she later married someone else.'

'Data,' said Samson. He had skimmed the next few lines. 'Listen to this. "In recent years, Arthur Mobius's fortune increased manyfold because of the success of Mobius Data Strip, a program designed to collect consumers' data from instalment plans, and in the mortgage and insurance industries. Mr Mobius devised algorithms for the analysis of that data." That's the motive – she wanted those algorithms, and fast.'

He bookmarked the story and started searching references for A. J. Mobius Data in the first years of the new century. The company was privately owned by Jonathan Mobius, Arthur's sister, Lilli, and Mila Daus, and little had been written about it. But profits were obviously large and, under joint CEOs Mila Daus and Jonathan, the AJM data expanded rapidly, picking up casualties of the dotcom crash that had owned valuable intellectual property. There were interviews in *New York* magazine and *Forbes* with Jonathan, who presented as the understated wunderkind of consumer data, but his father's widow was never mentioned. It was if she was the sleeping partner, whereas in fact she was building her own empire, based on the use of Arthur Mobius's programs, presumably leased at a favourable rate from the company she part-owned with the Mobius family.

Over the next half-hour, Samson used the skills he'd acquired as a banker to unearth a number of acquisitions made by a new entity, a company owned wholly by Mila Daus. Using the lustre of her second husband's name, she called it Mobius Pioneer Investment and purchased advertising and communications companies and software outfits, invested in financial apps and start-up internet banks. Samson assumed she had used Wall Street banks to finance the company's investments, some of which ran into hundreds of millions, but it was hard to tell which she was working with. There were few clues. A theme began to emerge. Besides the core business of acquiring, processing and selling data, another entity – MMM Data and Research – invested in environmental start-ups and those with adventurous R&D projects, particularly Low-earth Orbit satellite communications.

He had the sense that he was scraping the surface with her; that the level of activity and the number of acquisitions indicated a business acumen and wealth much greater than he thought possible for a woman who had arrived in the States with no money and no contacts. She had achieved many remarkable things, not the least of which was being both present and powerful in American society at the same time as leaving little trace, a most desirable state for an intelligence officer. There were very few words on Mila Daus, and no photographs, save the two that Samson had found published with the account of Arthur Mobius's death. She was spectral – the Ghost from the East.

While he worked, Ulrike got up and drifted around, distracted and muttering to herself. He suggested that he go back to the hotel and allow her to get some rest before the funeral, which was only a few hours away, but she shook her head and said, 'It helps, you being here. I'd like you to stay in the spare room.'

'That's fine,' he said.

'What did you find out about her?'

He closed the laptop. 'She's way too powerful to be seen as simply a Russian intelligence asset; a partner, more like. She's formidable, resourceful, deadly, brilliant and very rich – easily a billionaire by now.' He paused. 'All through his troubles, Denis sensed there was an unseen hand. It was Mila Daus. She's been working against him since he invested in one of her companies, TangKi, which was fronted by Adam Crane. It was her money that Crane was channelling to far-right groups in Europe. He stole from her and from the others unwise enough to invest in TangKi, but it was her scheme. And, of course, it was ultimately Mila Daus who organised the kidnap of Anastasia. Denis and Bobby knew all this, and they were going to reveal it, but I don't believe they were ready. And all these other names – did you have any luck working out who they were?'

She moved towards the conservatory door, clutching her cigarettes and lighter to her chest. 'The young people know all about it. They're coming to the funeral, so you can talk to them. You are now in charge of this, Samson. Anastasia has the money, but it must be you who decides what happens to all this information. Bobby would want that.' She leaned heavily against the door frame. 'Just before he was killed he told me that Daus used some of the old tricks the Stasi used.' She looked down. Her shoulders heaved and she let out a groan of anguish. Samson got up and went to her and held her. She sobbed silently for several minutes, shuddering with grief. At length she pulled free and dabbed her eyes with a cuff of her shirt. 'I haven't been able to do that before now. Sorry. Thank you. I am so sorry.' She looked away until he raised her head then shot him a fierce look. 'You get that bitch, Samson.'

'I'll do everything I can,' he said. He waited a few seconds. 'You were about to say something about old tricks.'

'She used blackmail in the same way the Stasi used it to get foreigners to work for them in the old days. It was usually about sex, or fraud – people's vices. She trapped people and forced them to help her. Bobby mentioned one man – a very well-known person in the United States, who had sex with an under-age girl. Mila set him up and he had to do what she asked when she confronted him with evidence.'

At that moment Samson's phone vibrated with a series of messages that had accumulated when he was sitting with Ulrike in the conservatory. One was from Macy and four were from Anastasia. He noticed half a dozen 'missed call' notifications. They'd been over a period of two hours. The first message read: 'Naji saw Stepurin's name at Vilnius airport hotel. Using his legit passport! We stole Stepurin's car! Call me!'

The second text read: 'Crossed Latvian border. We're near Bauska. Heading for Riga then Tallinn. We need help with border. Car has Estonian plates but Naji not registered owner. Does that matter?'

Third text: 'We've been followed since we stopped for fuel. Call me! What do we do?'

There was a fourth message, but it consisted only of random letters.

He dialled Anastasia's number on one phone and texted Tomas on another with the words: 'You up?'

When Anastasia answered, he said, 'Where are you? Are you still being followed?'

She consulted Naji. 'On the road to Riga. We got past the Latvian border on Naji's passport. He knows what to do at borders! Can't see anyone following, but we are going very fast.' Samson heard Naji's voice: 'Very slow. Just one ninety!'

His other phone sounded. 'Okay, I'll call you back.' He picked it up. 'Hi, Tomas, I need your help to get a couple of people you know over the Latvia–Estonia border tonight.'

Tomas took his time to respond. 'You are asking me for help to bring people into our country without delay. Who?'

'Anastasia and Naji. They're in a car belonging to Stepurin. They stole it.'

'So what are you giving us in return?'

'As much as Ulrike knows.'

Tomas didn't fall for that. 'I'd prefer to know what you know, Samson.'

'I'll tell you all I know, and that's not a lot.'

Tomas let out a laugh. 'What you know now is a fraction of what there is to know. What about the things you learn about in the next few hours and days? Will you give us access to those?'

'We can discuss it.'

'I believe that is a yes.'

Samson said, 'Yes.'

'Your friends need to go to Valka on the border. They are probably on the A1, so they will have to go across country to the A3. That will take them longer. I will need you to provide the registration of the car. When they get to the border, they will leave the car in Latvia and cross on foot. At the border they need to say, "Mr Sikula is expecting us." I'll need a phone number for them and they must share their location with me on WhatsApp. I'll see you tomorrow morning for the debriefing that you promise now. We have an agreement, Samson. That is good.'

Samson phoned Anastasia and gave her the instructions. For good measure, he asked her to share her location with him also – he needed to know how close they were to the rendezvous. He heard her relaying all this to Naji and telling him to slow down. 'He says we will be there in one and a half hours.'

He conveyed the information to Tomas then started watching the app for their location. A pulsing blue circle appeared near a town called Limbazi. He could see they were heading directly east and would hit the A3 at Valmeira. It occurred to him that if he was tracking Anastasia with such ease, it was very likely that Stepurin either had access to one of their phones or had a tracker fitted to the car he was using. He sent a message to Tomas. 'Can you give them cover before they reach the border?' Immediately the reply came.

'Not easy with this notice, but I will see what we can do.'

CHAPTER 25

Zoe

Speed was the only thing that separated them from the two cars that were, at most, only ten minutes behind them. That, and an unpredictable route which took them first north towards the border then east. They passed through shuttered parishes and municipalities whose names flashed into Anastasia's consciousness – Naukšēni, Kārķi, Vēveri, Ērģeme – and tore along dead-straight roads, the scent of forests and fields in springtime coming from the Audi's ventilation. Naji didn't talk, which was a blessing. She wanted him to concentrate. His driving terrified her, but she had quite given up trying to get him to slow down. She kept her eyes on her screen, knowing that Estonian intelligence and Samson were watching their progress. But, as Naji reminded her, that very same phone was likely to be revealing their position to the two cars in pursuit. It was almost certainly her phone that had led them to the farm in Macedonia, and, he added, the reason they were now running from Russian hit men. He also observed that a tracker might be fitted to a valuable car like this Audi Q7. They debated swapping to Naji's phone, but he said there were very good reasons not to give his number to KaPo, so they kept using hers.

They reached a string of small, darkened houses spread over about half a kilometre, a place that had neither name nor street lighting. About three hundred metres beyond the point where the houses petered out, there was a truck stop tucked into the woods, visible because of the neon light proclaiming the name Valdis Bar. They shot past it, then Naji abruptly pulled up and began to reverse. 'Turn your phone off, please,' he said. 'It is better for us.'

'What are you doing?'

'Wait for some minutes,' he said. He drove up to the building. Cars and a few small trucks were parked randomly at the front. Music and swirling lights came from inside. They could have been in Tennessee, she thought. Naji jumped out and went inside. Anastasia undid her seat belt and followed. But before she reached the door Naji backed out, propelled by a jabbing finger that belonged to a large man in braces and a leather cap. Naji put his hands up in surrender and started speaking rapidly in a mixture of Latvian and English, with a few German words thrown in. '*Das ist ein russisches Auto,*' he kept insisting. The man stopped and looked over to the Audi. 'You can have the car and this lady will give you €1,000,' said Naji, selling the deal with all the skill of his youth in Syria behind a cart full of second-hand trainers.

The man asked, '*Woher hast du das auto?*' Where did you get the car?

'*Wir haben es den russischen Gangstern gestohlen,*' said Naji with an enormous grin. We took it from Russian crooks. He added: 'We need to borrow another car to go to Valka.' Then he corrected himself. 'Rent a car from you, mein Herr.'

The negotiation went on for five minutes. The man began to find Naji quite the comedian and presently Anastasia handed over all the cash in her wallet — €1,300 — in exchange for the keys of an old green Passat. They were given the instruction to leave the car at the Alko 1000 market near the border post and place the key in the gap behind the rear bumper. Naji checked the petrol, kicked the tyres and got into the driving seat.

She shook her head. 'You need a rest. I will drive now, for the simple reason that I rented the car, and this gentleman doesn't want a lunatic behind the wheel.'

He rolled from the seat. 'Phone – have you turned off?'

She nodded.

About five kilometres along the road they saw two sets of lights close together, speeding towards them. 'I thought they were following us,' she said. 'They wouldn't be coming from the other direction, surely.'

'Headlights are different. Other people come from Russia. We are not so far from Russia.' Not far over that border, she thought, was the dismal forest where she had been held and tormented by the man calling himself Kirill. She found herself smiling at the memory of the preposterous little sadist in his hunting outfit.

They agreed it was best for them to get off the road. They took a forest track that led to a clearing where three trailers loaded with stripped tree trunks were parked. She steered behind one of the trailers so the Passat was hidden but she could still see the end of the track. She switched off the lights and reached for a bottle of water in the side pocket of her bag. Naji sank into his seat and rested his knees on the dashboard. He dozed, but she couldn't sleep and watched vehicles flash past the turning in both directions more times than she could count.

Samson saw that the pulsing circle had stopped moving and texted, 'Okay?' but got no reply. He wasn't going to start worrying yet. They would need to rest up.

Ulrike was looking at him absently. She was about to say something, but her head snapped up. '*Verdammt!* That's the garden door. I told them to stay away!' She moved to the conservatory and called out softly into the dark. A man's voice answered her. '*Mama, ich bin es – Rudi.*'

She shook her head and waited. Rudi came in first and kissed his mother on both cheeks. A few seconds later, in came Zoe Freemantle.

She took in Samson, nodded to him and moved into the centre of the conservatory.

'So, we meet properly at last – Zoe Harland. I owe you an apology, Mr Samson.'

'Harland?'

'Robert Harland was my dad. My mother's name was Freemantle. Didn't Ulrike tell you?'

'I was about to,' she said. 'I didn't expect you to come here. We had discussed that you were going to stay in the apartment for safety.' She looked at her son. 'Rudi, why did you come?'

He returned a rather hopeless look and said something in German that Samson didn't catch, but he saw the apology in his eyes. His mother nodded and turned to Zoe. 'You'd better explain everything.'

'Please do,' said Samson coolly, and sat down at a table, as it happened in the old Windsor-back chair that Harland had said was the only thing he'd kept from his life in Britain. But that turned out to be untrue. He had his spy mother's cookbook as well as an English daughter, one that he'd been hired to babysit.

'Are we smoking inside?' asked Zoe. 'Would you mind if I . . .?' Ulrike handed her the ashtray and her cigarettes.

She lit up, inhaled and smiled at Rudi, who was returning with beer from the kitchen. 'My father had an affair with a woman named Gillian, my mum. That was in 1990, when she was at the British embassy in Berlin. It was, shall we say, a very brief encounter. A fling. My mum was a career diplomat and she didn't want to marry him, but they pretended for a while so she could keep her job and her baby – me. I think they may even have lied about getting married.'

Ulrike nodded.

'Yes, they did lie, but who was to say otherwise? And after my birth, they went their separate ways and my mum was transferred to the embassy in Washington. She was talented, and they didn't want to lose her, and I guess my dad put in enough appearances to make everyone feel comfortable. My mother married a man called Billy Freemantle and everything worked out. Dad paid for all my education and, when I was eighteen, we started meeting up and, later, he helped me with some problems.' She glanced at Ulrike. 'Like my mother, I'm an addict. I still smoke and drink, but I don't do heroin.'

'But you use cannabis,' said Samson. 'I was out at the cabin earlier.'

'Oh, okay,' she said, unfazed. 'I think that was yours, Rudi.' She gave him a soft punch to his arm. 'I grew up in DC and New York, but mostly in Paris, where my mother and stepfather decided to live. He was an oil engineer with his own company. Retired early and devoted the rest of their lives to French society and getting plastered. They were socially grand, if you know what I mean, and had loads of money. They both died early. My mother's heart stopped when she was in the ocean at Biarritz in August and Billy had followed by that Christmas. I was at university in Paris at the time, and it's fair to say things got a little out of hand. But, hey, I completed my course, came top of the year and started a postgrad in experimental math. By that time I was using, and was screwing up in every way possible. But I got my masters. A couple of years later, Dad picked me up, got me into rehab and kept me kind of on the straight and narrow. That took two years, and he paid for it all because I'd been through all the money my mother left me. All of it!' She looked at Ulrike. 'Have I left anything out? Oh yes, my name is actually Zoe Harland, though I didn't tell my father about the change. And Rudi and I are an item. We've worked on my father's project for about eighteen months now, together with your Syrian friend and many others. I have the necessary skills, but Naji is at the superhuman level.'

Ulrike turned away and shook her head.

'And, as you can see, Ulrike doesn't approve. I guess it seems kind of incestuous that her stepdaughter is with her son. And she isn't happy about my past.' Neither Ulrike nor Rudi reacted. 'That's about everything,' she said, with a small concluding bow.

'And the apology?' said Samson.

'I told them at GreenState that you were stalking me, and I made out you were kind of a lech. Sorry. I know you had my back and that wasn't your kind of work, but I didn't know who you were until my father's friend Macy told me.'

Ulrike said, 'I must now try to sleep.' She moved to Samson and took his hand. 'Thank you for coming, and thank you for being the person you are. Your room, if you need it, is right at the top of the stairs. And if you're all going to talk all night, you need to do it quietly because I can hear everything in our bedroom.'

Samson tapped his screen. There was no movement.

'Are you watching Naji?' asked Zoe, getting up to try to see his screen. 'Is that what the call was about when we came in?'

He lowered the phone. 'No need to worry about that now. Shall we sit in the conservatory?'

'So you're the boss now?' she said, collapsing into the sofa next to Rudi and hooking a leg across his thigh. He thought she was a little drunk.

'Yes, and I need to know everything that you know – I mean, everything.' Samson took in Rudi Rosenharte, whom he'd fleetingly met in Berlin with Bobby and Ulrike. He was very tall and had a slightly Slavic cast to a face that was open and engaged. Willingness shone from his eyes, and sensitivity too. Where Rudi had bearing, Zoe was, despite her good looks, ill at ease and defensive in manner. He had noticed that part of her at GreenState, but he had imagined that she'd be more self-assured in conversation. They were a strikingly handsome couple.

'So is this it?' she said, picking up the *Nomenclature of Colours*. 'Is this the mother lode then? Did you find it out at the cabin? We thought something might be there. Can I look?'

Samson moved forward. 'I'll take that for the moment,' he said.

'It's got everything?'

Instead of answering her, he said, 'Let's start at the beginning. What was your role at GreenState? I assume you were investigating Jonathan Mobius, but had little knowledge of the other strands of your father's inquiry into Mila Daus, the person he had seen in Berlin and Mobius's stepmother.'

'And lover.' She unhooked her leg. 'You have to understand that for a long time we were looking for a way in. My father realised that we needed an entry point and that had to be GreenState, which of course is a front.'

'For gathering data?'

'Sure – Mila's a data junkie, but what's important about GreenState is that it's like a hidden dimension and she moves in it without anyone knowing she's there. And it's structured so that all these harmless souls beavering away to save the planet have no clue about what's really going on. You saw them! I mean, they're kind of pathetic. And, by the way, when you did your little searches about the company they picked that up straight away and it was a real help because, right then, just before my father was murdered, I thought they might be on to me. So you drew some fire there, which was great. I realise now that in those last few weeks my father understood that they would be getting close. That's why they put you in there, and I'm grateful for that, and to you because I know they twice tried to kill you. So, yeah, you have my thanks, Mr Samson.'

'Part of the service,' said Samson. 'What precisely were you doing?'

Rudi suddenly got up and announced, '*Ich bin echt müde.*' He was going to bed.

'Oh, okay. You want to sleep here. I'll see you in a bit.' She watched him go. 'He's beautiful, isn't he?' she said when they heard him on the stairs. 'We have a lot in common, and now it turns out both our fathers were killed by Mila Daus and her associates. Dad always said he thought she was ultimately behind the death of Rudi's father.'

'At GreenState, what were you doing?' repeated Samson.

'We needed to access Jonathan Mobius's communications and follow the trail to Mila Daus, as well as work out the relationship between different entities in her empire and, in some cases, prove ownership, or control. She's like a fucking mobster. She's into everything, and her influence goes way beyond her companies and GreenState. And yet there's no trace of

her. You've tried looking her up on the internet, right, and you found
that she doesn't really exist out there?'

'How did you obtain that access?'

'Firstly, I had to get a job in GreenState, which is easy enough, but we
had to put a lot of work into Ingrid Cole and eliminate from the Web as
much as we could of my wild years. There are people who can do this for
you. Denis paid for it. I had to win their trust at GreenState, which wasn't
that hard. I'd done some advertising work and I'm pretty good at data analytics. Eventually, we placed spyware on Mobius's devices and in the Green-
State server, all designed by Naji and Rudi. Then we just had to wait and
collect the information. Jonathan Mobius is really security conscious and
he's always fucking travelling, so that took the best part of nine months.'

'You accessed his phone and computers?'

'Yes, he has a vulnerability.'

'Meaning?'

'A weakness for chicks, plus he's a real bastard, which means he uses
them then drops them. Likes S&M, too. Likes to hurt people.'

'So you dated him?'

'Jesus, no! We fixed him up. We put someone in his way that could really
take care of herself and she slept with him and she got inside his phone.
She's a friend of Rudi's. So, once we got access, my work at GreenState was
to download as much as I could from inside the organisation, because they
had good firewalls and it was just a bit simpler from inside the building. But
we had to go gently, and of course I had my bloody job to do.'

'Had you completed the work when your father was killed?' Samson
asked quietly.

'Not quite – there was a lot of checking and assimilation to do.'

Samson thought for a few moments. 'So, the belief that Denis Hisami
had material in his briefcase that he was preparing to reveal must be wrong.'

'I don't know. Mr Hisami and Dad were making those decisions.' She
looked down and started stroking her knee nervously. 'I really loved my
father, you know. Maybe the only person I've actually loved in my life,

though Rudi comes close.' She stopped. 'He told me he was going to die. That's what made it so hard being in London. But I had to see it through for him. It meant a lot that he trusted me with it.'

'He knew you'd got what it takes.' He stopped. 'Your tradecraft is pretty good, Zoe.'

'Gave you the runaround, did I?' She smiled for the first time, and Samson began to like her.

'You did.'

'If Rudi hadn't been in London, I couldn't have done it.' She stopped, and their eyes met. 'We went to the cabin because we both wanted to be where Dad lived his last months. He was murdered there, but that wasn't the point. You probably know that Rudi treated him as his father and loved him, too. We wanted to feel his presence, see the light he painted, that kind of thing. You understand?'

'I do. What did you burn out there? I saw ashes in the fire.'

'Notes that Rudi kept from London. Nothing important.'

'Ah! What about the structure of this operation? How did it work?'

'There were four teams: Pearl, Pitch, Aurora and Saffron. Dad mimicked the cell structure that Mila had in place. Then there was Berlin Blue, which was run by Mr Hisami and Dad, because that was the apex. The reason we were all there.'

Samson pulled his laptop towards him and read out, 'Jonathan Mobius, Erik Kukorin, Chester Abelman and Elliot Jeffreys.'

'So, it is all in the book,' she said.

'Yep. And each of these men was running agents or people who'd been compromised by Mila Daus,' he said, and handed her the piece of paper. 'Ulrike just discovered this in your father's book.'

She took it and ran her eyes down the names. 'Yes, these people. But there are more, some we have only just found out about. I see the Special Adviser in Number Ten is here.'

'In Number Ten!'

'Yeah, Anthony Drax. Totally Mila's man.'

'That explains a lot. Did your father think that MI6 knew about Drax? The name meant nothing to me.'

'Yes, my father thought MI6 had their suspicions. The last time I saw him he was wondering whether to tip them off, but then the whole operation would have been blown, and he had no love for his former employer. There are bigger fish in the States. They have someone who works for the Director of Intelligence and a senior person in the National Security Council. Naji knows everything. We'd better pray he gets here. Now, can I look at the book?'

At first light Anastasia got out for a pee. The ground was wet with dew. There was a red stripe of rising sun beyond the trees and a remarkably loud dawn chorus. She returned to the car. Naji was awake and staring up at the sky through the windshield.

'Shall we go?' She handed him the water bottle. 'You okay?'

He nodded. 'I need to do what you just did.'

'Sure. It's four thirty. We can make it in an hour or so and then we just walk over the border.'

He shambled out and stood listening to the birds for a moment before urinating against the wheel of one of the nearest trailers. Why do men always do that? she asked herself.

He returned to the car, got in and slammed the door.

'Something wrong?'

He didn't reply.

'Naj, what is it?'

'We are going to a funeral of a good man. I liked Mr Harland. A lot! We talked like with my father.'

How could she be so blind? Of course, Harland was a substitute for the father he'd lost before he set off on his journey into Europe in 2015. 'Yes, I saw you together. I know you're going to miss him badly.'

He nodded. 'I miss Ifkar, too. Sometimes we go out into the forests and listen to the birds like this. "The birds are the friends of the stars." That is what Ifkar says. It is sentimental, but I like it.' He turned to her. 'I like Ifkar very much.' What was in his eyes was love, not mere affection. She said nothing but held his gaze. He nodded. 'Yes, Anastasia, in *that* way. And he likes me like *that* way. Is this wrong?'

'Of course not.' She kissed his brow and stroked his hair. 'Wherever a person finds love, that's good.'

'But it is bad. Ifkar thinks it may be bad.'

'Of course it isn't — it's how you both are. It's the most natural thing in the world.'

'Like you and Samson?'

She banged her hands on the wheel. 'Do you mind if we don't go there? I mean, it's, well . . . it's very awkward.' She started the engine. 'And I do love my husband. He's a courageous man.' She stopped and shook her head with frustration. 'Let's go. We have to crash that border.'

'Want me to drive?'

'No.'

She drove faster than she had the night before. Naji sat with his knees up, murmuring to himself in Arabic and English. They met no other vehicles on the way, which made them feel conspicuous. On the outskirts of Valga, he straightened and looked up Alko 1000 on his phone. 'There are two and they are both near to border,' he said, and showed her the map on the phone.

They decided on the one in the centre of town, a supermarket surrounded by a large car park about two kilometres away. Naji retrieved her phone from his backpack and waited for the network to show at the top of the screen.

Valga was a dreary place with waste ground between the houses. There was little sign of life at that hour, although they saw one or two pickups and tractors loaded with produce heading in the same direction as they were. They went slowly, feeling their way to the supermarket. Naji spotted a coffee stand on one of the deserted cross streets. It was open and serving labourers and farm workers who had parked their vehicles chaotically around the cabin. He suggested they grab something while they waited for her phone to begin sending their location. She still had no signal. 'We need to speak to them before we move,' he said.

She reluctantly agreed, and he hopped out at the stand and bought coffee and sweet pastries. The early workers in a gaggle around the cabin window immediately parted, believing, perhaps, that a young Arab in their town meant some sort of trouble. He returned, grinning, with two coffees and a pastry for himself and handed her a cup. Back in his seat, he unstuck the pastry from its paper wrap and looked over at her phone: it still had no reception. 'Turn it off then turn on again,' he suggested, with his mouth full.

'I hate waiting here,' she said, putting her takeaway cup into one of the holders. 'Shall we just get to the supermarket and leave the car? I'd feel happier.' She started the engine, but Naji insisted on finishing his coffee before they moved off, so she did, too.

They reached the supermarket – a long, low building, almost certainly a converted cinema – and circled the block before rolling into the south side of a car park where a man was loading flattened cardboard boxes on to a trolley. He stopped and looked up with interest, then away to the far side of the car park, where there were about half a dozen vehicles. Now messages began flooding into her phone. A glance told her they were from Samson and all more or less said the same thing. KaPo had intercepted phone calls and texts that suggested three separate teams were looking for them. They knew the model, colour and registration of the car and they were aware of the arrangement to leave it at the supermarket. Her only thought, as she slammed the car into reverse, was that the Russian teams may have staked out the larger Alko 1000 to the north of the town on the A3, because maybe that was where they had been meant to leave the Passat.

Naji had the map on his phone. 'Go right!' he shouted.

She dropped her phone in her lap and accelerated away, just as a silver saloon appeared in her mirror. At least one member of the Russian team

had been waiting in the car park. They had no distance to go, but the
pursuing car was already hard on their tail, trying to nudge the rear of the
Passat so as to send it out of control on one of the grassy areas on either
side. She anticipated the manoeuvre and braked sharply, letting a Mazda
with two men inside – the passenger on a phone – shoot ahead of them.
'Where do I go? Which way?' she shouted.

'Left at the end.'

She took off across the grass, causing the Passat to leap into the air
when its wheels met a hidden bump. Yet this didn't stop them, and she
was able to cross the rough ground and rejoin the road before a row of
lime trees. Now the street was more confined, with buildings on both
sides. Another car, a black Mercedes SUV with alloy wheels and darkened glass, appeared from their right and aimed straight for them. She
swerved and steered round the back of the SUV. Naji let out a whoop
of admiration.

'Doesn't feel like there's a border near here!' she shouted.

They reached a group of one-storey Communist-era apartment blocks.
Naji shouted 'Left! Left! Left!' But a third vehicle was heading towards
them from the right and she lost concentration for a split second, hitting
the kerb and causing the front near-side tyre to burst with a loud pop.
But they had momentum still, and there, not a hundred metres away, was
a gull-wing canopy straddling the road and a lowered barrier. She put
her foot down. The tyre made a rumbling noise, but she reached a good
speed. They flashed past three low white brick buildings from which men
issued, some with guns, all of them running towards the border post. On
the Latvian side of this normally sleepy crossing they knew nothing of
what was occurring, however the menace of the three cars in pursuit and
the distress of their quarry were plain and they raised their guns. The barrier was two seconds away. Suddenly it rose and the Passat sailed through
and came to a halt a few metres on. It was immediately surrounded by
men with guns pointing, not at Naji and Anastasia, but across the border
to the cars that had pulled up in a line about twenty metres away, all of

which was to the astonishment of an elderly tractor driver in a straw hat who had just crossed over from Estonia with a ram tethered to the front bar of his trailer.

Anastasia rested her forehead on the wheel and took deep breaths. Naji rubbed her shoulder. 'That is last time I am your passenger,' he said, echoing her complaint of the evening before. 'Here, you have missed calls.' He handed her the phone.

Samson had phoned. She called him back. 'We're through,' she said.

'I'm relieved. Tomas Sikula is there to meet you.' He paused. 'You'll need rest before the funeral. Conversation may not be such a good idea.'

'Of course,' she said. She understood exactly what he was saying.

The second call was from Dr James Carrew. He'd just sent a text. 'Emergency surgery in progress to correct heart irregularity. Situation became critical – we had to move quickly.'

She rang him, but got his message service, and there was no assistant at his office number.

CHAPTER 26

Funeral in Tallinn

Samson arrived at the headquarters of Kaitsepolitseiamet promptly at 10.30 a.m., an appointment that allowed Tomas Sikula time to travel by helicopter from the border with Anastasia and Naji, change and shower before arriving at the offices just outside Tallinn's old town. It was typical of Sikula to look as fresh as the morning dew after a sleepless night and also to choose not to mention the incident at the border, but that was because he'd probably drawn a blank with Naji and Anastasia, neither of whom Samson had seen. They were already resting at the Harlands' little green house, filling it to capacity. Naji, he had gathered from Anastasia's text, was more interested in the helicopter than anything Sikula had to say.

Samson was already in a suit and tie and clutching a bag with the sketchbook and Harland's last painting, which KaPo's director, Aaro Sollen, said he would very much like to see. Samson drew it out of the bag and rested it against the wall on a glass table in the conference room. They said nothing. The beauty of the study of a burst of light far out to sea overwhelmed the significance of the bullet hole at the bottom of the canvas, and that is the way Harland would have wanted it. It was his last painting – that was all – and it was magnificent. Samson told them it would be framed and placed in the exhibition for the opening later that day.

They sat down. 'There are formal requests from the British government for your arrest,' said Sollen. 'But since we are talking to a citizen of Hungary named Norbert Soltesz, I don't think we have to pay much attention to that.'

'They're behind events,' said Samson. 'Whatever happens will happen without the British government having the slightest influence.'

Sollen nodded.

'What *is* going to happen?' asked Tomas.

'I cannot say. Denis Hisami owns this information, but he's just had an emergency heart operation. I'm here to look after the interests of Harland's widow and Mr Hisami's wife. They should have increased security over the next forty-eight hours and, obviously, Ulrike needs looking after long term.'

'They will have everything they need. That part of town will be in lockdown. No one will get near the church or the gallery. Our President will be attending, so there would be security in any case, but we guarantee the safety of each one of you while you are in Estonia and, of course, we have Ulrike's best interests at heart. Is that satisfactory?'

Samson pulled out the *Nomenclature of Colours*. 'This is what Robert Harland gave his life for. There are seventeen names here, and each one is working for Mila Daus, a Russian asset who started her career in the Stasi and has since become a very powerful figure in the United States.' Sollen allowed a puzzled look momentarily to cross his face. 'It's unlikely that you've heard of her. But she's responsible for the kidnap of Anastasia Hisami nearly three years ago, the support of numerous far-right, racist organisations, the death of Robert Harland, the use of nerve agents in Congress and countless other deaths, which include all the suspects on the initial team of hit men.'

Tomas reached for the book. Samson placed his hand on it. 'All in good time. Happy to give you a copy of the relevant pages and the list we found at the back, but that's on the condition that you take no action and don't use the information in a way that will damage outcomes in the United States and United Kingdom. We – I – need to have a free hand.'

Sollen placed his fingertips together and looked out of the window. 'We thank you for this information, but let me ask you how you are going to prove this woman is a Russian asset, and that all the people associated with her are, in effect, working for the Russians? You have her name and an allegation. You have other names. What ties her to all these crimes? What ties them to her?'

'That's why I need a free hand.'

'You need to work quickly, and we will not stand in your way, or pre-empt actions. However, I want us to be informed of your findings as you proceed, the proof that you assemble. We may be able to fill in the gaps for you.'

Samson agreed that there would be contact between him and Tomas.

Sollen was silent for a minute before saying, 'And your troubles in the United Kingdom you ascribe to Mr Harland's Book of Revelations, which you have there. Who does he name in the UK?'

'Jonathan Mobius, a powerful American-born resident, and Anthony Drax, the Prime Minister's chief adviser. Those two we know about. There will be more.'

'The Prime Minister's adviser! That is really something. But, then, Russia has successfully targeted your country for many years, and the political establishment seems content with the interference because they believe it helps them.' He opened his hands incredulously.

'We live in strange times. But we're at the beginning of this. We have a long way to go.'

'No, Mr Samson, you're at the end. You either win or you lose in the next few days and, frankly, I cannot see how you win.'

The spies of Europe gathered at St Olaf's Baptist Church to celebrate Robert Harland's life. One of the outstanding intelligence officers of the post-war era had been assassinated in what were certainly the last few weeks of his life. The manner of his death made a difference, never mind the conviction in the judgement of most of those attending – whether they knew the details or not – that he had been killed in the course of his last great operation. That was somehow a given, even though it was well appreciated that he had been gunned down while painting.

A bell tolled from the tower of St Olaf's, once used by the KGB as a radio mast and observation platform during the Cold War. The streets were sealed off to allow cars to arrive at the door and deposit men and women who would rather not be gawped at. A lovely light, filtered by the lime trees in the churchyard, filled the entrance, where – unusually – the widow greeted each mourner. If there was a person she didn't know, the young officers from the Kaitsepolitseiamet checked an iPad, asked polite but firm questions and led them to a place in the church. Only one was rejected, and this turned out to be a German journalist.

Samson watched from a little way off. He'd got there early and was waiting for Naji and Anastasia. It would be the first time he had met her in over two years, but this wasn't on his mind. He wanted to see who was attending the funeral. Among the earliest to arrive, in search of a good place in the church, no doubt, were the British contingent – Peter Nyman, Lewis Ott and a young stiff from the Foreign Office. The youthful British ambassador came a little later in his own car, and he was followed by what Samson assumed were various members of the European intelligence services, though he recognised only one – a member of the DGSE, the French Director-General for External Security, whom he had come across in Macedonia. Then there were the old lags – Macy Harp, the Bird and several men in their seventies who Samson had learned from Ulrike had gathered in a hotel the night before to talk about old times, a reunion for the Cold War warriors that included former agents from Hungary, Czechoslovakia, East Germany and Poland. For the funeral, Macy was wearing a straw hat, as though attending the races; the Bird had a baseball cap that had faded from red to pink, which he doffed on seeing Ulrike before planting a kiss on both her cheeks. There were a handful of Estonian friends, who all knew each other, the couple from the art gallery, whom Samson had just met, and then Zoe and Rudi, dressed entirely in black to mourn the man they both regarded as their father. Zoe held her head up high and looked ahead. Rudi hugged his mother, who then placed a hand against his cheek as he stepped away into the shadows of the entrance.

There was one surprise, and that was Frank Toombs, who never knew Robert Harland, but who'd made an impression on Ulrike and was invited nonetheless. He wore dark glasses and a blue suit and was accompanied by one of the young Agency men Samson had seen in the anonymous building close to the American embassy in London. Samson began to think that Toombs must be more senior than he'd first imagined, and it was significant that Ulrike had invited him – possibly a signal to the British, for whom she had no love.

He moved closer to the church as police began to prepare for the arrival of the President.

'Still lurking, Samson?' came a voice from behind him. He turned to find Anastasia and Naji a few metres away. She approached and kissed him on both cheeks, stepped back with a radiant smile. 'It's good to see you, Samson. I thought we'd never get here, with Naji's driving.'

'We are here because of Naji's driving,' Naji said.

Samson smiled, and something moved in him, despite his very keen desire to remain as cool as possible. It was something like being reunited with his family, and Anastasia looked so utterly beautiful in the spring sunshine. A new line or two on her brow and at the corners of her mouth, but the strain he had noticed on the live stream from Congress was, surprisingly, not present.

'Hi, Naj,' he said, putting a hand on his shoulder. 'So good to see you both here. Thank you for bringing Anastasia safely.'

Anastasia was beaming. 'Shall we go in?' she said.

They turned to the church. 'How's Denis?' asked Samson.

'He's going to make it. The procedure was pretty simple, but it saved his life. The odd thing is that if they hadn't tried to kill him in Congress, he would almost certainly have died quite soon anyway. He'd like the irony. It turns out that it was extremely fortunate he was in the hospital.' They began to walk towards the church.

'He's still in a coma?'

'Yes, and they're worried about the long-term effects. God knows what's going to happen. But we must hope.' She grabbed his hand and squeezed it briefly then let it go. 'It's been very hard, seeing him like that.'

'Bloody awful for you,' he said, and turned to Naji. 'You and I have a lot of catching up to do, Naj, don't we?'

Naji nodded. 'You know how big this is, Samson? I mean, it's really super-massive.'

'I do, but I have no idea what we do with the information you have dug up, Naji. No idea whatsoever.'

Before they reached the entrance an electric vehicle pulled up and the President got out with her bodyguards. In the background was her husband, who arrived separately on a bicycle. She spoke to Ulrike for a few seconds, then the two women entered the church, the President taking Ulrike's arm. Samson, Anastasia and Naji followed and found space in the pews at the rear of the congregation.

The church was very light and plain with all the paraphernalia of modern faith– children's paintings of the holy story, developing-world project boards, leaflets and posters with smiling faces. There was no coffin, Harland having been buried by Ulrike, Zoe and Rudi in a ceremony immediately after the post-mortem – his wish, Ulrike had said. And, naturally, the order of service for a famous spy gave no hint who would be contributing. A list of music and readings was headed by a quotation from Cavafy – 'When we say "Time" we mean ourselves. Most abstractions are simply our pseudonyms. We are time.' Naji put his forefinger on this and showed it to Anastasia, and she nodded. At the bottom of the list was a drawing by Harland of a sea bird in flight.

Any idea that this would be a simple affair vanished with the beat of a half-muffled drum. The congregation turned to see a drummer and a four-man brass section – all wearing dark red cassocks – begin the slow march to Purcell's funeral music for Queen Mary II. The solemn pomp seemed most unlike Harland, who was simple in taste and expression, however it jolted the congregation to focus on the moment. Harland, in his own way, was a great man, and that was the theme of the welcome by the minister and of the President's opening address, in which she admitted that only on her election to office did she come to appreciate the service he had rendered to his adoptive country. She couldn't go into detail, but it was enough to say that he had helped more than any single foreigner to defend Estonia's fledgling democracy from those who even now worked to destroy it. Samson noticed Peter Nyman nodding vigorously at the front.

A choir sang, there were readings in German and English, one by Lewis Ott, who read Shakespeare's 'Fear not the heat o' the sun' with all the feeling of a customs officer, and a short speech by the owner of the gallery, who told how he had come across one of Harland's paintings fifteen years before and sought him out, only to find that Harland suspected him of being an enemy agent.

Then Ulrike read an account of meeting Harland in East Germany and how, in the wake of her first husband's murder, he became her protector and friend, and, by degrees, her lover and companion. It was unadorned testimony, without much colour or humour, but Samson liked it for that. At the end, she paused and looked around the congregation. 'Both my husbands were murdered, and by the same evil. Over thirty years separate their deaths, but I have reason to believe that the same people were responsible for their murders. Many of you here are engaged in the struggle that Bobby, Rudi Rosenharte and I committed to many decades ago in the GDR. I ask those present not only to seek justice for their deaths, but please – never give up. Bobby is with you because you are all that stands between civilisation and barbarism, between freedom and tyranny. And for that I cherish you, as I did my dear, beloved, sweet, eccentric Bobby.'

She stood silently for several moments. Samson caught Anastasia looking at him. She wiped away the tears that were coursing down her face. And then someone started clapping and the congregation followed and there were one or two muted cheers. It was a minute or two before the applause died down and Ulrike returned to her seat.

The last to speak was Macy Harp, who seemed caught off guard, as though he had only been asked minutes before. He had no notes and didn't seem sure where he should stand, so positioned himself between the two front pews in the aisle and began telling stories of Harland's staunchness, good judgement and exceptional tradecraft, as though reminiscing with a few intimates. 'Bobby was my lifelong friend. I loved the man,' he concluded. 'I respected him beyond any person on this earth. In his later years, he devoted himself to his painting and I saw much less of him, but these paintings are extraordinary, each one a revelation. They teach us about the hidden world we live in. It is vital that those of us who loved Bobby now honour his memory by ensuring that the largest possible audience is made aware of these revelations. We owe that to him.'

Half the congregation no doubt believed that this red-faced gentleman from England was merely paying homage to Harland's paintings, but the former and current intelligence officers present knew exactly what Macy was saying. Robert Harland's murder would not go unpunished. A smile twitched in the Bird's crazy old face.

Early that morning Ulrike decided that the art gallery was the only place large enough to hold the wake for so many and opened the exhibition to all. There would be a private event for a few of them later that evening. Naji, Zoe and Rudi went off to prepare. Samson told them that they would be going through everything and then they would decide on a course of action. They said others had come to Tallinn but had stayed away from the funeral because they'd never met Harland in person, although he was aware of each one of them. Samson agreed that they should be there too.

He followed Anastasia to the wake. He wanted to talk to her and see the paintings, which turned out to be much freer and more deeply felt than he had ever expected. The catalogue said each painting had been completed in a day and so the exhibition was a kind of diary of Harland's last anguished months, ending with the painting that Samson had brought in that morning, which now stood in the centre of the space, framed and untitled, fixed to a Perspex glass screen. Anastasia gazed at it for a long time and said it reminded her of one of Van Gogh's last pictures, 'Wheat Field under a Clouded Sky'. 'Look at the urgency. This is a man who's dying and knows he's seeing these things for the last time. It's incredibly moving.'

'Did Van Gogh know he would die?' he said.

'In the last letter to his brother, Theo, he said he was risking his life for his art. That letter was found on his body. I guess Harland risked his life for his art, painting out there, making this beautiful work with no protection.'

She didn't mention the bullet hole. It was left to Peter Nyman to do that. 'A very poignant symbol of Bobby's life and death,' he said, having approached them unseen.

'Not really,' said Anastasia, and went off to look at the other paintings.

Nyman wasn't put off. 'A word, Samson?' he said, not taking his eyes from the painting. 'It's very much in your interest.'

'You must be desperate, Peter. I mean, the arrest warrant! Pressuring a senior police officer to change her statement. What's that going to look like when people get to hear about it? Here's a promise for you and Ott. Unless you have that arrest warrant lifted, I will sink your fucking boat. And if you think that you and that upper-class fool can play games with me, I'll make sure that the names you are trying to protect, or are trying to deal with in your own way, will be made public, with all the evidence of Russian penetration at the highest level. Got it?' He turned away.

'Have it your own way. But this will not turn out well for you.'

'Don't threaten someone who's carrying a bloody big axe, Peter. First law of intelligence work.'

He was saved by the Bird, who had never encountered Peter Nyman before but knew exactly who he was and, more particularly, what he was. 'There's someone I want you to meet,' he said, steering Samson away. 'His name is Bruno. Macy and I had an interesting chat with him last night.' They walked towards a small man wearing a beret, a charcoal grey suit and bow tie. 'This is Herr Bruno Frick. He was a friend of Bobby's and they worked together in the GDR. Herr Frick was one of our best people there, until his network was rolled up and he was imprisoned and came across a certain female employee of the Stasi. He took some splendid photographs of her in 2019, which I believe you've seen.'

'Of course,' said Samson, gripping Frick's hand. 'Impressive work.'

The man's astonishingly blue eyes sparkled behind small square spectacles. 'And Bobby put them to a good use, I understand.'

Samson was aware of Nyman and Frank Toombs watching him from different sides of the room. 'Yes, Herr Frick, he did. But can we continue this conversation elsewhere? Maybe we could meet at the café in the Hotel Sweden two blocks from here in, say, ten minutes. I am going to bring a person with me who's closely involved in this work. Will that be all right?'

'By all means, but I do not wish to miss the exhibition.'

'It won't take more than half an hour.' He shook his hand as though to say it had been a pleasure meeting him and moved off to find Ulrike.

Herr Frick was already there when he and Anastasia arrived, a small glass of cognac in front of him, hands folded above his stomach and a beatific expression on his face. He offered them a drink and they accepted because the wine had been hard to come by in the crowd at the gallery. When Anastasia sat down beside him he looked pleased and patted her knee, which surprised her.

'Can I leap in with our problem?' started Samson. 'We can connect the woman known as Mila Daus to three husbands and multiple businesses as well as scandals but, apart from your photographs and your evidence that you saw her, we have nothing to say that she is the same person who was a senior Stasi officer at Hohenschönhausen prison. Ulrike can testify that she saw her there, but both your and Ulrike's testimony can be dismissed as unreliable, because of the mental stress you were under at the time, and it is over thirty years ago. We have to tie her to Hohenschönhausen and the Stasi if we are to make the case that she is Russia's primary asset in the United States, and do it so there can be no doubt. We've got just one shot at this.'

Herr Frick took a sip of his cognac and dabbed his lips with a folded handkerchief from his breast pocket.

'You know Leipzig?' he started. 'It is the city where Ulrike was born. Many beautiful things come from Leipzig, apart from her – Bach's music, for example. The 1989 Revolution was born in the square outside the church. And there is this. Actually, I should say *these*. He stretched to the pocket of the raincoat on the seat next to him and withdrew an envelope and a jam jar with a sealed top. He placed the jar on the cushion beside him and directed their attention to the envelope. This contains the proof you need of Mila Daus's identity.' He held the envelope horizontally and slid his entire hand inside, then brought it out with two cards held with a paper clip resting on the flat of his hand like a tray. 'This is the report of her arrest.'

'I don't understand,' said Samson.

'When Daus was nineteen and a student at Leipzig University she was arrested. The Stasi spotted her and decided to take a closer look. They sometimes did this to test a candidate's suitability and observe their behaviour under duress. She was arrested because she was with a disorderly group of students who were drunk. It was probably a set-up.' He turned over the first of two cards. There were three photographs in a row of a stern but pretty young student – facing the camera, in profile and half-profile. Underneath was her name, Mila Gretchen Daus, her address and date of birth – 20 August 1955. The document was dated 12 December 1974. 'Here in a margin note are the remarks of a senior officer named Colonel Joachim Ropp, and I quote, "This is the finest candidate that I have seen in ten years. Immediate recruitment recommended." But there is more.' He removed the paper clip and turned over the second card and held it up. 'Her fingerprints. She was arrested, so naturally they took her fingerprints.'

'Where did you get this?' asked Samson. 'She whitewashed her record and destroyed all the incriminating entries.'

'Maybe she forgot about the arrest. Even if she remembered it, she probably forgot that her fingerprints were in the records. To answer your question about where I got it, I stole it from the archive. Also, I stole this.' He held up the jam jar, which contained a ball of cotton wool that had yellowed with age. He placed it on the table and took some more cognac. 'It was one of the Stasi's most distasteful practices. When an interviewee or arrestee left the chair they had been sitting on, the Stasi took a swab from the seat using cotton wool which they immediately placed in a jar. They believed they were capturing the unique pheromones of an individual. Who knows what was in their minds? You will see the name is written on the label, and the date.' He smiled. 'It was actually on show in the former headquarters at Dittrichring 24, Leipzig, together with many other similar specimens. I happened to notice that this one's label was intact. A piece of good fortune – some would say divine providence. And it has never been opened.'

'But you're not suggesting that we can use this to identify her?'

'If these samples had any value, it has long since faded. But look closer.' He handed the jar to Anastasia. 'Do you see them?'

'What?'

'The hairs at the bottom! They are almost certainly hers, because the Stasi would never allow a sample like this to be contaminated by extraneous material. They collected her hair after the interview and placed it in the jar, quite unaware that science would later find a way of identifying someone by their DNA. That was a decade or so later. If this is her hair, it is conclusive of her recruitment by the Stasi and subsequent career.'

Samson sat back. 'I'm overwhelmed, Herr Frick. Did Bobby know you had this material?'

'Yes, but he didn't show any interest.' He stopped. 'No, that is a mis-representation. He said he would need these items at a later stage, but to be candid, I think he'd forgotten them, or did not properly recognise their importance.'

Samson looked at Anastasia. 'I think we need to find a lawyer to take a sworn statement from Herr Frick as soon as possible.'

'That has already been effected. I have deposited an account with my lawyer in Frankfurt and everything has been notarised to an international standard. The items were kept in her safe. Should I return them?'

'Will you entrust them to us, on the understanding that we will return them as soon as we can?' asked Anastasia.

The precise, courageous little man said, 'It will be my pleasure,' and patted her knee again.

She shook her head in mock reprimand.

'Ha, these days one is not allowed to acknowledge a beautiful woman like you. Forgive me, but it is my policy to show my appreciation. I have long since ceased to be a threat to the opposite sex, if, indeed, I ever was. Unlike Mr Samson here, who is too handsome for his own good. If you ever require my testimony in person, please be assured that I will come whenever and wherever you need.' He picked up the cognac again. 'I will send you by email the statement. It is not an easy document to read.' He looked down and took a sip. 'Mila Daus broke me – that is my story. I am not the person I was. Superficially, I am the same man who loves opera and orchestral music and the good things in life, but there is a hole at the centre of me. That is the only way I can describe it to you. The lies they told to my wife about my activities destroyed her also. She committed suicide in 1988, a year before the revolution.' He put down the glass unfinished and reached for his raincoat. 'Now I must go to see Bobby's paintings. I wish you good fortune.'

CHAPTER 27

Confession

They sat in silence after Bruno Frick departed, leaving a small card on the table with his name and email printed in an elegant typeface. At length Anastasia picked it up, smiled and handed it to Samson. 'He has class. Did you notice – no self-pity whatsoever.' She studied him with a smile. 'Ulrike tells me you want to run this from now on.'

'That was her idea, but you are paying for it and this is Denis's operation. I can walk away. I've done what I was paid for, though I wish Macy had told me that I was being used as the decoy for Harland's daughter.'

'You're not going to walk away. They've tried to kill you three times. It's not in your character to walk away.'

Samson disliked her telling him what was and wasn't in his nature. 'I don't think you have the first idea of what we're taking on. This is going to be hard.'

She straightened. 'No idea? I just saw my husband poisoned and his lawyer dying right in front of me. *Of course* I know how hard this is going to be. Don't be so bloody patronising.' She looked away.

'My apologies. I meant . . .'

'That's okay.' She smiled ruefully. 'I'm sorry. I need sleep, and I'm worried about Denis. Sorry. Just don't be an arsehole! This is your world, Samson, not mine. You run it, you decide, and you get that bitch.' She pointed to the envelope and the jar. 'We need to get these things in a safe place. Your hotel? Would you mind if I took a nap? Say if you do! Really!'

'Of course not. We've got time to kill and . . . it would be good to talk. Two years is a long time. I have things to say – clarifications.'

She made a face. 'I look forward to your *clarifications*.'

At the hotel, he pulled a heavy desk to block the door and opened the doors on to their balcony, where there were a couple of chairs. They went outside and sat down. The balconies either side were empty.

'You stopped calling me. Why?' she said.

'You didn't return my calls, so I waited until you were ready. I thought you needed space. It was all pretty agonising. Later, I saw a story about your work in Lesbos and you looked fine in the photographs, so I thought you were happy without me. I did think of coming to see you, but then I thought I'd be—'

'Getting in the way?'

'No, pressurising you.'

He got up and went inside to fetch beers from the mini-bar. When he handed her one, she said, 'I'm not going to sleep with you.'

'How do you know I want to?'

'It's the only way it works between us.'

He shook his head. 'I'm sorry you think that and, anyway, it's totally untrue.'

'Okay, I'm sorry. Bed is always out of this world. You know that. And it's always a temptation. But I can't while my husband is in a coma. He saved me and I can't betray him again. That's just how it is.'

'Really, it's no big deal.' He stopped to sip the beer. 'I love you and, to be honest, that is a big inconvenience in my life, but I get you don't want to and you don't have to mention it again.'

'Fuck off,' she said, and smiled.

He looked over the city's roofs towards Alexander Nevsky Cathedral. 'If you want me to try to run this, I will. But I'll do it my way, even though I'm not sure what that will be.'

Without warning, she said, 'I was pregnant. I lost the baby. It was from our last time together. Our baby. I had a miscarriage and I went to pieces. That's why I didn't call. Denis got me through it, although he must have known it was yours. He was magnificent, and I will never forget what he did for me. That's why . . . that's why we can't just hop into bed, like old times. I hope you understand, Samson.'

Samson's mother appeared in his mind: she had so wanted him to have a family with Anastasia, and before her death was endlessly pleading with him to win Anastasia back and marry her. 'I'm so sorry. I'm sorry that I wasn't there for you. I wish . . . I had no idea.'

'What could you have done? Really, there was nothing. It is the way things are with us. Bad timing. I understand that now.'

'I wish you'd told me.'

'What would have been the point, to make you feel bad and help-less? Besides, I couldn't talk about it. I had a breakdown, Samson. Me, the damned psychologist, with a breakdown! I was out of it. Being kidnapped and shot didn't help – that all came out. The shock, the terror, the sleepless nights. Classic PTSD, and losing the baby sent me crazy. Actually, I can't remember which was first, the miscarriage or the breakdown.'

He leaned forward, shaking his head, and took her hand. He began to say something but ended up again muttering that he was sorry.

'It's not your responsibility, and I know you did try to contact me. It was two years ago, and I recovered. I am myself again.' She made a dramatic flourish, as though taking a bow. 'But all that – the miscarriage and my breakdown – is why Denis didn't tell me that he was going after Mila Daus. I didn't even know her name until today. You see, he really does care for me and he didn't think I could take any more pressure. Turns out he was wrong about that – I seem to be okay after being chased by carloads of killers through two countries. Actually, three, if you count Macedonia.'

'I want to hear about Macedonia.'

'It was delightful. The farm is as it was, but there's a new barn that I suspect Denis paid for. There's much more to say, but I really have to sleep. Can I crash on your bed? I really can't say another word more.'

He led her to the bed and they lay down and he held her.

'Even this seems wrong,' she said. She wriggled round and looked up from his chest. 'I know you love me, Samson. I understand.' She turned again and wrapped his hand around her breast. You don't mind, do you?'

'No, I don't mind.'

She closed her eyes and was immediately asleep.

'I'll wake you in a couple of days,' he murmured.

At 5.35 p.m. Anastasia's phone went off. She raised her head from the bed then let it fall back, wrapping an arm across her eyes and groaning. She felt much worse than when they had lain down. Samson pulled his arm from beneath her and shook the circulation into his hand. 'Maybe you should see who called.'

She groaned. 'Water.'

He went to fetch a glass from the bathroom. 'I've just had a message from Warren Speight's office,' she said on his return. 'They want me to appear in front of Congress within the next seven days.'

He absorbed this. 'They surely can't question you on Denis's affairs when he's lying in the bloody hospital?'

She shook her head and dialled Jim Tulliver.

'What's going on, Jim?'

'They just called. The committee want you there Friday or Monday.'

'What are they going to ask me? I know nothing.'

'Speight is pushing for it. Did he give you any idea he was going to do this?'

'None.'

'Well, I guess you just go along and say you can't answer questions on things you don't know about.'

'He kind of trapped me with all that schmoozing, and I thought he was on our side and wanted not to persecute Denis. I don't understand. He went on about what was in the lawyer Steen's briefcase – you remember that? Said there was something in it to be used *in extremis* and asked did I know what it was.'

'Well, I think you should come back anyway. Denis is frail, but they think he's out of danger and his heart appears to be beating normally so that's good news. I'll talk with the lawyers, and we can get a damn great wall built around you. You go in and you say you would of course be honoured to help the committee, but since you had your own life and your own problems, how can you respond on things that you don't know about? That kind of thing. We'll get a statement drafted.'

'But I do know how much money we spent on relief and medical aid. And maybe I can give evidence to support that. Shall I call the staffer? He left a message.'

'Yeah, you do that. His name is Matthew Corner. I could send the plane, but it's going to be as quick for you to fly from Tallinn to Helsinki on the early flight, then to DC. There's a seat for you. I'll send details.'

'Did Marty Reid get in touch?'

'As a matter of fact, he did. He heard some rumour that Denis was out of his coma and he came to the hospital, only to find that Denis was in surgery. He wants to talk to you, but I stalled. Didn't tell him where you were. He's very anxious to help. Believes he has something new on the TangKi business; says he's identified the ultimate source of where the money came from to support European fascists.'

'Does that matter?'

'He seems to think so.'

'Do you trust him?'

'Denis has always had his doubts about Marty.'

Her phone was on speaker and Samson heard all this. He went to the desk he had dragged in front of the door and found some hotel notepaper in a folder. He wrote, 'Can you bring evidence to the committee?' And handed the paper to her.

She asked the question. Tulliver replied, 'I see no reason why not. You can respond to questions how you see fit, and you can support what you're saying by the submission of documents.'

'Okay. I'm going to speak with Matthew Corner, and I'll take that plane you booked.'

She hung up. 'Are you thinking what I am?'

'We can be ready by then. There is the very large issue of proof. We have to show that the woman now known as Mila Gaspar is *the* Mila Daus, and there's only one way of doing that, and besides, the only thing I have seen is a colour chart with names – some of them well known, others not. But there's no proof attached to them. It's nothing more than a list.'

'Naji has it all.'

'Yes, but there was a reason that Denis didn't use it. They weren't ready. Mila Daus knew this and moved to head them off. I don't believe she thought there was anything in that briefcase, and we know Denis's case had nothing important in it. Bobby was out painting. If he thought Denis was going to reveal everything in Congress, he would have wanted to be near a TV to watch it. There's nothing like that at the cabin.'

'Why use nerve agent? Why not shoot Denis on the way to Congress? We had no protection.'

'That's a very good question, and I've been thinking about it, because it seems too downright crazy for her. Also, as I keep on saying, the people contracted to kill me, Bobby and, I guess, you and Naji are all amateurs and gangsters. The Mila Daus that we know about would have made sure of the hit every time. There's so much that doesn't make sense. I repeat, we don't have a case against her.'

'You're forgetting about Naji.'

That didn't give Samson a lot of confidence, although it was true that Harland had trusted him. 'Yes, but I don't yet know what he has.'

She dialled Matthew Corner in Speight's office, put him on speaker and started explaining that she was out of the country attending a funeral of her husband's dear friend.

The staffer said, 'Hold it right there, I have Congressman Speight for you.'

Speight came on. Concern was expressed for Denis, pleasantries were exchanged, and a particularly hot spring day was commented upon. 'Mrs Hisami, I have spoken with my good friend Harry Lucas, who, you may recall, is the chair of our committee, and he is in agreement with me that we need to clear up one or two matters of detail. Then, I feel, we could put the matter to rest.'

'What detail? I cannot answer for my husband.'

'These would be matters that directly relate to you, Mrs Hisami, and I think we both know it's important for those around the globe who witnessed the shameful events of last week to understand that American democracy will not be cowed by an act of terrorism. Our flame will not be doused, if you follow my drift.'

She looked at Samson, who had certainly picked up on the use of the word 'douse' – a homophone for Daus. He thought it might be intentional and nodded to her. 'I understand you, Congressman. It will not be doused, but why the rush?'

'I knew you would grasp what I was saying. I hope that I can take this as your acceptance of our invitation. But we do need to expedite these matters. Much depends on it. My staff will be calling with the arrangements but, in the meantime, I'd like to leave you with this quotation, from a law enacted in the year of our Lord 1954. It concerns the evidence of witnesses to a congressional committee in respect of investigations concerned with national security subjects. And the matter in hand does seem to me, Mrs Hisami, to be one that falls into the remit of the Foreign Affairs Committee.' He cleared his throat and read, '"No witness shall be prosecuted or subjected to any penalty or forfeiture for or on account of any transaction, matter, or thing concerning which he or she is so compelled, after having claimed his privilege against self-incrimination, to testify or produce evidence, nor shall testimony so compelled be used as evidence in any criminal proceeding . . . against him or her in any court.'" He paused, 'I want you to be clear on the import of this passage, Mrs Hisami – it means you have protection.' After more silky reassurance, he bid her good day and rang off.

'Has he just offered me a platform to expose Mila Daus and her networks?'

'Can you trust him?'

'Shit, no.'

'Then we go ahead and assume he is part of her network and is trying to draw you out. But it's still an opportunity, if we can prove who she is.'

'Wouldn't it be something to get her there? I mean, actually in Congress. Get the bitch sitting where Denis was.'

He gave her a doubtful look. 'How would that happen?'

'When I get back I'll talk to Shera Ricard, our representative in Congress. But we aren't ready, and, shit, I'm not sure I can do this. I mean, you saw Speight chew Denis up on the stand. And it's not as though he is the only one that can ask questions. Maybe he's organising some kind of ambush with other members of his group.'

'Look, we should go,' he said, brushing down the back of his hair and looking around for his jacket.

She caught his hand. 'Can we really pull this off, Samson?'

'Let's see what we've got. We'll know in an hour or so.'

She held on to his hand. 'Thanks for being understanding about things. It's just not possible at the moment . . .'

'However beautiful you are, however much I exalt in sleeping with you, I have to tell you that sex is the last thing on my mind.'

'And I'm sorry for not telling you about the baby.' She stopped and smiled shyly. 'That's the last time I mention it. I've recovered. I'm no longer crazy. That's all in the past.'

Her attention went to the window, where a butterfly was trapped. She let go of his hand and took a few steps to let it out.

'What are you smiling for?' she asked.

'I'll tell you another time,' he said. 'We'd better get going.'

He dragged the desk back to its position and noticed that an envelope had been slipped under the door. Inside was a note from Ulrike explaining that she had changed the venue of the meeting. The address was on the other side of the old town. She stressed that particular care should be taken to avoid being followed.

CHAPTER 28

Open Toombs

Anastasia went on ahead. Samson paid his bill and joined the crowds of young Estonians in the streets of the old town on a warm spring evening. He'd gone no more than a hundred metres when an SUV pulled up alongside him and Frank Toombs got out. 'You want to be shot, Samson? I mean, what the hell are you doing?'

'Hello, Frank, what can I help you with?'

'Get in the fucking car.'

'I'm on my way to meet an old friend, so if you don't mind.'

He opened the door. 'You need to hear what I have to say.'

Samson climbed in and three younger agents got out. Toombs wore his usual expression of disdain, but Samson knew he wanted something. 'Okay, I'm listening,' said Samson.

'You're dumb to be walking around like that. You'll certainly not survive the next twenty-four hours if you stay here. The place is crawling with Russians who want you dead.'

'I hear you.'

'What are you going to do with it?'

'What?'

'The information you have.'

Samson gave a shrug and looked ahead.

'This is where we stand. I know that Robert Harland and Denis Hisami were in a position to reveal names of senior individuals in the US that have been compromised by Russia, or work for Russian interests as a matter of choice. We know that Congress was attacked to protect those names and, with Harland's death and Hisami's incapacitation, those parties believe they're now safe. Yet they'd be a lot happier if you and Anastasia were dead, too, and there's no doubt in my mind that they'll achieve that aim within a very short time frame.' He stopped and opened a window. It was warm without the car's air con. 'And I guess that applies to your people, too. They'd happily feed you into a woodchipper. But, hey, that's the British for you.'

'Maybe,' said Samson.

'Maybe nothing! They want to close you down – hence the arrest warrant – because they're desperate to keep it away from the Russians. At least in my country we have people who remember what the Cold War was about – Russia, Russia, Russia.'

'So?'

'Let's cut to it. This information is going to come out, and we need to know exactly who's involved. I want a list, a heads up.'

Samson was silent.

'In exchange, we'll provide you with protection.'

'Like the protection you've given me and Anastasia over the last few days?'

'You don't make it easy. By the way, I notice you never mention the kid – the Syrian kid.'

'He's unimportant.'

'The hell he is. We know he's crucial. We know, so please don't fucking tell me otherwise. But right now my concerns are bigger than how this young man has been communicating with Mr Hisami. I'm here to protect the American people. It's as simple as that. We can't have a drug-dealing

Balkan deadbeat walking into Congress with nerve agent again. It's not going to happen and we're taking steps to make sure that it doesn't.' He looked at his watch. 'At this moment interventions are taking place in Ukraine to eradicate that supply chain. I doubt there'll be many arrested alive. We're not fucking about.'

'And Anatoly Stepurin?'

'We'll get him. You were right – he's the paymaster, the organiser and planner. And he was the one who supplied the nerve agent, so he's a priority.'

'No, Frank, he's just a go-between and a slightly better class of assassin.'

'Whatever. We'll get him. Let's get back on track, Samson. The grown-ups in the US government, and there aren't too many of them . . .'

'Try my country!'

He looked irritated. 'The adults understand that foreign influence is preying on our weaknesses, corroding the foundations of the republic from the inside, whatever the folks at the White House say. We've got a problem with the British ambassador. He's spinning a fantasy about gang-sters and revenge to distract from the truth about Russian manipulation. The Secretary of State has bought it, and so has the White House. They'd rather do anything than offend Russia right now. So, if this material comes out half-assed, they can dismiss it and our only chance is blown.'

'So what do you want?'

'An agreement that you will give us notice of what you've got, and all of it!'

'What do you mean by notice?'

'As soon as you know – that has to be the deal.'

'If we're going to have an agreement,' said Samson, 'I don't want you getting in the way. You will also tell me of any pushback you're getting from the politicians. By the way, what's the hurry?'

'What do you mean?'

'You seem nervous, Toombs. I mean, you're pushing this.' And then he had a second thought. 'They're going to shut you down now you've nailed the supply line, and you know there's so much more. And you desperately need it to come out. They're telling you – job done!'

'Something like that, yes. But you have to tell me what you've got. I need to have ammunition and, in the meantime, I will guarantee your safety.'

'Others have offered.'

'Suddenly everyone wants you alive, Samson.'

'Fine – it's a deal.'

They shook hands and he left the car.

CHAPTER 29

Raw Data

The address on Ulrike's note was a drama school. The entrance was barred by an elaborate art nouveau metal gate. Samson pressed the bell and the gate lock was released. He entered a short, gloomy passageway and, after being asked by a young black British woman to switch off his phones and deposit them in a box, was directed to a rehearsal room at the back of the building. 'Have we met?' he said. 'I feel we have.'

'Maybe my twin, Jessie? She was working at GreenState. I'm Joy.' She led him to a rehearsal room at the back of the building, where Ulrike stood with her hands clasped like a welcoming headmistress. Behind her were the props from a production: an empty picture frame, suspended on wires, an animal skull on a cocktail table and a psychiatrist's couch. The chairs were organised in a crescent. A portable screen had been erected and Naji stood at a flat lectern with an open laptop. He raised a hand without looking up.

'This is Paul Samson, who some of you know,' said Ulrike. 'A dozen or more faces turned. Macy Harp gave him an awkward nod, and the Bird, still in his faded cap, performed a sort of salute. Anastasia, Zoe and Rudi were sitting together. Zoe got up and introduced the young people around her – Kurt, Joy, Jessie, Patrick, Craig, Leah, Magnus, Rose, Chris, Axel, Ibrahim and Marina. Samson lost track of who was who, but he logged that four were American, 'Finally, this is Merlin,' she said. Francis, the young gamer who had shared the overflow room with Samson at GreenState and introduced him to the concept of Düppel in the gamers' pub, nodded and flicked back his hair.

Ulrike dimmed the lights with a remote and moved forward into a pool of light. 'Samson is now going to take control of the operation. My husband would want this. I have spoken to Mr Harp and Mrs Hisami, and they're in agreement and believe it would also be Mr Hisami's wish.'

Samson turned to them. 'Okay, so we need – I need – to know everything. I guess someone had better take me through it. Naji, can you do that?'

Zoe spoke. 'We thought I would do the talking and Naji the slideshow, if that's all right with you. I now know everything Naji does. Okay, so the first thing those of you who haven't worked on this must understand is that the global environmental action group GreenState is a total fraud. All the marketing and branding says "We're here to save the planet and we've got a whole bunch of dedicated activists working round the clock in every time zone." That's bullshit. GreenState is a scam. It's a ruthless enterprise that soaks up money and data and allows Mila Daus and Jonathan Mobius to influence politics on both sides of the Atlantic, but, much, much more important, it is one part of their operation to gather high-grade intelligence for the West's enemies.

'GreenState is a brilliant cover operation, yet it provided us with a great opportunity to penetrate Mila Daus's organisation because it has inbuilt vulnerabilities, not the least of which is its size. This was Robert Harland's idea.' She stopped, looked around the young people in her audience, who had not been at the funeral. 'Most of you don't know he was my father. I want to say right now he gave what little remained of his life for this work and, because of that, Ulrike, Rudi and I were never able to say goodbye to him. That's one good reason why we absolutely *have* to see this through.'

She turned to the older faces. 'But GreenState and Jonathan Mobius are not the only part of this organisation. There are three other individuals in the United States who run their own networks and are entirely distinct from GreenState. You should think of GreenState as just one of four separate operations – okay?

'My father gave these four entities colour codes: 'PEARL GREY, PITCH BLACK, AURORA RED and SAFFRON YELLOW. On top of the pile, receiving all the information and controlling everything, was Mila Daus. My father named her BERLIN BLUE.

'What we did was to mirror Mila Daus's structure to find out what we could about these individuals. Then all the information went to my father and Denis Hisami, who built a picture of Mila Daus's activities. The people in this room – plus others who can't be here – worked separately and we had little contact with each other. Only Naji, Rudi and I had contact with all of you.

'It's really important to understand that our task was to acquire the raw data, the leads, the connections, the copies of emails and text messages, recordings of video calls, information about the money transfers, the dates and venues of meetings, plus information on Mobius's use of shell companies in London to launder money and distribute it. That was the basic material. We didn't do the analysis or piecing together. What we are going to show you now are some snapshots of Mila's network, but it is not – repeat not – the final product. I'm going to start with my own group, which investigated Jonathan Mobius – Pearl Grey.'

An organisational chart appeared headed by a photograph of Jonathan Mobius. He had changed little since the wedding of his doomed father to Mila Daus – slim, humourless and with a curl to his upper lip. Like his stepmother – with whom he still had some sort of physical relationship that Zoe described as 'Oedipal habit'– he was interested in three things: influence, political intelligence and data. The key people in his network were old friends. He had met Anthony Jerome Drax, one of two special advisers to the Prime Minister, in St Petersburg in the early 1990s, when he was seeking to recruit mathematicians for his father's business. Ben Bera of the Foreign Office and Joint Intelligence Committee – Samson had never heard of him, but Macy thought that maybe he had – was befriended at a party in New York a little later when Bera was working for the UN. Christine Carter, head of an Anglo-American trade organisation, Tanner Matlock and Jeff Koblenz – both from finance – all came later but were part of Mobius's circle for at least a decade. Of these three, Matlock was the most influential. He was on the governing body of the BBC and also on the board of Luminescence Analytics. The common characteristic was that they were all off-the-scale right wing. Zoe corrected herself: 'I'm not sure if it's accurate to call them fascist, neofascist or whatever, but they do all have contempt for democracy and people. It's all about power and winning.'

This power was exercised and extended socially with receptions at the Tate and the National Gallery, summer drinks parties in the Chelsea Physic Garden and seats at Wimbledon and Covent Garden. There were environmental awards, retreats and conferences; donations to think tanks located in the Smith Square area of Westminster, and favours done for members of the British political establishment. Near Arezzo, in Umbria, a restored Palazzo offered special respite to politicians, where it was likely they were compromised with young male and female members of staff, a mirror image of the operation at GreenState's Clouds Ranch in Idaho.

Naji projected a photograph of the man in Number Ten. Drax was in his mid-forties, with cropped dark hair, a bulbous nose and watery blue eyes whose lower lids sagged and gave for an unsettling stare. They heard that he checked in with Mobius at the end of every week, and then Mobius reported back to Daus.

Zoe went on: 'We've got emails and messages to receiving-only accounts that we believe belong to Mila, which usually followed these conversations. Of course, there is never any traffic from her. But the access she has to the inner workings of the British government is clear.'

Macy coughed and raised a hand. 'So, all this information goes to her,' he said, 'but do you know what she does with it? Have you got any sense of the ultimate destination?' He opened his hands and looked affably at the young people for an answer, and, there being none, continued. 'Put it this way, you have described the sort of business network that I come across all the time. Companies, industrial sectors and syndicates often gather intelligence and seek to bend the will of governments. If you have evidence that this information was going straight to Russia, well, that would be a different matter.'

Zoe looked down to hide her irritation. 'What we're showing you here isn't the final product, and, no, we don't bloody well know the end user of the information. But how many companies can you name that have people killed and kidnapped, smear opponents, use intimidation and blackmail, bend elections, bribe officials, soak up people's data without regard to law and regulation and use it against them? Even if this had absolutely nothing to do with espionage, you would have to classify what Mila Daus has created as a Mafia-level criminal enterprise. And no one has a clue about her, or who controls companies like Luminescence MB, Luminescence Analytica, MBX3, or even Luminescence MXB3, same as they don't know who actually owns GreenState, although we have established it is wholly owned by Daus and Mobius.'

She grabbed a bottle of water from her seat, swigged from it and resumed. 'Now we are going to move on to the States.'

Under the headings, 'Aurora Red', 'Pitch Black' and 'Saffron Yellow' appeared photographs of three men: Chester Abelman, Erik Kukorin and Elliot Jeffreys. They had the country neatly divided up between them. Abelman was based on the West Coast, Elliot Jeffreys in Washington, DC, and Erik Kukorin in New York. They ran three distinct operations, and there was little or no contact between them. If connections needed to be made, they went through Mila Daus. Apparently, the three had no interest in business whatsoever – Mila and Mobius handled all that. But Abelman, Jeffreys and Kukorin had millions at their disposal and lived the life of the top one per cent of Americans.

Unlike the deep-cover illegals that Russia seeded in the US in the 1990s and in the early part of the century, all three were born in America. No infiltration from Canada was necessary, no marriages of convenience between spies, and no making do with scraps of intelligence from the bottom of the food chain. They formed Daus's frontline from political conviction, which was about love of power and a straightforward loathing of liberal America.

'But do they know they are really working for the enemies of America?' asked Anastasia.

Zoe looked at the four Americans in front of her for an answer. The answer was – no, but Leah suggested that if they did know, it probably wouldn't affect them because they basically shared the worldview of the Russian leadership.

The Bird and Macy Harp exchanged looks and shook their heads. This wasn't a world they recognised.

Leah, Chinese-American, with a bob and eyes that shone from behind small, oval glasses, took over from Zoe to speak about Elliot Jeffreys. He was a lawyer from Chicago who had failed in the city's politics and moved to set up a small political consultancy in the K Street area in DC, helping Conservative allies in Congress with data and election strategy. He was the most powerful of the trio, though you'd never guess it looking at him. In the several pictures of him, he was short and plump, with no neck to speak of, and an execrable taste in ties and pocket squares. On his books, so to speak, were Mike H. Proctor, Deputy National Security Advisor, and Kirsten Donnelly, a staff member at the office of the Director of National Intelligence, which gave Daus access to what was going on in the White House Situation Room and the most secret concerns of America's Intelligence Community. His network included hundreds of people, who were attracted by his Conservatism, open wallet and cut-price consultancy fees. There was a dark side to Jeffreys, said Leah, and they had only got on to it through the suicide, a year ago, of a young Congressman named Sam Kuvin who they believed was filmed at Clouds Ranch with an under-age boy, then presented with evidence that not only had he had sex with him but had conspired in trafficking a minor from a neighbouring state. It was rare to acquire such detail, but Jeffreys had sent emails whose meaning could not be doubted, a rare lapse for him, and the boy, who was then sixteen, was active on social media. Leah said that the FBI were investigating and beginning to sniff around cases of entrapment by Jeffreys, their interest piqued by abrupt swerves in position, resignations, divorces and unaccountable wealth. Pointing to Jeffreys's photograph, she went on, 'This man right here is responsible for a lot of pain and corruption in America, but we believe that all the psychological pressure on individuals is orchestrated by Mila Daus. She picks the targets and works them over.'

California was Chester Abelman's realm. He ran GreenState West from a spacious building in Palo Alto, as Anastasia noted, not far from the offices of Hisami's own lawyers. Of mixed Jewish and Irish parentage, Abelman moved easily among the scientific community of the West Coast under the cover of GreenState's funding activities and the organisation's interest in the environment. Originally an academic at Stanford, he had set up GreenState West five years before and he and his socially active wife had made connections with the partners of a coterie of right-leaning entrepreneurs.

They ended with the Pitch Black network, which was smaller than the other three and also relied on a powerful wife, in this case Betsy Kukorin, a publicist from a conservative family in Ohio. Erik Kukorin, originally a cable-TV news producer, moved in the background, making connections at parties Betsy threw for her celebrity clients, a good cover for gathering intelligence on banks and hedge funds. There were some forty names associated with Kukorin's network, three of which were prominent Wall Street figures, including the head of a bank. Most of his activity, however, was in the large-scale financing of dark operations on the Web – false-flag Antifa sites and accounts, partisan provocateurs, YouTube channels that openly praised the Nazi 'experiment' and a myriad of Facebook groups pushing for one form of violent disruption or another. Kukorin had a television producer's eye for plausible, fresh-faced advocates among young fascists and backed half a dozen with enormous sums.

The last slide showed hundreds of names in the three networks. Macy raised his hand again. 'That's impressive. Fine work. But there's a great deal of difference between intelligence and proof. You can't publish a list like this and say all these people work for Mila Daus and are effectively betraying their country. How many of them are there by chance?' The Bird nodded and muttered something.

Samson stepped in to smooth the differences between the Cold War warriors and young hackers. 'I think we accept that this is a first draft, Macy, and that the complete work that answers these questions is with Denis Hisami. What do we have on Mila Daus herself? Where does she live? Where does she work? What's her routine? Does she travel much? We've heard that she's in London and Berlin – does she go to Moscow? And what about the foot-doctor husband? How does he fit in? Does he know about her past? Does he know that she's sleeping with her stepson?'

'That's Rudi's area,' said Zoe.

Rudi got up and stood in the pool of light beside her. He glanced at Macy and began speaking. 'Mr Harp, this is the woman who murdered your friend and my stepfather. Before that, she killed my father, Rudi, and she had a lot to do with the psychological torture and medical neglect that killed my uncle just a few weeks before the Wall came down.' He walked over to Naji and placed a hand on his shoulder. 'My friend Naji's dad was tortured and broken by a different group of thugs. We have an interest in this investigation. Yes, we seem young to you, but we have been through very bad times. We aren't frivolous and we haven't made errors. Now we will show you some photographs.' Ulrike smiled at him. Her eyes were filled with tears. Zoe laid her hand briefly on his arm.

A picture of a group of houses appeared. They were arranged around a rocky outcrop that overlooked mountains and forests as far as the eye could see. Each house had a separate driveway and parking area but no garden. The bluff and the house looked like the prow of a ship heading into an ocean of trees. In some places the houses incorporated parts of the sedimentary strata, giving the impression they'd grown out of the native rock.

'This is Seneca Ridge,' said Rudi. 'It's one and a half hour's drive from Harrisburg, Pennsylvania. There are seven houses and they are all owned by Mila Daus, through her husband, Dr John Gaspar. We have satellite imagery from six years ago showing the construction of passageways between some of the houses. The area has been landscaped so these are invisible. Gaspar owns a lot of land around the hill. A private road of two kilometres leads to the ridge. We acquired drone footage from a local man we hired last winter when the trees were bare. He was surveying the property for us from high up, operating at a thousand metres, which is way above the legal limit. That's why they didn't see the drone. We were fortunate. Watch this.'

Naji ran the footage. At first there was just a clear view of the houses in snow. From the left of the picture, three cars followed a pickup snaking up the metalled private road. The drone zoomed in as the cars peeled off and parked in different driveways. 'We think these two cars are her bodyguards and this one contains Mila Daus. Watch.' The rear door of a black Escalade opened and a woman wearing a scarf, dark ski jacket and black trousers got out. The man who'd jumped from the wheel of the pickup went to join her. He was in a cap and green jacket and was carrying a rifle case over his shoulder and a box with both hands. 'This is John Gaspar,' said Rudi. 'He's a gun freak. We think they'd been to a restaurant ten kilometres away and a gun range that he owns. It was a Saturday. The man we hired to take this film was using very good equipment so we were able to enlarge the images.' He stopped and nodded to Naji. Two close-ups showed the woman Samson had seen in the photographs taken by Harland's friend Frick. There was no doubt that they were looking at Mila Daus.

'They live here with a small security detail,' continued Rudi. 'She's at the Ridge two or three days of every week. Gaspar is there most of the time and doesn't usually travel with his wife, but sometimes they go together to Clouds Ranch in Idaho, where he hunts. The security detail always travels with his wife, so he's on his own when she's away. They almost never travel long distances by road. Instead, they take a helicopter from their own airfield three kilometres away and fly to the local airport, where she has a plane. But we get the impression that Clouds Ranch is her domain. It's where she does a lot of her business and hosts target guests.'

Macy and the Bird murmured their approval. This all sounded like more familiar intelligence work.

'What do you know about the foot doctor?' asked Samson.

'John Gaspar is fifty-five, ten years younger than his wife. He has his own life. He still practises at two local clinics. He spends a lot of time at the gun range. He deals in rare weapons and he takes hunting trips to Africa – which is amazing, considering GreenState's campaigns against big-game hunting. He collects vintage hunting rifles. We found this ad last week on a collectors' website.'

A screenshot showed a double-barrelled rifle in a case with two-inch brass ammunition lined up in front of the case. The advertisement read: 'The real deal. A 470 Nitro Express from 1909 in immaculate condition. All documentation is available, including the original sales invoice from William Evans Ltd of St James's, London.'

In the text below, Gaspar admitted that he was loth to part with the gun but the recoil was proving too much for his injured shoulder. He attested to the reliability and killing power of the weapon by publishing pictures of himself with a variety of slaughtered animals. Gaspar, always wearing a ridiculous camouflage hat, was photographed standing on or beside a dead giraffe, two buffalo, a warthog, a hyena and an elephant. The elephant had been stopped in its tracks and had ploughed an enormous rut in the red earth of the savannah. Around the dead beast was a shooting party of three men in hunting garb, Gaspar at the front, toting

the double-barrelled rifle. 'Disgusting!' exclaimed the Bird, which reminded Samson that the Bird had set up a wildlife sanctuary in Northern
Australia.

But Samson's attention was drawn to one of the men in the background
and he rose to get a closer look. 'Do you recognise this man?' he asked
Naji, pointing to the only member of the party not smiling, a stocky
individual of about fifty with a shaven head and heavy brow carrying a
gun that looked more suited to warfare than killing defenceless animals.

Naji enlarged the area of the photo. 'Yes, he was at the hotel!' he
exclaimed

'This, ladies and gentlemen,' said Samson, 'is Anatoly Stepurin, the
man who's responsible for Bobby's death and the poisoning of Anastasia's
husband.' He turned to Rudi. 'Well done. You've got the vital evidence
that proves the link between Stepurin and Gaspar. And the photograph
is dated. They've known each other for four years. That covers the time
of Anastasia's kidnap. I cannot stress how important this is. Thank you.
Thank you all.'

He stopped and thought for a few seconds before speaking again. 'So
Denis had all this, plus the information from his own inquiries. We're sure
he had nothing with him when he went to Congress, and if he had been
going to speak about this, he would need a lot of evidence with him. But
let me ask you – was he going to use it that day?'

'Naji?' Zoe said. 'You met Mr Hisami twice, you helped him on the
tech side?'

Naji didn't look up from his screen. 'I don't think so. Everything is
encrypted on a special laptop. This computer has never been used on the
internet and only Mr Hisami knows access code.'

'Oh, great,' said Macy.

'He has a device I adapted – an old calculator. I reprogrammed it.'

'His Tandy calculator!' said Anastasia 'The one in his briefcase!'

Naji nodded. 'You enter a twenty-digit number into calculator and it
will give you the code.'

'You have that number?' asked Samson, remembering that Naji had adapted an online game to hide the information he had stolen from hacking ISIS computers.

'No, Mr Hisami has the unlock code for the calculator.'

'He's in a coma!'

Naji shrugged. 'Yes, but I could maybe bypass . . .'

'The FBI have the briefcase with the calculator in it,' said Anastasia.

'Can you get it back?' asked Samson.

'Possibly,' she said a bit doubtfully, 'but that means Naji has to go to the States.'

'That will not be a problem for me,' said Naji.

CHAPTER 30

In pectore

They dispersed in ones and twos, and for the young this was a final parting. They were bound for destinations across Europe and few of them
would meet again. Zoe and Rudi were catching a ferry to Finland. Before
leaving, she came over to Samson and shook his hand. 'You're going to
get her, aren't you?' she asked.

'I hope so. I believe we can.'

'I know you will,' she said, and kissed him on the cheek. 'For my dad's
sake.'

Then Ulrike and Anastasia left together to meet up at the house with
Macy and the Bird, who had already taken off to find a drink. Samson
and Naji stayed behind to put away the screen and projector and order
the chairs. As Samson turned off the lights, he thought he heard a noise
from the small gallery above the rehearsal space. He put his finger to
his lips and waited. Naji nodded in the half-light – someone was there.
Samson indicated to the passageway and they made their way to the gate,
pressed the button to open it and banged it behind them. They moved to
the far side of the street and withdrew into a doorway, not far from the
drama-school entrance. After a few minutes Samson told Naji to go to

the house with his bag and enter by the garden entrance. He would stay because he needed to know who had been listening in.

It was a full half-hour before he heard the gate lock being operated and caught sight of Tomas Sikula pull up his collar and set off in the opposite direction. Samson dialled his number and watched him stop and search for his phone in his jacket.

'Keep it to yourself, Tomas,' he said.

'Ah, Samson. How good of you to call. Where are you?' He looked up and down the street.

'You'll get us all killed if that information gets out, Tomas.'

He let out a light, sardonic laugh. '*In pectore*, as they say in Rome. You realise that I was there with Ulrike's consent. It was the only way we'd allow a meeting like that to happen in our capital city. Besides, dear Samson, it saves you having to brief me tomorrow.' He was still searching the street.

'We're depending on you, Tomas.'

'You have my word. We have already made assurances to Ulrike. By the way, the drama school was my idea.'

'Then I'll say goodbye, Tomas.' Samson stepped from the shadows and held up a hand.

'You take care, Samson.' Tomas acknowledged the wave and turned to continue on his way.

Samson didn't go immediately to Ulrike's house but found a bar with tables outside and, after begging a cigarette from the waitress, he considered what he was going to say to Toombs. He had an agreement and he was prepared to keep to it as much as he could, but it was a delicate calculation.

He smoked the cigarette down to the filter, swallowed most of the wine in one gulp and dialled the number on Toombs's card.

'Yep,' said Toombs. Samson heard the sound of a lavatory flushing.

'Where are you?'

'Guess!'

'I'm calling to say we're going ahead.'

'I have absolutely no idea what you're talking about.'

'A few hours ago you said you wanted a heads-up and . . .'

'You're mistaken,' said Toombs. He grunted as if lifting something.

'This sounds like a bad moment. Maybe another time.'

'It's not a bad moment, I just don't understand why you're calling me.'

'I'll say goodnight then.'

'Goodnight.'

Samson hung up. Toombs had been shut down and was being extremely circumspect on the phone, though, clearly, he was in a bathroom and alone. Had the staff of the Director of National Intelligence got to the CIA? Or maybe it was the Deputy National Security Advisor, Mike Proctor? Either way, it amounted to the same thing. The argument to cease and desist was simple enough: the supply chain for the nerve agent had been notionally eliminated and the end user, Vladan Drasko, had died in his motel room, so the threat to Congress and the American people could be said to no longer exist, although of course Stepurin was still at large. The same instruction had probably reached the FBI. With its domestic remit, there was even less reason for the Bureau to pursue the case, particularly if the administration had embraced the argument that the affair had nothing to do with Russia, or its agents. In these circumstances, it was almost inconceivable that the results of Harland's investigation would be aired and acted upon, whatever the proof that lay in Denis Hisami's air-gapped computer. He got up and, finding he had nothing less than a €50 note, waved it at a waitress. She came over with a tray of dirty glasses, set it down and counted out €38. One of the notes fluttered to the ground. He picked it up and placed it on the saucer for her. She thanked him then something caught her eye. Her smile faded. He spun round. A man in a motorcycle helmet was approaching. His hand reached inside his jacket. Samson knew he was going to be shot at and his only concern was that the waitress wasn't killed too. He pushed her to the ground, knocking over two metal tables and the tray of dirty glasses. He heard a screech of brakes and shouting, looked up and saw the same SUV in which he had been subjected to Toombs's disdain a few hours earlier. The vehicle had slewed to a halt, blocking the path of the man in the helmet. Three young agents with Toombs surrounded him. Although they weren't openly carrying weapons, Samson knew they wouldn't be other than armed. The man was pulled to the side of the street, frisked and relieved of two guns. He was forced to remove his helmet and was struck three times on the back of the head. The agents led him down to the cobbles and propped his head against the wall. Samson had never seen the man before.

He helped the waitress to her feet and examined the heel of her hand, which had been cut by broken glass. He wrapped a napkin around the cut then held her shoulder; she was shaking a little. Two of her colleagues rushed out to help. Samson picked up his rucksack and stood back.

'Sir!' said the voice behind him. 'Mr Toombs repeats – if you want to get killed, you're going the right way about it. He says you should leave Tallinn immediately.'

'I will do exactly as he suggests. Thank you.'

'You're welcome, sir! There's one other thing. I have a message from Mr Toombs. He says, keep going. That's all. I hope it means something to you.'

'That's interesting. Tell him I plan to.'

The Americans returned to their car, having dumped the weapons by the tables. Samson hoisted his backpack and suggested that the bar owner call the police. It had been stupid of him to sit outside. He apologised to the mystified young waitress and left her a tip well in excess of the money scattered on the ground.

He took his time to circle through the city on foot to Ulrike's house. Apart from needing to shake off any tail, he had a lot of thinking to do. The message from Toombs persuaded him that it might now be possible to use Anastasia's invitation to appear at the Congressional Committee, but they had very little time, six days at the most. They'd need luck and a good plan.

He pushed through the unlocked garden gate at 11 p.m. Ulrike and Anastasia were still up and he could see that the Bird had spread himself out in the conservatory, almost supine on one of the two sofas. He was holding a glass up in his fingertips as if offering a chalice to the Lord. When Samson entered, he beamed an enormous, mad grin. 'Macy thinks I should come with you to the States. You'll need protection.'

Anastasia gave a discreet shake of the head, but Ulrike said she supported the idea.

'Quite so,' said the Bird. 'I still know a trick or two and, if I'm guessing right, you are going to need me in Pennsylvania.'

Ulrike said, 'Take him, Samson. He is very, well . . .' She searched for the right word then gave up. 'Violent.'

'Agreed,' said the Bird, admiring the colour of the slivovitz.

'Let's think about it,' said Samson.

'Well, I'm at your disposal. What's more, Macy – who's fallen by the wayside and returned to barracks – is paying all my expenses. And I have a passport that will be suitable.'

Samson didn't need to talk about the Bird's passport, but he asked what he meant nonetheless.

'I will use my brother Alyn's passport. He was in point of fact a general before becoming attached to a Bulgarian lass, over whom he has a head start of something approaching thirty years and with whom he is setting up home on the Dorset coast. He's very happy there and hasn't moved from the United Kingdom in a decade. His passport is as new.'

'Why is this important?' asked Samson.

'General Alyn is a gun enthusiast and well known for the barbaric practice of killing large numbers of grouse in August. I can quite easily stand in for him and bullshit about guns for an eternity. I've listened to the blighter often enough.'

'You stole your brother's passport!' Samson shook his head.

'That seems harsh. I prefer "borrowed".'

Samson hadn't forgotten that his Aymen Malek identity included an active membership of a shooting club at Créteil, outside Paris, something he occasionally referred to in his posts. The gun interest was something they might work up into a story because, one way or another, they had to gain access to the remote cluster of houses in the Appalachians. 'If you can get to the Watergate Hotel in DC, we may be able to do something.'

'I'm fine with that,' said the Bird, going through the preparatory motions of elevating his great bony frame to a standing position. 'I'll be at the Watergate whenever you need me, or at the Natural History Museum, which I have long wanted to visit.'

After his departure, Samson laid out the basic plan. The two women listened intently and suggested changes, most of which he accepted. It was a long shot. Success would firstly rely on Naji gaining access to Denis's computer, and no one knew where it was. It would have to contain substantiating evidence to allow them to convert intelligence to fully formed allegations. They would need support from at least one member of Congress, probably two or three. Anastasia's performance in front of the committee would require careful planning, courage and a cool head. Finally, one of the most difficult tasks was to find those people who would credibly identify Mila Daus from the 1980s and testify, at short notice, in Washington. Samson said they would need at least four individuals, including Ulrike and Frick, to appear in person at the hearing. He understood that was a tall order. Ulrike wished them good night and took her laptop to her room to set about finding those individuals who might testify to Mila Daus's history.

After finalising their travel arrangements, they retired at 1 a.m. There was not space for them to have separate rooms, so Ulrike went to the room they'd occupied over two years before. From both Naji and Ulrike's rooms they heard the clatter of keyboards. They undressed. Samson folded his suit and laid out his clothes for the morning.

'I don't know another man who does that,' she said from the bed.

He smiled. 'Habit. Saves thinking about it in the morning.' He paused. 'It's going to be all on you in Congress. Can you do it?'

'And I like the beard you're growing. Is that a beard, or just a failure to shave?'

He looked at himself in the mirror on the chest of drawers. 'The second, but I think I'll keep it.' He turned to her. 'Can you do it? I mean, Congress?'

'Yes, I believe I can. Daus is the cause of everything bad that's happened to us in the last three years. I want to be her nemesis. I want to see her fucking face. I can do it. I'll do it for Denis, for Bobby, for me.'

He sat down on the bed beside her, feeling he should tell her about the gunman the CIA had briskly disarmed outside the café. But instead he just said, 'You know it's going to be risky.'

She nodded.

He laid her hand on hers and held her eyes with his.

'I'm sorry not to have told you about the baby,' she said.

He didn't reply but pulled her gently towards him and kissed her forehead.

He went to the other side of the bed and lay down. She let her head fall back on to the pillow, but her eyes remained open.

'I'll turn off the light?' said Samson.

'Yes, please do.'

Some ten minutes later, when Samson was nearly asleep, she reached out to take his hand and brought it to her lips and held it there. 'I've missed you so badly, Samson,' she said. She let him go and raised her head. 'Are you asleep?'

'Nearly.'

She was leaning over him, her hair brushing his forehead. She kissed him and drew back. 'Well, are you going to cooperate, or not? This bed is to blame. It has so many memories for me. I need you, and that is all there is to it. Would you consider a dream fuck?'

'What's a dream fuck?'

'When you more or less do it in your sleep in the middle of the night and the next day you wonder about it because it doesn't seem real and you decide that you dreamed the whole thing.' This was delivered in an urgent whisper to his cheek.

He smiled in the dark, turned to her and found her wrist and pushed it down, then took her other hand, interlocked fingers and pushed that down, too, so that she was pinned to the bed. He kissed her and said, 'Like this?'

'I wouldn't know. I'm asleep,' she murmured.

PART THREE

CHAPTER 31

Locked in

Denis's eyes were open but he did not see. Anastasia picked up his hand and held it between both hers. It was the first time she had touched her husband since the morning of the attack. Jim Tulliver looked on from the end of the bed. The doctor who had taken over from Lazarus, Jamie Carrew, was on the other side.

'What's this mean?' she asked Carrew.

'We don't know,' he replied. 'He's made a really excellent recovery from the procedure, and his heart and breathing are much better. We're not able to assess any neurological impairment because we can't do that without Denis saying what he can and can't do or feel.'

'Can he hear us? Can he understand?' She looked down at him, appalled. 'Can you hear me, Denis? Will you squeeze my hand, like you did the nurse's, and tell me that you understand?' There was no response. She peered into his eyes. He shut them then opened them again very slowly. 'Are you trying to tell me something?' She waited – nothing came back. 'Is he locked in?'

Carrew said, 'Possibly, but there's nothing in the literature to suggest this is a result of being exposed to a nerve agent. Perhaps we should not have this conversation in front of him.'

'No, I think we should, because if he's in there he'll be working through this himself. He'll want to know what we're doing. He's not a child. If it's bad news, he'll want to know. So I'm going to ask you – did he have a stroke during the operation?'

Carrew shook his head. 'We checked. His brain is fine.'

'But it isn't, is it? Is there some kind of stimulus you can give him?'

'Not without knowing what's the matter.'

'Might he be braindead?'

'No, he doesn't need any help breathing. And as you see, he's opening and shutting his eyes. We're in the process of consulting experts across the country with a video link. I hope that's okay with you.'

She thought about that. 'I don't want any film getting out. Are you sure about security? It could have a devastating effect on his business and the livelihoods of a lot of people.'

It evidently hadn't occurred to Carrew. She looked at Tulliver, exasperated. 'Can you have our lawyers be in touch with everyone who's seen the film of Denis as he is now and make sure it's never shared?'

When left alone with Denis she started talking about the things that most interested him: a re-design of their garden at the Mesopotamia estate, a trip to Jordan they had planned, tennis, his library and the people who worked for him. And then she bent close to his ear and spoke about Harland's funeral and everything that had happened in Estonia. She kept checking his eyes, but there wasn't the slightest flicker of recognition in them; the pulse of his intelligence was absent and she began to wonder if Denis had actually disappeared.

When she spoke about the computer – the special laptop that had never been used on the internet and was reserved for the accumulation of evidence against Mila Daus – she was so close to him that her lips brushed the top of his ear. 'We need to find that computer, and then Naji will try the code that he developed to read what's on it. Without it we can do nothing.' She suddenly felt hopeless and sat back. Then she noticed that his eyes had turned to her and the look of indifference had momentarily vanished. 'You're there!' she said, and kissed him. 'Hash, I know you're there.' But the eyes clouded and, although they remained looking in her direction, his presence, if that indeed was what it had been, had receded.

She stopped talking and held his hand for the next half-hour. Only when Tulliver knocked on the glass door did she let go and rise. 'We need to speak,' he said. 'Martin Reid is here. Says he's got something important for you.'

'What? Can't you tell him I'm with Denis?'

'He says he'll wait. Any change?'

She shook her head. He looked away. She reminded herself that Tulliver was devoted to her husband. 'I know it's hard, seeing him like this. I'm sorry for you, Jim. You're going through a lot.'

He made a gesture to say that what he was feeling didn't matter.

'What's Reid want?'

'Says he knows what Denis was going to reveal. He's down the hall by the dispensing machines.'

She found Reid sitting with hands across his stomach, looking bad-tempered.

'Marty, it's nice of you to come, but I really should be with Denis at this time.'

'How is he?'

'The doctors are pleased with his recovery from a minor procedure. Things are looking good.'

'I heard otherwise.'

'Well, you heard wrong,' she said, folding her arms.

'You told me you were going to the West Coast, but then I hear that you're in Europe. I like to be told the truth, Ana. That has to be the basis of our arrangement.'

'What arrangement? You came to me offering help. You said you were outraged about what had happened and you would do everything in your power to support us. But there was no arrangement, Marty. None! And what the hell are you doing, tracking my movements? I don't have to justify myself to you. Now . . .'

'Forgive my manners, Ana, they're a habit of a lifetime of deal-making. I'm too harsh. I meant to be of some help. Please sit down.'

'And no one calls me Ana. What did you want to say?'

'I'm sorry. I was given to understand that's what your friends called you.' He looked downcast for a moment. 'This is a complicated business. I'm not sure what to say. My sense is that Denis was about to reveal the source of the funds in TangKi, which were definitely from within the United States and can be traced to a man named Chester Abelman. I have all the evidence.'

'Who is he?' she said, knowing perfectly well.

'He runs GreenState on the West Coast – a big wheel in the Bay Area, supports a lot of projects. And he's into every kind of business and investment; a big buddy of the Goodhardts – Alan and Lily. You know them?'

'No.' She took a seat opposite the vending machine. 'But GreenState is an environmental organisation – how would they be involved in supporting fascist troublemakers in Europe? It doesn't make sense, Marty.'

'I thought maybe you had it all figured out – that Denis had tied all the loose ends. But you say you don't. Anyway, the money trail is there and that does have implications.'

'In what way? The Foreign Affairs Committee are hardly going to be interested in some right-wing whacko pretending to be a liberal environmentalist. I don't think it's going to impress Mr Speight.'

'Speight! Do not trust that man. He's a goddamn snake.'

'You said that before. Look, I'm unlikely to. He was the one who forced Denis into the hearing and then cut slices off him.'

'So, you've heard nothing about GreenState?'

She shook her head. 'No.'

'But I heard Denis was investigating the organisation.'

She was about to ask him who he'd heard that from but stayed her hand. The old bastard was fishing, and she'd let him dangle his line in the water a while longer. 'My only concern is Denis's health,' she said. 'You may not know this, but exposure to nerve agents in the organophosphate group of compounds can cause serious cognitive impairment, chronic seizures, etcetera. We have no expectation that Denis will remember what he was doing immediately before the attack, still less why. Is that clear, Marty?'

'So, there's nothing that I can work with. I was hoping that my people might be able to access his computer.'

She laughed. 'As you know, Denis never, ever carries anything with him. He rarely uses a cellphone and doesn't even have a wallet. Everything that Denis's lawyer had with him in the briefcase was destroyed; the laptop and all the papers were incinerated. Sorry to disappoint you, Marty, but I have nothing to give you. Thanks for your offer of help, though. It's really appreciated, and when Denis is better, he'll be grateful that you stayed true to your friendship. It means a lot to him.'

'Thank you. I will continue my work. Let me know if there's anything you need.'

He got up, gave her a cattle rancher's handshake, grunted goodbye and left with rather less spring in his step than when they'd met there before. The titan of business looked rather uncomfortable, to her mind, brought low and in some way humiliated.

She called Tulliver to tell him about the encounter. 'I need to speak to you about something else too,' she said. 'I'll see you on the roof in five.'

They stood in the shade, out of the dazzling glare of the early-morning sun. 'I need my husband's computer. The one he used for all this.' Her hand swept across Capitol Hill. 'You know what I'm talking about, Jim. The laptop that's never been used on the Web.'

He said nothing.

'Do you know where it is?'

'I may. But you can't get into it.'

'Leave that to me. Where is it?'

'In New York – at least, that's the last time I saw him use it.'

'Off you go then.'

'I can have the plane bring it down here.'

'No. I need you to go and find it and bring it back yourself.' He looked doubtful. 'Jim, I'm not going to take no.'

'You know what's on it?'

'I do, and I think you should have told me.'

'Anastasia, I have absolutely no idea what's on there, but I know it's more than a hand grenade.'

'It is. So, you go and get it. You need to be smart, Jim. Don't use the plane. Don't take your usual phone. Go and come back by different means. I suggest you don't go to the apartment but get Angel to bring it to you.' Angel looked after the place for them.

He made to leave but she stopped him. 'There's more, Jim. How much was Denis paying Zillah Dee?' She'd met the former National Security Agency employee who owned and ran Dee Strategy after her kidnap to thank Zillah for her part in bringing about her release. She knew Denis rated her abilities and that he must have used her.

Tulliver grimaced at the question.

'So, she was working on this. How much?'

'About three, maybe nearer four million.'

'Jesus! That's lot of money.'

'Could be much more. I wasn't aware of all the ways he paid her. She set up a separate team, effectively a special operation. It was a big deal.'

'They were checking stuff the young team brought in?'

'I believe so, but Denis held it all. That I do know. He received hundreds of thumb drives that were destroyed after one use. They didn't transfer by email or over the Web and it was all encrypted.'

Tulliver knew a lot more than he'd ever let on, which annoyed her, but she said nothing because she needed him on her side and he seemed more willing now that Denis's recovery was obviously going to take a long time. 'I'll need to see her. Are you able to fix that in the next twenty-four hours?'

'Won't be a problem – she's in DC.'

He left and she called Matthew Corner in Warren Speight's office, with Martin Reid's warning ringing in her ears. Snake he might be, but she and Denis, who had, after all, been Mila Daus's primary target for the past three years, had nothing to lose. Corner put her through to Speight and it was agreed that she would appear in front of the committee at 2 p.m. on the following Monday. The chairman of the committee, Harry Lucas, had allotted two and a half hours.

'That's like a confirmation hearing,' she said. 'How will you fill it?'

'Oh, we're not going to have any problem with that, Mrs Hisami. I have plenty of questions, and I know that when my colleagues on both sides hear that you'll be appearing, there'll be no shortage of interest.'

'When will that be?' she asked.

'Considering recent history, we thought it advisable not to announce your participation in these proceedings until after the committee has risen for lunch. A few members will be informed ahead of time, but for the majority your evidence will come as a pleasant surprise.'

'Can I be open with you, Congressman Speight?'

'I would expect nothing less.'

'Please regard this as confidential. My husband is not at all well. They're not sure what's the matter with him, but he is not responding in the way they hoped. If his condition worsens, I will need to be by his side. I hope you understand.'

'I don't wish to presume, but it is my assessment that your husband would, in these dire circumstances, wish you to appear, even if things look very bad.'

'I need that option,' she said. It was not only an option to be with Denis, but one that allowed her to bow out of the hearing if things went wrong, or if they didn't manage to prise the secrets from Denis's computer.

'That's reasonable. I will tell Chairman Lucas.'

'Thank you. I want to say something else. When I met you I felt that I could trust you, Congressman. But since then I've been most specifically warned against doing that.'

He thought about this. 'I'm grateful for your candour, and you're right that in this line of work it's advisable to watch who you trust. But I have found that when two people have the same interests at heart and hope for a particular outcome, no matter where they start from, trust is never an issue. Do you play bridge, Mrs Hisami?'

'No.'

'A good practice in bridge is to trust your partner. Never assume he or she has made a mistake. Watch closely. Keep the faith and we will prevail. I'll see you Monday.'

From the rooftop, she phoned Special Agent Reiner. Three times it went straight to voicemail, so she left a message for him to call her on the fourth. It was odd that he hadn't been in touch since her return.

She returned to Denis's bedside and, between talking to him, played his favourite music. He was oddly catholic in his taste – AC-DC, Dire Straits, the Cranberries, Bach, Haydn and Mozart. As a young man, he'd listened to heavy metal on a Walkman when fighting in Northern Iraq, and it was still his practice, if he had something to think through, to go to the end of their property in Mesopotamia with his headphones on and look out at the ocean. She found a video that Denis admired of the Cranberries performing 'Zombie', a raw protest against the violence in Northern Ireland. At the end of the number her phone signalled an incoming call. It was Special Agent Reiner.

'You were trying to reach me, Mrs Hisami. What can I do for you?'

'Are you aware of my husband's condition?'

'I had heard, yes.'

'We're trying very hard to reach him and stimulate his memory with familiar sounds and objects, and I wondered if you could return his brief-case to me. I understand that you'll need to retain the calendar, but there are things in there that I would like to use to try to remind him who he is. Can you do that for us?'

Reiner coughed. 'That won't be possible, I'm afraid.'

'It's my husband's property, and you have all you need on the attack in Congress. I've given you as much help as I know how. The suspect is dead. Why?'

'The investigation is still ongoing. I'd truly like to oblige, but there's really nothing I can do at this time.' She thought briefly of asking for the calculator, but dismissed it as too risky. 'Was there anything else, Mrs Hisami? No? We will no doubt be in contact when we need.' No mention of what had happened in Macedonia. His manner was remote and entirely official.

She lowered the phone. Denis's eyes had turned to her and were watching.

Tulliver would normally catch the shuttle to Manhattan, but he'd heard the door-to-door limo service was as quick when you took into consideration delays and cab lines at La Guardia, so a car picked him up at his hotel half an hour after he left Anastasia. She was right to warn him about the phones, but he'd need one when he was in Manhattan to arrange a rendezvous with Angel. He'd brought an old phone and it was on charge at the USB port in front of him. The driver, a big talker named Andy, was eventually asked to keep quiet and Tulliver used the time to catch up on sleep.

He called Angel when they'd passed through the Lincoln Tunnel, but someone named Manny answered.

'Is this the Hisami residence?' he asked.

'Think so, yes.'

'What do you mean, you think so? Where's Angel?'

'Angel is illegal.'

'What?'

'Angel is with ICE – they say he is illegal. I am Manny, from Nicaragua. His friend. I watch place for Angel. He is in jail.'

'Are you at Mr Hisami's apartment now?'

'No, at home.'

'Why did you say you were? How long will it take you to get there?'

Manny had problems of comprehension but finally it was established that he was in the Bronx and it would take him forty-five minutes to an hour to reach Tribeca. He promised he would leave soon. Tulliver repaired to a sports bar and watched baseball. It was over ninety minutes before Manny phoned to say he was in the apartment. He had some bad news, however. Someone had been there and the place looked a mess.

Tulliver went to see what kind of mess before using Manny's phone to call Anastasia. 'They had Angel arrested on a phony immigration offence and tossed the place,' he said, surveying the empty drawers, upturned furniture and gutted cushions. 'Maybe you should check Mesopotamia.'

Anastasia muttered, 'Got it,' then hung up.

Tulliver began his search. First he looked beneath the top of the elaborate drinks table, but someone had already lifted the bottles and decanters and checked the space below. He went to the office. The five or six desktop computers used by Denis's staff when they were crashing a deal were all askew. He had no doubt their passwords had been hacked and their hard drives stripped. An Apple laptop Denis used for business had gone, an iPad also. The box files had been opened and papers dumped at the bottom of the shelves, plainly unread. In the small library all the books had been pulled from the shelves and left in heaps. There was no attempt to hide the search, or the desperation behind it. Manny came to ask if he should start clearing up the kitchen, or wait until Angel was released later that day.

Tulliver did a double take. 'Why didn't you tell me that Angel was being released?'

He pulled out his personal phone. There was brief message from Angel's wife in Spanish.

'You get some big-shot lawyer and Angel is free, right?' said Manny with a broad grin.

No such lawyer had been employed, but Tulliver didn't bother to question that.

'Call Mrs Lopes and tell her to get Angel here as soon as possible.' This he did, then stomped off, bow-legged and cheerful, to deal with the kitchen. Manny was more maintenance man than major domo, but when Angel appeared three hours later his talents were needed. It was Angel's idea to follow the electricity. If there was a computer hidden somewhere, it would, given Mr Hisami's fastidious nature, be on charge. They began to check all the sockets in the apartment. Manny, with a headlamp fixed around his reversed baseball cap, traced every flex and cable along ducts, behind radiators and through wardrobes and cupboards. At midnight they found what they were looking for – a socket in the office that had been hard-wired with an extension lead that vanished under the reclaimed oak panel floor. Manny followed it with a wire tracker to an air-conditioning vent on the wall. He unhooked the grille, peered inside then felt the top of the vent. A grin spread across his face. A disguised security drawer. There was a lock but no key. He forced it open easily with a pry bar and the drawer, in which lay a pristine laptop, slid out.

Tulliver unplugged it and slipped it into a padded envelope. He thanked Manny, gave him a hundred-dollar note and asked Angel to remain.

'Tell me about the lawyer, Angel,' he said when Manny had gone. 'I want to know everything about your arrest and release.'

Cuth Avocet liked to do crossword puzzles and he sent what he insisted later was an ingenious clue by text to Samson. 'Meet oldest bird in conservative surroundings.' Samson knew to go to the Museum of Natural History and without much trouble found his way to the dinosaur wing, paid for by the late David H. Koch, one of the ultra-Conservative Koch brothers – thus, the 'conservative surroundings' – and to a cabinet of four fossils, the last two of which clearly had feathered wings. In front of these stood the Bird, in his oversized trainers and faded cap, mouth open in wonder.

'Are you the fossil or the oldest bird?' said Samson to his back.

'Contemporaries,' he replied, turning with an unhinged look of joy. 'Good trip? No problems with our friends in the Office?'

Samson moved close to him. 'Nyman and Ott are going to be a problem here in Washington. They're working against us through the UK ambassador and the White House. The CIA has been called off and Anastasia thinks the FBI have been told to find other things to do. They refused to give her the briefcase, by the way.'

'That's a pisser,' said the Bird, turning back to the cabinet and the fossil of a small dinosaur frozen in balletic pose. 'But I'm sure my new friend over there will get round that.'

Naji was examining a cabinet of marine dinosaurs. He wore ear buds and hadn't seen Samson. 'We did a deal,' continued the Bird. 'Yesterday was spent in the National Air and Space Museum and today is dinosaurs and large mammals.' He laughed. 'He's a hell of a character. We attended a lecture with an astrophysicist named Sanjana Vadiki – no, I hadn't heard of her either – but Naji had and engaged her in a debate about the na-ture of gravity in black holes. She tried to find out who he was, but we thought it best to leave before he got too deep in.'

'How are we fixed with the foot doctor?'

'He took the bait good and proper. My brother's name and rank are what did it. I don't think I told you that Alyn makes Mussolini look soft. Having acquainted himself with Alyn's barbaric slaughter of deer and birds, he's gagging to meet me and talk weaponry. We're on for the morrow. He has asked details about you, so I suggest you brush up your profile.'

'Are we meeting at Seneca Ridge? That's crucial.'

'He hasn't given me an address. We need $20,000 cash deposit if we're going to talk business about the Nitro Express. He wants to see the money and know we're good for it. That's our entry ticket. I'll arrange that with Macy this afternoon.'

'I'll explain on the way. Nine o'clock at your hotel. I'll bring the car.'

'Needs to be showy,' said the Bird.

Samson glanced at him with some amusement. 'So I don't let you down, Cuth?'

Naji wandered over and gave Samson a fist bump. They adjourned to the café, where Naji consumed three Danishes and a lot of Diet Coke. Samson aimed his words at the table. 'The laptop is on its way now. Can you get into it without the calculator?'

Naji threw his head back. 'It'll take a long time. Mr Hisami is the only one who knows the code for the calculator, and that will take me hours to bypass.'

'What about the computer? Can you bypass the need for a code?'

Naji shook his head slowly. 'There are two things we need, and we don't have either. We can't yet prove Mila Daus was once a Stasi officer and we don't have access to the evidence of her networks. We don't have the code and the laptop is somewhere between New York and here, so we concentrate on exposing Daus. For that I'll need to see the film of Seneca Ridge again. Can you send it to me, please?'

Naji slid a thumb drive across the table. 'This is all footage from the drone. Close-ups, also.'

'That's helpful. You'll need to watch it, Cuth.'

'Already have. Lots of good film of her.'

Samson got up. 'We'll speak later.' He gave the Bird a tilt of the head to suggest that maybe they shouldn't be running around town too much before the committee hearing. The Bird nodded.

CHAPTER 32

Seneca Ridge

Samson watched the footage early the next day in his room, with coffee and a bowl of fruit and granola. He'd had no contact with Anastasia but had received messages from Tulliver overnight informing him of the situation with Denis and the successful search for 'a lost item' in New York. By return, Samson said he knew things were difficult at the hospital but asked him to make sure that she would be free later.

The film of Seneca Ridge was more recent than the one shown in the rehearsal room – the woods had filled out and the trees around the houses were in leaf and cast deep shadows. From the dates on the footage Samson realised that Mila Daus appeared with her bodyguards on Friday evening at around six or Saturday morning at eleven. She always dressed in dark colours, usually brown or black, and invariably wore sunglasses, but once or twice there were clear images of her from an angle, so it was possible to identify her without any doubt. From the flight log of Learjet 60 XR, Rudi Rosenharte had learned that she invariably flew in from DC, Boston, MA, or Richmond, VA, where her businesses were mostly located. Occasionally, weekend guests arrived at the same time or a little after her. He concluded that she almost certainly wouldn't be there that day, which was a Thursday.

Gaspar and his weekend wife seemed to occupy adjacent houses on the property, while the prow of Seneca Ridge, with its views over a small, meandering river and tracts of forest, was reserved for guests. The security presence was light, essentially just two men at any one time. Three utility task vehicles were parked behind Gaspar's house and trails led down from the rocky outcrop of Seneca Ridge into the woods. Most of the service activity – the arrival of catering staff in a blue van and maintenance men and deliveries – also took place behind Gaspar's quarters. Samson guessed the foot doctor ran the household for her.

He had time before taking delivery of the rented Range Rover to look through footage of the comings and goings at the weekends, with some close-ups of guests arriving. He searched for the balding, shaven head of Anatoly Stepurin but, unsurprisingly, failed to find him. Yet there was a large man who lumbered with his feet pointing outwards and wore a cap that gave Samson pause. His face was hidden but there was something familiar about him, and Samson instantly remembered Ulrike telling him about the famous businessman who had been compromised with a young girl. He clipped that part of the film and sent it to Anastasia via a messaging app.

He felt there was little hope of accessing and organising the information on the computer before her appearance at the committee's hearing, but if they could prove who Mila Daus was, that would go a long way to disrupting her operation. He changed into his blue suit jacket, a clean pair of trousers, a blue shirt and coffee-brown silk tie. For the first time, he combed and shaped his new beard, which was no novelty for him. His entire time in Syria and Northern Iraq, searching for Ayshel Hisami, he hadn't shaved. He gave himself a parting, which he never usually bothered with, and put on the slightly blue-tinted glasses that changed his appearance so well. Overnight, he had done a lot of work on two social media sites, fleshing out his business life with mentions of deals and banks he was working with, dropping the names of famous investors. He also worked up the gun-club aspect, using stills from videos of the gun range at Club de Tir Sportif de Créteil and photographs of targets, guns and men brandishing pistols. There were also heavy hints about his admiration for Le Pen's National Front. He sent the biographical information to the Bird, who passed it on without links to the foot doctor, who would doubtless conduct his own quick checks and feel the more reassured for having done so.

Anastasia saw a message from Samson at 8.30 a.m., a couple of hours after he had sent it, and looked closely at the few seconds of film. At first, it meant nothing to her because he hadn't explained why he'd sent it. Then it dawned that she should concentrate on the central figure in a group of three walking between a black vehicle and one of the houses at Seneca Ridge. The individual carried a jacket over his arm, held out in front of him, and walked in a particular way, at the same time both awkward and determined. It reminded her very much of the man who had twice visited the hospital in the last ten days, offering her support and all his resources, but had not in fact produced anything of use. She replied: 'Marty Reid.' At which Samson sent her an exclamation mark then a beat later another message: 'Do you think he could be the businessman she compromised with an underage girl? Does that seem possible with Reid???'

She thought about that. 'Maybe' she replied.

'I have an idea,' wrote Samson.

Minutes after this she received another text from him but from a different number, asking her to a quick breakfast at Place du Café, ten minutes' walk from the hospital. She shouldered her bag, touched Denis's arm and said she would be gone for forty-five minutes. There was no response and she left the room without a backward glance. Sometimes she felt he was there with her, but that morning there had been no hint that he understood what was going on around him, no sense of that watchful intelligence. Later that day he would have a brain scan, to see if he had in fact suffered a stroke during the procedure to regularise his heartbeat, which was now the doctors' preferred theory: 'Ischemic infarctions in the territory of the middle cerebral artery,' as Carrew had put it, without a trace of his habitual optimism.

She was glad to be outside and walked briskly, working through the implications of Reid's behaviour. His attempt to gain her confidence had been so clumsy she had always half suspected him, and had said nothing of importance to him. Yet he'd gained knowledge of Denis's condition, and that must have been relayed to Mila Daus. The less immediate question was how long he'd been working with her. Did the relationship go all the way back to the business at TangKi, when a co-investor and Denis's friend Gil Leppo seemed to be the lone traitor who had conspired in her kidnap to put pressure on Denis? And she wondered how Samson could use the information about Reid's relationship with Mila Daus.

The Place du Café was a large, busy establishment with orders being shouted out and a churn of young Beltway professionals carrying non-disposable coffee cups. She took a table at the far side of the café, ordering from the waitress as she sat down, coffee and toast that she was unlikely to eat. There was no sign of Samson. Two boisterous young men in their thirties jumped on the table next to her. A woman, also in a suit, joined them, and they chatted about the unprecedented spring heat and a tennis tournament in which they'd all competed. Then they left. She glanced at her phone. There were no messages. She called Samson and got his voicemail. 'I'm here,' she said, rather forlornly, because she had felt a lift at the idea of seeing him. They hadn't seen each other since Estonia, and they needed to talk, though she wasn't sure what she should or could say. She waited a few minutes, accepted a refill, toyed with the toast and called again. Nothing.

Her phone vibrated. 'Where the hell are you?' she demanded.

'The item you asked to be returned,' said a woman's voice. 'It's beneath the banquette to your right.'

Anastasia felt below the banquette. It was a briefcase – Denis's briefcase.

'Have you located it, Mrs Hisami? Good. You have a great day, now.'

She brought the briefcase to her own chair and put money on top of the bill. As she looked for her waitress, she saw Special Agent Reiner turn, fold a copy of the *Post* and look at her over his glasses. He nodded to her, got up and walked out.

She left the Place du Café a few minutes later and waited outside until she saw a red cab, which she hailed. She told the driver to circle while she made calls. She dialled Tulliver, without success, then got Samson, who was driving and on speaker, and told him about the text sent by the FBI pretending it was from him and the briefcase.

Samson understood immediately the significance of the briefcase covertly returned to Anastasia by the FBI. It chimed with the CIA's intervention in the street in Tallinn and the news that a lawyer from one of the most expensive firms in Manhattan had been hired – God knows by whom – to spring Angel so that he was free to help Tulliver locate the computer. They now had everything except the code to access the computer and proof of Daus's identity. These were enormous challenges, but what he dwelt on as they headed on the 270 to the city of Frederick was what the covert help from two intelligence agencies meant. He sounded out the Bird and got a surprisingly cogent answer. 'Those two senior officers wouldn't be acting without the knowledge of their superiors so that means there's a struggle inside Executive with the British sucking up to the White House, which, for reasons we cannot fathom, is keen to keep Russia out of the story of the attack on Congress.'

'What are those reasons?'

'Too soon to say,' said the Bird. Samson glanced over. The madness in his eyes for once was replaced by thoughtfulness. 'But if we can prove Daus is the former Stasi beauty queen and that she's actively working for Vlad the Impaler, a lot of the rest will take care of itself.'

The traffic was heavy and just past Frederick they came to a stop with an accident involving a truck and a boat transporter. The boat, which had fallen from the trailer into the bank to the right, reminded Samson of his trip across the North Sea.

'Ah yes, Gus. He died, you know. A heart attack the day after you left,' said the Bird.

'I'm very sorry to hear that. What about Fleur?'

'She gets the boat, and her freedom. Gus was a very brave man, but extremely keen on the sauce and an absolute demon to live with on a boat, I shouldn't wonder.'

'I'd have liked to have known about his drinking.'

He passed a hand across his forehead. 'Slipped my mind. A lot going on, what with Macy and so forth.'

'Macy and so forth?'

'I am afraid Macy is on his way out. Like Bobby, he's been given a few months. But in Macy's case there's absolutely nothing to be done. It's his liver. He's given it quite a pasting these last few years.' The Bird looked at him. 'I'm sorry, but I thought you needed to hear. He wants you to know, but he's never going to tell you himself because he's that kind of bloody fool Englishman. He has plans for you to take over Hendricks Harp and he was asking me what I thought about that when you bowled into the office the other day. Loves you like a son, he does.' He stopped. 'You'd do well, running Hendricks Harp.'

Samson felt a profound sadness wash over him. Macy was, in truth, the best friend he had, but the idea of succeeding him at Hendricks Harp was ridiculous. It wasn't him.

'I know you're very fond of him,' the Bird continued, 'even though Macy is on the slippery side.'

'Yes,' said Samson, to both those things.

'Everyone's moving on – Bobby, Gus, and now Macy – and they're leaving the fight to the likes of you and those impressive young people I met in Tallinn. Same fight, same old enemy.'

They stopped on a rural road so that the Bird could watch a bull elk sloshing in a stream a little distance from the road. He took the opportunity to relieve himself and, as he did so, shouted over his shoulder that the Lakota tribe, members of the Great Sioux nation, valued the elk for its sexual prowess; male babies were given an elk tooth to ensure lifelong courage and potency.

The entrance to Seneca Ridge was so inconspicuous they missed it and had to turn back. They found the gate and a lodge hidden around a bend. A man wearing a green jacket with 'Seneca Ridge Staff' printed on the breast pocket looked at their passports, made a note of the Range Rover's plate and called up to the ridge, as he put it. The gates opened and they travelled up the winding drive to the cluster of houses they knew well from the drone footage, parked and got out. The door to Gaspar's quarters opened and a man in hiking clothes and lightweight boots exited, his hand outstretched.

'It's an honour to meet you, General,' he said. 'Glad you could make it.' He did not offer a hand to Samson, but merely nodded in his direction and turned towards the open double doors. The Bird shook his head and winked at him.

They entered a wide hallway with walls filled with old guns, cases of medals, and nineteenth-century photographs of hunters standing on and around slaughtered animals. Further on, there were displays of Bowie knives, a moccasin jacket with tassels and a confederate cap and flag. Samson took in Gaspar: an edgy manner, bodybuilder's neck and forearms, a small, downturned mouth and eyes set too close together. He was as tall as Samson yet seemed to be overly conscious of the Bird towering over him. Apart from his very blue eyes, Gaspar was unremarkable – more like a construction worker or a plumber than a doctor, certainly not someone who seemed capable of ordering the murder of Robert Harland and the attack on Denis Hisami in Congress, or, indeed, the subsequent liquidation of all the deadbeat assassins hired by his hunting buddy Anatoly Stepurin. And there was no suspicion in his eyes whatsoever, even though he had apparently signed off on the contracts on Samson by Miroslav Rajavic – the Matador – and, subsequently, the Dutch lowlife Pim Visser. Samson doubted whether he ever knew these names, so remote was he from the actual fact of the killings and attempted killings.

'I have something to show you, gentlemen,' said Gaspar, moving them on from the displays in the hallway. 'We can take a glass of lemonade while we talk about the gun.'

They turned into a huge room that made the Bird gasp. From floor to ceiling were arranged severed heads, stuffed bodies, amputated limbs, stretched hide and mounted skins; and tusks, teeth, tails and claws – evidence of Gaspar's lifetime asymmetric war against the animal kingdom. It was a revolting sight. The Bird looked up at the head of an elephant; next to it the heads of a rhinoceros, a hippo and a buffalo, each with its mouth agape, eyes replaced with lifeless glass. 'You killed all these?' he said.

'Yep, every last one of them.'

'And the leopard?' said the Bird, turning to the wall on the left, where the big cat posed on a branch.

Gaspar nodded. He had his hands in his pockets and rocked on his heels, partly to seem taller but also from excitement and pride. 'The elephant, rhino and buffalo were all nailed with the Nitro Express.'

'Were they charging you?' asked the Bird with a deadly cool.

'No, General, they were not. But they were close. I was in some peril.'

The Bird looked round silently. His eyes fell on a stuffed crocodile at the far end of the charnel house. Its mouth was open to accommodate a bottle of Glenmorangie whisky on a small silver platter.

Samson saw that he could stand it no more. 'Perhaps we should look at the gun,' he said.

A wooden case had been laid on the table with three sizes of ammunition lined up in front. Gaspar opened it reverentially and out fluttered the bill of sale from more than a century before and details of the weapon's ownership since. Gaspar handed them to the Bird, who passed them to Samson. 'My friend here will examine these. He's the expert. He's one of the best shots in Europe, though is far too modest to say so.'

'Oh, right,' said Gaspar. This was the first time he had really acknowledged Samson.

Gaspar picked up the gunstock and barrels and snapped them together,
then fitted the forend to the underside of the two barrels. He hefted it,
broke it open to reveal the twin chambers and handed it to the Bird. He
selected the largest bullet, which was over three inches long. 'With this
gun, I recommend this 450 Nitro Express black powder cartridge, which
propels a .458-inch-diameter 480 grain bullet to a muzzle velocity 2,150
feet per second.'

The Bird nodded as though he knew what the hell Gaspar was talking
about, examined the workmanship and engraving and looked down the
chambers. He gave it back to Gaspar.

'As a matter of fact,' continued Gaspar, 'I had quite a bit of fun in
Africa showing this weapon to a friend of mine who doubted its destruc-
tive power. There was this baboon out on the savannah. I loaded one of
these babies into the breach, took aim at said baboon and fired, and, well,
there wasn't a lot left of that ugly old monkey.' He stopped. 'Lemonade,
gentlemen? Where's my lemonade? Where's Hector with my goddamn
lemonade?' He went to the door and yelled.

A small Hispanic man bearing a tray appeared with a flurry of apologies, set it down and poured the lemonade. He handed a glass to Samson
and Gaspar but missed the Bird's hand and the lemonade spilled on to
the green baize of the tabletop. In his rush to mop up the spilled liquid,
Hector knocked over the bullets that had been carefully ranked by size
by Gaspar and they clattered on to the floor.

'My fault,' said the Bird, stooping to pick them up. 'Entirely my fault.
Must be the thrill of seeing this beautiful gun.' Samson saw him palm two
of the bullets and wondered what he planned to do with them. But his
attention went to Gaspar, who had put the rifle down and was looking
furiously at Hector. 'You can leave,' said Gaspar. 'Take your money at
the end of the week and do not come back. Just leave!'

'But it was my fault,' said the Bird.

Gaspar shook his head. Hector left. 'Okay, so let's go and try her out. You want to shoot the gun, right?' He slapped his forehead. 'You brought the deposit money, should you wish to buy this beauty. Twenty thou was what we agreed.'

'Mr Malek has the money.'

'You want to see it now?' asked Samson. 'I can easily go and get it.'

'You left twenty grand in the car? Jeez!'

'You have good security,' said Samson.

'Maybe you should go and get it. Meet us out back. It will be obvious to you. Take the path between the buildings, Mr Malek.' Gaspar mispronounced the name May-lek. That he was a racist prick and treated him like the help did not bother Samson in the least. He needed to look around. He left by the front door and retrieved two bundles of hundred-dollar bills in a transparent envelope from the locked glove compartment of the car, divided them and put them in his inside pockets. He saw he had messages, one of which was from Zillah Dee. 'Meet tonight or to-morrow?' Samson replied, 'Tonight.'

He locked the door and took the path between the buildings to the service area at the back, which formed a kind of alley. His behind resting on the strata of rock that jutted from the ground, left by the builders as an interesting effect, Hector was smoking and looking absolutely desperate.

Samson stopped by him. 'I'm so sorry about that.'

Hector looked up. He didn't bother to conceal that he'd been crying. He shook his head and tried to pull himself together. Samson placed a hand on his shoulder. 'It was completely unfair.'

'Thank you, sir. It is my daughter. She needs treatment for cancer. I had this job and one at the store to pay for it. Now I have just one job and that doesn't pay well.'

Samson stepped back. 'I'll give you money.' He opened his jacket to reveal one of the wads of cash. 'I just have to show Gaspar I've got it with me. If you meet me here later, it's yours.' Hector didn't know what to say. 'But I wonder if there's something you can do for me.'

Hector nodded, now open to any hope.

'I'm an investigator, and I need to prove something about Mr Gaspar's wife. Can you get me something with her DNA on it? A comb, a hair-brush or a toothbrush – anything that definitely has her DNA. Hair would be really good. A jumper might do it.'

Hector considered this. 'How much money do you have?'

'I have twenty thousand on me. I will give you half whatever happens, because there's no question in my mind that the person whose money this is would want you to have it. I will give you the other half if you manage to come up with something. I don't want to put you in any danger, but if you think you can manage it, I'd be very grateful.'

Hector looked away and thought. 'Okay, I do it. They are not good people.'

'Believe me, I know this, Hector. We have a deal. You keep an eye out for our return and I'll make sure you have that money.'

He found the Bird and Gaspar talking beside a Pinzgauer, a German utility vehicle. The Bird was already looking pretty weary but Gaspar was so keen to impress he hadn't noticed. They all got in and set off down the ridge, following a track into the woods. Gaspar was opening up with unmediated theories about black people, Mexicans, Jews and Arabs then suddenly brought the vehicle to such a shuddering halt that the gun case and metal ammunition box slid from the seat beside Samson. Gaspar, now wearing wrap-around reflective sunglasses, jumped out of the vehicle and jogged to a grassy patch in a clearing thirty paces from the track. 'You gentlemen need to look at this!' he called out.

They climbed down reluctantly. In the tall grass, a bear had keeled over on its side and expired. One massive front paw was raised, as if trying to ward off its attacker. 'Have a guess what killed this sucker?'

'You?' said the Bird, quietly.

'Kind of, yeah! That little plug in the ground you see right there is an M-44 trap. The animal comes along, chews and pulls at the bait, and bang!

The spring-powered ejector is triggered and sends a plume of cyanide into the animal's face. This site right here has killed two bears, a coyote and a bob cat.' He looked down at the bear. 'That's the biggest yet – six hundred pounds or more.'

'Aren't these illegal?' asked Samson, as appalled as the Bird.

'No sirree! Not if you have contacts in the Wildlife Services Agency. Hell, I'm doing their job for those sons of bitches.' He made a call to his staff and told them to dispose of the bear and charge the M-44 with a new capsule of poison. Then his eyes followed a movement in a glade dappled with spring sunshine. A deer looked inquisitively in their direction. 'A Northern white-tail,' said Gaspar. 'Go get the gun. May-lek and I can show the general what killing power looks like.'

Samson didn't move.

'Didn't you hear me, May-lek?'

'It's *Malek*, Mr Gaspar, and I did hear you, but that animal will be gone before I return. And we really want to see the accuracy of the Nitro Express on the target you promised us.'

Gaspar wasn't listening. He had pulled a pistol from his pocket and, seconds later, fired. The deer jumped and tore off, uninjured. Samson caught a look of hatred briefly flood the Bird's face. 'Not now,' he said under his breath as they walked back to the vehicle. 'Focus on what we came for. There's been a development. When we get back, delay him for ten minutes inside the house.'

A target had been set up a little way on, but before Gaspar put the gun together he wanted sight of the money and made some show of counting it. They fired the gun with different sizes of ammunition, the longest shells giving a kick twice as powerful as the two-inch ones. The Bird, who, like his brother, was a very good shot, effortlessly blew an almost circular hole with six bullets in the centre of the target. Samson did less well but bettered Gaspar, who reminded them he was selling the gun because of a shoulder injury.

On the way back the Bird said, 'The second trigger is not quite what it should be, old chap. A bit sticky, wouldn't you say? Can your gunsmith look at it?'

'Are you kidding me? It's in perfect condition, General.' Gaspar was outraged.

'Well, it's just my impression, but otherwise I like the gun. What do you say, Aymen?'

Samson agreed and said he thought it worth the price of $75,000.

Nothing more was heard from Gaspar until they reached the Ridge. He said he would look at the trigger and maybe use a little oil. They'd talk it over inside; maybe the General would like a fine malt whisky he'd opened.

Samson got out, said he'd go back to the car to check something, and headed for the passageway.

He found Hector waiting in the spot, a bag at his feet. 'I have what you want,' Hector said.

'That's terrific. What did you get?'

'Razor for the legs and a comb for the hair. In freezer bags.'

'You got these items pretty quickly. How did you do that?'

'Martha, the maid, brought them to me. I pay her. It was hard because Mrs Gaspar, she is here.'

'Gaspar's wife is here now!' It was a Thursday. Daus wasn't meant to be at the Ridge.

Samson looked him in the eye, saw nothing to mistrust and handed him the money.

'She is with Mr Gaspar and your friend in the den right now.'

'How do I go back in – through the front?'

'Ring the bell – someone will come. Maybe Martha.'

He went to the car and locked the two freezer bags and the rest of the money in the glove compartment. He waited for a couple of minutes in the hope that the Bird would extricate himself, but the risk of Mila Daus testing his story was too great to leave it any longer and he went to ring the bell. Within a few seconds a young maid in uniform opened it. She was flushed and darted a look of terror at him. 'Martha?' he said quietly. 'Is she with them?'

She nodded, wrung her hands and indicated the way.

'Don't worry about a thing.' He hissed then asked loudly, 'Where's the general?'

Mila Daus stood at the far end of the room, arms crossed, each hand resting on the opposing bicep. She was looking at the Bird, who'd flung himself down in a leather chair and was descanting on boar hunting in Hungary, a whisky in his hand. She looked up with sudden focus when Samson came in.

'This is Mr May-lek,' said Gaspar, 'the general's driver. Speaking of help, I let Hector go.'

'Hector?' she murmured.

'He's gone. It doesn't matter. A servant.'

'There will be no problem for lunch?' she said, still without acknowledging Samson verbally, although her gaze had not left him.

'I got it covered,' said Gaspar. Out in the woods, Samson had wondered what Mila Daus was doing with this crude, parochial and not very bright individual. It was now clear. Gaspar ran things for his wife as a major domo and, when required, he did her dirty work. There was no hint of an equal relationship between them.

The Bird coughed. 'Aymen is my driver and friend. He's in banking. Lives in France.'

'Actually, I am more involved in politics now,' Samson said, not wishing to be tested too closely on banking.

She took this in with a nod. 'How interesting,' she said. 'Which party?'

'*Le Front*,' replied Samson. '*Le Front National* but at the local level.' He didn't want to be caught if she tried out some names on him.

She moved closer. 'But you are an immigrant, no? From which country? Algeria? Morocco?'

'No, Madame, Lebanon. But I am French, as were my parents.'

'But why are you involved in *Le Front National* if you are from a family of immigrants?'

He had offered his hand. But she neither took it nor returned his smile. 'The truth is I am French and I feel French,' he continued. 'My parents taught me the value of work. Like them, I've worked hard and now I am very concerned about the state of my country and the millions who feel they have a right to rely on the generosity of the State.'

She didn't react to this.

He smiled awkwardly. 'I'm sorry, I don't know your name.'

'This is Mrs Gaspar, May-Lek,' said Gaspar. 'My wife.'

'A pleasure!' He gave a tiny bow and glanced at the Bird who wore his hangdog look. 'I think we should be going, General.'

'You seem familiar to me,' she said to Samson. 'I know you from some-where.' She moved closer, into the light of the recessed spotlight to get a better look at him. 'Where have I seen you?'

Samson grinned. 'Perhaps we have met before. Who knows?'

'Aymen is quite the society man. He gets about, Mrs Gaspar,' said the Bird.

It was now his turn to study her and he did so candidly, as though try-ing to place her. He thought she'd maybe had some work done around the eyes and mouth and that the frown lines had been smoothed. Up close, her extraordinarily pale skin looked thin, papery. The whites of her eyes had suffered some discoloration; brownish veins were showing at the corner of each eye. However, the pupils were youthfully unclouded and as unforgiving, no doubt, as when they settled on a victim in the Stasi prison. Her pupils oscillated slightly, both with scrutiny and calculation. 'No,' he said in conclusion. 'I feel sure we've never met.'

Again she didn't react. Maybe these silences were an error-forcing tech-nique. He returned her a pleasant look and opened his hands accommo-datingly. It was then that he understood that the only life in her face was to be found in the eyes. Her eyebrows and mouth, carefully delineated with make-up, hardly moved, even when she spoke, and they gave no hint of what went on in her mind. Her face was an icy mask. And there was something else. When she spoke to assert that she was never ever mistaken in matters of recognition, he noticed the smell of her breath, the smallest hint of corruption.

She took a step closer and began to speak rapidly in French, asking him where he lived. She knew the 14th arrondissement quite well. How far did he live from the Gare de Montparnasse? Did he frequent the famous Lebanese restaurant in the 14th? He replied no, he had never been to Chez Marc Libinais and, anyway, he preferred French cuisine to Lebanese. The restaurant that she referred to was in the 15th, and quite far from his apartment in the Rue Hallé, as was the train station, which was mostly in the 15th. He answered a couple of questions about his life in banking without hesitation but when she tried to return to politics, he said with good-natured exasperation. 'It's almost as if you were testing me, Madame.'

Samson had looked into the eyes of some bad people in his time, but this woman was something else. She made his flesh crawl, not out of fear, he reflected, but revulsion. It was as though her gaze alone was enough to poison a person. He had noticed Gaspar's nervousness. The man knew exactly what his wife was about and Samson was sure that she absolutely terrified him.

'It's obvious that you have a busy schedule,' said Samson.

'Indeed, we shouldn't detain you any further' said the Bird, slapping his leg. He put his glass on the table and scrambled up.

'The Nitro?' said Gaspar. 'What about the rifle?'

'I'll come back next week,' said the Bird. 'Get the trigger fixed and I'll be pleased to take it off your hands.'

They bid Mila Daus goodbye, the Bird giving one of his weird salutes, and headed for the door, where Gaspar started up about the deposit. The Bird said that wouldn't be appropriate just yet and they exited before he could protest further.

The Bird got in the car with a look of dark abandon. 'In all my years, I've never met a more gruesome couple,' he said. 'To think they ordered the death of my dear friend, well, it makes me very angry indeed.'

Samson reversed out and moved off without hurry. 'What the hell were you doing in there, Cuth? You made yourself pretty comfortable.'

'She was there when we got back so there was no escaping.'

'Did you get anything?'

'They've got politicians flying in for a big do on Saturday. And they've got someone coming today. She announced that before she saw me. There seemed to be something up, if you know what I mean. All hands on deck, and so forth. And she's in Washington the first half of next week.' He winked. 'That's what we call intelligence work, Samson.'

'Anything else?'

'Terrible breath. Smells like roadkill,' he said, wiping his face with a folded red-spotted handkerchief. He glanced at Samson. 'She's a real bad'un. Wicked beyond words. We've got to fix those two,' he concluded with a fierce look.

'We certainly do,' said Samson quietly.

CHAPTER 33

Angel

Anastasia sat with Denis for most of the day and the evening. She talked to him, but stopped when she ran out of things to say or felt she might be boring him. What could be worse than having to listen to someone when you wanted to sleep or be with your own thoughts and being able to do nothing to stop them talking? She held his hand and stroked his forehead and spoke about the solar-powered calculator, showing it to him in the hope of a response. When the nurse came in – a less frequent event now, which she read as resignation on the part of the medical staff – she slipped the calculator into the inside pocket of a light jacket she wore in the particular chill of the air conditioning in the room.

When the police guard shift changed in the afternoon she noticed that had been reduced too. Now there was just one uniformed officer by the elevator and he was playing a game on his phone whenever she passed. She went to the canteen twice for coffee and to keep in touch with Naji, and Samson, who was on his way back from Pennsylvania with news. But there was no word from Jim Tulliver. He had indicated that everything was okay in the morning but hadn't been in touch since. That worried her.

At seven the doctor appeared, but he said little. She again asked what could be done. He looked blank. The scan had shown no abnormalities whatsoever. For the moment they had no option but to make sure Denis was comfortable and wait for signs that he was emerging from the trance. He asked her if he slept. No, he hardly ever closed his eyes.

She did, though. When the doctor had gone she napped for half an hour. She was woken by a nurse with the news that Mr Angel from New York was waiting to see her. She went out and found Angel in the hallway with a bag. 'Angel, how nice of you to come.'

'Mrs Hisami, we need to speak.' He looked around. 'In private.'

'Okay, why don't you come and see Denis? We can talk in his room, and I think it would be good for him to hear another voice. Would you mind that? He's really not well, so prepare yourself.'

'First, I need to tell you that Mr Tulliver is in hospital.'

'Jesus, what with?'

'He was attacked last night in the street outside the apartment.'

'Come to the room – we'll talk there.'

Tulliver had left the apartment before Angel. They had agreed to meet up near a sports bar half an hour later so that Angel could hand over the computer, but Tulliver never showed. Angel waited at the bar. He tried calling him, but there was no answer. In the morning he realised he had been using the wrong number. He tried several times more before the police broke into the phone and called him. Tulliver had been badly beaten and was unconscious in New York-Presbyterian Lower Manhattan Hospital. Angel understood that Tulliver's attacker thought he was carrying the computer, or was in possession of some valuable knowledge, so he'd decided to catch the train straight away and bring the computer to her personally. He felt it was best not to call her.

'Do you know how Jim is?'

'I called from the train station but they wouldn't tell me because I'm not a relative.'

Angel gave her the direct line for the ward where Tulliver was being treated and eventually Anastasia persuaded a duty doctor to give her an update. Tulliver had been beaten unconscious and had suffered brain swelling. He was still in a coma. He had three fractured ribs, a broken hand and contusions all over his back and sides. The police reports said there were two men and they had used baseball bats. If they hadn't been disturbed, he would probably not have survived the battering. The doctor said they were anxious to trace his next of kin. Anastasia knew Jim had a sister in Kentucky named Hope. She called Denis's office in LA and left that task with them.

While she was speaking, Angel had sat down by Denis and had started talking to him normally, as though nothing were wrong. Anastasia noticed that Denis's eyes had shifted to focus on Angel and, moreover, they were engaged and he appeared to be listening.

'Tell him about Jim,' she said. 'It's really important that he knows what's going on.' Angel looked doubtful. 'Go ahead. And don't hide anything from him – he's still your boss and he wants to know.' She leaned over and squeezed Denis's hand. 'We're going to win,' she said. 'I promise we are going to win.'

She mimed to Angel that she was stepping outside to make some calls. He nodded and picked up the hand she'd just held. She'd be surprised if there was anyone on the planet more empathetic than Angel Oliviera.

They were both convinced they had been followed from Seneca Ridge – not an aggressive pursuit, by any means, but a definite weight on their tail which they both sensed. When they hit DC, the Bird suggested that Samson drop him at Union Station Bus Terminal and he'd lose himself in the crowds: it was vital not to lead anyone to Naji Touma's hotel. Samson did so then took the Range Rover to his hotel garage, left the fob and documents with the attendant, called the rental company and went for a walk. He had plenty of calls to return. He spoke with Ivan at Cedar, who had left three messages. The office and the restaurant had been raided that morning. Computers and documents were seized by the police, who had shown a warrant to Ivan that stated that under Section 15 of the Police and Criminal Evidence Act the Metropolitan Police would search the premises for evidence of an unspecified indictable offence. Ivan sent him a photograph of the warrant with a note saying they'd forced entry into his flat in Maida Vale. This was confirmed in a message from his tenant, Derek, who had observed police that morning removing folders but little else. They had already searched the place once, after the death of Pim Visser, and had found nothing, so all this was a feeble attempt to intimidate him.

There were much more pressing matters on his mind. In his bag was the sample jar containing the old cotton wool swab and a strand or two of hair belonging to the young Mila Daus that Herr Frick had handed over in the hotel in Tallinn. Against all his wildest hopes, he had managed to acquire two more samples of Daus's DNA, that is, if he hadn't been sold a pup by Hector and the maid at Seneca Ridge. Everything relied on a match being found between the two sets, separated by nearly forty years of history. Without this, the allegations against Daus herself and the high-ranking officials and businesspeople on both sides of the Atlantic would implode.

At nine fifteen, at her request, he began sharing his location on a messaging app with Zillah Dee as he moved through downtown Washington. That way she could watch to see if he was being followed then choose her moment to make herself known. She called it her 'mobile rendezvous'. At nine thirty-five two SUVs pulled up beside him outside Ford's Theater, the place, he noted on a plaque, where President Lincoln had been assassinated in April 1865. A door was pushed open and he was invited to climb in. 'Good to see you, Samson. I almost didn't recognise you with that beard.' Zillah gave it her appraisal. 'Yeah, I think it's working for you. Pity about the grey.'

Very little had changed in her appearance since they worked together during Anastasia's kidnap – the same practical yet high-end wardrobe, the

same short, asymmetrical hairstyle and string of tiny pearls. The brisk
manner hadn't changed either, although was that warmth he spotted in
those neutral grey eyes? He thought so.

'We have a lot to discuss,' she said. 'I have hired some space.'

When Zillah said 'space' she meant several different suites of offices
that had been rented for a few hours and which allowed her choice and a
last-minute change of venue.

They went to a boardroom in a former hotel. It had reproduction
pictures of twentieth-century politicians on the walls and in a corner a
vase of bird-of-paradise flowers and palm fronds that trembled in the air
conditioning. The room smelled of air freshener. Two of her staff busied
themselves with coffee and water.

He delved into the backpack and produced first the jar containing the
hair sample and the swab, then the zip-lock freezer bags with the shaver
and the comb. 'I'm looking for a match,' he said, 'but I need the sample
jar intact with as much hair left in it as possible.'

Zillah picked it up and curled her lip at the yellowed cotton wool.
'What the hell is this – urine?'

'No, age! The important thing is the hair in the jar.' He explained how
the Stasi had tried to capture people's essences before DNA science was
properly developed and had included a DNA sample in the jar. 'I need to
know whether the hair matches. On this hangs everything.'

She picked the jar up and squinted at it. 'This doesn't prove anything –
who's to say where these samples came from? And even if you do get a
match, that doesn't prove they're from Daus. These items were all stolen,
right? It only works if you can absolutely prove where the jar came from
and that the things in the bag were hers, or you get another sample from
her in front of witnesses – you yank her hair out or you take a swab in
her mouth. And that does not seem feasible.'

She was right, but Samson said that for his own peace of mind he had
to know she was the same person who had terrorised dissidents in the
Stasi jail.

'Okay,' she said, passing the samples to one of the young men who hovered but never said anything. 'What else?'

'We need to go through what you researched for Denis, what your brief was and how you delivered the information to him . . .'

Until I have confirmation from Denis Hisami or Jim T., I can't discuss the details of our work.'

'I'm running it all now,'said Samson.

'I haven't heard that. Literally, the only people in the world that I would accept instructions from are Denis or Jim. They're the guys who pay me and I'm adamant about maintaining client confidentiality.'

'If I get Anastasia on the phone . . .'

'Nope. Doesn't work. She was never involved in the investigation and she's not my client.'

'She has power of attorney.'

'Then she has to show me those papers. I'm sorry, Samson, but I'm not going to bend the rules.'

'Okay, I'll get Jim to sort it out.' He turned to the matter of the famous businessman. 'Ulrike mentioned that Bobby told her about a famous busi-nessman who had been set up with a young woman who was under-age. This was thought to have taken place at Clouds Ranch. I have an idea who it might be. Martin Reid.'

'You want confirmation, or are you telling me?'

'So it was him. Have you seen the film they used to blackmail him?'

'Yes, it's with Denis. We don't possess copies.'

'Because you undertook to deliver all your research on thumb drives and keep no evidence whatsoever.'

'That's correct, but Denis's research team had got most of the evidence. We did some supporting work.'

'But you saw it.'

She nodded. 'It ain't pretty and, taken as a whole, he's one of the least important names. He's a billionaire, and he has the resources to defend himself. Why're you interested?'

'He was one of the traitors at TangKi. He knew about Anastasia's kidnap and he had the gall to sit next to her at a GreenState fundraiser a couple of years later and gain her sympathy by talking about the deaths of his son and wife. He was getting close to the Hisamis for a reason. Now Daus is using Reid to find out whether Denis is going to recover, and, also, how much Anastasia knows. So, he's a way in and we can use him. But we need to have the film in our back pocket and he has to know that we would use it.'

'You be careful. He's a brutal motherfucker.' She looked up at the two young employees who were still in the room and jerked her head imperceptibly towards the door. They left. 'So how are you going to play it? I don't have the whole picture, so it's hard for me to see a strategy.'

Samson poured some coffee. It was going to be a long night. 'We need to get Daus in the room.'

'Which room?'

Samson grinned. 'I can't tell you – client confidentiality.' He paused. 'It works both ways, Zillah. I was employed by Denis, too.'

'Okay,' she said. 'But here's a word of warning. People in the government want this to just go away.'

'I gathered.'

'They don't want the mess.'

'That includes sheltering Daus's assets in the office of the Director of National Intelligence and on the National Security Council?'

Any hint of warmth in her eyes now evaporated. 'I have to work in this town. I am not going to piss off the entire intelligence community unless my life depends on it. In fact, my life and my company depend on not pissing everyone off at the same time. You follow?'

'No, I don't. You're on our side. Your client is lying in hospital in a coma and his lawyer and Robert Harland are dead. This is to say nothing about the deaths across Europe of the men John Gaspar hired. These people are spies, and they're acting like gangsters. They're fucking your country over. A lot of young people, earning far less than you, have risked their lives to penetrate and investigate Mila Daus's organisation. They obtained the information that you checked that's now on Denis's computer, which we can't currently access because Denis can't speak. But those young people went undercover without training or back-up. They took the risk, while the conventional agencies that are meant to protect society sat on their hands.'

'Then get it from those brave young people.'

'We have a lot of it, but you know that one half doesn't work without the other. We need substantiation, the proof you were paid millions of dollars to find.'

She knitted her fingers and rested her chin on them. 'Just get Jim to talk to me, but in the meantime, you, Anastasia and the Syrian boy need to find someplace safe. I may have an idea about that.'

'I didn't tell you he was here.'

'You didn't, but if I know, you can bet others do. We'll work on that hideout.' She got up. 'I'll be in touch when I have results from the DNA test. Should be sometime tomorrow.'

She offered him a ride but he said he would use the room to make some calls, if that was okay. She left. He wasn't happy with the encounter and he was sure Zillah wasn't either.

Only then did he remember what the Bird had told him that morning — Macy Harp was terminally ill and had only months to live. He phoned him. Imogen answered and put him on. 'How are you doing?' asked Samson.

'Cuth told you? Good. I knew I could rely on his indiscretion. Saves me having to go through it all with you.'

'I'm so sorry. I had no idea . . .'

'That's because I didn't tell you. It was a race between me and Bobby but, sadly, he won.'

'How long have you known?'

''Bout six weeks. Look, I'm sorry for not filling you in about Zoe being Bobby's daughter. Felt bad about it. I hope you understand.'

'Not an issue, now. Though it was. Is there anything to be done?'

'Treatment? Good heavens, no. We're past that stage. Nothing to do apart from seeing old friends and having a good few summer months on the racecourse, for which reason I am flying to the States. It's the Preakness Stakes next Saturday – the second leg of the Triple Crown – and that is held at Pimlico outside the fair city of Baltimore, a few furlongs from where you are.'

'What are you up to, Macy?'

'Apart from watching Bronzino Star, the three-year-old colt that just won the Kentucky Derby, I have a proposition for you. Did the Bird tell you about that, too?'

'Yes.'

'Well, let's talk about it while I'm there. I think you'll like what I have to say. You know I don't have any heirs apart from my utterly hopeless nephew, Gregory, and you really are the nearest thing I have to a son.'

This put Samson on alert. 'That's very kind of you, but I'm going to ask again – what are you up to?'

'Nothing, Samson.'

'There is one thing you can do for me, and that's talk to Zillah Dee. She says she can't help me until she has either Denis or Tulliver's sign-off. Frankly, I think she's been warned off. She needs to get with the programme, as they say here.'

'Right, I'll do that now and I'll call you when I get in tomorrow evening.'

The line went dead. As usual, Macy had hung up without warning.

Samson walked round the room with a coffee in one hand and his phone in the other. Two calls to Anastasia's number went straight to voicemail. He waited for a further half-hour then considered walking over to the hospital. There was only one thing to do that evening and that was put Hisami's calculator and computer in Naji's hands. He checked in with the Bird – everything was all right – and left the room to walk back to his own hotel.

At ten thirty Anastasia called and told him that Tulliver had been beaten unconscious in a side street in Tribeca and was still out of it. He was likely to recover but would be in hospital for at least ten days. He wasn't carrying the item he had gone to New York to collect, however: that had just been delivered safely to its owner.

'I need to take delivery. Should I come to you?'

'It doesn't feel right to leave now. Denis is responding to Angel – that's the man who looks after the apartment in New York. Let's do it in a couple of hours.'

'Okay. Two things. First, do you have any proof of power of attorney? And, second, I want you to consider how we best handle Martin Reid. You know him better than any of us. Do we threaten him with what we know or do we seek to persuade him?'

'I'll think about that. Denis and I both have digital copies of the Enduring POAs for each other.'

'Send it to Zillah Dee. I'll need to take delivery of those items this evening.'

They agreed to speak in an hour or two.

Anastasia was used to the hush that descended on the corridors of the hospital in the evening, but the lone police officer was nowhere to be seen and she became convinced that Denis was in danger. They had killed one man in hospital who had been under police guard and she had stupidly told Reid that the doctors were pleased about Denis's recovery from a minor operation, implying that he was conscious and very much on the mend. That news would have reached Daus. She called Special Agent Reiner to see if he could arrange for more officers, but didn't raise him. She went to the nurses' station but found no one in authority. Then she called Dr Carrew's cellphone and told him she needed Denis moved immediately for his safety. Carrew became pompous about the hospital's ability to keep her husband safe. After all, hadn't they done just that when she went to Europe, leaving her husband to face a medical emergency by himself?

'I'm not really asking you, Dr Carrew. I'm telling you that this must happen. I have good reason to believe that my husband is in grave danger, and we need to move him now. His right-hand man, Jim Tulliver, was beaten senseless in New York last night and is now also in a coma.'

'But there are police officers watching the floor.'

'I'm in the corridor and I can see no security whatsoever. I believe we need to move him right now. I am thinking only of my husband's safety. Please hear me on this.'

She ended the call and went back into the room. Denis was still looking fixedly at Angel, who was chattering about his wife's failure to notice she was pregnant with their third child. She peered at him and smiled. 'Are you coming back to us, Hash? I do hope so.'

Angel said, 'I know he is. I see it in his eyes.'

'Angel, you give us hope.' She went to the other side of the bed and sat down. 'Hash, I need to move you. You probably can't remember why you're here, but the danger isn't over and I want to make you safe until I get more security here.' Angel looked alarmed and sat down.

They were there for another two hours before nurses and an overseer came to move the bed and all the equipment. While they waited she sent the POA to Zillah Dee and said that she needed at least two security guards at the hospital by morning to watch over Denis. The move was completed by eleven. Angel pulled up a chair and rested his head on a cushion to watch Hisami.

'Are you going to be all right there?' she asked him.

'Maybe he will say something to me.'

'I pray he does.'

She went to the nurses' station and asked the duty supervisor not to update the change of room in the records until the morning. Without looking up from her screen, the woman said it would be impossible to ignore hospital procedures. Anastasia let her bag drop to the ground and told her about the millions of dollars Denis had given in memory of his sister to the health group of which this very hospital was a member. If the hospital wanted to continue to benefit, the supervisor would do this one thing for her husband – it was all she was asking. The nurse eventually agreed. Anastasia thanked her and walked away, not feeling particularly proud of herself. She phoned Zillah Dee and left a message reminding her about security. The POA was already in her inbox.

She took the elevator to the car park and headed for the ramp that led out to the street. As she exited she heard an engine start. She looked back. A Suburban parked in a bay at one end had its lights on but wasn't moving. She dialled Samson and quickened her pace.

'I have both items with me,' she said.

'Okay, share your location with me. I'm not far away from you . . .'

'There's someone in the garage. They're watching me, I'm sure.'

'Get out of there and find cover. There's a park near the hospital. Go there.'

She ran in the direction of the park, where, from the rooftop of the hospital, Tulliver had spotted a hawk hunting for vermin. It wasn't large, but it was at least dark. Once there, she opened up the app and, shielding the light from her phone as much as she could, wrestled with the procedure for sharing her location. She waited, looking out from the bushes. Several times a car – almost certainly the Suburban – passed the park in both directions, moving without hurry or, it seemed, much purpose. She felt the old terror of her kidnap return – the shallow breaths and the fizzing panic in her head. The car passed for a third time and she strained to see two men searching the night. She called Samson. 'They're definitely looking for me. Where are you?'

'I can see the car. I'm in the park. Be with you in a sec.'

There was a loud crash, and then another. Something had hit the car. It braked, swerved a little then tore off.

Samson ran up to her and she couldn't do other than fall into his arms. 'You okay?' he said.

'Jumpy. What the hell hit that car?'

'I have a good cricket arm.'

She let go of him and stood back. 'What's that mean?'

'I can throw a ball accurately. I aimed a couple of rocks at the passenger's side.'

She gave him the bag. 'I don't know how we can do this by Monday. I mean, it's all so damned complicated.' She stopped. 'I was thinking about Marty Reid.'

'Ulrike told me that there's film of him with an under-age girl. And Zillah confirmed it but not in detail. She was seventeen, and that counts in the State he was in at the time, and also in the one where his private plane picked her up. He trafficked a minor across a state line for the purposes of illegal sex. That's something we have on him.'

'Okay, so leaving aside the gross behaviour and criminality, the one thing I know about Reid is that threatening him will get us nowhere. He's been winning against the odds his whole life.' She stopped. 'But he's a patriotic American citizen and I don't think he wants to be in this position, which is, essentially, betraying his country to a foreign power.'

'Does he know he's betraying his country?'

'That's a good question,' she said. 'Maybe he just thinks she's a right-wing nut like him. What if we don't use the film but, instead, appeal to his love of country?' She shivered and clutched her arms tight.

'Love of country,' mused Samson. 'Not sure that's going to work. How's Denis?'

She gave him a look of anguish. 'He's responding to Angel, but no one understands what's wrong.'

'I'm so sorry.'

'About the other night . . . I feel so . . .'

'It didn't happen. You dreamed it. Look. I need to get these to Naji. I'll walk you back.'

At that, her phone pinged with a message from Zillah Dee accepting the proof of Power of Attorney. She would have bodyguards in the hospital by morning.

CHAPTER 34

Blink

The next day there were efforts by Samson's team across three different lo-
cations to unlock or reassemble the dossier that Denis Hisami and Bobby
Harland had put together. They already had a lot – the entire presentation
in Tallinn, for one thing – but Samson read everything with a rigorous
eye for proof, and little made the grade. Zillah went through as much
as she and her staff could remember, matching it with the discoveries
of Pearl Grey, Pitch Black, Aurora Red and Saffron Yellow, the teams
specialising in the activities of Jonathan Mobius, Erik Kukorin, Chester
Abelman and Elliot Jeffreys.

Across two hotel rooms, Naji constructed wigwams from clip coat hang-
ers and a sheet. Even though he had no intention of using the Web on the
laptop, he had read somewhere that hotel rooms were sometimes fitted with
minute surveillance cameras. He pointed out to the entirely sceptical Bird
that Edward Snowden had hidden under sheets when on the run in Hong
Kong. The Bird ordered breakfast in both hotels and sat sprawled, looking
at the ceiling with the gun that had taken him precisely one hour to buy on
the street in Columbia Heights. Naji was beginning to have doubts about
the Bird but decided to make allowances because he had been Harland's

good friend. Before Samson had come with the computer and the calcula-tor, the Bird had talked of their times together, his and Harland's. The Bird was definitely the oddest person Naji had spent time with, but clearly he had admired Harland as much as Naji had, and once the computer arrived he was too busy to worry about him, or consider, eyeing his footwear with the professional eye gained as a boy selling dead men's shoes in Syria, whether his enormous trainers had been specially made.

At the hospital, Anastasia spent most of the day with Denis. Angel said he would stay as long as it was necessary, and they took it in turns to sleep in the tiny room, which Anastasia had kept on. But Denis never slept. His eyes were moving more now, although it still took an awfully long time for him to respond by shifting his gaze to the speaker. For that reason, in the new room, she and Angel decided to talk from only the chair on his left. There was both understanding and incomprehension in those eyes, yet, in truth, never much hope. Angel was astonishingly good at keeping his interest, much better than Anastasia. She again told Denis they needed the code for the calculator but didn't press him – what was the point when he couldn't answer?

That evening Samson texted her to say that there was a match between the two DNA samples – the nineteen-year-old student who'd been ar-rested by the Stasi on 12 December 1974 was the same person who had shaved her legs and combed her hair at Seneca Ridge. She called him.

'I'm relieved, and not just for the obvious reasons,' said Samson. 'I paid twenty thousand of Denis's money for that. Half of me thought I was being had.'

'You deserved to be, for taking that risk.'

'Zillah says this won't cut any ice and we'll need to take a sample if we get her in the room, but that of course is impossible. But I have another idea, which I'll tell you about when I see you. By the way, you need to start thinking about talking to Reid. Maybe tomorrow evening.'

They ended the call and she walked the corridors of the hospital, nodding to the three members of Zillah's security team and two new faces at the nurses' station. They seemed better disposed to her since her disagreement with the supervisor. She tried then gave up trying to plan the conversation with Reid and went to the area by the vending machines and called him.

'Marty, I felt our last meeting went badly and I wanted to apologise.'

'Oh, that's quite all right, my dear. You're under a lot of stress.'

'I have some news and wanted to deliver it personally, but I guess you're out of town.'

'I'm not far away. In Virginia.'

'But I don't want to ruin your weekend. Maybe it should wait until next week.'

'What's this about?'

'Denis.'

'Not bad news, I hope.'

'On the contrary, things are good. But it's something that I can only speak to you about in person.'

'Maybe I can drop by the hospital tomorrow afternoon.'

'At what time?'

'Say four.'

'I'll see you then.'

She hung up then became aware of Angel signalling to her with a frantic smile. 'What is it?'

'Mr Hisami is communicating.'

They tore back to the room. Denis's eyes were turned to the speaking chair. She was horrified. He looked paler and the flesh on his cheeks sagged, as though his body had suddenly resigned itself to paralysis. 'One blink for yes, two for no – right, Mr Hisami?'

A slow blink followed.

She sat down and took Denis's hand. 'Oh, Hash, I can't tell you how relieved I am.'

Blink.

She kissed him, something that she hadn't done since the attack because of the risk of contamination. Angel said he would be down the hall and left.

'Do you know what happened to you? Why you're here?'

Blink, then two blinks. He knew something, but not all. She repeated everything she'd told him before, holding his hand and looking into his eyes. Occasionally, he blinked when he already knew something; he used the double blink if he wanted explanation and enlargement. Because she had moved him and either she or Angel had been with him all that time, she felt there was no risk of being bugged, which she'd half suspected in the other room. Even so, she spoke quietly about her trip through the Balkans, seeing the farm where he had rescued her, Samson and Naji, then the race through the Baltic States with Naji stealing a car and bursting through the Estonian border. His eyes watched her without blinking. He was taking it all in. Sometimes his pupils dilated and she wondered if this was love for her or the realisation of his imprisonment.

She had spared him the details about the killing of Robert Harland on the same day as his appearance in Congress, but she told him now and described the funeral and the encounter with Herr Frick. 'And we know everything, Hash,' she said. 'What you and Bobby have pulled together is so impressive.' He blinked. She told him about the attack on Tulliver and Angel bringing the computer on the train. 'We'll talk about that later maybe,' she said. 'Jim will be okay, but he's going to be out of action for a while so I'll have to handle things. I hope you're good with that.' Blink. 'There's a lot of business stuff I have to go through with you.' Two blinks. 'Does that mean you want to do the business stuff now?' Two blinks.

'I don't want to tire you with all these questions.' Two blinks. 'Shall I go on?' Blink. 'Would you like a freshener for your mouth?' Blink. 'And some water?' Blink. 'Can you drink through a straw?' Blink. She pressed the call button. The nurse came and Anastasia told her to phone

Dr Carrew and bring water and freshener. She turned to her husband. 'Would you like a shave? I know you hate the feeling of stubble.' Blink.

A razor, brush and soap were found and Anastasia set about the task expertly, for, in the last days of her domineering, faithless father, she had shaved and washed him, though she had no love whatsoever for him. She asked the nurse, who looked on admiringly, if she could soak a small towel in hot water so she could press it to Denis's skin. When she'd finished, she stepped back and smoothed his hair forward. 'You look more yourself now. Open wide,' she said, tickling his chin. 'Come on, Hash. I know you can open your mouth.' But he couldn't, so she opened it for him and swabbed his gums and the inside of his cheeks then sprayed a little breath freshener on to his tongue. 'Better?' Blink.

She sat down and smiled at him. His eyes watered. Tears ran down his cheeks. She kissed him and dried his cheeks with a tissue then held his hand. 'We're going to survive this somehow,' she said. 'You're going to get better and we'll have that holiday in Jordan that you promised me.' Two blinks. 'We have to be positive, Hash. We have to be!' Two blinks and his eyes moved away. It was a little while before they closed and, for the first time since her return, she saw him sleep.

She waited for half an hour then went out into the corridor and phoned Samson to tell him that Denis was communicating but he had changed drastically in the last twelve hours. 'I think he just wants to die,' she said in a whisper. 'He's given up.'

'What do the doctors say?'

'Dr Carrew is coming. He's got people to dinner, but says he'll come by when they've gone.'

'I'm sorry to ask this, but is there any way you can find out the code to enter into the calculator?'

'He's asleep. And he can only say yes or no by blinking. And there's no guarantee he remembers it. Maybe the nerve agent has taken its toll.'

'I don't want to put pressure on you, but we do need to get into Denis's laptop. I can bring Naji with the calculator. Denis likes him. They worked together to make this code and, of course, now Naji can't break it.' He paused. 'Sorry, I know I'm pushing, but you can ask him, can't you? Allow him to make the decision.'

In the middle of the night, and after Carrew had spent an hour examining Denis with questions that required only the answer yes or no but added to his obvious perplexity, Anastasia did ask her husband, half expecting him to close his eyes and go back to sleep. But the question drew a single, definite blink and sudden miosis in his pupils – a narrowing with which she was all too familiar, one which conveyed the strength of her husband's feelings.

Samson brought Naji over to the hospital but decided to stay outside Denis's room. Naji shambled in, smiled and sat down beside Denis. They looked at each other long and hard, and much passed between them – not just their shared history in which both the young boy and the seasoned commander struck at an ISIS terrorist at the same moment in a barn in Macedonia, or the time when Naji, on the old rail bridge at Narva, diverted vast amounts of money electronically to the mafia shooter in payment for three well-aimed bullets that killed Anastasia's Russian kidnapper and saved her life, but perhaps a deeper connection between two people who had escaped the violence of the Middle East as young men and, with their high intelligence, had found a life in the West, even though there would always be something about them both that was dispossessed, uprooted.

'Hi,' said Naji, eventually.

Denis gave him a single blink and Naji held up the calculator in his left hand. Denis blinked again.

'You have twenty digits. Is that correct?'

Blink.

'I point finger at each number and you tell me when I have right one.'

Blink.

At first it went well: Naji noted down 40782366. Then Denis's response time slowed and Anastasia began to worry the effort was too much for him. His breathing seemed to have become shallower and his face was drained of colour. It took minutes to acquire the next three numbers – 4, 5 and 9. Then Denis looked away. After a full minute his eyes returned to Naji and he gave three blinks.

'What do you mean?' asked Naji.

He waited. So did Denis, gazing at him.

'Do you want me to use another key?'

Blink.

Naji looked at the keypad. 'Memory key?'

Two blinks.

'Square root key?'

Blink.

'Ah! So you need the square root of 40782366459, right?'

Blink.

'And that gives us 2019464445317124 – but that's only sixteen digits. So we have to find four more digits, Mr Hisami.'

He returned to the keypad and they added 1, 1, 2 and 0, which took little time because Naji started with the lower numbers. He now had a twenty-digit code on the piece of paper and entered it into the calculator. The moment the final zero was keyed in the digits were rearranged into the code that would unlock the computer. Naji made a note of it and handed it to Anastasia, who folded it and placed it in her back pocket. She gently moved Naji out of the way and sat down beside Denis. 'What is it, Hash?' she asked, again taking his hand in both hers.

His eyes rested on her, but they seemed distant and she wondered if he could see her. And she didn't like the short, shallow breaths, which seemed to have grown more irregular in the last minute or two. She glanced at the monitors and saw that his heart rate had slowed. She pressed the call button and told Naji to go and find a nurse quickly, but before he had moved to the door they heard shouting from the corridor. She let go of Denis's hand, jumped up and pushed Naji aside so she could block the door. The shouting continued – several voices demanding that someone put down their weapon. She cracked open the door but could see nothing, so moved a little way out. Nurses had surrounded a man in blue scrubs, face mask and theatre cap. All had guns drawn. One of the nurses, also in a face mask, patted the man down from behind while another moved closer to him, aiming a gun with two hands at his forehead. The search ended with a pistol equipped with a silencer, a large wad of medical dressing and a vial being thrown on to the linoleum. The vial rolled away and was snatched up by one of the nurses.

This had all taken place just beyond the nurses' station. Anastasia saw Samson, together with two of Zillah's guards, rising from the floor, where they had presumably thrown themselves when undercover police intercepted the man in scrubs. Special Agent Reiner appeared from behind the station with two men who looked like detectives. One of these stepped forward and pulled the mask from the man's face. Naji, who had slipped out of the room behind Anastasia, recognised him as the man who had checked into their hotel at Vilnius and whose key fob and car he had stolen. With the mask hanging from his neck and face turned to the ground, Anatoly Stepurin was handcuffed.

Anastasia glanced back through the door at Denis and realised something was wrong. His eyes were turned upwards and his mouth hung open. The pallor of death had taken hold of his face. She shouted for help. A nurse ran towards her, followed by a duty doctor who had come to see what the shouting was about. The nurse began CPR, pushing down on Denis's chest with both hands, while the doctor moved a defibrillator to the bedside, turned it on and placed the pads either side of his chest. He consulted the monitor and told the nurse to stand back so he could deliver the electric shock. He felt for a pulse at Denis's neck but, failing, listened through his stethoscope to his patient's chest, his eyes fixed on the ceiling. He shook his head and called for help. An adrenalin shot was needed. This was administered, but to no avail. Denis's body bounced lifelessly on the mattress as the nurse continued the rhythmic compression of his chest. Denis Hisami had passed from this life the very moment the man who'd come to kill him was apprehended.

And she had not said goodbye, hadn't said she loved him and respected him above every man she had ever known, although those things were in her mind when the commotion had started out in the corridor and she'd stupidly gone out to see what was happening. She recoiled, her hands covering her face, her mind flooding with regret and guilt and shock. She looked again at his face, swamped by shock and an odd disbelief. Never for one moment had it occurred to her that she would lose him.

When Samson got out of the elevator, having handed Naji over to the Bird so they could go back to the hotel they were currently working in, he was met by Special Agent Reiner. It was past one in the morning and Anastasia was still in the room with Denis's body, which had yet to be removed to the morgue. She had said she needed this time with him and the hospital authorities didn't press the matter.

Reiner and Samson went to the room where she slept. 'We need to know all about this man – everything you have on him.'

Samson looked at him with disbelief. 'Is that so? Seems to me you used Denis as bait to catch him. You withdrew the officers when his wife returned from Europe and waited, sure they would try to kill him. That was pretty risky behaviour – you put other people's lives in danger.'

Reiner mumbled a demurral that included the phrase 'national security', but it didn't add up to much.

'You were here all the time. Your agents in the garage were following Anastasia until they saw me hurling rocks at them. You set her up. She could easily have been killed.'

Reiner ignored this. 'There's a question of evidence about this individual.'

'Toombs knows all about him. Why do you need me?'

'Things are difficult, as you know.'

'They've shut him down and he's forbidden to cooperate with the Bureau. And from what I hear, you're overstepping the mark by carrying out this operation.'

'It's a criminal justice matter. We were intercepting an assassin.' He smiled, and went on: 'What do you want?'

'Time,' said Samson. 'About sixty hours.'

'Go on.'

'Denis's death will be announced tomorrow morning by his office on the West Coast and they will state that he died from an underlying heart condition, which is the truth. This was how Stepurin planned to make it look. I don't know what was in that vial, but I guess it's something that interferes with the rhythm of the heart and causes cardiac arrest. We want the people who are paying Stepurin to believe that he succeeded in killing Denis without being detected. And for that you need Stepurin to make a call tonight.'

'Why?' said Reiner.

'We need them to think they've won, that with the elimination of Denis Hisami and Robert Harland the threat no longer exists.'

'And what does that serve the American people?' asked Reiner. 'Because that's my job.'

'A job you are being prevented from doing. High-level penetration in the US and the UK by the same network is deemed to be just too damaging to both governments, and you were taken off the case.' He leaned forward and spoke confidentially. 'I don't know you, and you don't know me, but we do kind of recognise each other. What I'm asking you is to give us sixty hours and we'll try and break this thing open. Then the people who have blocked a legitimate investigation on behalf of the American people can go fuck themselves, because you will have to act on the knowledge that's in the public domain. Look, you're on our side. I know that!'

'How do you propose we persuade Stepurin to make that call?' asked Reiner.

'Keep him out of the criminal justice system and put him on ice, which isn't so hard because he is, after all, a Russian spy. Tell him that if he makes that call, there could be a deal – maybe a swap – and he can go back to Russia or Cyprus, wherever the hell he's based. That's credible – he knows the last thing the Russian government wants is for him to be questioned in an open court. He has to make the call tonight, and to the right number. Not some fucking number he pulls out of the air.' He took his phone out and gave him Gaspar's cellphone number.

Reiner thought about it. 'Okay, what are you going to do in these sixty hours?'

'Draw them out in the open, but it will take a lot of luck, and it all hangs on Anastasia. As you can see, she's extremely upset. I'm not sure she'll be up to it.'

'You know her well – what's your bet?'

Samson got up, went to the basin and poured himself a glass of water. 'She's been through a lot, and everything she's suffered has been caused by the woman whose name neither of us has mentioned. Mila Daus.' He watched for a reaction, but there was none. Samson was convinced Reiner knew the name but he wasn't going there. 'I think she'll be up for it. I know she will, but we need the weekend.'

'And what happens if she isn't?'

'Nothing! We'll go back to pretending that Russia hasn't got its people at the top of the American and British governments. And all those bit players who feed information into an enormous human eavesdropping operation will be free to continue to betray their country, whether they are doing it consciously or not.' He sat down. 'Imagine this situation in the eighties or nineties. It's impossible to conceive. What happened? Why did we roll over? How did we let them do it?'

Reiner looked at him. 'Do you have a drink?'

'Yes, there's a bottle of Scotch beside your chair.'

He grasped the bottle – Anastasia had consumed about a third – and went for one of the glasses wrapped in cellophane. 'It's more complicated than you think, Samson. People in our administration, the Russian government and the UK government are all unified at this time by a desire to see you, the Syrian boy and Mrs Hisami taken off the map. You need to hide and keep your cellphones switched off, and stop using the internet. That's my advice to you for the next sixty hours. Get the hell off the grid.'

'So you'll get Stepurin to make the call?'

'Here's the deal. I will make sure that call happens tonight, but you have to give me the entire dossier before it's made public. I mean everything! I need to know what's going down.'

'Okay. That won't be until after the weekend. But you'll let me know about the call either way, yes?'

He nodded. They shook hands and Reiner got up, contemplated the rest of his whisky, then washed it down the sink and rinsed out the glass. A careful and considerate man, Reiner.

At that moment they heard shouting. It was Anastasia. He ran the length of the corridor and tore past two nurses who had emerged to see what was causing the second disturbance of their shift. From Denis's room hurried two men, both in jackets and ties, pursued by Anastasia, who was brandishing one of the hospital's now empty drip stands. They brushed past Samson, one of them, absurdly, putting on dark glasses as he did so.

He reached Anastasia. She was heaving with anger and exertion.

'I went to the bathroom, came back and found them searching the room. They were about to search the body.' She shook her head, put the stand down and told the nurses that everything was all right. They looked doubtful, but left.

Samson and Anastasia turned to Denis's body. Shrunken, and without the slightest hint of the energy that had propelled him from the dust and chaos of Kurdistan to the very top of American society, he was unrecognisable. Anastasia expressed what Samson was thinking. 'This isn't him, is it? He's gone. He wouldn't want us here. I think we should leave.' She stood up, looked down at him and kissed his forehead. Then she slipped both hands under his body.

'What the hell are you doing?' he hissed.

She withdrew the computer and put it in her shoulder bag. 'If I'd come back a minute later, they would have found it.' She looked at Denis once more, touched his folded hands and mouthed goodbye. 'It was the only place I could think of. And Denis would have found it funny,' she said, turning to the door.

'I thought Naji had it.'

'He didn't take it when he left and, as I sat here with Denis, I began to think he'd want me to handle everything now.' She closed the door behind her and didn't look back.

Reiner had gone but when they reached the elevators Samson received a text: 'That was Homeland Security.'

Anastasia and Samson slept for a few hours in a large suite in the Jefferson Hotel. He held her for most of that time and whispered to her, and in the morning she asked him to make love to her. Before dressing she sat on the side of the bed and phoned Marty Reid to tell him to bring the meeting forward and that it would take place in one of the Jefferson's business suites. She ended the call before he could protest for a second time that it would take him two hours at least to reach DC by car; after his son's death he didn't take helicopters.

They had rearranged it so that the announcement of Denis's death would be after Reid's arrival, partly to see whether he already knew, in which case he had spoken with Daus or Gaspar, who could only have been informed that Denis was out of the way by Stepurin. On the advice of Macy Harp, who had arrived at the hotel and ordered himself breakfast, they would only play tough and use the existence of the film if absolutely necessary. Macy's experience of questioning and turning traitors in the Cold War suggested that pressure worked best if it was implied. 'The looming threat is always more terrifying than the stated one.' He was greatly saddened by Denis's death, but that didn't inhibit a cold assessment of the challenge. 'You lead,' he said to Anastasia. 'It's fine to have Samson in the room with you, but use the position you're in. If Samson talks too much, Reid will see it as a challenge. But you are grieving, and that will make him listen. It's going to be hard, but use the history of the Cold War. Fighting communism means something to someone of my and his generation.'

There was no hint of Macy's terminal illness in his manner, or his choice of a cooked breakfast.

'We're going to have to make ourselves scarce until Monday. What are you going to do for the weekend?' asked Samson.

'Cuth and I have plans to meet up with one or two old chums from the Agency in the eighties. Should be fun. And we thought we'd take a look at the spectacular countryside at some point.' This was said into a plate of hash browns and sausage. When he looked up, he ignored Samson's stare.

Reid arrived in golfing attire and a poor mood. He was shown into the meeting room, where there was coffee and iced tea and a selection of sandwiches. He gave Samson a suspicious look and sat down. 'What is it that you so urgently needed to tell me in person?' he asked.

He hadn't asked about Denis, or why they were meeting at the hotel rather than the hospital.

'You haven't heard?' Anastasia said.

'Haven't heard what?'

She waited and searched his face. Samson had already decided that he knew.

'Denis died last night, of natural causes. His heart just stopped. Sadly, no one was with him, but we believe it was peaceful.'

'I'm so sorry,' said Reid. 'Of natural causes . . . and you say you weren't there. So distressing for you, Anastasia.'

'Yes, I wish I had been able to say goodbye and tell Denis how much I loved and admired him.'

'Terribly sad. Thank you for telling me. When are you announcing this?'

'About now.' She looked at her watch.

'Was there anything else? You told me you wanted to speak in person before Denis's passing, so I guess there is.'

'What do you know about Denis's work over the last few years, Marty?'

'He's made a very good comeback with some sound investments, which I have sometimes followed.' He smiled. 'I always thought I knew the media and the music business, but Denis beat me to a couple of good deals.'

'His other work.'

He looked perplexed and shifted in his seat. He was a tall man, but when he was sitting his stomach bulged over his waistband and it evidently made him uncomfortable. 'I don't know what you're referring to.'

Anastasia leaned forward with her hands clasped. If Reid had been half as alert as he thought he was, he might have asked why this grieving widow looked so composed. 'Like you, Denis was a patriot. He cared profoundly about liberty and democracy. He loved this country – it gave him everything.' Reid nodded. 'So when he discovered a network of foreign agents that had infiltrated the highest councils and agencies in the land, he was determined that it should be exposed. That's why he died.'

'Network?'

'Yes, led by a woman named Mila Daus, also known as Mila Muller and Mila Mobius. She was a member of the East German security service – the Stasi.' She stopped and looked for the tell, which came in the form of a brief fluttering of his left eyelid. 'It's a very effective network based on a classic cell structure. Everything feeds into her and her stepson, Jonathan Mobius. People worry about cyber, but Denis and his friend Robert Harland, also murdered, knew that if a foreign asset is in the room with the most powerful people in the land – the bankers and politicians and intelligence officials – then hacking is child's play. For over thirty years,

Daus has been feeding secrets and intelligence back to her Russian handlers. Her influence increases by the day. We're at the point when she can do just about anything she damn well wants, including contaminating the heart of American democracy with nerve agent.'

'Why are you telling me this?'

'Because you're one of her people, Marty.'

'How do you reach that bizarre conclusion?'

'Because we know, Marty! Denis knew, too.'

There was no eruption, but the blackest look entered his eyes and his mouth resolved into a tight, lipless, downturned line. 'I like you, Anastasia, but don't mistake me for some liberal sea sponge. I am not in the habit of rolling over. I never have and I'm not going to start now.'

'Yes, Marty, you'll nail me to a prairie washboard, etcetera. I notice you didn't deny your association with Daus. You couldn't very well do that, could you? Because there are pictures of you together.' Samson glanced in her direction. This wasn't going the way they had agreed.

Reid worked his way to the front of the leather armchair and launched himself forward with a grunt. 'I'm not going to listen to this. You'll be hearing from my lawyers.'

Anastasia didn't move, didn't even look up at him as he stood. 'You aren't going anywhere, Marty.' She held up her phone. 'Because if you do, the evidence of your entrapment will be published within the hour.' She waited a beat. 'But why are we concerned with this? Why don't we just talk about the damage being done to the country you love?'

He stood stooped, exuding a kind of raw, primitive aggression. 'She's a business associate. She knows thousands of people.'

'I want you to meet someone,' she said. 'Would you do me that favour?'

This certainly surprised Samson, but then in the brief meeting with Macy he had noticed the flash of steel when Macy suggested Anastasia give the computer to Zillah Dee for safekeeping. Anastasia was keeping the computer and doing things her own way. And why not? This was her husband's legacy.

Anastasia sent a text and within a couple of minutes the door opened and, to Samson's considerable astonishment, Ulrike entered.

She looked at her most regally beautiful as she offered Reid her hand and a charming smile. Samson changed chairs so she could sit next to the one Reid reluctantly re-occupied. 'You've got ten minutes,' Reid said. 'Ten minutes before I rain down hell on you.'

'Ulrike is the widow of Robert Harland,' said Anastasia. 'She was the most important Western spy in East Germany in the closing months of the Cold War.' She lost her husband two weeks ago. He was shot in cold blood while painting in the countryside. She wants to tell you her story.'

Ulrike began in 1989 and, because she could tell a story clearly and without superfluous detail, Reid was soon listening. She spoke of meeting her first husband, the risks they took while working with the CIA and MI6 to seize, in Leipzig, an Arab terrorist sponsored by the Stasi, her capture and confinement in a Stasi jail and her first encounter with the ice-cold supervisor of interrogations, Mila Daus. Then came the fall of the Berlin Wall, her release and her marriage to Rudi Rosenharte, which was followed by his murder and her eventual marriage to Robert Harland. That she had lost two husbands to Daus was stated as a matter of fact; she did not dwell on it. Rather she talked about her work with Western intelligence services – she emphasised her dealings with the CIA – before the Wall came down. She went on to detail her experience looking at her file in the Stasi archive which, because of Daus's obsession with data, was a revelation about their power.

'And this was before the internet became part of all our lives,' she said. 'Now Mila Daus collects the data of American citizens with perfect ease.' She stopped. 'I know you are an important and busy man, sir, but I want to tell you about the archive. Victims of the Stasi were allowed by the authorities to inspect their own file at the archive in Berlin. I went there and found the details of my life – my boyfriends, my dental appointments, my mother's illnesses, her love of canaries, references to my college project, my taste for making clothes and the money I made from selling them, the name of our neighbour's dog, my absolute failure at any sport, my love of Bach – honestly, they knew more about my life than I did, and that was before I was working for the West.'

Reid plainly wondered why he was being told this.

'When I was in the archive I met a woman who was about ten years older than me. She's the sort of person you see in a bus line anywhere in Germany, utterly ordinary: a pleasant face yet eyes that betrayed her struggle. She was sitting near the desk I was using and suddenly she began to cry. I went to comfort her and she told me her story. I won't trouble you with too much detail, but this woman was arrested for making a joke in a store about the Party leader, Erich Honecker. She was put in Hohen-schönhausen jail, where she became one of the first subjects of Mila Daus. She was there for two years and was only released when her husband had divorced her and gained custody of her daughter and son. She never saw them again, even after the liberation. And you know why? Mila Daus told her husband that she had betrayed him with another woman and that she'd had many lesbian lovers all through their marriage, which was untrue. She was barred from the weddings of her children, has never met her grandchildren and has led a life of lonely destitution. Until she read her file and saw that Daus had persuaded her neighbours and friends to collaborate in the lie, convincing her husband that she liked women, she never knew the reason. And now he's dead and the children will still have nothing to do with her.

'It's a small story from the Communist era, but it tells you of the kind of pain that is Mila Daus's life's work.' She had held her hands together. Now she leaned forward and touched Reid's wrist. 'She murdered the only two men I ever loved. She murdered first the father of my son, then his stepfather, whom he loved very much.'

'I'm sorry, but this has nothing to do with me.'

'But it does, Mr Reid. I can see that you are a good man and you've had your share of pain and loss. But now you need to help us expose this woman and save your country. You are the only person who can do this.'

'I'm not in a position to help.' He had admitted nothing, but Ulrike's sympathetic appeal had eroded his resistance.

'But you *are* in a position to help us, sir,' said Samson. 'All we want is for you to bring Mila Daus to the Foreign Relations Committee on Monday afternoon in Room 2172 of the Rayburn Building.'

'Why would she do that?'

'Because she will hear Denis's reputation being destroyed,' said Anastasia. 'For her, it will be the ultimate victory.'

'By Warren Speight? You know my feelings about him.'

'Yes, by Speight and others.'

'I have absolutely nothing to hide,' said Reid. But the titan of American business didn't look convinced of that. If he had nothing to hide, why was he still in the room?

'When we talked at that fundraiser,' said Anastasia, 'I really felt we had a connection. Can I just ask you to do this for Denis and me, after everything that we went through?'

Reid was about to say something, but a knock at the door broke the spell and he began to shuffle forward out of his seat. One of Zillah's bodyguards came in and bent down to whisper to Anastasia. Samson could hear that Homeland Security agents were in the building. The Agency, routinely used as the presidential enforcers, was demanding entry to the suite that Samson and Anastasia had used under the name of Zillah's personal assistant. Her people had already got Naji out a half-hour before, and Mr Avocet had left with Mr Harp some time ago.

Anastasia rose to make a final plea, but it was Ulrike who hooked her arm with Reid's and walked him from the room. They didn't hear what she said to him, but they saw him with his head bowed and shaking before they were led by two of Zillah's men to a car waiting in the service road at the back of the hotel.

Zillah was in the front passenger seat on the phone with a laptop on her knees. 'It's all kicking off, but it's only the waterheads at Homeland Security who really don't have a clue,' she said. 'Ask them to beat up protestors and they can just about do that, but anything else and they go to pieces. If it were the Agency, or the Bureau, we'd be in trouble.' She turned round for the first time. 'But they're taking the weekend off. And so are we. You're going to spend the next thirty-six hours on *Ariel II*.'

'That's your boat?' asked Samson, the memory of crossing the North Sea in *Silent Flight* fresher than he'd wish.

'My *new* boat! You'll like her – roomy, very sleek and beautiful to behold under full sail. The love of my life.'

Ariel II was moving sedately across the wind, some distance off shore, where the Potomac and Anacostia rivers meet the Washington Channel. They boarded a small launch, driven by a tanned blonde woman in a dark blue windcheater with *Ariel II* printed on her breast. 'This is Daphne, your skipper today,' said Zillah. 'I'll join you later in the weekend.'

Before he got on board Samson received a call from Ivan at Cedar telling him that Peter Nyman urgently wanted to be in touch. He explained to Anastasia that he needed to return the call to find out what Nyman wanted before they left. 'They're going to track the phone you use to call back,' said one of the bodyguards and handed him her phone. 'Try this.'

The number rang: an American dial tone. Nyman was in the States. 'How can I help, Peter?' said Samson.

'Denis Hisami is dead, and we think that should be an end to the matter.'

'Who am I to argue with that? If you think the matter is over, that's fine.'

'The British government is working to resolve certain aspects of this affair and we do not need your interference now.'

Samson grinned at the phone. 'It's not my interference you have to worry about. Maybe you should look east, and, by the way, I literally have no plans other than a weekend in the Blue Ridge Mountains.'

'When are you returning to the Washington area?'

'Sometime next week.'

'That hardly seems likely.'

'Whatever you say,' said Samson.

'We take a rounded picture of the events of the past two weeks. But the Americans are very angry indeed and I cannot guarantee they will be as understanding. Your life is at stake.'

'Are you threatening me, Peter?'

'No, you're putting your own life at risk. You need to come in. Clear the air. If you have your country's best interests at heart, you'll do as I ask. We can arrange a place. Number Ten wants certain assurances and those need to be given today.'

'I'm afraid that's just not possible.' Samson hung up and handed the phone back to the bodyguard. 'They're worried as hell, but I don't think they have any idea what's going to happen.'

'Nor do I,' said Anastasia.

CHAPTER 35

Sunset on Potomac

They sailed south on a warm westerly breeze generated by a massive storm system in the south. Naji was allowed to steer for fifteen minutes and Anastasia captured it on a phone. 'Not bad,' she said out of the corner of her mouth to Samson. 'A few years ago he was an unaccompanied minor, caged in a refugee camp in Lesbos because he kept on breaking out. Now he's steering a multimillion-dollar yacht down the Potomac. Seems like he was right to escape.'

She hadn't said much since the meeting with Reid, which she believed had gone badly. 'Did you notice his hand was shaking?' she said. 'His right hand has a tremor and he had to hold on to it with his left. Ulrike saw it too, but do you know what? I think he's much more frightened of Daus than he is of us or anything we might do.'

'He may calculate that the only way for him to end that fear is to help us,' said Samson. 'But I guess he has to be absolutely certain she's going to be destroyed. He has to see the stake through her heart, or at least know it's poised above her.'

'He has the power to finish us with one call,' said Anastasia. 'He's the only person outside our group who knows that something may happen in Congress on Monday. If he tells her, we're finished.'

She went below with Denis's laptop, refusing all offers of help and saying she needed to go through the files and begin to distill Denis's work into something she could present. She had to be completely on top of the information, know every detail inside out and have the connections imprinted on her brain so that she could answer questions fired at her by hostile members of Congress.

In the early evening, Samson suggested she came on deck for some air. 'What's up?' he said.

'Can't say,' she replied, and took the bottle of beer that he offered. 'It's not what you expect,' she added.

Naji, who had been helping her below, joined them. They looked across the water to an enormous facility on the Virginia side of the Potomac. 'That's Quantico,' Daphne called out from the cockpit. 'Where I did my time.' It figured that Zillah had an ex-fed as skipper.

'The files are devastating.' Anastasia looked down at her beer. 'There are just so many people that Daus has suborned and entrapped. And the data! I never got this part of it before, but she's accumulated tens of millions of people's personal details, and she uses it to push the line that's advantageous to her friends in Russia. Honestly, I'm surprised there's anything resembling democracy in this country or the UK. It's baffling that those guys' – she flung her hand at Quantico – 'are letting it happen.'

'Maybe they're not,' said Samson. 'They may have been helping all along,' he continued. 'The CIA saved my life in Tallinn. No doubt about it.'

Naji got up from the cabin roof and went to talk to the crew.

'Has he read all the stuff?'

'No, he didn't know what was input from the American end. That went straight to Denis.'

'So you're the only person who knows what's in it.'

She nodded.

'We have to give it to the FBI if we go ahead on Monday. Sorry, I had to do a deal.'

She looked irritated. 'Was that strictly necessary?'

He waited a moment. 'How else was I going to get Reiner to make Stepurin put in a call to say he'd killed Denis? Stepurin made that call late last night. So Daus believes her man murdered him. And that's important for her sense of being in control of things on Monday.'

A cooler breeze from the bay, bringing the smell of the ocean. The sky and water turned a dark mauve. The sails were dropped; *Ariel II* was now pointing straight into the wind, and the engine was started.

They looked across the river in silence. Presently, he turned to watch Anastasia. Her jaw jutted out slightly and her mouth was set firm. She dragged her eyes from the water and returned his gaze with a brief, grim smile. 'You're wondering if I'm going to be okay,' she said.

'Are you?'

She shrugged. 'Whatever it is between us, I loved Denis. You understand?'

'I do.'

'It was shocking to see him like that. I was mortified for him, a man of such dignity and power lying there like a fucking dried-up, dead old mummy. I owe him everything – he saved me, and his money has saved thousands of people.' She looked down.

'He was an extraordinary man. Few of us are ever going to make his impact.'

'I betrayed him with you, and now I'm going to betray him again. I have read things that I never wanted to know about.'

'What things?'

'I can't talk about them.'

Her phone pinged with a message. 'I need to make a call,' she said, then jumped up and went forward, steadying herself against the motion of the boat with one hand on the forestay. He watched her. She seemed to be agreeing to something. She hung up, looked down at her phone and began to read. Then she made two more calls and returned to his side.

'They've moved it up. I'm on at 10 a.m. It's not advertised. They're going to make a last-minute change to the schedule. I've told Ulrike, and she'll work on persuading Reid to bring Daus. But that's not going to happen, is it? I'll prepare a simple presentation, but I have to understand the whole thing.'

She went below again and Samson wandered back to the cockpit as Daphne pulled back on the throttle to slow the yacht. They dropped anchor a little further on, in the lee of Liverpool Point, within sight of the Mallows Bay Ghost Fleet, the resting place of scores of ships from the First World War. The lights of a small craft sped from the shore across the water, which was unruffled by wind or current. 'That's Zillah,' said Daphne, and told the crew to lower the landing platform at the stern. Sails were stowed, ropes coiled, the anchor was checked and the deck washed down.

Zillah hopped on to the stern boards and gave a thumbs-up to the man on the rigid inflatable. She handed her backpack to one of the crew and stepped up, smiling. In the years dealing with this strangely concealed, neutral person, he had never seen such unguarded joy. She evidently did love her boat.

It was still warm in the shelter of the bay so a table was set up in the cockpit and the crew went to prepare dinner. Anastasia emerged looking red-eyed and they sat down with another beer. Naji was apparently taking a nap in the forward cabin, where she had been working.

'Okay, so I've got a lot to tell you,' said Zillah. 'Jim Tulliver is out of his coma. He is recovering faster than they anticipated. He has some memory loss, specifically about what happened to him on the night, but more generally about how he came to be in Manhattan and what he did for Denis. His sister informed him about Denis. She had to – it's all over the news and he'd see it on the hospital TV. He's devastated.

'The media is looking for you, Anastasia. And so is Homeland Security. But before I get into that, you'd better tell me what you're planning because I can't do my job if I don't know the full facts.'

They went through it all, picking up each other's thread. The names of Reid and Speight gave Zillah no confidence whatsoever. If it were up to her, she wouldn't have told Reid, and Speight was so damned sinuous even he didn't know his next move.

'So we need to get you into the decontaminated Rayburn by early morning. That's going to be hard, but not impossible. We can start by doing a number of things. You should organise a media conference for yourself for 9 a.m. Pacific Standard Time on Monday at Denis's office. When you've done that, I want you to switch off all your devices and give them to me, with your passcodes. But you'll need to make one more call. You're going to dispatch Denis's jet to the West Coast with one of my people, who will start sending emails and texts from you the moment they land. I suggest you compose those tonight. They need to be in your voice. Maybe thank them for their support at this time. If you're able to talk about funeral arrangements, that would be great. Put in as much personal stuff as possible. The plane should leave at around midday tomorrow and I will have the devices picked up before we weigh anchor.' She turned to Samson. 'And you need to turn off your devices now. Naji also.'

'They're secure,' said Samson. 'I'll make sure Naji does, though he isn't going to enjoy life without the Web for twenty-four hours.'

'So, this is where we are right now. Reiner and his team have all been furloughed or transferred. Agent Paula Berg has been moved to San Antonio. Frank Toombs is indisposed. He may have been re-tasked, or suspended. I don't know which at this time. Homeland Security under Michael Selikoff is running everything. Selikoff is a very smart lawyer out of the Southern District in New York. If you put the entire staff of Homeland Security in a stadium, Selikoff would have ninety-nine per cent of the brains. He is close to the White House – very close – and he is working with the US Marshals. I don't know how they justify this, but that's the way things are these days. State and Justice are out of the loop and the only thing that matters to the people at the top is making sure you don't use anything that may have been left to you by Denis.'

'You think they're working in collaboration with Mila Daus,' said Samson.

'Absolutely not! I don't think anyone really appreciates who she is. And if they knew what Toombs and Reiner undoubtedly suspect, they wouldn't touch her. This is a defensive action to protect themselves. They don't understand much, but they grasp enough not to want exposure and scandal.'

'Like the British, although they understand it much more.'

'Which makes it even more of a betrayal,' said Zillah. 'But this here, in the United States, is an outright disgrace. I have never seen anything like it.'

'Is Daus aware of all the activity?' asked Samson.

'She'd have left the country by now if she were.'

'And Stepurin?'

'We don't know who has jurisdiction on that. Word is that he might just be given bail and quietly allowed to leave the United States. But the people at the top don't know he's the one who shipped in the nerve agent and hired Vladan Drasko. Toombs and Reiner do, however. So, the administration would be making a huge, dumb-assed mistake if they freed him.'

Paella, salad and more beer arrived. The crew sat with them to eat. It was only then that Samson noticed that all four carried weapons beneath their *Ariel II* jackets.

Next day, at 7 a.m., as the tide rushed into the bay, Anastasia's devices were exchanged for a printer and leads. She wouldn't use the ship's WiFi to connect the printer to the computer because of the risk of a hack, which Naji assured her was entirely possible. She had worked for several hours overnight and produced a document distilling the main discoveries in the order she wanted to introduce them. Sitting next to Samson, she read it over and over and kept on going back to reduce and re-order. She gave part of it to Samson. He was impressed and said so. The plan was to circulate the statement shortly after she had answered questions, which would mean a large number would have to be printed for members of Congress before she reached the building, because she sure as hell wasn't letting the master copy or the computer out of her hands. They argued over what to give Reiner, Anastasia maintaining that his suspension made the deal void. A deal was a deal, Samson said. He hadn't risked his life several times over the last couple of weeks to start reneging on an agreement with an ally, which, in any case, might benefit them. If he had the material before the hearing, he could argue with his bosses that he had been right all along and that everything was about to be made public.

She again found herself apologising. 'It's all on me.'

'Yes, it is. And I wish it weren't, but you're the only one who can do it. I'll be right behind you.'

'However much I prepare, it can all go wrong with one question.'

'Have you talked to the Congresswoman you mentioned – Ricard? Can she help?'

Anastasia snorted a laugh. 'Turns out Shera took two hundred grand from Abelman via GreenState. I guess Denis knew that when he was talking to her. And Reid! Jesus, the film is utterly disgusting. That ugly old man fucking that poor young girl, and from behind! I mean, you know what he was doing!'

'Please!' Samson looked away. 'You've done all you can. Let's go sailing. Forget it all for a few hours.'

The anchor was snagged on an old cable that led from the wrecks. Zillah took half an hour to free it, moving the boat backwards and forward on the engine and eventually raising the sails and turning the boat away from the wind to free it, a high-risk manoeuvre. She steered *Ariel II* downstream into the tide and wind and they tacked across the broader reaches of the Potomac, heading towards Nanjemoy Creek and the Maryland–Virginia state line, where Samson took over and sailed close-haul with his eyes never leaving the luff of the main, as Fleur had taught him. Anastasia and Naji sat nearby, looking up at the sails. She had her arm round his shoulder, which, unusually for Naji, didn't seem to bother him. They had been much closer since the flight from the Balkans to the Baltic.

At midday, they turned for home and ran before the wind with the sails stretched out like wings. They reached Washington just after nightfall and moored a hundred metres offshore. It was then that the detailed planning began.

CHAPTER 36

2172 Revisited

She wore the dark dress she'd used for Harland's funeral, and a lightweight jacket and a silver necklace that Denis had given her. It was his first gift to her – not at all valuable; she always kept it in her washbag. Zillah had equipped her with a pair of lightly tinted glasses and a baseball hat, also black. Over her shoulder she carried the bag that contained Denis's computer and twenty copies of her statement – a further forty would be printed when Anastasia was sure they would be needed. At Security, she was required to take out the computer and turn it on, which wasn't a problem. No one among the Capitol Police, the journalists on their phones, the aides and congressional staff scurrying hither and thither recognised her. It was Monday and things were a little slow, the more so because storms in the South, stretching up to the Carolinas, had delayed flights into the capital.

They went to the back of Room 2172 and sat down. Anastasia noticed that a few things had changed. The carpeting around the witness desk had been replaced with a slightly darker shade of blue and the desk itself was new, longer and narrower. She assumed that the contamination had been limited to the desk and where Denis and Steen had fallen and, of course, Steen's briefcase, which had been destroyed. There had been no trace found on either her or Tulliver's clothing.

The schedule announced two witnesses for the session 'Assessing American Policy in Northern Iraq' – the Honourable Alison Carney, Acting Assistant Secretary, the Bureau of Middle Eastern Affairs, US Department of State, and Dr Sheila McNeill, Professor of Middle East Studies at the University of Texas at Austen. Harry Lucas would be in the chair. A note at the bottom of the page stated that witnesses might be added.

They waited for twenty minutes before a young man appeared from the curtain behind the chair's position and placed papers on Lucas's desk. Other staffers materialised with papers and one or two representatives took their seats. Harry Lucas came out and sat down, consulted two staff members with his hand over the microphone. There was no sign of Warren Speight. Anastasia knew he would take the seat immediately to the chair's left. Lucas spoke.

'We have some problems with the weather this morning, ladies and gentlemen. We are waiting to hear from Ranking Member Speight, who is on his way from the airport, and from the witness Dr McNeill, who is delayed for the same reason as he. I am sorry to have to tell you that the other witness, Alison Carney, appears to have had an accident. I'll get back to you in fifteen.' He rose and left.

'McNeill never got on the plane, and I believe that Carney is Frank Toombs's partner,' whispered Zillah to her.

The public seating areas were still almost empty, as were the three rows reserved for members of Congress. Samson, Naji and the German nationals being brought by Ulrike would not enter room 2172 until Anastasia had been called as a witness. They waited, Anastasia's trepidation rising by the minute. She hadn't struggled like this since receiving therapy for the PTSD that followed her kidnap and the loss of her baby, both of which she had blamed on herself in the mangled thought processes of that time. As she had spiralled deeper into depression, so deep that a smell, a noise or a word would set off panic and result in aggression aimed at Denis, he'd found a clinical trial for the use of MDMA – ecstasy – for trauma sufferers, and he had moved heaven and earth to have her enrolled. Just three treatments of eight hours, in which she lay wrapped in a light blanket between a male and female psychologist, had brought about a miraculous change. Apart from the insight into her own mind, she realised its great potential for all those refugees suffering from PTSD that the Aysel Hisami Foundation sought to treat. She and Denis had been trying to find a way of legally using the Schedule 1 Controlled Substance.

Thus she distracted herself thinking of the foundation and consciously recalling what she had experienced in those hours, and in a few minutes she had regained a measure of calm and, more importantly, purpose.

Lucas and Speight came in together and sat down. Lucas said they would have to abandon the morning's planned session, but that not all was lost. He looked around.

'I understand that we do have a witness in the room who can help this committee's deliberations. Would Mrs Anastasia Hisami please stand up and be recognised.'

Anastasia rose. 'Thank you, ma'am,' said Lucas. 'I am going to put it to the members present that we call you forward.' He looked along the benches and received several nods from both Democrats and Republicans. 'Please come and take your place,' he said.

She went forward with the bag and sat down at the table, propping it against her chair. She placed her hands together, briefly noticing the dreadful state of her nails, and nodded to Lucas.

'I want to draw the committee's attention to the fact that you lost your husband just forty-eight hours ago, and that you have agreed to continue, as far as you are able, giving the evidence that Mr Hisami was providing when he and Mr Steen began to sicken from the poisoning that killed him and was almost certainly a contributory factor in your husband's passing last Friday evening. I first wish to convey the condolences of the committee to you, but also to state our gratitude that you have chosen to return so soon and support the democratic process that we all believe in. I thank you, Mrs Hisami, for that.'

So far, Speight had only looked up from his papers once and he hadn't acknowledged her during a brief sweep of the room, where there was now much activity. Journalists were competing for seats while photographers took up positions on the floor in front of her. TV cameras were being set up left and right. If there had ever been any doubt in her mind, she now knew that every word she said would be on the record.

Harry Lucas held up a hand to suggest he would not start until everyone had found a seat and the slight hubbub had died down. She looked round and saw Samson and Naji enter. Samson was having a word with one of the officers and pointing to the front. The officer was shaking his head. He left Naji with Zillah and took one of the chairs on the aisle three rows behind her. She saw Ulrike shepherding a group of five people, two women and three men, including Herr Frick, into the back row.

She occupied herself by taking the copies of her statement from the bag, laying them face down on the table in front of her and squaring them off neatly.

'Settle down,' said Lucas to the room. 'I am now going to turn it over to the Ranking Member for his opening statement.'

'Thank you,' said Speight slowly, and looked up from his papers. 'I want to associate myself with the chair's remarks. I was saddened to hear of your husband's death, Mrs Hisami, and I endorse the chair's sentiments about the courage you show in coming here so soon after. Yet I feel bound to warn you that the process of democratic inquiry is not always kind, even in these woeful circumstances. I must press you on the matters we were addressing when that shameful attack took place. You understand that?'

She nodded but felt her hands suddenly grow cold, a sign of anxiety she hadn't managed to shake off even with therapy.

'You will recall that I was pursuing a line that connected your husband's activities in support of Kurdish forces this year to his period as a commander of considerable daring and ruthlessness in the 1980s, when, as a young man, he took part in actions against Saddam Hussein's forces and was closely associated with the CIA.'

'That is true,' said Anastasia. 'A senior officer testified in a hearing in New York to challenge my husband's detention by the Immigration and Customs Enforcement two and a half years ago. My husband worked closely with the CIA and during that time was an important ally of America.'

'But the fact is that ICE lawyers got the wrong massacre in that hearing, and your husband was allowed to walk free. The Agency's informants made a mistake on the dates and doctored the written evidence as well. Is that true?'

Samson saw Anastasia's head go down. She said nothing. Had Speight tricked her into believing he was somehow on her side, only to revisit the allegation surrounding the massacre? He was aware of a slight disturbance behind him and looked around to see a tall man, well dressed and with an air of entitlement, moving to two spare seats on the right of the public area. It was Jonathan Mobius, and he was followed by Mila Daus. She was wearing a well-cut two-piece in dark, smoky blue. Samson thought – *Berlin Blue*.

At that moment, he saw a woman he knew to be working for Zillah Dee leap up and hand something to Daus, who shook her head and gave it back to her. He knew this to be a shiny black Chanel powder compact that would be spirited away for fingerprint analysis. He kept his head down but allowed himself one more look at Daus. She was saying something to Mobius, who nodded and smiled. Then she smiled, closed her eyes and threw her head back. If the circumstances had allowed, there would have been a hearty laugh to accompany all this. Martin Reid had done a good job. They had come to watch the public evisceration of Anastasia and were evidently looking forward to it.

'In your own time,' said Speight quietly.

'Yes, sir, I'm thinking,' Anastasia replied, and remembered his remark about the silent alliance between bridge partners. 'Never assume your partner has made a mistake.' She had no option but to trust him, yet it was a few seconds more before she finally answered his question with a simple, 'Yes.' There was a murmur around the room.

'Thank you for that,' said Speight, so quietly that the stenographer looked up. 'Can you tell us exactly what your husband's involvement was and how that connects to the allegations that he supported the Kurds?'

'My husband was involved in the execution of forty Iraqi soldiers in early 1995. It's true that the information provided to the court in New York was erroneous and the evidence brought by ICE, in effect the Department of Homeland Security, was a clumsy forgery. Documents were altered in a font that did not exist at the time of their creation.' She looked down again. 'However, I can confirm that my husband took part in a war crime. He was commander of a group operating in Northern Iraq. Forty Iraqi soldiers surrendered to his company and they were all executed.' Samson caught Daus's quiet look of triumph.

'On his orders?' pressed Speight.

'Yes, I only learned the full facts after his death.' She stopped. 'It explained a lot to me. I believe it weighed on Denis his entire life and was the driver in the enormous amount of charitable work he undertook. I looked at the figures over the weekend. He gave away nearly 3 billion dollars.'

'And that massacre, that war crime, is why he changed his name from Karim Qasim to Denis Hisami?'

'Yes, I believe so.'

'But you say there's no connection between this atrocity and his recent support for the Kurdish people.'

'They weren't motivated by the same fanatical nationalism, if that's what you intend to imply. The murder of those young men was committed during a fast-moving battle taking place on many fronts.' She paused. 'Denis was an American patriot, but he was also Kurd and believed in the right of the Kurdish people to self-determination. After the Kurds helped the US track down Saddam Hussein and successfully fought ISIS, albeit with the loss of eleven thousand lives, America abandoned them to the Turkish forces. Denis believed that the recent attacks by the Turks on Kurdish lands were laying the ground for the genocide of his people, and he decided to do something about it.'

'He gave his people money.'

'Yes, for medical supplies and infrastructure.'

'And weapons?'

She was looking down. 'Yes.'

'How much?'

'From the notes he left, I would estimate it was two hundred million, a quarter of which was designated for medical aid.'

'And you have learned all this since your husband's death.'

She nodded. 'Yes.'

'I thank you for your candour, Mrs Hisami. This is obviously an extremely difficult time for you.' As Speight said this, his attention went to Harry Lucas, who was listening to a thin, hawkish-looking man with an entirely bald head. Samson felt his phone vibrate with a message. It was from Zillah: 'Something's going down.'

Before he could look up, four men had moved behind Anastasia. She turned her face to them with a look of pure anger. One man had his hand on her shoulder. It was shaken off.

Lucas exploded. 'This is an outrage. I have to inform members of the Committee that this is Mr Selikoff, the Director of Homeland Security, who informs me he is carrying out an interdiction to arrest our witness and seize material that he claims is vital to national security.' He stood up and faced him. 'But this is Congress, sir, and the Executive does not have the power to interrupt proceedings, still less to arrest a witness giving evidence. You will leave this committee room now.' He pointed to the door. 'Go now!'

Selikoff straightened, surveyed the room and began to speak but was quickly cut off.

'Mr Selikoff, you have to be elected by the American people to make speeches from this platform,' roared Lucas. 'Leave the room and remove yourself and your agents from this building.' He ordered the Capitol Police to escort the Homeland Security agents from the room. Uproar ensued, with members of Congress jumping to their feet, shouting and pointing. Selikoff gave a signal to his men, one of whom reached down to pick up Anastasia's bag and remove the computer.

'Put that down,' said Lucas, now holding the microphone to his lips. 'Return that to Mrs Hisami.'

They took no notice.

'Thank you, Mr Chairman and Members of Congress,' said Selikoff. 'We will not trouble your proceedings further. We have got what we came for and we will doubtless speak with Mrs Hisami later.'

With that, the five men marched from the room with Denis's computer, pursued by journalists and TV cameras. Near the door they passed a man wearing a suit that Samson immediately recognised. No one in Washington wore a suit like that. It was Peter Nyman, who turned with an expression of grim satisfaction, but he did not register Samson with his beard.

Samson's eyes went to Mila Daus, who was leaning forward so that Mobius could speak to her ear. She appeared utterly composed, though was also plainly mystified by what she had just seen. And that interested Samson. He remembered Zillah Dee being categorical that Mila Daus and the government were not working in concert and that they were ignorant of each other's agenda. She didn't get up and leave because, like everyone else in the room, she wanted to know what would happen next.

Samson went to Anastasia and crouched down beside her so he couldn't be seen from the back row by Daus. 'What do we do now?' she demanded. 'They've got everything.'

'You have your notes, and they can't access the information on the computer.'

'But the proof!' she hissed. 'We don't have the complete dossier and we don't have the proof.'

'Daus is here with Mobius. She's to your right, at the back. All Ulrike's people are here, so we can still spoil her bloody day. Go to it. I'm here for you.'

Harry Lucas had brought the gavel down several times. Samson went to his seat. Lucas boomed, 'This committee will come to order!' The noise died down. 'What we have just witnessed is a constitutional outrage, the like of which has never been seen in the history of the Republic. The Ranking Member Mr Speight and I will need to consult the Speaker about the violation of Congress and the challenge to America's democracy. I propose we adjourn.'

He was about to take the views of both parties when Speight interrupted. 'If I may, Chairman?' Lucas nodded. 'I think it would be advisable to find out why Homeland Security believed it was necessary to storm in here and seize Mrs Hisami's property before our eyes, and to enquire about the laptop they removed and what is contained therein.' The slow, modulated Southern voice stilled the room better than Lucas's gavel and, since every member was asking themselves exactly those same questions, a quick consultation produced a vote to remain in session.

But Lucas insisted that he must confer with the Speaker, leading figures in both parties and the Capitol Police. In the meantime, Room 2172 was in lockdown. People could leave but they would not be allowed back. If they wanted to use the bathroom, that was too bad – they would have to forego attendance at the session. As the only witness, Anastasia was offered the members' facilities.

She hoped to meet Speight on the way to the washroom but saw no one. Unsurprisingly, Shera Ricard the freshman Democrat Congresswoman representing California's fourteenth district, who had taken money from both Denis and Mila Daus, had made herself scarce that day.

She had a pee, then sat on the lavatory with the lid down. The hand holding her phone shook. She'd expected Speight to touch on the massacre, for he had hinted as much on the phone, but she had no idea how painful it would be to admit to Denis's most guarded secret so soon after his death, a secret that she was only just beginning to process. Though it was obvious from Denis's precise account on the laptop that these were things that he had prepared himself to admit, it still felt rotten and disloyal. She had trashed her husband's reputation for good, yet the revelations about Daus's network that justified doing this were now lost. Without the computer and painstaking detail of Denis's files, no one would believe it. Her testimony was basically useless. But then it occurred to her that the reason she was in this state was Mila Daus. Denis's death, her kidnap, even the loss of her baby, were all directly Daus's doing. Samson was right – they could at the very least expose her.

She heard voices as two people entered the bathroom. She withdrew her legs so they couldn't be seen and waited. There was a sound of a tap running, then she heard a woman say, 'Senator Speight says to tell you that it's all going to plan.' There was a murmured response which she didn't catch. Then she heard the door open and close. The sound of the hand dryer followed. She waited. As soon as she heard the door a second time, she rushed from the stall to look down the corridor. A woman in a floral dress with pale blue cardigan, who had been standing behind Speight for most of the hearing, was walking back to Room 2172. Who had she been talking to? What did it mean when she said it was all going to plan? She went back and rinsed her hands in warm water, noticing an odd mixture of perfume and staleness in the bathroom and returned to the committee room.

Lucas was in position and consulting with the Clerk of the Committee and her deputies. Most of the members had returned, but Speight was nowhere on the dais. Then she saw him, at the far end of the members' chairs, talking to a tall man with his back to her. Speight seemed to be enjoying himself. He turned to check how things were going, realised he should resume his seat, shook the man's hand and punched him lightly on the bicep. As he moved away, he threw a look past the man, grinned and raised his hand to someone – just a lift of the fingers, but a wave nonetheless. His interlocutor now turned and Anastasia recognised Jonathan Mobius. The person to whom Speight had semaphored his good wishes could be none other than Mila Daus. That was who the aide had been speaking to.

Anastasia whipped round to Samson, who had seen all this, and made a helpless gesture. He replied by indicating that there was something on the desk in front of her. She found a folded sheet of paper. In Samson's neat hand were the words: 'Martin Reid found washed up on bank of Shenandoah on Sunday morning. Reported heart attack after entering cold water on Saturday afternoon!'

She read it twice in disbelief. If Reid was dead – whether by murder, suicide or accident – why was Daus in the committee room? He had been the person tasked with persuading her to attend. Had he had time to make his case to Daus after leaving the meeting with her, Samson and Ulrike and before entering the waters of the river? It seemed unlikely. Questions swarmed in her mind, particularly concerning the reassurance she'd overheard in the bathroom. She was about to turn to Samson when Lucas gavelled the room to order and began speaking.

'Members of Congress, ladies and gentlemen, what we have witnessed today is an offence to the Constitution of the United States of the gravest order. It is without precedent. I have consulted with the Speaker and she has made her feelings clear to the White House. I am pleased to say that we have the support of both sides of the house in our resolve that this committee must now prove to the world that the United States Congress will suffer no trespass or breach of its ancient rights by the Executive branch or any federal agency. I remind everyone in this room that one agency, and one agency alone, has jurisdiction in Congress, and that is the United States Capitol Police, which have powers in the District of Columbia, as well as across the United States, to protect and safeguard Congress and its members. The USCP is the full service – that is, independent – federal law enforcement agency that answers to the legislative branch, *not* the President. The Speaker and I have instructed the Chief of the USCP to secure Room 2172 for the period of this testimony. We are in lockdown. No one will leave or enter this committee and that restriction will be rigidly enforced by the USCP. That will include certain cable-news channels, which have made urgent applications to the Speaker, the Clerk and my staff.' He stopped and looked fiercely around the room. 'This is the second time evidence on these matters has been interrupted by outrage. There will not be a third. I hope I make myself clear.' He glanced to his left. 'Ranking Member, you were saying . . .'

Lucas didn't notice the lanky youth in an oversized jacket walk hurriedly from the back of the room and sit down beside Anastasia with a computer decorated with a sticker that read: 'The Singularity Starts Here.'

'What the hell are you doing?' she said to Naji.

'Everything's here,' he said. 'I copied it two nights ago when you were sleeping on the boat.'

'It seems we have another witness, Chair,' drawled Speight. 'In any case, I yield my time. The questions I suggested can be asked by anyone.'

Lucas now bore down on Naji. 'Who, sir, are you?'

'Mrs Hisami's adviser, Mr Chair,' replied Naji, pleased that he had some of the protocol right and smiling idiotically.

Lucas shook his head and blinked several times. 'You're younger than my grandchildren. You don't look like you have any advice to give Mrs Hisami.'

'But I do,' said Naji, bridling. 'I am Naji Touma, and I am the only person here that has seen the Kurdish people fight ISIS.'

'Is he your adviser?' Lucas asked Anastasia.

'He is who he says he is, but he's not my adviser and he needs to return to his seat right now.'

Naji got up.

Samson glanced over at Daus, who for the first time was beginning to look concerned. He kept watching as Lucas turned to his right and called on Abigail Hunter, the Democrat representing Nevada's fourth district.

In her late thirties, with blonde hair, small, polygon-shaped glasses and an earnest manner, Hunter looked surprised to be called but quickly recovered and said, 'I'll follow the Ranking Member's suggestion. Why were Homeland Security here and what is on that computer?'

Anastasia paused. She didn't know where to start.

'You may answer now,' said Hunter.

'My husband, together with many others, but chiefly a former senior intelligence officer named Robert Harland who was murdered on the day of the attack here, was investigating a very large network of influence within the government, agencies and business. I believed that computer held the only copy of the dossier they had been compiling for the past two years.'

'Have you entered evidence into the record? I have seen nothing.'

'No, but I can certainly do so now. I was expecting to be asked and have prepared copies of my statement. They're right here,' she said, hefting the bundle in front of her. 'More will be made available.'

A brash young congressman from Arizona named Daniel K. Nolan, who she had noticed was never still, put up a finger and said, 'Point of order, Chairman! Why are we listening to this? What conceivable relevance does all this have to America's relations with the Kurdish people? Secret networks, computer dossiers – I mean, I am lost. Motion to dismiss.'

Lucas turned to him with a withering look. 'This is not a legal case and there's nothing to dismiss. We are the legislature, not your courtroom, Congressman and, yes, you are overruled.'

Nolan didn't take the putdown well and sat with his arms folded, looking furious, thus attracting the attention of the cameras. But it was plain that some members thought he had a point, particularly an old congressman from Pennsylvania who was nodding vigorously, and another from Idaho named Ed Riven, who turned from the row below the dais to shake Nolan's hand.

Samson received a message from Zillah, who had scrambled back into 2172 just before Harry Lucas's lockdown. 'We need to speed up.

Those two guys are in Daus's pocket. She donates to their campaigns in Pennsylvania and Idaho. Mobius is texting the whole time. They are going to play rough. We don't have much time, especially when they see the papers. BTW the fingerprints on the compact match. She can't deny who she is.'

The tension in the room was palpable. A member of the clerk's staff, a heavy white guy with a paunch and an audible wheeze, took his time collecting the papers, and counting them. He indicated that there weren't enough. Zillah went to Samson and gave him the freshly printed copies, plus a zip-lock clear plastic envelope. Samson nodded to her. She was right. It was time. He took the papers to Anastasia and placed the envelope and the bag he had carried into Congress on the seat beside her. 'It's all there when you need it,' he said. He didn't care whether Mila Daus saw him because she couldn't leave, but her attention was focused on the papers being distributed and she seemed to be urging Mobius to get hold of a copy.

'Who is this?' Lucas called out to Anastasia.

'He works for me, Mr Chairman. Just an employee, no one important.' Even now she had time to have a dig at him. That was a good sign.

Many of the representatives now had the papers and were reading, some flipping through skimming the contents, others reading from page one.

'Is it still my time, Chair?' asked Abigail Hunter.

Lucas nodded.

'Mrs Hisami,' she began, 'I have just spent a few minutes with this, but these are astonishing allegations.' She looked down. 'You are naming four individuals as running key networks in Washington, London, New York and on the West Coast with a fifth in charge. You accuse two highly placed individuals in the National Security Council and in the Office of the Director of Intelligence and, in the UK, you suggest the Prime Minister's right-hand man is a Russian spy.' She looked up. 'There are very well-known people on these lists. I won't name them but, honestly, how can you make these allegations that they are part of a vast network servicing a foreign power?'

'Because it is true.' She kept her voice low and controlled. 'These days the public and media focus on cyberattacks and hacking, but Denis and Robert Harland knew that what matters is real people who have access to the highest councils of the land.'

'You are saying that this is a huge network of spies feeding information to the Kremlin? There are scores of Americans involved!'

'Yes, and Britons as well,' said Anastasia. 'You want to know why a man shoved papers covered in nerve agent into my husband's hands? This is the reason. They believed he had this evidence with him on that day. He didn't. You want to know why one of the greatest intelligence officers of the Cold War was shot in cold blood on the same day? This is the reason. People have died to bring this information to your attention. My husband was as good a person as a man with his past can be. He gave his life for it because he believed in this country. You want to know why Homeland Security entered this room, against all constitutional norms, and seized that computer? This is the reason.'

'Are you suggesting Homeland Security is working for the Russians?'

'I am suggesting that the administration does not want this information to come out, which is different. I am suggesting . . .'

But she was silenced out by several members waving the papers and shouting. Lucas was looking left to the Republicans and right to his own party, and didn't see Jonathan Mobius approach the dais and speak with Riven and Nolan. They nodded and consulted with three other colleagues. Mobius returned to his seat, Samson craned to see Mila Daus, who glanced at the door, where three large USCP officers stood barring the way. Then she clasped her hands between her knees and looked down. Mobius whispered to her and she nodded without looking up. They were trapped, but they weren't beaten. They had a last throw of the dice.

Nolan was shouting the loudest and eventually got Lucas's attention. 'Chair, I believe the congresswoman is out of time.'

'She has a minute to go.'

'Nevertheless,' said Nolan, 'I have to remind the Chair of this committee's rules.' He put on his glasses and held up a book handed to him by a staffer. 'I'll read two sections from the Committee Rules. "The majority may vote to close the hearing for the sole purpose of discussing whether evidence to be received would endanger national security, would compromise sensitive law enforcement information or violate Paragraph Two." And, sir, I am going to read you Paragraph Two. "The Committee may vote to close a hearing whenever it is asserted by a Member of the Committee that the evidence or testimony at a hearing may tend to defame, degrade, or incriminate any person."' He looked up. 'What I have in front of me, Chairman, fulfils all those requirements, to say nothing about the risks to national security if you continue on this course. You have to take a vote. The rules require it.'

'I will take advice,' said Lucas, closing his hand over his microphone and leaning towards the unreadable face of Warren Speight.

'May I continue while you do that?' asked Nolan. He didn't wait for an answer because he was clearly out of order. 'Mrs Hisami, is it true that you have recently suffered serious mental-health issues – a complete nervous breakdown – and that after treatment failed you engaged in a controversial therapy involving the party drug MDMA, otherwise known as ecstasy?'

'Yes,' she said. 'It was a controlled medical trial.'

'Is it fair to suggest that you have made these allegations while you're not only grieving for your husband but also under the influence of this drug?'

'Absolutely not! I finished treatment two years ago. And I didn't make these allegations, my husband did.'

'Your husband, *the war criminal*,' he said, and sat back. 'I yield.'

Lucas looked around. 'I think the representative has a good argument for a vote on the grounds that this hearing risks defaming or denigrating people who cannot defend themselves. We'll leave the National Security aspect out of it because none of us is in a position to say what impact these papers may have.'

'I may be able to help in that regard,' said Speight, waggling a pen between his index and middle finger.

'Would you mind if we just take the vote, Mr Speight?' asked Lucas, now very much at the end of his patience.

'Nope, you go ahead, Mr Lucas.' He lounged in his chair and, unlike everyone else present, appeared completely relaxed.

Anastasia watched him and for one infinitesimal moment she thought she saw some encouragement directed at her. Before she had time to consider her next action, she was on her feet. 'I have some things to say before you take your vote. I don't wish to talk about myself, or my pain, but it is true that Denis and I have been through a rough time these past few years, and now my husband is dead. He didn't survive the struggle with an immensely powerful enemy, an enemy that threatens us all. That enemy is in this room, sitting with us now, quietly and patiently working out her escape route with the man who is her stepson, but also her lover and fellow traitor. The vote you are about to take is their escape route.'

She picked up the two bags and pulled out the jam jar stolen by Herr Frick from the display in Leipzig and turned to face the back of the room. 'Over there sits Mila Daus, a self-made billionaire, although it is fair to say she did have some help in acquiring her wealth from two rich husbands, named Muller and Mobius. Mila Daus started life in the German Democratic Republic as a member of the Stasi secret police and was the organisation's most terrifying and cruel servant. She destroyed people's minds for the cause. The lives of literally thousands of political prisoners were wrecked by this woman before she was even thirty-five years of age.'

'What is that you are holding?' snapped Lucas.

Without turning, she replied. 'Proof that the woman sitting over there is the same person who committed these crimes. It contains a hair from a young student the Stasi arrested because she had been talent-spotted. That was the way the Stasi got to know people. The hair was an accident, but the DNA in this sample matches hairs collected by my associates at her home at Seneca Ridge just four days ago. They acquired two samples and the match was perfect in both cases.' She held up the bag containing the woman's razor and comb. 'But that's not all. As a matter of course, the Stasi fingerprinted everyone they arrested.' She held up the arrest sheet. 'Here are the fingerprints of that young woman.' She picked up the zip-lock bag. 'And here are her fingerprints, taken from a woman's compact Mila Daus handled less than two hours ago in this room. They are a match and, lest there be any doubt about that, I believe we have mobile footage of her handling that compact.'

Daus sat with her head down and did not react, but Mobius rose and shouted, 'You are defaming an innocent woman and an American patriot! Shame on you! Mr Chairman, you cannot lock us in here and subject us to these slurs. This isn't justice.' He looked down at his phone. 'We both need to leave right now. We are dealing with a serious data breach of our companies' servers and closed data. I demand that we are allowed to pass without being obstructed, or else you will be hearing from our lawyers.'

'I have no idea who you are,' said Lucas, 'but you have no right to speak unless asked, still less to threaten Congress in that manner.' He looked down at Anastasia. 'All right, Mrs Hisami, I think we have heard quite enough. Please take your seat while I hold the vote.'

'I will not,' she said. Samson saw the flash of aggression that occasionally showed itself in their fights and had undoubtedly got her through her kidnap and incarceration in Russia. She was in command and the room was hers. 'People are here today who were broken by this woman and can identify her.' She turned. 'Would you all please make yourselves known?'

Led by Ulrike, the five elderly Germans who had been sitting around Mila Daus, and, in one case, in the chair next to her, rose to their feet.

'The lady at the front is Ulrike Harland,' continued Anastasia. 'She is the widow of Robert Harland, killed two weeks ago by a gunman. Her first husband was murdered by Daus's Stasi associates in the nineties. She will introduce the others.'

Lucas was muttering his disapproval but, caught up in the drama of the moment, was too slow to intervene.

Ulrike began to speak. 'This is Frau Lauerbach. Lilly was held in Hohenschönhausen prison then in Bautzen prison. She was released after four years of mental torture overseen by Mila Daus.' She indicated another woman, a fragile, bird-like creature who stood with the aid of a cane. 'Johanna Feldman was accused of crimes against the state. She was imprisoned for five years and has suffered numerous breakdowns since her release. She never married because of her mental-health problems.' She pointed to Frick, who had come spruced up in a three-piece suit and bow tie. This is Bruno Frick. His wife killed herself a year before the Wall came down.' She touched the shoulder of a tall man in a checked sports jacket. 'This is Tobias Nest, a musician who was prosecuted for antisocial activities and imprisoned for four years. His wife divorced him after Mila Daus, in the guise of a social worker, informed her that Herr Nest was a paedophile. And finally, this is Ben Rugal.' She turned and smiled at a man with a cap mark on his forehead and a deeply tanned faced below. 'Herr Rugal is a farmer. One night he gave shelter to a young student who was on the run from the Stasi. He was sentenced to three years for aiding and abetting the student. His wife died of cancer while he was in prison, for which reason she was denied all treatment.'

The room had fallen silent. No one moved. The six German citizens looked at each other, slightly at a loss to know what to do. Then all turned to Daus and each spoke the words agreed on beforehand.

'*Ich identifiziere Sie hiermit als die Stasi-Offizierin Mila Daus.*' Ulrike explained to the room that this was a formal identification.

Daus looked up uncomprehendingly and, without the slightest recognition, although she knew exactly who Ulrike was and darted a brief venomous look at her.

'Okay, that's enough,' said Lucas. 'We will now have our vote on whether to suspend hearing the evidence of this witness. Does anyone want to speak before I take the vote? The issue is simple enough. Does the continuation of Mrs Hisami's evidence unfairly defame, degrade or incriminate those named in these papers?'

No one spoke and forty-seven representatives voted. Warren Speight was among the first to indicate that he agreed with the motion. It was carried with an overwhelming majority.

'That seems to settle things,' said Lucas. 'Mrs Hisami, we are grateful for your attendance this morning. Thank you. I hereby end the session.'

Anastasia looked round to Samson. He shrugged. There was nothing to be done. Then her eyes came to rest on Naji, who was looking down at his phone with a broad grin, completely unaware of what was going on around him. Daus and Mobius had got up and were moving to the door. Anastasia turned to get her things together then became aware that Warren Speight was speaking.

'Excuse me, Chairman,' he was saying. 'I have a note of what we just voted on. We voted to suspend *hearing the evidence of the witness*, not to suspend the session.'

The room went silent again. Lucas looked at his notes and glanced at the clerk, who nodded.

'And at the bottom of the schedule I see that it expressly states that more witnesses may be added.' He held up the schedule and pointed to the words. 'And I do have two more witnesses for this session. They have only just emerged, but they are relevant to the subject under discussion.'

Lucas sighed. 'Very well. We'll take a vote on the principle of whether we should consider the evidence of two further witnesses. But it will have to be brief. We only have forty-five minutes remaining.' Seeing that the Ranking Member had been tough on Anastasia and had voted for a cessation of her evidence, his side were inclined to support him, as were a majority of Democrats, who did so out of curiosity, because Speight refused to name the witnesses until he had the endorsement of his colleagues. The motion to hear two more witnesses was carried. Anastasia saw Speight's aide, Matthew Corner, disappear behind the curtain. She sat down, but Lucas suggested she leave the witness table and, if there weren't a chair available, an officer would move one of the witness chairs to a suitable position. She saw no reason why she shouldn't now sit beside Samson on the aisle and pointed to the spot. Before sitting, she smiled at Ulrike, who, like the other five victims, remained standing – a living memorial to the thousands of people who had passed through the Stasi's prisons, she thought.

In the time it took the man to move the chair and satisfy himself that it would not obstruct the aisle, two men had come through the door on the far-right-hand side of the dais, walked to the table and taken their seats.

As Lucas said, 'Please state your names,' Anastasia recognised them from the backs of their heads.

'Special Agent Edward Harold Reiner.'

'And I am Frank Toombs.'

'Mr Reiner, you are a long-standing Federal Agent, serving with the FBI for twenty-five years. And Mr Toombs, you are senior member of the CIA with twenty-two years' service, both in the field and at Langley. Is that correct for you both?'

'Yes, sir,' they both said.

'Lucas isn't reading from notes!' Samson whispered. 'He knew!'

'Since this is your idea, Ranking Member,' continued Lucas, 'I suggest you proceed, unless of course there are any objections from our colleagues.' He looked up and down the lines of members. 'Please go ahead.'

'Gentlemen, please state your current status,' said Speight.

They looked at each other. Toombs spoke first. 'I was given notice of likely termination this morning from my job at the Central Intelligence Agency in Langley, though as yet I have received nothing in writing.'

'I'm glad to hear that last part,' said Speight. 'Special Agent Reiner?'

'I'm on paid leave of absence and I expect to be redeployed to Seattle,' said Reiner.

'And can I confirm that you were both working on the matters that we have touched upon this morning before you were threatened with termination and suspended? You have both been watching the live feed – yes?'

They nodded.

'And have you seen the material that is before us, the distilled version? And before you reply, I want to make quite sure that you understand that this committee has voted to support the principle that no one should be defamed, degraded or incriminated by these proceedings.'

'We have seen all of the material,' said Reiner. 'By which I mean everything on Mr Hisami's computer. It was delivered to me early this morning.'

Speight nodded and weighed his next question. The room held its breath. 'To the best of your knowledge, has the American government been penetrated by a network operated by and for the benefit of the Russian government, an operation run by five key players that has spread its tentacles and corruption through the top of our society, as well as using its considerable resources to gather personal details of millions of Americans under the guise of environmental and climate-change campaigns?'

'Yes, to all those questions,' said Toombs. 'Special Agent Reiner and I have been informally working on this for some time, though it took us a while to put everything together. However, it is right to state we were way behind Mr Hisami's investigation. That is what broke this open.'

Lucas cleared his throat. 'May I ask you gentlemen a question? Was the attack that took place here roughly two weeks ago carried out by the people you were investigating?'

Toombs looked at Reiner and answered. 'Yes, it was a coordinated assassination of Mr Hisami, Robert Harland and a man who has worked closely with both – Paul Samson, a former officer in MI6 in the UK.'

'And Mr Samson was the only one to survive,' said Speight.

'Yes,' said Toombs. 'Without Mr Samson and many others, including, obviously, Mrs Hisami, none of this would have seen the light of day. Paul Samson is right here in this room, if you want to thank him.' Samson looked down as the journalists scanned the room for likely candidates.

'And you were stopped from pursuing the investigation because someone was pulling strings behind the scenes?'

'We cannot speak to the motives or indeed the fact of any cover-up, but they have the dossier now and I believe resignations and arrests are already taking place.'

'That's good to hear. And what now for you both?'

'We're waiting to hear,' said Toombs. 'Though my seniors won't be pleased to see me here.'

'Well, I guess that's just too bad. Congratulations on a fine job, the two of you, and also to Mrs Hisami and Mr Samson. I have no further questions, Mr Lucas.'

The stunned silence that followed was broken by a moan from Daus's direction. Samson and Anastasia jumped up to see her levitate from her seat, fight through the standing figures around, cuffing Ulrike in the process, and tear to the front, where she stood berating Warren Speight. 'You are a traitor. I will destroy you.'

Speight pulled the microphone towards him. 'That is an epithet that surely applies to you more than me, ma'am.'

She went on shouting. Unperturbed, he shuffled his papers, rose and paused for a moment to seek out Anastasia's face in the crowd jostling to see and take pictures of Mila Daus. And, when he found her, he placed his hand on his heart and bowed, as they do in Afghanistan, where Speight had briefly served his country as a reservist and learned a whole lot more about chemical weapons. He looked up and mouthed the words, 'You won!'

CHAPTER 37

Old Friends

Macy Harp and the Bird were unaware of the drama unfolding in Congress. They were travelling through wooded landscape in the rental car, each with a cup of coffee in the beverage holder. They did not speak but occasionally glanced at each other and grinned. After many operations during the Cold War the once inseparable spies were working together again.

For much of the weekend they'd recced the area north of Seneca Ridge, probing tracks that looped through the woods and weren't visible on the public satellite photography of the area, which had all been shot in the summer months. They went unhurriedly, stopping to look at an otter lying in the sun on the bank of a stream and a bald-eagle nest. They had plenty of food. Macy had loaded up at a high-end food store in DC and the Bird made a neat little fire that was as hot and efficient as it was small. He fried steak in a skillet that he'd bought on the way in an outdoor sports store. They were content, like two boys playing hooky, and they talked of old times, going back forty years and more. Macy drank his fair share, while the Bird watched him with a wild affection. How many operations had they done together? the Bird mused. Something like twenty, the most hair-raising of which, they both agreed, had been undertaken in the winter, on a boat skippered by Gus Grinnel, when they searched for, and found, a man in a canoe with a tiny home-made sail off Sassnitz, on the East German coastline. They drank to Gus and to their old friend Bobby.

By mid morning they were in position. The Bird winked at Macy and got out of the car. With the pistol he'd bought on the street in Washington tucked in the back of his waistband, he began the long trudge up to Seneca Ridge. It took about forty minutes to reach the incline to the houses. He walked two thirds of the way to the top then waited in the shade of a broad leaf oak, watching for any movement. There was none. He knew that Gaspar had no appointments at either of the two clinics because those were only held from Tuesday to Thursday. He approached the Pinzgauer truck, looked around and went to the door Gaspar had used to exit the building, which he'd noticed wasn't locked. He entered and headed straight for the den, where two computer screens sat on a desk.

The Bird was so quiet that Gaspar didn't hear him. He was concentrating on one of the screens, a pair of reading glasses on the end of his nose, chin up and stroking his collarbone absently.

The Bird coughed quietly and said, 'Good morning Dr Gaspar.'

'My God, General! Where the hell did you spring from? Have you come to buy the gun?' He rose and folded the glasses. 'They didn't tell me you were here.'

The Bird moved towards him, gun drawn, and said, 'I have come to talk about my friend Bobby Harland, the man you had shot two weeks ago.'

Gaspar spluttered that he didn't know what he was talking about. Had the General lost his mind? What the heck did he think he was doing, walking into his home with a gun? He made for a pistol in his desk, but the Bird moved quickly to bring the gun down on his bare arm. A small gash appeared. Gaspar looked astonished. He reached for the phone. The Bird stopped that, too. He now saw that Gaspar had been watching the stream from Congress being aired by Fox News. Anastasia was sitting alone at a table. Someone was asking her a question. The Bird nodded and smiled. This was the first he knew of what was happening in Congress.

'You know her?' said Gaspar incredulously.

'Yes, she's a remarkable young woman. Now pick up the gun case over there and walk to the door. If you do anything but walk and breathe, I will shoot you in the back of the head.'

'Are you taking the gun?'

'To fill a room like this with dead creatures?' He looked from the elephant to the leopard then back to the rhinoceros head. He shook his head. If Gaspar had glanced at the Bird's eyes instead of the street gun, he would have seen a look of great sadness, as well as disgust.

The Bird pushed him out of the house to the Pinzgauer, where Gaspar made as though he had forgotten the keys. 'They're where you left them, clipped above the sun visor.'

They drove to the spot they had stopped before, where Gaspar had excitedly climbed down. Waiting there was Macy Harp, sitting on a tree stump with his loafers resting on a boulder. He was peering at an anthill. The Bird, who never noticed much about a person's mood, saw how content he seemed. Now he looked up and squinted at them in the sunlight. 'So this is the fella who killed my friend Bobby,' he called out. He got up and ambled over, picking his way through the grass, which had already grown tall in the spring warmth. He reached them and looked at Gaspar. 'It's funny,' he said, addressing the Bird, 'when you meet a real bad'un, how profoundly unimpressive they always are.'

Gaspar shrank from him. He saw in the cheery, rubicund features something that really frightened him. 'I haven't got long to live, Mr Gaspar,' started Macy conversationally. 'A matter of weeks, they tell me. I have no pain – nothing like Robert Harland endured in his final days – so I count myself as fortunate.' He looked around him. 'But, when you're dying, you see the wonder of things with such clarity. Bobby was painting when your man executed him, completing a work of sublime beauty. I can't paint, but I have been watching those ants over there for nearly an hour and, to be honest, I haven't spent a happier hour in the last forty years. Ants are quite simply marvellous, aren't they?'

Gaspar glanced at the Bird, as an improbable haven of sanity. The Bird handed the pistol to Macy and set about fixing the barrel of the Nitro Express rifle to the stock and fitting the forend under the barrels.

'What do you want?' asked Gaspar. 'Money? I can give you more money than you could dream of.'

Macy smiled. 'It must be evident that I have no use for money.'

'Normally, I'd take you up on that,' said the Bird. 'I could use a substantial donation for my place. I have a zoo and conservation projects that absolutely burn money.' He looked down both barrels. 'But, well, it seems I can do more for conservation and the wildlife right here with you.'

'You have no ammunition,' said Gaspar. 'Let's talk this over. Come on, fellas. You don't want to do this.'

'Oh, but I do have ammunition.' The Bird put his hand in his pocket and held out his hand. Two large shells rolled across his open palm. He inserted them in the barrels and snapped the rifle shut.

'You going to shoot me with that?'

The Bird shook his head. 'You start walking over there. Follow the deer track. If you want to run, please feel free to do so. Sporting chance, and all that.'

'You can't be serious,' said Gaspar.

'I am,' said the Bird. And for the first time the smile vanished from his face. 'Go!'

Gaspar took a few steps, looking back at the rifle, then a few more. People and animals had flattened the path. It was tempting. He could make a dash for it. He ran thirty paces, picking up speed, then ducked down, took a firearm from his ankle holster – Bird had known it was there – turned and fired wildly in their direction. Macy ducked, but the Bird didn't move. Gaspar ran a few more paces, and only then did the Bird raise the rifle. He didn't aim at the figure fleeing chaotically through the dappled light, but rather at a spot a little ahead of him, and loosed off two shots in quick succession. The sound was deafening. Realising that he hadn't been hit, Gaspar shot over his shoulder twice more and kept running – straight into the plume of cyanide gas that had been ejected from the baited M-44 trap that had so recently felled a six-hundred-pound bear. Exactly three paces beyond the trap he staggered, performed a grotesque pirouette, clutched his throat and fell forward.

'That's for Bobby,' murmured Macy.

'And for the baboon,' added the Bird. He lowered the gun. 'And the leopard, the warthogs, the rhino, the buffalo, the elephant, the bears, the deer and the croc.' Indistinct sounds came from the grass up ahead of them, but very soon there was silence. 'We'll wait for the gas to clear,' he said, beginning to wipe down the gun and the shells with a newly laundered red-spotted handkerchief.

A few minutes later a breeze shook the leaves above where Gaspar had breathed his last. The Bird went over to the body, with the handkerchief pressed to his face, and laid the rifle near the outstretched hand that held the Saturday-night special. He took the little pistol in the handkerchief and unfastened the ankle holster with one hand. He removed his cap and placed the gun and holster in it, and peered at Gaspar's face. The same foam was visible on his lips as had appeared on the bear's muzzle. Having checked the scene once more, he turned to Macy.

'Spot of lunch, Cuth?'

'That'd be perfect,' replied the Bird, and they walked to their vehicle, hidden a little way down the track. He used one of the food store's bags for the handkerchief, cap and gun and holster and placed it in the trunk for disposal later.

'Shame about the cap,' said Macy, 'I'd become rather fond of it on you.'

'Had you,' said the Bird, with his usual untamed pleasure. 'How nice of you to say so. I saw a rather nice one in the camping store. Thought we might drop in on the way back, if that's all right with you.'

EPILOGUE

From Room 2172, Anastasia and Samson were more or less propelled into the lobby, where the media jostled around them. Anastasia let go of Samson's arm and said, 'You don't want your face on every news channel. I'll see you in a few moments.' He made his way to the back of the crowd and watched Ulrike gather the German witnesses around Anastasia, who stood looking into the camera lights. When eventually the noise had died down, he heard her say, 'The dossier speaks for itself. I stand by all the information that my husband and countless others have assembled. It is now for the American and British people to make up their minds about Russian penetration of their governments, and the scandal of the governments' cover-up.'

Samson was aware of a voice at his side. 'No doubt you're proud of what you have done.' It was Peter Nyman.

'No,' said Samson. 'I'm proud of what Anastasia has done. Very proud.' He turned to see Nyman's tight-lipped, drained expression, smiled and shook his head.

'You don't give a damn, do you? I mean it's all out there – everything.' He swept his hand over the crowd.

Naji had only just told Samson what had happened. When Homeland Security stormed into 2172 and seized Denis's laptop, Rudi Rosenharte and Zoe Harland had pressed the button and released everything on the Web. By sharing it through a peer-to-peer network they eliminated the need for a vulnerable central server and ensured that Denis Hisami's dossier couldn't be taken down or sabotaged. The whole thing was being amped up across social media.

Samson smiled again. 'I understand perfectly what's happened, Peter. The entire British establishment, including you and Ott, would prefer to take a few discreet actions then forget the whole affair. But a younger generation are outraged, and it was in their power to make sure nothing was swept under the carpet. That makes you seem, well, a bit obsolete, Peter.'

'You think you're going to get away with this? These matters were being dealt with at a level that you cannot even comprehend. Don't you see? It was all in hand.'

'That's bollocks, Peter.' Samson moved off to listen to what was going on.

Ulrike had spoken. Now a CBS reporter called out a question to Anastasia. 'Why should anyone believe the evidence of a war criminal?'

'Because my husband was prepared to give his life for the country that became his home.'

'Is it hard to mourn someone with that kind of past?'

'Of course not,' she fired back angrily. 'He did more good than most of us. He lived with his own terrible guilt, but also the pain of what had been done to his people for centuries, and to his sister, who was murdered by Islamic State. He was America's friend. Don't ever forget that.'

Anastasia had signalled Samson with a look that she was winding up when a woman reporter from Fox News asked, 'Did you order the destruction of the server and internal networks at GreenState?'

'I didn't order anything. I have absolutely no idea what you're talking about. That's all I have to say.' Samson moved to her side, and Zillah led them from the building.

'What was that woman saying about GreenState?' asked Anastasia.

'Let's talk outside,' said Zillah. She turned to them both once they were through the doors. 'Naji and his friends hacked the GreenState servers and published all the data in redacted form to show how the organisation has siphoned millions of people's private information from social media accounts and a bunch of different commercial entities.

'Actually, it's kind of funny. They sent an email to everyone in GreenState's database with an apology, a copy of their data and advice on how they might join a class action against GreenState and its hidden affiliates. Everything is laid out – people's ethnicity, education, sexual orientation, family members, income, political views and relations with authority, institutions and local communities. Interestingly, it's precisely the kind of information that was gathered by the Stasi in East Germany. They've also provided an account of how each individual was targeted with special ads by parties and campaigns. This is a big deal. It's likely to get as much attention as what went on in there.' She jerked her head towards Room 2172.

They went to a large suite in the Jefferson. A conference call was booked with Tulliver, who'd managed to follow the morning's proceedings from his hospital bed. As pressing for him were the problems set off on the first day of business since Denis's death. Billions in assets needed to be stabilised and bankers and investors reassured. It was agreed that Rick Blumenthal, Denis's effective deputy, would take over for one month, while Tulliver consulted lawyers about the legal implications for Anastasia and the business. Tulliver had access to the will, he said, but had never read it. Anastasia was ignorant of the contents. It had never occurred to her to ask about it.

Zillah received a text asking whether Naji was available for an interview with her former bosses at the National Security Agency. They wanted to hire him and give him and his family American citizenship. Halfway through a room-service burger and fries, Naji raised his head and said, 'Another "A" and I'd do it. NASA, yes; NSA, no.'

'The NSA can be pretty persuasive, and they'll put a lot of pressure on you. I'll tell them you're going to think about it. But my advice is – stay clear. You, particularly, wouldn't enjoy it. There's a five o'clock flight to Berlin that connects with a service to Riga. I figured you'd want to leave.'

'I'll put him on the plane myself,' said Anastasia.

Naji nodded and returned to focus on the burger and his phone.

'They want a meeting,' said Zillah, 'that's the Agency and the Bureau. Here. Around six.'

On the return from dropping Naji at Dulles, Anastasia found Samson in the lobby, trying to get hold of Macy. 'People are recognising you,' he said, noticing the looks coming from around the lobby.

'Yeah, I had that problem at the airport. I told them I just looked like the bitch in Congress.'

That made him laugh out loud.

Zillah caught them outside the conference room she'd hired and told them the news that Gaspar had been found dead from poisoning at Seneca Ridge. 'It looks like an accident, but of course they don't believe that. They're really pissed because he's a key witness. And Mila Daus has vanished.'

Now Samson knew exactly why he hadn't been able to get hold of Macy and the Bird, but his expression gave nothing away as he walked into the room. He smiled to Toombs and Reiner, who had plates and napkins in their hands and were hovering over a room-service trolley of sandwiches and snacks. 'We were just saying what a fine job you did today, Mrs Hisami,' said Toombs. 'Having those German people come was an inspiration. Truly affecting.' He took a bite of his sandwich. 'So, where are we going to start?'

'With me,' said Reiner, stirring the ice in his Scotch. 'You've heard about Gaspar?'

'Just now,' said Samson.

Reiner explained that the M-44 trap had been triggered by a stray bullet. 'We are one hundred per cent sure he was killed. I mean who the fuck goes hunting in the woods with a weapon like that, especially one that he couldn't fire properly because of an injured shoulder? Yes, we saw the ad where he talked about the reason for selling the gun.' He sat down, sipped his whisky and studied Samson. 'And frankly, I find it incredible that a guy like Gaspar brings just two shells and fires both of them at a cyanide trap he knows is there because he fucking well put it in the ground.'

'What am I meant to say?' asked Samson.

'You went out there to collect Mila Daus's DNA, so . . .'

'Yes, four days ago, and you know where I've been since.'

'Right,' said Reiner. He glanced at Toombs, who shrugged. Zillah gave them wine and they joined Reiner at the table. 'Okay, so I will be brief. Stepurin is talking. He denies having anything to do with the nerve agent, but we know otherwise. He hasn't yet been charged because we want him to think he can talk his way out of this, and we are getting good material. He confirms that John Gaspar was the paymaster, but he won't say anything about Mila Daus. Denies ever having met her.'

'You know where she is?' asked Anastasia.

'We think we do, but I'll come to that. You were right in thinking that Gaspar and Stepurin connected on the big-game circuit. All the murders were signed off and paid for by Gaspar. Stepurin confirmed this. On the key people in her network, Erik Kukorin, Chester Abelman, Elliot Jeffreys and Jonathan Mobius have all been arrested, and we are talking to all their contacts. The British want Mobius, but they aren't going to get him. And the big fish here – Mike Proctor, the Deputy National Security Advisor, and Kirsten Donnelly, from the office of the Director of National Intelligence – they're with us right now. They say they had no idea they were helping the Russians. Actually, we were aware that both were compromised sometime back, so that story isn't going to work for them. In the UK, the PM's adviser, Anthony Drax, is under arrest, but

Ben Bera – the guy at the Foreign Office – has vanished. We believe he's in Russia, but the Brits aren't saying anything.' He shook his head. 'There's literally nothing that Drax and Bera didn't know, or couldn't find out. It's a fucking disaster over there, but really serious for us, too.'

'You say you knew about Proctor and Donnelly,' asked Samson. 'How far back?'

He smiled. 'Frank's your man. Frank made all the running at the start, so I'll let him answer.'

Toombs grunted. He seemed in no better humour than usual. 'We were aware of leaks of highly classified information a year back and I was certain they came from Donnelly's office, but I didn't know how to proceed because she was close to people in the Agency – high-up people – so I consulted a friend of mine and he pointed me in the direction of the political consultant Elliot Jeffreys. My friend knew that Donnelly and this man Jeffreys were close. Jeffreys intrigued me because of his enormous Rolodex and the money he was spending. The income from that consultancy nowhere near matched the money he was splashing around. Then we realised it came from Mila Daus, though we had literally never heard of her before.'

'Where is she?' asked Anastasia.

Toombs allowed himself a smile. 'She had it all figured out. She told Mobius she'd meet him to do a joint media statement in the Rayburn before they left the committee room, then she went to the bathroom. She got out of the building with the help of the staff of one of her friends on the committee. Within the hour she was on her way to Cuba. We think she's headed to Moscow. Mobius was left holding the baby and, naturally, she didn't give a damn what happened to that fool of a husband, although he was probably already dead by then.'

'Was Denis going to make any kind of allegation the day of the attack?' asked Samson.

'No, we're sure of that. He didn't have the back-up material in either briefcase. We had a guy in a chemical-warfare suit check what was in Steen's before it was burned. There was nothing.'

Samson shot a look at Anastasia. 'Then why didn't you tell us this?'

Reiner rubbed a finger in the corner of his eye. 'We were finding our way, just like you, I guess.'

Samson frowned. 'When was your inquiry shut down? Who ordered that?'

'Exactly five days ago – Wednesday last week – and it came direct from the White House. There was absolutely nothing we could do, but with you two taking the strain, we knew we still had a chance. All we needed was for you to get into that computer and appear in front of the committee.'

'And Homeland Security?' said Samson. 'What was their role?'

'They were on the other side in this war, working directly for the White House.'

'But you couldn't rig this all on your own,' said Samson. 'There were too many variables, too much that could go wrong, or that you couldn't predict. Until I gave you the dossier there was so much you didn't know and, besides, it didn't contain anything about the East German witnesses, the DNA and the fingerprints on the old arrest sheet. You didn't know that we could prove who she was. So, the idea that you were orchestrating all this doesn't hold water.'

'That was quite a coup,' said Toombs. 'We were greatly impressed by your work on all that.'

'I repeat – you couldn't have done this all on your own.'

Reiner looked at his watch and glanced at Zillah. 'Perhaps we should all get another drink.' He pushed a bowl across the table. 'Potato chip? They're excellent.'

Anastasia accepted a refill from Toombs, her eyes working furiously. 'Are you going to answer Samson's question?'

'Nope,' replied Toombs, and turned to the drinks tray. Samson watched as he poured rye whisky and red vermouth into a cocktail glass then searched the tray for a bottle of angostura bitters, discovering one at the back, together with a jar of maraschino cherries. The room was silent.

'He's here,' said Zillah, looking up from her phone.

A few moments later, Matthew Corner opened the door, stepped aside to allow his boss, Warren Speight, through and closed it behind him.

'Good evening, ladies and gentlemen!' said Speight. He offered his hand to Samson, apparently the only person he didn't know, and swept the room with a broad smile, which came to rest on Anastasia. 'If I may say so, ma'am, you were truly magnificent this morning. Your poise was awesome – the perfect bridge partner.'

Toombs handed him the drink he'd mixed.

'The best Manhattan in Fallujah! Thank you, Frank.'

'You know each other,' said Samson.

'We go a long way back. We met when I was serving in Iraq.' He placed the drink on a leather coaster and sat down.

'You're the friend Frank consulted about Elliot Jeffreys,' said Samson.

'Correct,' said Speight. He stroked the table with his fingertips. 'My role in this should never be spoken of outside this room. Is that okay with you, Mrs Hisami, and you, Mr Samson?'

They nodded.

'I don't have a lot of time, so maybe I should cover the main points and you can ask questions. My purpose was simple. I had to win your trust at the same time as keeping a line open to Mila Daus. A year back, I met with her and she tried to make me one of her people, as she did with every lawmaker. Jeffreys offered me help on data in my district, and money and support staff for my re-election campaign. I was invited to their places in Utah and at Seneca Ridge – in fact, I was at the Ridge just this last weekend. I went for lunch with two colleagues of mine. You saw them doing Daus's bidding in the committee this morning – Congressmen Riven and Nolan. I wanted to get her to attend today, and those two gentlemen were very helpful in that endeavour. I couldn't have done it without them.' He squeezed his eyes at them and sipped the Manhattan.

'That was Mila Daus,' said Anastasia. 'You had to get me into the room as well. Is that why you came to the hospital? Were you making some kind of assessment of me?'

'Exactly right. I had no knowledge of you, though I learned from Frank that you had been through some tough times and that you were smart and resilient. But I didn't know *you* and I wanted to get a sense of who you were.'

'And you asked me to appear in front of the media at the hospital that day so Daus saw you were talking to me. Is that right?'

He nodded. 'She was obsessed with you and Denis. It was her weak point. My task was to persuade her that, if she came to Congress, she'd see Denis's reputation destroyed for ever. In fact, she provided me with some of the material about the incident in Iraq. Once she knew that Denis was dead and she thought Stepurin was responsible, she couldn't resist coming to see it all play out. This was like her victory lap.'

'So, her presence today had nothing to do with Martin Reid?' asked Anastasia.

'No, she used him to find out about Denis after the attack. That was all. Marty Reid had no sway over her whatsoever. In fact, she held him in contempt.' He paused. 'It was a sad story, but he was a bully and a son of a bitch and there won't be too many mourners at that funeral.' He leaned forward and looked directly into Anastasia's eyes. 'I am sorry that we had to go into what happened in your husband's former life. I am afraid it was unavoidable.'

'Thank you. Denis had prepared a statement on his computer that left no doubt about those events.' She didn't use the words 'massacre' and 'war crime', but in his notes Denis hadn't shied from them.

'There is one thing I don't understand,' said Samson. 'Why did you start pushing Denis on those events in the hearing on the day of the attack? What were you trying to do?'

'There were two reasons. I spent time in Iraq, and I saw atrocities committed by both sides. This is not something that I was prepared to overlook, even though I knew some of the information came from Mila Daus. Second, Denis needed to get it out of the way before we started talking about systemic penetration by Russia.'

'You are speaking as if you had some idea of what he had on that computer and, moreover, that you knew he wasn't going to use it that day,' said Samson. 'How did you know all that?'

'We talked.'

'You talked! When?' demanded Anastasia.

'Two nights before the attack. He knew I was going to push him on Iraq. He agreed that was necessary before he made these allegations. It was the thing that Mila Daus held over him and he needed to get that out of the way.'

He rose and went to take Anastasia's hand. 'I have a tight schedule of TV appearances. Suddenly, the conservative from the South is the hero of the liberal media. You were magnificent today. You've done this country a great service. Thank you, and thank you all.' He nodded to Toombs, and left.

Anastasia smiled at Samson and got up. 'That explained a lot. Look. I have some things I need to do. I have to go.' Samson gave her an enquiring look. She shook her head. It wouldn't involve him.

She didn't explain outside the room either, but she didn't have to. He knew. He hugged her and told her he loved her. 'I know it,' she said. They kissed and she walked away.

Late that night, Anastasia took off in Denis's jet with his body. Over the Atlantic, she looked out at the dawn rushing towards the plane, then glanced at the casket at the rear of the cabin. She had wanted him to be with her and now murmured her gratitude to him. Despite everything in his life and her unfaithfulness and love for Samson, she still loved Denis. She loved him and revered him. And she told him so. The secrets they'd kept from each other didn't seem at all important.

They refuelled in Cyprus and took off for a place on the far eastern side of the territory in northern Iraq, where the Kurds desired to create a fully independent state. They touched down and taxied to a spot in front of a rudimentary terminal building. Word had spread. Thousands of people had made the journey in pickups, battered cars and even tractors to pay their respects to their hero. On a baked apron, Anastasia watched his casket being unloaded then placed on the back of a large black pickup, where it was draped with the Kurdish flag – a sunburst on red, white and green bands. It was there, with the wind tearing at the black scarf she wore over her head and dust devils racing across the tarmac, that she felt she had done her duty and returned Denis to his people. She was offered a seat in the vehicle travelling behind the pickup in a long chaotic cortège that snaked across the desert and through villages where little crowds had assembled with flags. They headed east, gathering more vehicles along the way, until they came to a village cemetery where his ancestors lay, shaded by almond and olive trees. On the grave marker, his people gave him back his name – Karim Qasim. It pleased her because she had always preferred it to his adopted name, although she would, of course, keep Hisami for herself.

Acknowledgements

Writing a book in lockdown means there are fewer individuals than usual to thank because talking to people face to face and travel were not possible. However, I say thank you to my wife, Liz, who cooked for me every evening, listened patiently and advised on my plot problems and put up with me returning to my shed for a final hour or two at the end of the day. I would also like to express my gratitude to Jane Wood, my long-term editor and friend, who brings such clarity and good judgement to a work of fiction. She is the best. And, finally, I offer a deep, socially distanced bow to my agent Rebecca Carter of Janklow & Nesbit. Without them, this book would not be in your hands.